Sage watched a tall man dressed in jeans and a blue chambray shirt make his way forward. From her position in the front of the crowd, she noted his long, lean build, wide shoulders, and thick, wavy black hair. When he turned to face the crowd, she saw that he had blue eyes. Striking blue eyes, the color of Hummingbird Lake in summer. His face was a study of sculpted angles and masculine planes that the artist in her itched to sketch. In a tone just shy of miffed, she observed, "So, that's the great Colt Rafferty, hmm?"

Ali looked at her friend in surprise. "You have a problem with him?"

Sage shrugged. "I've never met the man."

Lori Reese sighed. "Dr. Rafferty is the reason I decided to go to college. I'm hoping all my professors look like him."

Sarah slung an arm around her daughter's shoulders and said, "If all your professors look like Colt Rafferty, I'm going to enroll in classes myself."

Leaning forward, Sarah added to Ali, "Sage has had a stick up her butt about Colt ever since one of his carvings beat one of her paintings for the blue ribbon at the summer arts festival last month."

ALSO BY EMILY MARCH

Angel's Rest

Hummingbird Lake

An
Eternity Springs
Novel

EMILY MARCH

BALLANTINE BOOKS • NEW YORK

A Ballantine Books Mass Market Original

Copyright © 2011 by Geralyn Dawson Williams
Excerpt from *Heartache Falls* copyright © 2011 by Geralyn Dawson Williams

Published in the United States by Ballantine Books, an imprint of The Random House Publishing Group, a division of Random House, Inc., New York.

BALLANTINE and colophon are registered trademarks of Random House, Inc.

This work contains an excerpt from the forthcoming novel *Heartache Falls* by Geralyn Dawson Williams. This excerpt has been set for this edition only and may not reflect the final content of the forthcoming edition.

ISBN 978-0-345-51836-1

Cover illustration: Robert Steele
Cover design: Lynn Andreozzi

Printed in the United States of America

www.ballantinebooks.com

9 8 7 6 5 4 3 2 1

Ballantine mass market edition: April 2011

For Amanda.
Welcome to the madhouse
otherwise known as our family.
We love you!

O N E

September

The echo of the gunshot jerked Sage Anderson out of her nightmare. Her eyes flew open. She lay in the darkness, panting, sweating, her heart pounding in fear, her hands clenched into fists. *Oh, God.*

The images. The sounds. *Oh, dear God.*

It was a dream. Just a dream. One of those old, horrible, terrifying nightmares that had haunted her since the events she dreamed about had been her reality.

Slowly the past retreated. Her pulse calmed and her fingers relaxed. At that point, the shivering began, a reaction to both the chill in the room and the aftermath of the dream.

Sage rolled up and reached for the bedclothes she'd kicked off the end of the bed during the dream. This was the first time in months that she'd been plagued by one of these nightmares. She had thought she'd put them behind her.

"I am so totally done with this," she said aloud as she yanked up the sheet, tugged up the comforter, and fished for her discarded socks at the bottom of the bed. When she finally cuddled beneath goose down and Egyptian cotton, she turned her head into the pillow and tried to cry.

She badly wanted to succeed in the effort, to sob and

wail and release these vicious emotions churning inside her. As usual, the tears wouldn't come. In the past few years she'd managed to find catharsis in tears only a handful of times.

When her eyes remained stubbornly dry and the possibility of sleep appeared completely beyond reach, she focused her attention on more pleasant thoughts. She thought about weddings. Her best friend's wedding. Well, one of her best friends, anyway.

Yesterday Nic Callahan had returned to town and reconciled with her husband. They planned to reaffirm their wedding vows at St. Stephen's church later this morning prior to the grand opening celebration for Angel's Rest, Celeste Blessing's healing center and spa. Sage was thrilled for Nic and Gabe. She was pleased for Celeste and excited for Eternity Springs. Today promised to be a lovely day.

And I'm not going to let a bad dream ruin it.

With that determined thought uppermost in her mind, she glanced at the bedside clock, where 4:07 glowed in red numerals. Today promised to be a lovely day—and a long one, she realized with an inner sigh. She knew she wouldn't get back to sleep at this point.

Sage sat up and took stock of her options. She could read or watch TV or surf the Net. She could catch up on paperwork or tackle the painting she'd begun yesterday for her upcoming show in Fort Worth. Except she wasn't in the mood for the first three, and she needed to let that painting sit for a few days. Something wasn't working with it, and experience had taught her that walking away for a day or two almost always helped her figure out the fix.

Her thoughts returned to the wedding, and at that point she knew what she wanted to do. She'd grab a new canvas and see if she could create a gift for Gabe and Nic to mark their special day. She'd do something simple, but light and bright and beautiful.

"Perfect." She blew out a breath, rolled out of bed, and headed for the studio she'd set up in the cottage's second bedroom. This was what she needed now—something positive to think about, a task to take her out of the shadows and away from the pain and the past.

In the studio, she placed a blank canvas on her easel and studied it, opening her mind to inspiration. She shied away from one image that hovered in her head, a leftover from her nightmare. Instead, she thought about Nic and Gabe and the obstacles they'd overcome while finding their way to today. She opened her mind to the promise of their bright and happy future, and inspiration flowed. An idea took shape in her imagination. She picked up her paintbrush and went to work. When she stepped away from her easel three hours later, she studied the finished painting and smiled. "Good job, Anderson."

She had managed to shake off the lingering ugliness of her dream and create something she knew her friends would treasure. All before breakfast. "Not a bad start for the day."

She showered and dressed and had just decided to toast a bagel when, to her surprise, someone rapped at her front door. Warily Sage peeked through the window blinds.

Celeste Blessing stood on her front porch, a canvas tote bag in one hand, a relaxed smile upon her face. She had gorgeous silver-gray hair and youthful, sky-blue eyes. This morning she wore a stylish bright red jacket, and gold earrings shaped like angel's wings dangled from her ears.

Sage relaxed. When she grew up, she wanted to be just like Celeste. The woman was the kindest, friendliest, smartest, and most active senior Sage had ever met. She rode a Honda Gold Wing motorcycle for fun, watched DVDs of *The Mary Tyler Moore Show* for entertainment, and never missed a Sunday at church or failed to give her opinion about the preacher's sermon. It had been her idea to turn the Cavanaugh House estate into Angel's Rest Healing Center and Spa, and construction alone had already proved a boon to the economically depressed town even before today's official opening.

The townspeople loved Celeste for doing her part in rescuing Eternity Springs. Sage loved Celeste for herself. In many ways, she was the mother and the grandmother Sage had never had.

She opened her door with a smile. "Celeste. What brings you out this way?"

"The Landrys offered their vacation home as an overflow facility for the center, and since we're packed to the rafters with the grand opening, we'll need to use it tonight."

The Landrys were a lovely family from Texas who owned the only other house on Reflection Point, the narrow little peninsula where Sage lived. "I wanted to stop and drop off a little welcome basket," the older woman continued. "When I saw your light, I decided to come beg a cup of coffee."

"I'm glad you did. I was about to toast a bagel. Care to join me?"

"Actually . . ." Celeste held up the tote bag. "I happen to have breakfast fixings with me. Care if I make myself at home in your kitchen?"

Sage blinked. "That's fine with me, but, with the grand opening, aren't you swamped?"

"Everything's under control, and frankly, with all the hustle and bustle, I'm glad to have a few moments of peace and quiet out here at Hummingbird Lake. I have bacon, eggs, a loaf of bread for toast, and a jar of homemade strawberry jam."

"That sounds much better than a bagel." Sage eyed the bag appreciatively. "Tell you what. My stovetop is persnickety when it comes to heat regulation. You have to talk to it just right. Why don't you let me man the frying pan while you handle the toaster?"

Celeste's blue eyes twinkled. "An excellent plan."

Sage took the tote bag and led Celeste through the cozy little cottage to the kitchen, where the women went to work. Their conversation centered around the two main events of the day, but when they sat down to eat, Celeste sipped her coffee and introduced a new subject. "How are you feeling, Sage? You look a bit tired."

She attempted a dodge. "I got up early and painted a gift for Nic and Gabe."

"That's nice," Celeste said. "Although I'm sure they wouldn't have wanted you to miss sleep because of it. This wedding is a last-minute thing, after all."

"Actually, a nightmare woke me up. I couldn't get back to sleep." Sage set down her knife, surprised at herself for admitting the truth. She never talked about the nightmares.

"Oh, you poor thing." Celeste clucked her tongue. "I'm so sorry. Does that happen often?"

"No, not really." Sage took a bite of jam-slathered toast and realized that something about Celeste invited confidences. She was simply so easy to talk to. After savoring the flavor of springtime in the jam, she swallowed, sipped her juice, then added, "Since I moved to Eternity Springs, I sleep pretty well. I think the mountain air is magic."

"Eternity Springs is special," Celeste agreed. "I've said it before and I'll say it again. This valley nurses a special energy that soothes troubled souls—if those souls open their hearts and minds to the possibilities."

Sage couldn't argue against it. Heaven knows the town had been working its magic on her these past few years. She'd been a basket case, running away from life as she knew it, when she literally arrived at a crossroads on a Colorado mountain road and turned left, ending up in Eternity Springs.

She couldn't explain it to anyone—she couldn't explain it to herself—but she'd known in her bones that the left turn had been the rightest turn of her life. Call it instinct or intuition or a message from her very own angel, but Sage had understood that she was meant to live and work in Eternity Springs, at least for a little while.

So she'd moved here and made friends here. She'd made a life and a career here. Except for the occasional nightmares and flashbacks, she was happy here.

"Eternity Springs has been good for me. I predict your healing center will be a wild success, Celeste."

"I completely agree. Those who open themselves up to all that life has to offer here will find great rewards. You remember that, Sage. Now, let me help you with the dishes. Breakfast was simply divine."

"It did hit the spot. Thank you for providing both the idea and the supplies."

"You're very welcome. I'm a big believer in having protein for breakfast, especially since you and I have a packed day ahead of us."

Sage didn't argue with her, but she didn't anticipate her own day being all that busy. Other than showing up at St. Stephen's thirty minutes early to help Nic dress, the only tasks on her docket were to witness the wedding and stroll Celeste's estate as a guest at the grand opening. She didn't intend to open Vistas, her art gallery, at all today.

After Celeste left, Sage wrapped her gift for Nic and Gabe in plain brown paper and fished a red marker from her junk drawer in order to draw hearts as decoration. When the memory of a homemade valentine that had giraffes sporting heart-shaped spots drifted through her mind, she sucked in a breath.

"Stupid dream," she muttered, then gritted her teeth as the pain washed over her. Following a dream, invariably the memories stayed around like a hangover. Not all memories were bad, but the good ones seemed to be buried beneath the mountain of ugliness she'd brought home from Africa.

Sage set down the marker and walked to her kitchen window, where she gazed out across Hummingbird Lake toward Eternity Springs. Taking in that view went further to rid herself of that hangover than ingesting any painkiller ever could.

"Forget the nightmare," she murmured. "The sadness ends now."

Well, at least for today. Today was going to be a wonderful day. This was Nic's real wedding day and the culmination of Celeste's "Angel Plan" for the economic survival of Eternity Springs. It was a day for celebration—not one for nightmares and heartbreaking memories—and it was time she headed for the church.

As she retrieved her car keys from her bedside table, she stared longingly at her pillow and added aloud, "A day for celebration, and maybe a nap."

A hand slapped Colt Rafferty's ass and jolted him out of his dream. It had been a good dream, too. Warm sun and a sugar sand beach. A beer in his hand. Half-naked women jumping to catch a Frisbee, jiggling. Loved that jiggling.

"Roust your butt out of bed, boy. The trout are calling our names."

Colt growled into his pillow and bit back the caustic words he would have spoken to any other man on earth. This man, however, was his father.

He cocked open one eye and groaned. "It's still dark."

"Of course it's still dark," Ben Rafferty said. "Have you forgotten how to fish? We need to be at the water at dawn."

Colt's flight out of Washington yesterday had been delayed by weather. It had been midnight before he'd made it to Eternity Springs, almost two before he'd hit the sack. What he needed was sleep. "Angel Creek is right outside."

"I fished the creek yesterday while I was waiting for you to get here. If I'd known you'd be so late arriving, I'd have gone up north and tried my hand at the Taylor River. I've been itching to fish there for years. We don't have time for that today, though, so I'm thinking we should fish Hummingbird this morning. It's only ten minutes from here, and with the grand opening kicking off at noon, this will be a busy place this morning. Fishing should be done in peace and quiet." Then, in a quieter tone, he added, "We only have today together, son. I don't want to miss a minute of it."

At that, Colt rolled out of bed.

Twenty minutes later, they stood along the bank of Hummingbird Lake and made their first cast of the morning. With it Colt felt the warm, gentle blanket of peace surround him. His dad must have experienced a similar sensation, because he sighed and said, "This comes close to being a religious experience."

"Yep. And I've been away from church for too long."

Ben Rafferty glanced at him. "How long has it been since you've visited Eternity Springs?"

"Three years. Haven't been back since I took the job in D.C."

His father shook his head. "That's a crying shame, son."

Colt had to agree. Colorado always had been special to him. His family had vacationed in Eternity Springs every year when he was a kid, and he'd loved everything about the town. He'd started working summers up here his last two years in high school and continued that all the way through college and even grad school. His mom always said that the reason he'd stayed in academics as long as he had was because he wasn't willing to give up his summers in the mountains.

"I wish this trip could be longer," he admitted. "If my appointment next week was for anything other than testifying before Congress, I'd skip it."

"That's a difficult class to cut." Ben Rafferty, high school science teacher, nodded sagely.

"It's a dog and pony show, is what it is. A pain in the ass." After a teaching stint at Georgia Tech, Colt had taken his Ph.D. in chemical engineering to the CSB, the U.S. Chemical Safety and Hazard Investigation Board, where he investigated industrial explosions. He loved the work—solving the puzzle of what happened in an incident and why and determining how to avoid a similar accident in the future—but he hated the hoops he and his team had to go through to get anything changed. They could write wonderful reports about their findings, but unless that led to change, what good did they do? "Let's not talk about work anymore. It'll spoil my appetite for my fish. I'm here today, and I intend to take full advantage of it. A little dose of Eternity Springs is better than nothing."

"Amen, son."

Thinking he'd had a hit, Colt tugged on the line. Nope. Nada. He made another cast, then laughed. "Know what I was dreaming about when you woke me up this morning? Senior trip."

Ben Rafferty gave a long-suffering sigh. "And people think preachers' kids are wild. Teachers' kids are ten times worse."

"Aw, c'mon, Dad. I wasn't wild."

Ben snorted. "Sure you were. You were also the most

stubborn, hardheaded, determined boy on the planet. Once you got an idea in your head, there was no stopping you. Don't see how that's changed, either."

"Being tenacious is an asset in my work."

"Sure made it a challenge to be your father."

After that, conversation lagged as the two men went about the serious business of fishing. For that stretch of time, Colt was as happy as he'd been in months. *I really need to get to Colorado more often.*

"Woo-hoo," Ben called out, snagging Colt's attention as he landed the first fish. "Better get to work, boyo. I'll be having myself a fine trout breakfast and you'll be eating cereal."

"Not gonna happen." Colt proved his claim by catching the next two, which led to some good-hearted grumbling from his father.

Time passed and Colt soaked in the peacefulness of the morning. The air carried the tangy scent of a cedar campfire, and above him a hawk soared on a subtle breeze. Worries about the upcoming committee meeting nagged at the edges of his brain, but as Ben Rafferty pulled another rainbow from Hummingbird Lake, Colt lifted his gaze toward Murphy Mountain, tucked his worries away, and allowed Eternity Springs to work its mojo on him. He was here, fishing with his dad. Life was good.

"I'm glad you could make it up here this week, Dad."

"I am too, son. Wish the rest of the family could have come along as well, but your mom insisted that you and I needed some"—he smirked and stressed the words—"male bonding time. Personally, I think she's laying the groundwork to take a girls' trip with your sister. I've heard them whispering about a spa weekend."

"If Mom and Molly want a spa holiday, they should come up here. I have it on good authority that Angel's

Rest has hired the best masseuse this side of the Mississippi."

His dad glanced over at him. "Speaking of Angel's Rest, when do I get to see this sign of yours? Ms. Blessing went on and on about it and about your artistic talent yesterday when I checked in."

"She was happy with the sign."

"Happy? Now there's an understatement if I've ever heard one. She told me that you have enough talent to make your living as an artist."

Colt shook his head at that nonsense and changed the subject. "I don't know about you, but I'm thinking it's about time for breakfast."

"Sounds good." His father jerked his head toward their fishing creels. "You clean 'em, I'll cook 'em."

"That's a deal."

Back at the carriage house, with the aroma of fried trout drifting on the morning air, Colt looked through the kitchen window toward a mountainside gone gloriously gold with the color of aspens in autumn and smiled. The town's newly adopted slogan couldn't be more suitable: *Eternity Springs—it's a little piece of heaven in the Colorado Rockies.*

"I love it here, Dad. I need to visit more often."

"Then do it."

"How? My job is in D.C."

Ben Rafferty slapped him on the back. "You'll find a way to get what you want, son. You always do."

TWO

The marriage ceremony at St. Stephen's couldn't have been more lovely, Sage decided. Nic made a gorgeous bride, all ripe and plump and pregnant, and Gabe looked happy and relaxed and finally at peace. She mentioned as much to her friend, Sarah Reese, as they left the church and began the half-mile walk to the healing center on the opposite side of Angel Creek.

"Gabe is happy, he's crazy in love," Sarah said, her Liz Taylor–violet eyes gleaming with delight. Her short dark hair crowned an angular face and gave her a sassy look that matched her personality perfectly. Today she wore a yellow sundress and strappy heeled sandals, and she carried a bridesmaid's bouquet of daisies. "Of course, Celeste would point out that it's Eternity Springs doing its healing thing."

Sage twirled her own daisy bouquet as she thought of the conversation with Celeste earlier that morning and nodded in agreement. "I think she has something there."

Sarah shrugged. "I don't know. That's a little woo-woo for me. We're not Shangri-La. There are plenty of miserable, unhappy people in Eternity Springs. I have two words for you: Marlene Lange."

Fiftysomething and never married, Marlene made her living as a realtor, piano teacher, and choral director for the school. She rarely smiled, regularly offered her caustic opinions when they were neither needed or appreciated, and often took offense over ridiculous, imagined slights.

"Poor Marlene," Sage said. "She had dreams of singing professionally. Did you know that? After her father had his stroke, she stayed here to help her mom care for him, and she ended up caring for her aging parents until she'd aged herself."

"And grew bitter and unhappy and mean—thus making my point."

Sage could have voiced the obvious—that Sarah was walking the same road and she should take care that Eternity didn't gain a bitter baker along with its bitter realtor—but today wasn't the day for that. She kept her mouth shut.

Sarah continued, "I think the healing center is a great idea, but if it's successful it will be because Celeste threw enough money and manpower at it to make it work, not because of some happy-mist cloud that descends upon our valley."

"You're right." Sage nodded, conceding the point. "Nevertheless, I have good feelings about the healing center's success. I think people who visit will be glad they came, and they'll spread the word. I believe Celeste's Angel Plan will put Eternity Springs on the map."

"We're already on the map," Sarah countered. "Only problem is, we're a speck of dust. A pinpoint. But maybe now that we have an angel dancing on the head of our pin, we're going to grow to be a real dot. If we become a dot, maybe I can make a living here working only one job instead of two."

Sarah owned the Trading Post, Eternity's only grocery store, opened and operated by Sarah's family since 1894. A single mother of a high school senior and staring college tuition in the face, Sarah had begun baking desserts for the Bristlecone Café about five years ago to supplement her income.

Curious, Sage asked, "So if you had a choice, would you rather quit baking or stop selling groceries?"

"Groceries," Sarah answered in a heartbeat. "If I won the lottery tomorrow, I'd hire a manager for the store, build a commercial kitchen, and bake to my little heart's content." Noting Sage's smile, she asked, "Does that surprise you?"

"Not at all. You are as much an artist with shortening and flour as I am with paint."

Sarah preened a little bit. "That's a lovely thing to say. Thank you."

Both women turned their heads when a red BMW convertible pulled up beside them and stopped. The driver was Sarah's daughter, Lori. Ali Timberlake's son, Chase, a student at the University of Colorado at Boulder, sat in the passenger seat. The two had begun dating over the past summer when Chase worked at the Double R Ranch outside of town.

"Well, now," Sarah said, her brows arching. "Does Ali know you're driving her car, young woman?"

"Yes, of course." Lori tucked a strand of long dark hair behind her ear and grinned. "Don't I look good behind this wheel, Mama? I think I need a car like this to take off to college with me next year."

"And I need Jimmy Choo shoes to wear next time I go mountain climbing, too. Now, where is Ali?"

"My mom is right behind you." Chase hooked his thumb over his shoulder. "She said she'd rather walk. Good decision, I say. With all the traffic in town today, you walkers are liable to beat us there, anyway."

Sage glanced back over her shoulder and saw Ali Timberlake approaching. As the convertible pulled away, she and Sarah waited for their friend. A frequent visitor to Eternity Springs, Ali lived in Denver with her husband, Mac, a federal court judge.

"What a great outfit," Sarah observed, eyeing Ali's

knit sweater jacket and slacks. "Ali always looks so stylish and put together. Perfect hair, perfect makeup. That blond bob of hers is never mussed. She's pure class. I hate her."

"Me too."

"Sage and I decided we hate you," Sarah said cheerfully as Ali joined them.

"Oh?" Ali asked, nonplussed. "Why is that?"

"You always look so good, you put us to shame."

At that, the newcomer grinned delightedly. "What a lovely compliment. Thank you for the hate."

"You're welcome." Sarah looped her arm through Ali's and they continued toward Angel's Rest.

"I didn't see you at the church," Sage said to Ali.

"I was almost late," Ali explained. "Caitlin's cross-country team had a meet yesterday that ran long, so I didn't drive in until this morning." She grinned a bit sheepishly, then added, "I didn't have to stay till the bitter end of the race, but since this is her senior year, I didn't want to miss a minute."

"I totally understand that," Sarah said.

For the rest of their walk, the three friends discussed Nic's wedding and Celeste Blessing's uncanny ability to have anticipated that Nic would need a wedding gown when she was nine months pregnant. They crossed the footbridge over Angel Creek and joined a growing crowd of visitors, where they mixed and mingled and settled in to enjoy the celebration.

The bells of St. Stephen's church rang the noon hour as Celeste stepped up to the temporary podium erected at the entrance to her property. Watching her brought a smile to Sage's face. For this town and its citizens, Celeste had been Santa Claus, a fairy godmother, and Glenda the Good Witch, all wrapped up in a bow. When she gracefully brought her arms out as though she were a dove unfurling her wings to take flight, Sage corrected herself. Celeste Blessing was Eternity Springs' angel.

"Welcome, friends, neighbors, and special guests," Celeste declared, her blue eyes sparkling. "God has blessed us with a glorious day, has He not?"

She paused while the crowd clapped and cheered, then continued, "It's been an exciting year for Eternity Springs as we put our recovery plan into action, and I think the first order of business is to give ourselves a round of applause. Once the decision was made to move forward with the idea of establishing a healing center and spa in our fair town, everyone pitched in to make it a success. Now we have this beautiful facility, a thriving economy, and a growing population. Are we good, or what?"

As the crowd erupted into more cheers and applause, Sage scanned the estate, reflecting on the change a year can make. The centerpiece of the Angel's Rest property was the mansion previously known as Cavanaugh House, which had been built by Ali's ancestor in the 1880s. Spruced up by its new coat of paint, new shutters, new roof, and one entire new wing that replaced the section that had burned down almost a year ago, the house gleamed in welcome. New landscaping on the estate included inviting, bubbling pools in the hot springs park area, designed by Gabe Callahan. Recently constructed cottages and dormitories offered appealing accommodations to guests, and a small but efficient staff was in place and ready to see Celeste's vision fulfilled. Sage was glad to be part of it.

"Now, my fellow citizens of Eternity Springs," Celeste continued with a twinkle in her eyes. "Before the party gets started, I'd like you to recollect back to that town meeting just about a year ago when this town's future appeared so bleak. If you'll recall, I stood before you and said that Eternity Springs didn't need the state of

Colorado to build a prison here to save the town. I believed then and I believe today that in order for our town to thrive, it needs to free itself from the prison of its past and utilize the gifts a generous and loving God has bestowed upon it.

"I hold that Angel's Rest offers a tool to assist Eternity Springs in doing both. Now, though our journey forward has begun, our winter is not yet behind us. We continue to face the challenge of overcoming our fears, foibles, and failings. I stand here before you today asking each of you to reach inside yourself, take ownership of your personal power, and trust it. Explore the forces of good awaiting your participation. The rebirth of spring is closer than before. Have faith, offer thanks, and believe in Eternity Springs."

Sage glanced around and smothered a smile at the skepticism and confusion painted on many of townspeople's faces. Celeste spoke with authority, and in the past eighteen months the people of Eternity Springs had come to respect her and listen to her, even if they didn't always understand her.

From her position at Sage's side, Sarah asked, "Does that make you want to run off and paint a picture like her speech did last year?"

Sage laughed. "No. I've already indulged my creativity today. Besides, I smell barbecue and I'm ready for lunch."

At the podium, Celeste continued. "As some of you may know, I commissioned a sign to be created by a longtime seasonal member of our Eternity Springs family, Dr. Colt Rafferty. Colt is a brilliant man, an engineer and former college professor who now serves the citizens of our country as a safety investigator out of Washington, D.C. But at heart, Colt is an artist who creates magnificent carvings from wood, a man whose soul is fed by all the wonder that is found here in Eternity

Springs. Colt and his father, Ben, another frequent visitor to our town, have joined us for today's celebration. Colt, would you step up here and assist me with the unveiling, please?"

Sage watched a tall man dressed in jeans and a blue chambray shirt make his way forward. From her position in the front of the crowd, she noted his long, lean build, wide shoulders, and thick, wavy black hair. When he turned to face the crowd, she saw that he had blue eyes. Striking blue eyes, the color of Hummingbird Lake in summer. His face was a study of sculpted angles and masculine planes that the artist in her itched to sketch. In a tone just shy of miffed, she observed, "So, that's the great Colt Rafferty, hmm?"

Ali looked at her friend in surprise. "You have a problem with him?"

Sage shrugged. "I've never met the man."

Lori Reese sighed. "Dr. Rafferty is the reason I decided to go to college. I'm hoping all my professors look like him."

Sarah slung an arm around her daughter's shoulders and said, "If all your professors look like Colt Rafferty, I'm going to enroll in classes myself."

Leaning forward, Sarah added to Ali, "Sage has had a stick up her butt about Colt ever since one of his carvings beat one of her paintings for the blue ribbon at the summer arts festival last month."

"I haven't had a stick up anything," Sage fired back. "I simply didn't think his work belonged in the local artists category since he skipped coming to Eternity Springs for three summers in a row. How can someone be considered local if they're gone for three years?"

"Local or not, he is one fine-looking man," Nic observed. Sage watched Colt Rafferty's large, tanned hands grasp the cord attached to the canvas covering the sign. Celeste signaled for the middle school band student to begin the drumroll she'd arranged. The sound vibrated through Sage, and anticipation swelled within her. Suddenly she felt as if she stood at the edge of the observation point up on Sinner's Prayer Pass, and when she tangibly felt Celeste's knowing gaze upon her, she had but one thought in her mind.

Uh-oh.

Colt's gaze fastened on the redhead near the front of the crowd, a beacon of fiery beauty amidst a sea of attractive blondes. *My oh my.* The already gorgeous mountain scenery had been upgraded significantly since his last visit to Eternity Springs. Slender but deliciously curved, the woman had flowing auburn hair that made him think of a medieval heroine in an Edmund Blair Leighton painting. Big green eyes, fair skin, a faint dusting of freckles across her nose.

He wondered who she was.

Then Celeste gave him the nod, and he turned his attention to the business at hand, giving the rope a hard yank. The canvas slipped, the sign was revealed, and Celeste waved in a flourish and declared, "Welcome to Angel's Rest!"

Colt watched the crowd's reaction with a measure of professional pride as they viewed the bas-relief figure of an angel in repose in front of a bubbling mountain brook, the words *Angel's Rest* a cloud in the sky. He saw his dad beam and the redhead's eyes round with reluctant appreciation. He read her lips as she said, "That is gorgeous work."

At the podium, Celeste tapped on the microphone to recapture attention, then said, "I want you all to take a close look at the detail and artistry of Colt's design. It's a masterpiece, truly. Now, what you don't know is that Colt donated his work to Angel's Rest in support of our mission. Isn't that lovely?"

As Celeste led the crowd in applauding him, Colt shifted his feet, gave a little embarrassed wave, and wished he'd thought to ask that she keep that quiet.

"Without further ado," Celeste continued, "I invite you all to eat, drink, and be merry and enjoy our grand opening celebration. Lunch is ready to be served, and music and dancing will begin at two on the grassy area around the gazebo. And of course, the hot springs park designed and constructed by our own Gabe Callahan is open and ready for anyone who wants a nice therapeutic soak. Welcome, all of you, to Angel's Rest. Thank you so much for coming."

As the crowd near the sign began to disperse, Gabe Callahan called, "Hey, Rafferty. My wife is too busy with girl talk to break away for lunch, but I'm headed for the barbecue line. Do you and your dad want to join me?"

Colt glanced at Ben, who interrupted his conversation with the mayor to say, "You go on. I'm getting a fishing report."

"I'm there," Colt replied to Gabe. "It smells wonderful, and I heard a rumor that there's ice cream from the Taste of Texas Creamery for dessert."

"Yep. Rocky road."

"My favorite."

The two men made male small talk—they discussed the upcoming Denver Broncos game—as they made their way to the food line. Callahan had served as Celeste's general contractor during the renovation and construction, so Colt had spoken with him on the phone a number of times about the design, delivery, and installation of the Angel's Rest sign. They'd met in person for the first time today.

"So, when I saw you bright and early this morning you didn't mention you were on your way to get mar-

ried to Nic Sullivan. Congratulations. I've known Nic
since we were kids. She's a great woman."

"Thanks," Gabe replied. "We're happy. I'm very
lucky."

He and Gabe both looked across the crowd to where
Nic, Sarah, the classy blonde, and the stunning redhead
stood laughing with Sarah's daughter and a young man
who Colt assumed was Lori's boyfriend. Nic looked like
a fertility goddess, he thought. "When is the baby due?"

"Anytime now," Gabe said. "And it's babies. Twins.
We're having twins."

"That's exciting."

"I'm scared to death."

"I can imagine. Do you know if they're girls or boys
or one of each?"

"No, Nic wanted to be surprised," Gabe said. "Do
you have children, Rafferty?"

Colt could have explained that he'd married right out
of college but that his wife had wanted to wait to have
kids, which turned out be a blessing because the marriage didn't last. However, he was a guy, so all he said
was, "Nope."

Then, again because he was a guy, he asked, "Who's
the redhead?"

Gabe's lips twisted in a slow grin. "Sage Anderson.
She's a good friend of Nic's. She's an artist and owns
Eternity Springs' art gallery, Vistas."

"Oh yeah?" Colt said. Celeste had been pushing him
to contact the owner of Vistas about exhibiting some of
his carvings. Maybe he'd do that. "What medium?"

"She's a painter. Her career has really taken off in the
last year or so. She has a big show coming up in Texas
later this year. She's great. A really nice lady."

Hmm. Really? She'd sure shot daggers at him—for no
reason at all that he knew of. As he and Callahan
reached the front of the barbecue line, Colt filled his

plate, then glanced over his shoulder for one more look at the lady.

She stood conversing in a group of a half dozen or so women. Laughing at something Sarah Reese was saying, she looked so gorgeous that she stole his breath away.

On second thought, some of his wood carvings really were pretty good. "Maybe after lunch, you could introduce us? I want to show her my . . . etchings."

Gabe snorted a laugh. "Only if I can hang around and see her reaction when you say that to her. Shoot, Celeste didn't need to pop for a band. Something tells me you and Sage can provide all the entertainment this town needs."

THREE

Sage sensed the wood-carver's gaze upon her and sti-fled the urge to turn her head and stick out her tongue at him. She'd never said so much as hello to him, and he still managed to push her buttons. "Fool," she murmured.

"What?" Sarah asked.

"I was thinking about the hot springs pools," she improvised. "Gabe's design has made them so inviting."

"I totally agree," Sarah said. "I think that—oh, Anna is waving at me. She's watching Mom today for me, so I'd better go see what she wants. Save a place for me in the barbecue line, would you?"

"Sure," Ali told her. As Sarah hurried off, Ali brought the conversation back to Gabe's landscape design. "I especially like the rock work around the pool that's off by itself."

"I haven't seen it yet," Nic said. "I learned early on that the smell of sulfur and pregnancy don't mix for me."

A note in Nic's voice had Sage giving her a close look. She spied lines of tension on her friend's brow and around her mouth. Something was up. Softly she asked, "Nic?"

Nic pasted on a bright but not quite genuine smile. "In fact, even though the prevailing breeze shoots the sulfur fumes away from the estate, I'm catching a few

whiffs now, so I think I'll change my venue for a bit."
Nic linked her arm through Ali's. "I haven't seen the
wedding gown quilt our Patchwork Angels bee completed. Ali, could I talk you into showing it to me?"

Sage thought Ali might have picked up on something
in Nic's demeanor, too, because she looked hard at Nic
for a moment before brightly saying, "I'd love to show
you. It's in the Aspenglow suite, and it's one of my very
favorite rooms at Angel's Rest."

Nic glanced at Sage. "You'll come with us?"

"Absolutely."

Nic called out to Gabe, "Honey? I'm going up to the
house with Ali and Sage to see our completed wedding
gown quilt."

"Okay."

The three friends made their way toward the old Victorian mansion, others slowing their progress with
greetings, comments, and questions. Once, Nic stopped
beside a cottonwood tree and rested her weight against
it, her eyes closed, breathing deeply.

Sage checked her watch, and Ali mouthed the words,
"Oh no." By the time they reached the house and entered through the kitchen door, Nic's expression had
tightened. The moment they were alone, Sage stated,
"You're in labor, aren't you?"

Nic chewed her lower lip and grabbed the handle of
the refrigerator for support. "Yes, I think I am. Will you
check me?"

Ali's eyes widened with concern. "Um, don't you
think we should call the doctor?"

Nic and Sage shared a look, then Sage said, "Actually,
I am a doctor. I trained as a pediatric surgeon, but I've
delivered my fair share of babies. I'll ask you to keep
that to yourself, Ali. Now, let's get you upstairs, Nic."

Ali held back any comment until they'd entered the
Aspenglow suite and she shut the door behind them.

Then as Sage ducked into the attached bathroom to wash her hands, she said, "I admit I'm surprised, Sage. Reassured for Nic, but surprised."

Her voice tight with pain, Nic said, "It's her deep, dark secret."

Ali stripped the beautiful wedding gown quilt off the bed and helped Nic onto it, asking, "Why is that?"

"I don't know."

"I don't talk about it," Sage told them when she reentered the bedroom. "Especially not now. We have bigger fish to fry."

Ali started to leave the room, but Nic said, "No, Ali. Stay. Sage might have delivered babies, but you've had them. I'd appreciate your input on this."

Moments later, Sage scowled. "For crying out loud, Nicole. You must have been having contractions at the church this morning. You're in active labor. We need to call for the helicopter."

"It's that close?" Nic asked as Sage offered her a hand to pull herself up to a seated position.

"Only if you don't want your babies' birthplace to be the top of Sinner's Prayer Pass. You are too far along to risk going in the car."

"Oh, dear. I really didn't think this was it. I've had so many aches and pains and pressure that I kept thinking it would stop like all the other times."

"This time it will stop with two babies being born," Sage told her. "Not before then."

"So, okay. Let's call for the helicopter." Nic grimaced as another pain hit her, then said, "Gabe probably won't be happy."

"No, he probably won't," Ali agreed.

"I don't have my camera, either." Nic pursed her lips in a pout. "Do you think Celeste has one around here that we could borrow?"

"I have one in my purse downstairs," Ali said. "I'll get it for you on our way out."

As Sage phoned for the medical helicopter, Ali walked with Nic toward the staircase. Halfway there, Nic stopped abruptly and said, "Oh my."

She glanced downward as fluid gushed from between her legs.

Ali took one look and called, "Sage? Her water broke."

At that point, Nic gasped and bent over, her pain obvious. "Oh . . . Ali. I can feel . . . oh. Oh, whoa. Whoa. Whoa. They're coming. They're coming now!"

Sage took one look at Nic, and her stomach rolled. *No, no, no.* She didn't want this. She couldn't do this. For a few long seconds that lasted like hours, she was back in the stifling heat on a rutted dirt path, supporting the weight of a laboring mother walking to assist nature's work.

The sound of her name was a gunshot. "Sage!"

She jerked back to the present. Nic. Her friend. *I have to do this. I promised her. I can do this. I will do this.*

Sage reached down deep inside of her, past the fear and the ugliness and the grief, to find Dr. Anderson. "Okay, I guess we're doing this here," the physician said. "Ali? You want to go get Gabe?"

"I'm on my way."

Gabe Callahan was talking with Henry Moorland, owner of the Double R Ranch, repeating the story about the time he and his brothers had had the bright idea to ride a local rancher's bull. "Two of my brothers are identical twins," he said, grinning at the memory. "Mark and Luke peeled off their shirts and went into the pasture and—"

He broke off abruptly when he heard Ali Timberlake call, "Gabe!"

He whipped his head around at the note of urgency in her voice. The moment he met her concerned gaze, he started moving toward her. "Is it Nic?"

"She's in labor. The babies are coming. Now."

Gabe took it like a punch to the gut. *She's in labor. The babies are coming.* "Okay, I'll go get the car."

"No, Gabe. The babies are coming *now*. There's no time. Don't worry, though. Sage is with her." Lowering her voice, Ali added, "She's a doctor."

Don't worry? Don't worry? Grimly he asked, "Where is she?"

"Up at the house."

He took off running.

He covered the distance to the house in record time, and bounded up the steps and into the house. "Nic?" he shouted.

"Up here, Gabe," Sage called.

He had a lump the size of Texas in his throat as he took the stairs three at a time, following the terrifying sounds of his wife's groans and Sage Anderson's calm voice. "That's good. You're doing fine, Nic. Now, push. Push, push, push. Take a breath. Push, push, push."

She's pushing. In that second, due to previous experience and the refresher childbirth class he'd taken in Gunnison this past summer, Gabe recognized that the situation was indeed too far gone to transport her to Gunnison. That meant no hospital. They were doing this here. *Thank God Sage is a doctor. Please, God. Please, please, please, please.*

He burst into the room. "Nic?"

"Wash your hands, Gabe," Sage instructed. She was behind Nic on the bed, supporting her body while she pushed. "That's it, sweetheart. You're doing great. Now rest."

Gabe ducked into the bathroom and hurriedly washed his hands, then rushed back to Nic. "Are you okay?"

"So far, so good." She smiled up at him tremulously. "I'm sorry, Gabe. I didn't mean to do it this way."

"That's okay. I'll yell at you about it later." Without being told, he took Sage's place and supported his wife just as she sucked in a breath. "Here comes another one."

From that moment on, time passed in a weird progression of agonizingly slow seconds and fast-as-lightning minutes. The dressing table mirror was arranged in such a way that he could see what was happening at the bottom of the bed, and he only vaguely noted that Ali Timberlake arrived with a camera in hand.

"Did you track down the supply cart?" Sage asked her.

"Yes. Celeste is on her way with it now."

"Oh, heavens," Nic said, panting.

"Get her up," Sage instructed. "There you go, girlfriend. Push, push, push."

Gabe kept his gaze glued to the mirror. Nic moaned and groaned.

Sage encouraged, "Attagirl. You can do it, Nic. We're almost there. Almost."

Nic let out a scream and a little head popped out.

"Dear Jesus," Gabe prayed as seconds later Nic gave another push and the baby slid out into Sage's waiting hands.

"We have a girl," Sage said.

For a heartbreakingly long few seconds, nothing happened, then Gabe and Nic's daughter drew air into her lungs and let out an angry mewl.

Crying and laughing at the same time, Nic said, "She sounds like a little lamb."

"So says the veterinarian," Sage said as she tucked the little one securely into the crook of her arm. "Ali? How long will it take Celeste to—"

"I'm here." The older woman blew into the room

pushing a medical cart. "I decided it was easier to bring the whole thing. Colt carried it up for me. What do you need?"

"Sterile scissors, to begin with," Sage said.

With Celeste acting as a competent assistant, Sage saw to the baby's immediate needs, then handed her to her mother. "You three say a quick hello, because there is more work here to be done."

Tears were flowing down Nic's face as she cradled their daughter against her. "Oh, look, Gabe. She's beautiful. Isn't she beautiful?"

She was a wrinkly, squiggly thing covered with blood and cheesy-looking stuff, but he agreed. "Absolutely gorgeous."

Love filled his heart as he watched his daughter and her mother, and when the memory of another birth arose in his mind, he refused to let it steal his joy. He would never forget the son he had lost or the woman who had given birth to him, but this was a moment for the future, not the past. Then Nic let out another groan, and he focused his mind on the present.

"I need another pair of arms here," Sage said. "Celeste? Ali? One of you take the baby."

"Let me," Sarah Reese said. Just when she'd joined the gathering, Gabe didn't know, but he was glad to have her here. It felt right for Nic to have her closest friends with her now. Sarah held out her arms and cradled the baby, now swaddled in the receiving blanket Celeste had brought along with the medical cart. "Well, now. Aren't you the prettiest little thing?"

"A little angel," Celeste said.

At that point things got busy again. Twelve minutes later, Nic delivered Gabe's second little girl.

By that time, a crowd had gathered downstairs and the helicopter was waiting to take them to the hospital. After a brief discussion and a phone consultation between Sage and the obstetrician in Gunnison, the decision was made to send the bird back without any patients. Nic and the girls were doing fine.

Nic and the girls. His girls.

Emotion shuddered through him, and Gabe closed his eyes and fought back tears. Celeste shooed him out of the room to announce the births to those gathered downstairs while the women tidied up. He was glad to have a brief escape. He needed to get hold of his emotions before he broke down and bawled like a baby.

Walking to the landing and gazing down at the gathering in sort of a shell-shocked gaze, Gabe felt a sense of belonging that went all the way to the bone. As he fumbled for words to express himself, Lori Reese lost patience.

"Well?" she demanded. "We heard crying. What did she have?"

His smile broke like sunlight on Easter morning. "Girls. Nic and I have girls. Mama and babies are doing great."

A cheer went up, and Gabe gave a little wave, then turned away. He didn't want anyone to see the tears he no longer could quell. He retreated down the hallway toward the room where his family awaited, then collapsed against the wall. He closed his eyes and his fingers found the small silver medal he wore around his neck, the gift from Celeste designed by Sage that the older woman had called the "official healing center blazon awarded to those who have embraced healing's grace."

Gabe didn't know about that. He wore it as a symbol of his own rebirth. He was John Gabriel Callahan, son, brother.

Husband.

Father.

When he opened his eyes, Celeste stood before him,

her smile warm, a tender look in her eyes. "Congratulations, Gabe."

"Thank you. Thank you for everything."

"You are very welcome. Now, you have three ladies waiting on you inside. The three of you need some alone time."

"Okay." He pushed away from the wall, but before he could take a step, Celeste placed her hand on his arm.

"You should get in touch with your family, Gabe. Tell them your glorious news."

He nodded. "You're right. I'm ready. I think I'll do that. Or, better yet, once the girls are old enough to travel, I think we should pay them a visit." A wistful smile touched his lips. "Maybe for Christmas."

"Yes. The season of miracles. It's fitting."

Gabe bent and kissed her cheek, then walked into the bedroom, where Nic had one baby at her breast. Sage sat in the rocking chair with the other. The babies appeared to have been washed, and Nic's hair was freshly brushed. "You are so beautiful," he said to her.

Sage rose from the rocker. "It's about time you came back, Daddy," she said, handing the baby over to Gabe. "I have it on certain authority that there's a plate of barbecue waiting for me downstairs in the kitchen. Holler if you need me, but I don't expect you will."

As Sage quietly left the room, Gabe kicked off his shoes, then sat beside Nic in the queen-sized bed. "I love you, Nicole Callahan."

"I love you, too, Gabe Callahan."

He smiled from one baby to the other. "I want to say that to these little bits, but I don't know what to call them. Do you?"

"I thought . . ." Nic glanced up at him. "Maybe after our mothers?"

Gabe thought back to when his mother was still alive,

and his father's pet name for her. "Meg, for Margaret? Or Mary."

"Meg, I think. And Carolyn for mine? Meg and Cari Callahan?"

"Works for me. What about middle names?"

"Hmm . . ."

"I have an idea," Gabe said, gazing at his girls. "It's probably hokey."

"Tell me."

"I don't know—I guess it's the Eternity Springs influence—but somehow it just feels right."

"What feels right?"

"I think—if you don't mind—I'd like their middle names to be Faith and Joy."

"Oh, Gabe. That's sweet. A little hokey, but that's what makes it perfect. I think Margaret Joy Callahan and Carolyn Faith Callahan are our names. You choose which baby gets which name."

Gabe frowned as he studied his daughters' identical little faces. "We're gonna have to mark them somehow so we don't get them mixed up."

Nic shook her head. "Their cries are different. Our firstborn is louder."

"Which one is she?"

"The one you're holding." She waited a beat, then added, "Sarah put a dot of fingernail polish on her toe just in case."

"Starting on makeup already." He sighed. Then he pressed a kiss to his firstborn daughter's forehead. "Okay, then let's name her Cari. It comes first in the alphabet. That'll help me remember."

"Don't be silly. You won't forget."

She was right. He had been blessed with another chance at happiness, and he intended to treasure it, revel in it, from this moment forward. He wouldn't forget a minute of it. John Gabriel Callahan's heart overflowed.

Here, in this one little corner of the big wide world, he'd found his faith, his joy, and his love.

Sage's stomach was about to erupt. She'd held off her nervousness, nausea, and panic during the heat of the moment, but once the emergency was behind her, she began to lose it. Seeking fresh air, she exited the house by the back door and fled from the crowd toward the mountain behind the estate and the cover of the forest.

She made it as far as the carriage house apartment. Ducking around behind it, she bent over double and vomited. When she was finished, she leaned against the house, closed her eyes, and shuddered.

A male voice she didn't recognize said, "Please tell me it wasn't the barbecue. I had two helpings."

The wood-carver. Of course. That was just her luck. Her cheeks stinging with embarrassment, Sage warily opened her eyes. He extended his hand, offering her a dampened washcloth. She accepted it, wiped her brow, then said a bit crankily, "Where did you come from?"

"I'm staying here in the carriage house." He waited a beat, then asked, "Are you okay?"

"Yes. I just . . ." She exhaled heavily as the memories gnawed at the edge of her consciousness, so she welcomed a distraction. "You shouldn't have entered the arts festival contest as a local."

He frowned. "What arts festival?"

Her fingers were beginning to tremble. She narrowed her gaze and focused on Rafferty. "The one last month where you won the blue ribbon."

"I didn't enter any contest."

"It was your work." She recalled the image of the artwork and concentrated on it. "It was beautiful. A segmented vase made of madrone, tulipwood, wenge, and maple."

"Shaped like a hot air balloon?" he asked.

"Yes." In her mind's eye she saw a balloon floating over a bloody killing field. Sage fisted her hands so tight that her nails drew blood from her palms. *Stop it!*

He shrugged. "I gave that to Celeste as a gift. I certainly never intended to show it." He rubbed the back of his neck, then asked, "Did she sell it?"

"No. It's in the Aspenglow suite at the main house. With its blue ribbon." Her chest grew tight, and it was difficult to breathe. "Could I have a glass of water?"

"Sure. Come with me."

He led her inside the carriage house apartment and to the kitchen, where he filled a glass with water and offered it to her, saying, "You're acting kinda cranky about that blue ribbon."

"I like to win." She took a sip, then waited a moment to make certain it would stay down. Her mouth tasted sour and she grimaced.

"There's a toothbrush in a guest basket in the bathroom if you want it."

"Thank you," she said quietly.

In the bathroom, she brushed her teeth, rinsed her face, then stared into the mirror. Instead of her own reflection, she saw . . . carnage.

It hit her then, the full-blown panic attack. Hyperventilation. Racing heart. Dizziness. Tight throat. Sweats.

She must have made some sound, because as if from a great distance, she heard him knock on the door and call her name. How long that went on, she didn't know, but at some point he was there, staring at her, frowning at her.

"You okay?" When she didn't answer, simply stood there shaking, he said, "Stupid question. I'll call 911."

He started to leave. She made a jerky grab at his arm and croaked out, "No."

He studied her. "You're not having a heart attack, are you?"

When she shook her head, he took hold of her arm.

"Okay, then. Since you're a physician, I'll take your word for it and chalk this up to a panic attack, with which, unfortunately, I am all too familiar. But if you keel over dead, you're not allowed to sue me. C'mere, you need to sit down before you fall down."

"You know about me?" she managed to ask as he guided her into the living room. "Being a doctor?"

"Word got out during the excitement."

"Oh no," she said, whimpering. "I don't want that. They'll ask me. I can't talk about it."

"It's okay. You don't have to talk about anything. That's one of the great things about having freedom of speech—you have the freedom to shut up, too." He sat in a rocking chair, then tugged her down onto his lap.

The tiny little part of Sage that could still think decided the man was being way too familiar, but the rest of her didn't care. She clung to him like a lifeline. He smelled of wood smoke and emanated safety. His arms offered sanctuary that she couldn't resist.

"I delivered those babies," she murmured, fighting back the memories washing over her, dark and ugly and full of despair. "Two healthy little babies."

"That you did." He held her and rocked her and murmured soothing sounds against her ear.

Slowly, ever so slowly, the past retreated and the panic dissipated. Sage could breathe again. At that point, a river of despair washed through her and with it, finally, came tears. A flood of tears.

She sobbed against a stranger's broad chest as if her world had come to an end. In many ways, that's exactly what had happened. A little more than five years ago, the world as she had known it ended on an African savannah.

"Let it go, sweetheart," Colt Rafferty murmured. "It's poison when you keep it inside. Get it all out."

So she did. She cried for the children. Cried for her

lost career. Cried because sometimes evil won. She lost all track of time, but for these stolen minutes, for the first time in a very long time, she felt safe and protected and not so alone. Throughout it all, Colt continued to rock her.

Finally, when the storm of tears had expended all their fury, she rested, completely spent. Colt allowed her a few minutes, then said, "A big part of my job is solving puzzles, so I'm inclined to explore what happened here. I know that you are Sage Anderson, owner of the gallery in town. I know you are a painter and have a competitive artistic streak. Today you served as Nic Callahan's obstetrician and delivered her twin daughters, but after keeping your cool throughout, you fell apart. That makes you interesting, Sage. Fascinating."

"I don't talk about it," Sage said, knowing she should move but not quite ready to do so.

"That's okay. Puzzle solving is more fun when you discover clues all on your own." With that, he put his fingers beneath her chin, tilted up her face, and kissed her.

She tasted minty fresh and surprised. *Okay, make that shocked,* he revised after she broke speed records scrambling off his lap.

"I'm not a puzzle," she snapped. "I'm a . . . a . . ."

"Doctor?" he suggested.

Her mouth moved, but no words came out.

"Artist who craves blue ribbons?"

Her chin came up. "I'm a woman."

He grinned. "Yes, you are definitely a woman. A beautiful, intriguing puzzle of a woman—who I suspect hasn't been kissed in far too long."

Satisfaction washed through Colt as her pale complexion flooded with color and her limp, weary posture grew straight and strong. "Bite me, Rafferty."

His laughter followed her out of the door.

Colt didn't see Sage Anderson again before he departed Eternity Springs the next day. But in the days and weeks that followed, he thought of her often.

He truly did love puzzles.

FOUR

December

Fat, white snowflakes floated down from the night sky and iced the gingerbread on the Victorian-era storefronts and houses in downtown Eternity Springs. At just after three in the morning, the temperature hovered around zero and the streets of the small mountain town lay silent and empty but for the three inches of new snow that had fallen since midnight. Out at her cottage on Hummingbird Lake, Sage dreamed she was back in Africa.

The flatbed truck roared into the small village and stopped outside the plain mud-brick structure that today served as a medical clinic. Sage glanced up from the child whose leg wound she'd just cleaned and stitched as a half dozen Zaraguinas jumped down from the truck and marched inside brandishing guns. One of the rebel gang members shifted his gaze between Sage and her fiancé, Dr. Peter Gates, and barked out a demand in Sangho. "Which is Dr. Sage?"

Peter shot her a warning glance as he stepped forward. "I'm Dr. Sage."

The Zaraguina frowned, then put his gun barrel against a toddler's head and asked her mother, "Is he Sage?"

The mother trembled, her eyes wide with fear. "No. She is."

As the rebel shifted his gun toward Peter, Sage stepped forward. "No! Hurt him and you might as well kill me, too. I won't help you if you harm him. What do you need?"

Tension shimmered in the air like heat waves. "You are a surgeon?"

"Yes."

"So am I," *Peter lied, drawing the rebel's attention back to him and making Sage want to kill him herself.* "I can do anything she can do. I'll go with you willingly if you need assistance. Guns aren't necessary. We are with the Doctors Without Borders organization. It's part of our mission to provide independent and impartial medical aid. Politics don't matter."

The rebel's gaze went flat and cold. Sage's knees turned to Jell-O. He rolled his tongue around his mouth, then spat on the floor. "The woman comes with us."

"That would be a mistake." *Peter lifted a hand and took a step forward.* "I'm a better doctor—"

As happened more and more often, the echo of the gunshot jerked Sage out of her nightmare. She lay in her bed breathing hard, her pulse pounding, actually smelling the stink of gunpowder, until terror dissipated, reality returned, and exhaustion and despair overwhelmed her.

She hadn't managed five hours of uninterrupted sleep at a time in months. And to think that prior to the Callahan girls' births, she'd believed that she'd almost defeated her monsters. She'd believed that her spirit was healing.

How wrong she had been. All it had taken was the delivery of two beautiful little girls who would grow up happy and healthy and loved and the demons came roaring back. Ever since that day, she'd spent most of her nights painting.

Purging.

Tonight would be no different. After tossing and turning, then considering and rejecting the temptation of sleeping pills—she'd been down that road before after her father died, and it wasn't a healthy route for her to take—she finally admitted that additional sleep was beyond her reach. Climbing from her bed, Sage pulled on her warmest robe and slippers, then padded to her studio, where she switched on the lights and placed a blank canvas on her easel. In keeping with her mood, she painted only in shades of red and black—the colors of violence.

Over the next five hours she poured out her inner rage, her fury, and her pain onto the canvas and exorcised the memories—at least for a little while. She rid herself of monkey chatter and lion roars. Rid herself of rain-soaked jungle and hot savannah. Rid herself of screams and the haunting melody of little voices singing childhood Christian hymns. When she finally stepped away from the easel, her right arm ached and her eyes felt gritty, but the door to the past was firmly shut. Exhaustion hit her like a fist. She thought longingly of her bed, but she didn't have time for a nap today. She had to be in Gunnison by noon to catch her flight, and she still had to pack.

She looked forward to the trip to Fort Worth and the reception for her show at Art on the Bricks gallery. Not only was Steve Montgomery one of her early supporters, he was an all-around nice guy. He reminded her of her father, which was totally weird because except for the similarity in age, broad-shouldered build, and graying hair, the Colonel couldn't have been more different. Steve was kind and indulgent, and he laughed easily and often. Her father had been the typical army leader—

tough, tenacious, and hard-charging. He didn't tolerate mistakes, lazy afternoons, flights of fancy, or cowardice.

No wonder he'd so often looked at Sage as if she were a changeling.

Which made her wonder why she thought of her dad every time she spoke with Steve. "Your mind is a scary place, Anderson," she muttered as she cleaned her brushes.

She spent the next hour packing and tidying her home, then departed for the airport. After a relatively smooth travel day, she arrived at the Dallas/Fort Worth airport and caught a cab to the boutique hotel in downtown Fort Worth where Steve had booked a room for her. She did manage a thirty-minute nap before Steve picked her up and took her to the gallery, where they spent a few hours finishing up last-minute show arrangements.

Later over dinner, Steve studied her over the top of his glass of wine and said, "What's wrong, darling? Are you unhappy with the show design?"

"No, it's wonderful. I told you I loved it."

"Then what's wrong? You seem to have lost your sparkle."

She reached out and squeezed his hand. "I'm sorry. I'm tired. I didn't sleep well last night."

"Well then, let's get you back to the hotel and you can make an early night of it. In fact, have the concierge schedule a massage and facial for you tomorrow, too. My treat."

Sage grimaced and reached for her purse and a mirror. "I must really look bad."

"No, no, no. You're lovely as always." He signaled for the check and added, "I just want tomorrow to be fun and relaxing and special for you."

That evening, Sage managed six whole hours of sleep and awoke feeling like a new woman. She spent the morning with a sculptor whose work Vistas represented, then kept her spa appointments and snuck in a movie—an amusement she missed living in Eternity Springs—before returning to the hotel to prepare for the big event.

Following a twenty-minute, hot-as-she-could-stand-it shower, she turned off the water and grabbed a fluffy white bath towel in the luxurious bathroom of her suite. Once she'd dried the water from her body and slipped into her robe, she used a hand towel to wipe the steam off the mirror. She peered at her reflection and sighed.

The facial and massage had helped, but it would take a miracle application of makeup to hide the results of weeks of poor sleep.

"You can do this," she lectured her reflection. "You'll go to this reception and you'll be charming and witty and no one will know that you are running on fumes."

She did her hair and makeup and had taken a seat on the side of the bed to don her hose when her cell buzzed. Expecting it to be Steve, she didn't bother to check the number before she answered. "Hello?"

"Sage? It's Rose."

Sage closed her eyes. Everything inside her went tense at the sound of her sister's voice. "Hello, Rose. This is a surprise."

The surprise of the century, in fact. She hadn't heard from Rose since when? The brief duty call last Christmas?

"I have news I thought you'd like to know."

"Okay," Sage warily replied. She waited, but the line remained silent. "Rose?"

Her voice tight, Rose finally said, "I need to tell you . . ."

"Yes?"

Her sister blew out a sigh. "I keep up with the newspapers in places where we used to live. I saw that Mrs. Ayer passed away."

It took Sage a moment to make the connection. Mrs. Ayer had lived across the street from them when the Colonel was stationed at Fort Bragg. She'd babysit Sage in the afternoons after school until Rose got home from tennis practice. She was nice. She'd made outstanding chocolate chip cookies. "I'm sorry to hear that. She must have been in her eighties by now."

"Ninety-one. The obit said she died of natural causes."

"I see. Well, she enjoyed a long life." And why was Rose using this as an excuse to call?

"Yes, well, I thought you should know."

But that's not why you're calling. Sage's hand tightened around the phone as her thoughts spun. Rose might have called to question her, to argue with her, or to scold her, but not to pass along old neighborhood news. That wasn't Rose.

Sage's relationship with her sister was complicated, to say the least. Rose Anderson, M.D., was six years older than Sage and in some ways more mother than sister, having stepped into the role at the age of eleven when their mother died. Even after Rose followed their father's footsteps into the army, she'd kept in relatively close contact with Sage. She'd been disappointed when Sage chose not to enter the armed services, but she'd been thrilled the day Sage had been admitted to med school.

The break between them occurred when their father suffered a stroke after Sage had returned from Africa and events spiraled out of both sisters' control. Sage couldn't tell Rose about her exchange with their dad, and Rose had said and done some things that Sage found unforgivable. Contact between them since had been short, sparse, and fraught with tension. Each time it happened, Sage wanted to get roaring drunk.

"Okay," Sage said finally. "Thanks for telling me."

"You're welcome. Sage, I, um, need . . ."

Sage waited a long minute, and when Rose didn't continue, she prodded, "You need what?"

"I, um . . . nothing. Never mind. I have to go. Goodbye."

The dial tone sounded in Sage's ear.

She counted to five, then exhaled a heavy breath and threw the phone down against the pillows. What was that all about? She blinked away the tears she wasn't aware had pooled in her eyes. "Excuse me, but she's the one who cut me off at the knees. She's the one who turned her back on me, not the other way around."

She shoved a foot into one leg of her pantyhose and almost tore a hole. Since it was the only pair she had with her, she was more careful with the other. She finished dressing, slipping into her favorite emerald green cocktail dress and a sparkly pair of heels that she acknowledged did wonders for her legs. Picking up her lipstick, she stood before the mirror and stared at her reflection. "Forget it. Forget her. This is your night."

She smoothed the bronze shade over her upper lip, then her lower. She rubbed her lips together, smoothed the color with a fingertip, then repeated, "It's your night and no one is going to spoil it."

At the downtown Fort Worth steak house following a mouthwatering rib eye and an excellent Napa Valley cab, Colt Rafferty surreptitiously checked his watch as his dinner companion asked, "Shall we order dessert?"

"Whatever you'd like, Melody."

Melody Slaughter was a lovely woman about his age, a happily married mother of three and a marketing director with a local defense industry contractor. As the senior planner for the safety seminar he'd attended today, she'd secured the speakers for the event and had invited Colt and his two fellow presenters to join her for dinner. He'd been the only one to accept.

"I shouldn't," Melody said, offering a sheepish smile. "But the chocolate cake here is divine and I have no willpower at all."

"Then by all means, let's order dessert." He signaled the waiter and smothered his impatience. She was a nice lady, friendly, intelligent, and interesting. Under other circumstances, he'd have been happy to prolong the meal. But ever since he'd scanned the society section of the local newspaper while waiting in the hotel lobby for Melody to arrive, he'd been anxious for the meal to be done. He had somewhere he wanted to go. Someone he wanted to see.

He gave their dessert orders, then Melody said, "At the risk of sounding like a suck-up, I want to tell you again how informative and fascinating I found your presentation today, Colt. You really know how to get people's attention."

"Graphic photographs will do that."

She shook her head. "No. The photos were part of it, true, but it's the narratives that will haunt me. So much tragedy that a little bit of planning and precaution could have prevented. What you said, the way you said it, connected with people. They won't forget it."

"Good. Maybe they'll be more aware and save me some work."

"You mean save lives."

"The less work my team has, the better."

"Amen to that. I have to admit, though, your presentation leaves me a bit nervous. My husband is a sales rep for a plastics distributor and he's in and out of a lot of factories. I hope they're all doing what they're supposed to be doing safety-wise."

As Colt searched for a more comforting response to that than *Probably not*, their desserts arrived. The interruption made it easy to change the subject, so after the waiter poured coffee and departed, he asked, "Are you familiar with an art gallery called Art on the Bricks?"

She brightened. "I am. The owner is a baseball fan. He has tickets in the same section as ours at Rangers Ballpark."

"Is the gallery far from downtown?"

"No, it's a five-minute car ride from here. It's near the Kimbell Art Museum."

Colt nodded. He knew where the Kimbell was located. He'd passed it on the way from his downtown hotel to the speaking venue. "I saw a newspaper ad about a reception they're having tonight. It's open to the public and I'd like to go. Would you care to join me?"

"I'd love to join you. Thank you."

"Your husband won't come after me with a gun or something for keeping you out longer than expected?"

She laughed and rolled her eyes. "Nothing to worry about. He had poker night earlier this week when our two-year-old was teething, so he owes me."

They talked about her children as the valet brought her car around, then on the short drive to the gallery she asked him about the reception. "Are they showing a new artist?"

"Yes. A woman from a little town in Colorado where I vacation, Eternity Springs. Her name is Sage Anderson. Are you familiar with her work?"

"No, I'm afraid not, but I do know Eternity Springs. It's a great little town. We spent a week there a few summers ago. Out of the way and not much to do there, but it's so gorgeous, so beautiful."

"Yes, it is." And so was one of its residents. Sage Anderson. Dr. Sage Anderson. He couldn't wait to see her again. Colt and Melody discussed Eternity Springs until they arrived at the gallery and discovered that they shared a few acquaintances, most memorably the mountain man who went by the name Bear. "My husband hired Bear as a guide to teach him and our eight-year-old how to fly-fish. He's quite a character. He and our son hit it off, though, so Bear took us up to his private land to fish. It has to be one of the most beautiful places on earth."

"Oh, yeah? I've never been there. Where is his place?"

"Up by Heartache Falls."

Colt flashed her a grin. "Thanks for the tip. I'll have to see what I can do about wrangling an invitation my-self next time I'm up there."

The gallery's parking lot was filled to overflowing and Melody drove around a bit before finding a space. "So, is this artist a painter? A sculptor? What are we going to see?"

"She paints, but I didn't notice the name for this show, so I'm not sure what we'll see."

Something emotional, he expected. Dramatic. He wouldn't be surprised to see boiling seas or tumultuous skies or even abstract art as long as it was full of motion and energy and depth. He'd wondered about it, and half a dozen times he'd started to indulge his curiosity and Google her, but the part of him that appreciated fine art wanted to wait and experience her artwork firsthand. He believed that seeing her work would tell him so much about her.

Pieces for the puzzle.

They reached the gallery door. Colt opened it for Melody, then stepped inside after her. Despite the crush of people in the room, his eye was immediately drawn to the centerpiece of the show. He gaped. *What the hell?*

"Isn't that beautiful?" Melody said at his side. "The colors are fabulous."

"It's . . . fairies. And butterflies."

"Yes, isn't it fun?"

He struggled for a response. Fairies. Butterflies. Sweetness. Finally he shrugged. "It's . . . okay."

Melody looked at him in surprise. "Well, that's a ringing endorsement."

"It's not what I expected. It's . . . nice."

From right behind him, he heard a familiar voice snap, "Rafferty? Did you just say my painting is nice?"

FIVE

Colt winced. *Ah, hell.* She'd heard him. Pasting on a smile, he turned . . . and all but swallowed his tongue. She wore a green cocktail dress that hugged her delicious curves and made her eyes glow like emeralds.

Or maybe it was the temper snapping in her eyes that made them gleam.

"Hello, Sage."

Sage folded her arms, lifted her chin, and demanded, "What do you mean 'nice'?"

Colt faced a choice. He could lie to her, tell her she misheard him, slather her with flattery, and perhaps pull himself out of this hole. But, frankly, he didn't want to do that. He tried never to lie, and he thought this woman deserved better than that from him.

"It's . . . pretty," he said. Glancing around the gallery, he spied another five or six paintings and had the same reaction. Pretty and whimsical. Passionless. Not the sort of thing he'd expect from a woman who'd shown the depth of emotion she'd demonstrated when he found her crying behind the carriage house at Angel's Rest. That woman had emoted from every pore. "They're pretty."

"Pretty," the artist repeated as if he'd insulted her firstborn.

"Hey, the world needs pretty." He snagged two glasses of champagne from the tray of a circulating server and handed one of them to Melody, asking, "Don't you think?"

"Well, um, yes," his clearly uncomfortable dinner date replied.

Sage's eyes narrowed to slits and raked him head to toe. Colt wondered if he should check himself for laser burns.

Her voice tight, she asked, "What are you doing here?"

"It's a public gathering. I saw the ad in the paper. I'm in town for a meeting." He gestured toward the ill-at-ease woman at his side and added, "Sage Anderson, meet Melody Slaughter. Melody has visited Eternity Springs and she knows Bear."

At that, Sage dismissed him, turned to Melody, and spoke graciously. "It's lovely to meet you. Thank you so much for coming."

Melody's distress disappeared. Curious amusement replaced it as she glanced from Sage to Colt, then back to Sage again. Then with genuine warmth she said, "I'm so glad to be here. I want to tell you that your work"— she gestured to the centerpiece—"warms my heart and lifts my spirits. It makes me smile."

Sage beamed with pleasure. She shot Colt a look just short of smug. "Let me show you a painting over here. It's my favorite."

She slipped her arm through Melody's and led her away from Colt. As he watched the women go, his gaze dipped to the swing of Sage's hips while his lips twitched with a smile. He sipped his champagne and wandered in the opposite direction, thinking he'd take a closer look at these fairies of hers.

The majority of her paintings sported tags marking them as sold. Appreciating that success, he lifted his glass in silent toast to her marketing acumen, then studied the work. He'd give her an A+ on effective use of color and texture, an A on composition, an A- on originality. But where was the emotion? Where was the energy?

The Sage Anderson he knew could do better than this.

He moved closer to one work and read the label. *Pixies at Play.* How ridiculous was that? What was the difference between a pixie and a fairy anyway?

Not that he had anything against fantasy. Colt liked a good fantasy as much as the next man, but this work simply didn't do it for him. He studied the painting in front of him, noted the tiny eyes and little wings peeking out from behind a pink hibiscus flower, and shook his head. *Maybe it's a girl thing.*

Or maybe painting fluff is how she copes. "Hmm," he murmured to himself. Interesting idea.

Turning away from the paintings, he glanced around the room looking for both Sage and Melody. The crowd had thinned out in the few minutes they'd been here. He glanced at his watch. Only fifteen minutes left if they kept to the advertised time.

He didn't see the guest of honor, but he did spy Melody conversing with an older couple. He wandered over to join her, and she introduced him to a local oilman and his wife. Colt learned that the couple already owned two paintings by Sage Anderson and had purchased another here tonight. "I smile every time I look at an Anderson," the oilman said. "In this day and age, smiles are something to value, don't you think?"

"I can't argue with that," Colt said, meaning it. That was the second "smile" comment he'd heard. Maybe he should give his position a bit more thought.

They made small talk for a few more minutes, and then the other couple took their leave. Melody turned to Colt and said, "I probably should be going soon, too."

"All right. Why don't we track down the elusive artist and say goodnight?"

It hadn't escaped Colt's notice that while Sage continued to work the room, she managed to avoid whatever section he occupied. He wished she hadn't heard him express his reaction toward her work, but at the same time, her hostility intrigued him. Challenged him.

He positioned their approach so that Sage couldn't see them coming and scoot away. Eavesdropping on her conversation, he discovered that she, too, was staying in a downtown hotel. *Well, now. That's convenient.*

He smothered his grin when Sage turned toward them and her smile momentarily faltered. Melody said, "I need to get home, but I wanted to tell you I'm so glad to have met you. I would love to own a painting of yours someday, and that I absolutely plan on visiting your gallery next time we're in Colorado."

"Thank you so much," Sage replied. "It's been lovely to meet you, too, and I do hope to see you in Eternity Springs."

She once again favored Colt with one of those fake smiles. "Have a good trip back to Washington, Rafferty."

"Why, thank you, Sage. I so appreciate your good wishes."

Colt took her hand, brought it up to his lips, and kissed it. "It's been a revelation."

She snatched her hand back, and Colt halfway expected to see her wipe it off on her dress. He couldn't help but chuckle as he and Melody made their way back to her car.

"That was entertaining," the lady observed as she slipped her key into the ignition. "I am so glad you accepted our speaking invitation, Colt. For many reasons."

"I take it as a personal challenge never to bore my dinner dates," he drawled. Melody laughed and pulled out onto the road, and Colt added, "Seriously, though, I appreciate having had this opportunity. You've given me something to think about where the job is concerned. I can see that doing this sort of outreach might be effective for our team."

She dropped him off at his hotel with the promise to stay in touch, and Colt watched her car pull away from the curb. After checking with the bellman for the address he needed, Colt decided to walk. It was a great evening weatherwise, with mild temperatures and only a gentle breeze. Strings of white lights hung in the trees lining the streets, and an active nightlife gave Fort Worth an appealing downtown. He'd always liked visiting here as a boy. It's a shame he didn't get here more often.

He arrived at his destination in under ten minutes, and he was pleased to discover a restaurant next door with outside seating. Colt ordered a beer and sat down to enjoy the evening and await Sage Anderson.

"You were a rousing success, darling," Steve Montgomery said as he pulled his car to a stop on the side street next to Sage's hotel. "Are you absolutely certain I can't take you to dinner to celebrate?"

"I'm certain. I'd probably fall asleep in my salad." Sage leaned across the seat and kissed his cheek. "Thank you again for everything, Steve. You are my hero."

"I love you, too, dear. Have a safe trip home and I'll talk to you next week."

Sage waved good-bye as he drove off, then turned the corner to enter her hotel. She hadn't lied about being exhausted, but she was always exhausted. Mainly she'd skipped dinner because after two days away from Eternity Springs, the walls of the city were closing in on her. And this was only Fort Worth, Texas. Imagine what she'd feel in New York. As nice as the reception had been—well, except for that one not-so-nice surprise—

she'd had her fill of people. Right now all she wanted was to hole up, order room service, and find her quiet.

Then a voice intruded. "Well, now. Isn't this an amazing coincidence?"

Sage froze in her tracks. Colt Rafferty stood on the other side of a short iron fence marking a bar's sidewalk seating. "No. I can't be this unlucky. I can't!"

He tossed cash onto his table, then easily swung his long legs over the fence. "Now that hurts my feelings."

"Good. We're even, then." She started to brush past him and into the hotel lobby, but he caught her arm.

"Let me buy you dinner?"

"No, thank you."

"C'mon. I want to ask you about your art."

She gaped up at him in amazement. "I'm tired. I want peace and quiet. Why in the world would I let you browbeat me about my work?"

"I don't intend to browbeat. I have honest, serious questions. This is your opportunity to show me what an idiot I am."

"Now that has some appeal," she admitted.

He grinned. "If you want peace and quiet, then walk with me down to the Water Gardens. It's only a couple of blocks and it makes you forget you're in the middle of a city. It's a shame not to enjoy weather like this. Why don't you go up and change and I'll get the restaurant here to make us sandwiches?"

She hesitated, wondering why she even considered it, but finally agreed to go. "Give me ten minutes."

"You won't stand me up, will you?"

"While the idea amuses me, no. *I'm* not rude."

Upstairs, she pulled on jeans, a knit shirt, and sneakers. The casual clothes immediately relaxed her, and she decided she was glad she'd accepted his offer. She'd intended to visit the Water Gardens on previous trips to Fort Worth, but she'd never followed through, mainly because she seldom had free time during the day and she wouldn't go into any park—no matter how closely patrolled—by herself after dark.

Sage took the stairs down and spied Colt waiting for her by the elevator. The man truly was hot. He'd been fine to look at wearing jeans. In a suit, he was *GQ*-cover-model pretty.

Seeing her, he grinned, and she decided that the wink of a dimple at the corner of his mouth made him danger-ous. She'd always been a sucker for dimples.

He'd come up with a canvas backpack that he carried slung over one shoulder, and his suit coat and tie had disappeared. The sleeves on his white dress shirt were turned up, the top two buttons released. Despite her best intentions to resist his charm, her stomach did a little flip-flop.

"Ready?" he asked.

Sounds of laughter and music floated on the evening air, and they walked without exchanging conversation. By the time they approached the entrance of the park, Sage's appetite had returned. "What's for supper?"

"Turkey sandwiches."

"Cool."

Colt placed his hand at the small of her back and guided her toward the Active Pool, designed as a canyon lined with rushing water. Rectangular stone blocks cre-ated a staircase of viewing platforms that allowed water to travel beneath visitors who descended to the bottom pool, almost forty feet down. Nighttime lighting made the spot breathtakingly lovely. "This is nice."

"Yeah, it is. I love the sound of rushing water. It re-laxes me." He pointed toward the lower pool. "Would you like to go down there to sit and eat, or do you pre-fer it up here?"

"Here is good."

He led her around the edge of the stone canyon to a

spot away from another couple and a family with two young children also enjoying the site. They sat, and he unzipped his backpack and handed her a paper-wrapped sandwich. "So, Anderson, talk to me about your work. Why fairies?"

"Why not fairies?" she fired back. "They are fun, fancy, fantasy. They play to my strengths as an artist. I get to experiment with color and motion." She gestured toward the water spilling down the steps. "What has the architect achieved with this creation? Speaking for myself, his work inspires me. It soothes me. It speaks to my senses and it makes me smile. I've had people use those same words in response to my pixie paintings."

He nodded. "I heard people say it tonight, that your work makes them smile."

"That's a wonderful compliment."

"Yeah, it is. I'm not saying otherwise."

Sage took a bite of her sandwich, then sipped from the bottle of water he'd provided. "No, you used the words *okay* and *nice*."

"And *pretty*. I said they were pretty, too."

"Careful there, Rafferty," she drawled. "Your effusive praise will embarrass me."

"Hey now. For a creative person, aren't you being a bit thin-skinned? Isn't putting up with criticism part of the job?"

She wrinkled her nose and shrugged. "Frankly, that depends on who is doing the criticizing and whether or not I respect him."

"Zing." He made a show of wincing.

"Look, I will admit that finances play a part in what I do. Making one's living as an artist requires a measure of practicality to coexist with the artistic muse. I paint what I paint now because I'm building a brand that's been well accepted by the art world. I'd be a fool to abandon it at this point."

"That makes sense."

"Yes, it does," she replied, proud of the way she'd made her points.

She took another bite of her sandwich and focused on the water cascading down the terraces and steps below her. The effect was mesmerizing, and she could feel the tensions of her day melt away. She'd enjoyed the reception. She'd been thrilled by the positive responses and sales, but being "on" wore a girl out. It was nice to sit here and share a sandwich and trade insults with a handsome man. Almost made her feel mellow. "This really is a great spot."

"I'll show you the rest of the gardens after we finish supper. If you're still talking to me, that is."

Sage gave him a sidelong look. "Are you gonna make fun of my paintings?"

"Nope. But I am going to confess that I went to the reception tonight with the thought of buying one. I've thought about you a lot since September. I liked the idea of having one of your paintings hanging on my wall." He finished off his sandwich, then added, "But I can't do fairies, Sage. Or butterflies. Don't you paint anything else?"

A vision of her nightmare paintings floated into her mind, but she firmly shut them out. "I don't want to be on your wall, Rafferty."

He waggled his brows. "Holding out for my bed, are you?"

"Very funny."

He rolled to his feet and slung his backpack over his shoulder, then held out his hand to her. "Let me show you the other pools. The Quiet Pool at night is one of my favorite places in town."

She put her hand in his, and he pulled her to her feet. He kept a firm grip on her hand as they crossed an open area to a pool with multiple fountains, and Sage's artist's eye noted the visual illusion of a floor of tiles created by sprays of water collapsing in on itself. "How fun. It looks as if you could walk right across it."

As they moved closer, their path took them beneath the spreading branches of oak trees. Away from the cascading water of the Active Pool, Sage now became aware of the squeaks, whistles, and croaks of birds in the trees above. *Must be dozens of birds,* she thought.

"Down this way," Colt said, leading her toward a set of stairs that narrowed as they descended, the spatial change intensifying the noise made by the birds. At the bottom, a turn took them into a sunken garden where water flowed down angled walls and tall, knobby-kneed cypress trees ringed a rectangular turquoise reflecting pool like sentries. "Oh, the colors," she murmured.

"I knew you'd like this."

They were alone. Hand in hand, they strolled beside the pool, where an elevated bank rose a foot or so off the ground. The nighttime lighting was muted but for the underwater lights that caused the water to shimmer. Despite the noise from the flock of chattering birds above, the place was tranquil and serene—and also the most romantic spot she'd found herself sharing with a man for years.

She turned to discover him watching her. "You brought me here with an ulterior motive, didn't you, Rafferty?"

"Yep." He reached for her free hand and tugged her around to face him. "I've replayed that kiss we shared in September dozens of times in my mind. Refresh my memory, Cinnamon."

Rafferty wasn't the first man to assign her a nickname based upon her hair color, but he did get points for originality. Cinnamon. She kinda liked it.

His hands moved to her waist and he pulled her close, aligning her body to his so that her soft, feminine curves met his firm, masculine angles. Her heartbeat began to thrum and she lifted her arms, swaying into him, clasping her hands behind his neck.

His lips brushed across hers, just a whisper, but enough to cause heat to flare within her. Then, again, as soft as a feather, testing and teasing and prolonging the anticipation.

She'd missed this, Sage admitted as she allowed her hands to skim across the breadth of his shoulders. His clever fingers answered by skimming up and down her spine, leaving tingles in their wake.

He nibbled her lips, traced them with his tongue, then finally, *finally,* fitted his mouth against hers and swept Sage into a storm of pleasure.

A glorious warmth flowed out from her center as she lost herself in the moment. Colt Rafferty might be at times obnoxious and infuriating, but my oh my, the man knew how to kiss. He bombarded her senses in a way that praised and promised and proved irresistible. Only a fool would avoid this caress, this mouth, this man.

He wasn't in any hurry, savoring her mouth in such a way that allowed her to savor in return. To take pleasure in the strength of his embrace. To relish the taste of him, the scent of him, and to bask in the sound of his desire.

He wanted her. She felt it in the taut muscles and hard angles pressed against her, heard it in his low-throated moan. She listened to him. Listened to the sound of . . . birds . . . hundreds of birds above her. Around her. Screeching birds. Shrieking monkeys.

Stinking bodies.

Harsh hands.

Brutal men.

The rebels' truck threaded its way through the jungle on the rutted road. Sage sat wedged between two dirty, sweaty men in the cab. The driver never looked her way. The other man never stopped leering.

The sound of the jungle closed in on her—pants, snorts, caws, chatters, cackles, and roars. Her mouth was dry. Her heart pounded. She'd never been so frightened in her life. A brutal hand grabbed at her breast. Sage closed her eyes and prayed.

The driver barked an order too fast for her to follow with her limited command of the language, but after giving her one more squeeze, the hand released her. She released a breath she hadn't realized she was holding.

They traveled for an hour, then two. She needed to pee. Between the stink and the fear, she feared she might vomit. The damned monkeys were driving her mad. Finally the driver braked and turned onto a path, then stopped. The men in the truck bed bailed out. Groper opened his door, grabbed Sage by the upper arm, and pulled her from the truck. He shoved her in front of him, pointed toward an armed gunman, and barked a word she did understand. "Go."

Okay. I'm okay. She silently repeated the words she'd kept running through her mind since they marched her away from Peter. *This isn't a random kidnapping. They want me for a purpose.*

Noting that the rebel who took up position behind her carried her medical bag reassured her that it was the truth.

Sage swiped a hand across her sweaty brow, then swatted at an insect the size of a small bird buzzing around her. Okay. I'm okay. I'm done being afraid. They're gonna do what they're gonna do and I'll deal with it.

If only the birds and the monkeys would stop their incessant clamor.

After what was probably a fifteen-minute hike, they broke from the trees onto a clearing. Sage counted seven huts. The Zaraguinas led her toward the largest of the huts, set off to one side, where the leading man knocked on the door.

A moment later the door opened. Murmured words were exchanged, then Sage was shoved inside—where the rebel leader, Ban Ntaganda, lay on a blood-soaked bed. He pointed a bloodstained finger toward her and said, "Dr. Sage."

"Sage? Sage?" Hands gripped her shoulders and shook her. "Sage! Holy crap, what did I do? It was a kiss. Just a kiss. I didn't grope you or anything. Don't scream like that."

She emerged slowly from the flashback. Not Africa, but not home, either.

"Sage?"

Not Ntaganda. Rafferty. Colt Rafferty. *I'm in Fort Worth.* Those weren't gunshots. City workers fired air guns downtown at night to chase the grackles away. The birds made a huge mess and created a health hazard. She'd read about it in the newspaper.

"Okay. I'm okay," she said, repeating her litany aloud.

"Why did you scream? What's wrong with you?"

"I'm okay."

"So you've said a dozen times, but I'm not believing it. I think we'd better get you to a doctor and—"

"I'm a police officer. Step away from the lady, sir," demanded a loud, forceful voice.

"Hey, I need help here," Colt replied.

"I said step away, sir."

Colt muttered a curse beneath his breath, then held up his hands and backed away.

"Ma'am? You screamed. Can you tell me what's wrong? Was this man attacking you?"

She'd screamed? Sage glanced to the right to see a uniformed officer walking toward them. "No, no. I'm fine. I'm sorry. He didn't do anything wrong."

"Then why the scream?"

Sage looked back toward Colt. His jaw was set, but beyond that, she couldn't read his expression. Clearing her throat, she offered the cop a shaky smile. "It was a rat. A rat ran across my foot. It scared me. I'm sorry for the commotion."

He continued to look suspiciously at Colt, who hadn't moved. Sage moved forward and slipped her arm through his, adding, "I've always been deathly afraid of rodents."

After a long moment, the cop nodded. "All right, then. We haven't had a rodent problem here, but I'll be sure the right people hear about this. You two enjoy your night."

"Thank you, we will," Sage said. Turning to Colt, she asked, "Ready to go?"

"Absolutely," he replied, his voice grim.

They headed for the nearest exit, a staircase across the pool from the one they'd descended, and they didn't speak again until they'd exited the Water Gardens and were back on the city street. There, Colt shoved his hands in his pockets and asked, "Do you want to explain what just happened?"

Sage opened her mouth to speak, but then exhaustion overcame her. Muscle-draining, bone deep, debilitating. She didn't think she could move another step. "I'm sorry. I'm so sorry."

"Talk to me, Sage."

"I can't. I'm so tired. I need to go to bed. Could you help me get a cab?"

"Your hotel is two blocks away."

"I can't make it, Colt. Please? Just . . . forget it. Forget me. I can't deal and I need to go to sleep."

Sage knew that cabs weren't all that easy to find in

Fort Worth, but luckily, they were across from a high-rise hotel, complete with a cab queue. Colt set his jaw even harder, then nodded curtly. He whistled and waved over a cab, and when it arrived, he opened the door for her, then shut it behind her, not quite a slam, but close.

He gave the driver a twenty and her hotel's name, saying, "Keep the change but watch and make sure she gets inside, okay?"

"Sure, man. Thanks."

To Sage, he said, "This is my hotel, so I'll tell you good-bye here."

"Colt, I'm sorry, I'm just so tired."

"Doesn't matter. Goodnight."

Then he was gone.

SIX

❦

February

Shortly before seven following yet another bad night, Sage washed red and black paint from her brushes and sighed. Maybe she should throw in the towel and go back on sleep meds. Maybe they wouldn't affect her so badly this time.

She tidied her studio, then dragged herself to the kitchen to put the kettle on. She'd make chamomile tea. Maybe break her rule about no daytime naps. Why the heck not? Staying awake wasn't helping at all.

She'd just flipped on the gas burner beneath her teakettle when her phone rang. Her stomach sank. Nobody called this early—except for Rose. Her sister had called three more times since reaching out that first time when Sage had been in Texas. The calls all had been awkward, strained, and strange. Sage simply wasn't ready to tackle that relationship tiger, though she had made an effort herself by calling on Christmas.

Checking caller ID, she saw Celeste Blessing's name and number. Relieved, she lifted the receiver to her ear and forced a brisk, energetic tone. "Good morning, Celeste."

"Is it?" her friend answered. The comment caught Sage off guard, but before she could frame a response, Celeste continued, "We are on our way with yogurt, granola, fruit, and fresh bread still warm from the oven. Put on a pot of coffee, would you, please? We'll be at the door in ten minutes."

The phone clicked and the dial tone sounded in Sage's ear. Lowering the receiver, she scowled at it. What in the world was this all about? She hadn't forgotten a meeting, had she?

Ten minutes gave her just enough to time to take a speed shower, pull on jeans and a sweatshirt, get the coffee brewing, and fortify herself with half a cup of tea. She heard a car pull into the drive as she stored her latest painting out of sight. Sage grabbed a hairbrush and tried to tame the tangles in her hair as she headed to the front of the cottage, where through the plate glass window she spied not only Celeste Blessing but Nic Callahan, Sarah Reese, and Ali Timberlake, too.

Her core group of friends presenting themselves at her doorstep uninvited? And why was Ali in Eternity Springs on a snowy Tuesday morning? This couldn't be good.

Sage pasted on a smile as she flipped the lock and opened the door. Frigid air rushed in. "Isn't this a nice surprise?"

Sarah Reese took one look at Sage, then spoke to Celeste. "You were right. She looks terrible."

"Well," Sage said as the women filed through the door into the gallery. "Aren't you just full of friendship this morning?"

"Yes, as a matter of fact, I am." Sarah disdainfully wrinkled her little nose and held up a white paper sack. "In addition to the healthy stuff, I've brought cinnamon rolls."

Sage shifted her gaze to Nic, who was studying her worriedly. Ali Timberlake gave her a tentative smile and asked, "Shall we go to the kitchen?"

Officially out of sorts at this point, Sage murmured, "Can I stop you?"

"Nope." Sarah flashed a smile that had more teeth than was friendly. "This is an intervention."

An intervention? Sage closed her eyes. *Wonderful. Just flippin' wonderful.*

"Yeah, an intervention. Ali's made a special trip for it."

Ali smiled reassuringly. Sage sighed and followed her friends to the kitchen. Celeste's brow knitted in a frown. "It's freezing in here."

"The heater can't keep up. I'm having a new system installed, but Jimmy Turnage is backed up. No telling when he'll get around to me." Since her table only seated four, Sage grabbed her work stool from her studio, placed it at the table, and snagged the first cinnamon roll out of the sack. She took a bite of the sinfully sweet roll, savored the taste for a moment, then faced the proverbial music. "So, dare I ask why you concluded that an interference—"

"Intervention," Sarah corrected.

"—was appropriate? What, you found out about my dark chocolate M&M habit?"

"Dark chocolate is good for you." Celeste smiled her thanks to Sarah as she served them all a mug of fresh, steaming coffee, then continued, "Actually, sweetheart, a guardian angel whispered in my ear that your light was on most of the night again. As your friends, we are concerned."

A guardian angel? More likely somebody up for a midnight snack. Although Sage's cottage was isolated from town, her lights shone like a lighthouse beacon across Hummingbird Lake, especially in the off-season, when hers was one of the few occupied lakeside residences.

"You've lost weight, and there's not a makeup on the

market good enough to cover the dark circles beneath your eyes," Nic added, snagging a carton of strawberry yogurt and a spoon from the center of the table. She crossed her legs, gave her blond ponytail a toss, and settled back in her chair. "Believe me, I know. Since the twins were born, I've tried every combination of foundation and cover-up out there."

Ali selected a banana while gazing longingly at the cinnamon rolls. "The girls tell me you haven't come to quilt group since before Thanksgiving, Sage. That's not like you."

Even as Sage opened her mouth to defend herself, Sarah went in for the kill. "Most telling of all, you haven't said word one about your gallery showing in Texas. You've gone out of your way to change the subject or ignore the question when someone asks about it. Did you think we wouldn't notice?"

Nic touched her forearm and asked, "What happened in Texas, Sage?"

"It was a man, wasn't it?" Sarah asked. "Who was he? What did he do? Did he hurt you, Sage?"

Nic set down her yogurt. "Honey, are you pregnant?"

At that, a laugh burst from Sage's mouth. She understood why Nic's thoughts would go there. A year ago Nic had had her own Christmas season soiree and ended up the mother of twins. "I wasn't hurt or impregnated. Nothing bad happened."

"Then what happened, dear?" Celeste asked. "You haven't been yourself since you came back from your show. Is it career-related trouble?"

"No." Sage recognized that concern, not nosiness, lay behind her friends' questions. While she appreciated that they cared, she had no intention of sharing the full story. She'd never told anyone the entire nightmare— not her colleagues, not her therapist, not even her sister. She simply couldn't.

So she gave them what she could. "But you're right, I haven't been myself. My sleep cycle is all out of whack and I'm not sleeping well. When I do sleep I have horrible dreams, and that exacerbates the problem. I'll get back to normal eventually, but in the meantime . . ." Sage shrugged. "I'm cranky."

"Can't you take pills to help you sleep?" Sarah asked.

"I could. I don't want to go down that road if I can avoid it. In the past, they've turned my nightmares into Nightmares."

"Is there anything we can do to help you?" Sarah reached across the table and touched Sage's arm. "We're worried about you."

As the others nodded their agreement, warmth washed through Sage. She loved these women. She truly did. "I'm okay. No need to worry. Just bear with me a bit. One of my sister's favorite sayings is 'This too shall pass,' and I know that it is applicable in this case. I've been down this road before. I know what to expect."

The others all shared a look, then Sarah asked Nic, "What do you think?"

Nic shrugged. "I'm a veterinarian, not a psychologist or a sleep specialist."

"Or a man," Celeste observed. "That's what Sage needs. A good man. A good marriage."

Amusement gleamed in Ali's eyes. "Now there's a thought, Celeste. Good sex does make a girl sleep like a baby."

"True," Nic agreed, smiling smugly.

"Now, that's just rude." Sarah turned to Sage and said, "I don't know about you, but I'm getting tired of these giddily happy married women lording their sex lives over us."

It was a running jest between them. Sage knew her friends were trying to lighten the mood.

"Yep. I don't like it either." Sage polished off her cinnamon roll, then licked her fingers while the others continued their banter. Just when she'd begun to hope that the intervention part of the morning was behind her, Sarah had to circle around to the topic once again. Darn her, the woman was a terrier.

"I hate that you're having trouble sleeping," Sarah said, "but I don't think it's a good excuse for you to go hermit on us. This isn't like your bouts of creativity, Sage." Gesturing toward the studio walls, she added, "I don't see new paintings stacked up."

That's because I keep them hidden away. Sage couldn't bring herself to destroy or paint over all of the nightmare canvases, but she couldn't bear to look at them, either. No way was she going to make their existence public.

Rather than address the topic of paintings, she tossed a proverbial bone. "You're right, Sarah. I'll make an effort to get out more. Okay?"

"You'll join us for the Patchwork Angels meeting next week?" Celeste asked. When Sage hesitated, she added, "Please, Sage. For me?"

Sage couldn't say no to Celeste. "I will."

"Promise?" Sarah folded her arms. "No convenient burst of I-must-paint-because-my-muse-demands-it?"

"I promise, Sarah. I'll come to quilt group."

After that, talk shifted to Nic's babies and Sage gratefully concluded that the intervention had now eased into a coffee klatch. Relaxing, she sat back, sipped her tea, and told herself she'd get through this rough patch. After all, she had the dearest, most caring friends in the world on her side, along with the haven that was called Eternity Springs.

Still, a little sleep wouldn't hurt.

Colt Rafferty held his breath as he reached the summit of Sinner's Prayer Pass during the third week of February. The road was well maintained, but the switchbacks in winter were a heart attack waiting to happen. He hoped his tires held. He really hoped his brakes didn't quit. When he hit an icy patch and skated toward the edge of the road—the edge of the mountain—he sent up a prayer and decided that whoever had named this pass certainly called it right.

Colt had made this drive dozens of times before, but never in the dead of winter. Never in ten-degree weather. Never with snow deep enough to swallow his rental SUV. This would be his first trip to Eternity Springs during the off-season. When his boss told him to go someplace to cool off, he couldn't think of a more fitting place to go. As his back tires fishtailed, he muttered, "Hope that wasn't my last fitting thought."

Colt was coming off the most difficult stretch of weeks he'd experienced since coming to the CSB. Two horrific accidents, eighteen deaths that could have and should have been prevented, and a bureaucratic wall of red tape and politics that made him see red and, unfortunately, lose his temper.

Well, sliding off the road here on Sinner's Prayer Pass would at least get him out of the lawsuit that was probably coming. He'd really screwed up when he threw that punch at the OSHA guy.

But dammit, he was sick to death of the agencies all working both sides against the middle, and he'd finally erupted. He'd just ended a phone call to Melody Slaughter in which he'd had to tell her that the chemical spill that had killed her husband and eleven others the previous week had been completely avoidable had the OSHA inspector done his job.

"I don't know why I even try," he muttered as he downshifted. What good were they doing, really? Only a small percentage of their recommendations ever made it into regulation. Only a percentage of those regulations were being followed in the field. "Why should they follow regulations when it's easier to bribe an inspector instead?"

That was the piece of news he'd received that had led to the meeting that led to his blowup. Were there no good, honest people in the world anymore?

Yes, there were. That's why he was headed to Eternity Springs.

Having been given two weeks of forced leave, he'd booked his flight to Colorado, and since his usual rental was closed for the winter, he'd called Celeste Blessing to arrange for a place to stay. He'd asked for one of the outlying cottages on the Angel's Rest property, but after Celeste explained that a church group from Kansas had rented the entire facility for a week, she suggested alternative lodging that she believed would suit his needs perfectly. She'd volunteered to make all the arrangements for him and instructed him to stop by Angel's Rest to pick up a key.

He couldn't wait to get there. He'd flown to Denver last night, then headed into the mountains this morning. He'd added at least an hour and a half to the trip by stopping to admire the snowy vistas at least half a dozen times since entering the mountains. He was hungry, craving a strong cup of coffee, and nursing a strong sense of anticipation. He loved Eternity Springs, its people, and their small-town values.

Life wasn't gentle in the mountain valley—especially not this time of year, he imagined—but in many ways, life was kinder there than elsewhere. People didn't cut other people off in traffic in Eternity—there wasn't any traffic. They weren't rude to strangers, because the only strangers were tourists and tourists were the economic lifeblood of the area. And of special appeal to him, here people said what they meant and meant what they said. The only spinning done in Eternity Springs was done by skaters on Hummingbird Lake in winter. They damn sure wouldn't take bribes and look the other way, putting lives at risk.

Finally he rounded the hairpin curve that offered the first sight of the little town nestled in the narrow valley. Once again he pulled to the side of the road and took a moment to soak in the view. "It's a postcard," he murmured. Gorgeous. Beautiful.

Special.

Mountains filled with evergreens and snow ringed the narrow valley with a small town nestled at its center. Unlike other times of year when nature painted a myriad of colors across the landscape, today white was the predominant color, with a spattering of blue, green, and yellow on the wood siding of the Victorian-era homes in the center of town. Smoke rose from redbrick chimneys, and he counted five snow-dusted church steeples reaching toward heaven. At the far end of town, Hummingbird Lake lay beneath a sheet of ice.

As Colt watched, the doors to the school opened and children came pouring out. He grinned like a kid himself as he pulled back onto the road and completed the final short leg of a long journey.

When he drove past the city limits sign, tension rolled off his shoulders and his spirits lifted. Coming here had been a good decision. The right decision. He'd always wanted to see this place in winter. And he had a score to settle with the redhead, too.

"Sage Anderson," he said aloud. He'd thought about her off and on since their little tête-à-tête at the Fort Worth Water Gardens in December. Once he got over the shock of having the woman let loose with a blood-curdling scream while he was kissing her, then being called out by the cops before he figured out what was wrong, he'd recognized that she'd provided him a big fat piece of the puzzle she presented.

Consider the circumstances. They'd been alone together in a dark outdoor venue. She'd gone from being enthusiastically responsive to scared to death in a heartbeat. That pointed to a flashback of some sort. He suspected the odds were pretty good that at some point in her past she'd been sexually molested or assaulted.

Some men were pigs. Some men were even worse. With any luck, during the next two weeks he'd have the opportunity to prove to her that he was one of the good guys.

Just another reason to be happy to be here in Eternity Springs.

He made his way down Cottonwood Street, then crossed the bridge over Angel Creek to Angel's Rest, where he glanced with a sense of artistic pride at the sign he'd carved. Damn, but he did good work. During the design process he had envisioned it with snowdrift on the flat edges, but the reality of it looked even better than he'd imagined.

He continued up the drive to Cavanaugh House, the original structure at Angel's Rest and the hub of the healing center. Parking his rental in the designated parking area, he was pleased on the town's behalf to see so many other vehicles in the lot. He opened his door, took a deep breath of the clean, crisp mountain air, and smiled. How could fifteen-degree weather make him feel so warm?

His heart lighter than it had been in weeks, Colt walked up the front walk and climbed the porch steps. The small sign beside the doorbell read *Welcome to Angel's Rest. May your visit here be peaceful.*

Colt stepped inside and was greeted by a teenage girl he recognized from his last visit. She'd worked at the local ice cream parlor. "Hey, Mr. Rafferty."

"Hi . . . Elizabeth, isn't it?"

"Yes sir. Ms. Blessing said I should expect you. She's

in the upstairs parlor, and she said to send you up after I present your special welcome gift." She stepped from behind the desk and gestured toward the library. "If you'll wait for a moment?"

"Sure. Thanks."

Colt went into the library and smiled at the collection of angel figurines decorating the fireplace mantel. Also new to the decor were a trio of framed historical photographs depicting scruffy-looking men in front of a mine shaft, St. Stephen's church, and a view of the valley he recognized as having been taken from Murphy Mountain. He stepped closer and studied the men in front of the mine. Could these be the town's founders? He tried to recall what he'd learned from visits to the local museum, where his mother had dragged her uninterested offspring who wanted nothing to do with learning on vacation days. Hadn't there been three men in on that silver strike?

At that point he heard Elizabeth's footsteps and he turned toward her to see her approach wearing a mischievous grin and carrying a bowl. "Don't tell me. Is that . . .?"

"Taste of Texas rocky road," she confirmed, handing him the bowl of ice cream. "Celeste loves it as much as you, so she laid in a supply."

"The woman is an angel."

"She says it's never too cold for great ice cream."

"A brilliant angel."

Elizabeth laughed. "She's waiting for you upstairs. Feel free to take your ice cream with you."

Colt climbed the stairs and followed the sound of voices down the hall to the parlor. He paused in the doorway and grinned. *Well, well, well. If it isn't sweet, intriguing Sage. Isn't this handy?*

He savored another bite of ice cream, then said, "Good afternoon, ladies."

Celeste looked up, and her face lit with a smile. "Colt! You made it. How was your trip?"

"Long," he replied, looking expectantly toward the redhead, who wasn't meeting his gaze. "Worth it, though, when I have such a delicious treat waiting for me at my destination."

"The ice cream is wonderful, isn't it?"

"That, too."

Celeste smirked and said, "Colt, have you met my friend Sage Anderson? She is Eternity Springs' artist in residence."

"We met last fall at the grand opening, and . . ." He hesitated until she darted a wary look his way. *So she's kept quiet about seeing me in Texas. Interesting.* Allowing his smile to warm, he added, "It's a pleasure to see you again, Sage."

She mumbled something and still didn't meet his eyes. Her cheeks flushed with color that betrayed her embarrassment.

Celeste carried on as if she hadn't noticed her friend's lack of enthusiasm at his arrival. "I am trying to select a new painting for this parlor," the older woman said. "Sage has brought me a lovely selection of Sage Anderson originals, but I'm afraid I'm having a horrible time making up my mind. Take a look at these, Colt. What do you think?"

She had placed five canvases against the near wall. Colt glanced at them, then at Sage, then back at the paintings again. These works were done in the same vein as the ones he'd seen in Fort Worth. He couldn't help himself. He shrugged and repeated the comment he'd previously made: "They're . . . nice."

Then he took another bite of ice cream, giving the spoon a slow lick as he waited for her to react. He knew she'd remember the previous exchange, and he expected her to turn on him, scratching and hissing.

Instead, when she finally looked at him, he saw the sheen of tears in her gorgeous green eyes. Immediately he felt like an ass. He hadn't meant to make her cry. He'd been teasing. Didn't she know that?

Where was the woman whose eyes had shot fire at him in Texas?

"Thank you." She dismissed him with a polite smile, then turned to Celeste. "I think the butterflies work best in this room, Celeste. Why don't we hang it and let you live with it awhile? If you decide it doesn't suit, we'll switch it out for another one."

"Yes, I like that idea." Celeste beamed. "Thank you, dear. Colt, can you do the honors for me? You'll find a hammer and nails downstairs in the kitchen drawer beside the refrigerator."

"Sure. I'm on it."

Actually, he was glad to escape the room. He needed a little time to think. How had he misread Sage Anderson so completely? He'd thought she liked to scrap and scrabble. Man, he couldn't do anything right where that woman was concerned.

Then, because he *was* a tenacious man, as he descended the staircase he said to himself, "Guess you'll just have to try harder."

In the kitchen, he discovered the healing center's director, Hunter Casey, pouring a cup of coffee. Colt understood that Celeste had lured Casey away from a facility in Southern California. The two men visited a few moments, and Colt congratulated him on Angel's Rest's at-capacity occupancy rate while he rinsed his now-empty dessert dish. When Elizabeth ducked in with a question for her boss, Colt made his way back upstairs with a tape measure, a hammer, and a couple of nails. He wasn't entirely surprised to discover that Sage had bolted in the interim.

"I didn't mean to hurt her feelings," Colt told Celeste.

"She's not herself these days."

"Oh? Why not?" He measured the spot and marked the wall with a pencil.

Celeste clucked her tongue. "I don't like to gossip, but I'm quite concerned about her. Our Sage is in a dark place. I know she's fought long and hard to escape it, but the solitary struggle is weighing her down. I think she needs help finding her way into the light."

Colt placed the nail. A dark place? From what he'd seen, he couldn't argue with that. "She's living in the right town. Eternity Springs helped me when I was in a bad place."

"Oh, really?" she asked. "When was that?"

Colt rolled his shoulders, his way of acknowledging the scars that crisscrossed his back. "Back in high school, my best friend and I were working after school jobs at a furniture plant when combustible dust exploded. He was killed. I had some minor burns, but they healed fast enough. It was my head that gave me trouble."

"You came to Eternity Springs?"

"Yep." He hammered in the nail. "My dad helped me get a summer job at the Double R. I made my peace with the past and found my future up on a mountaintop that summer."

"I see," Celeste said as she handed Sage's butterfly picture to Colt. "That's why you studied engineering? Why you are working in Washington?"

Colt hung the painting, then got down from the step stool she'd provided. "It's why I became an engineer. I'll admit I'm not so sure why I'm working in Washington, but that's another story." Moving back, he studied the painting and said, "You know, the butterflies aren't half bad."

Celeste slapped him on the shoulder. "Be nice, Colt

Rafferty. Now, come with me and I'll get you the keys and directions to your rental."

As they made their way downstairs to the office, she explained that the place she had arranged for him was a cabin out at Hummingbird Lake, an eight-minute drive from the center of town. "You're on Reflection Point, with only one other house near you. There are a couple of lovely trails out that way that are maintained during the winter for hiking and cross-country skiing. One of them goes up to Heartache Falls, which is one of the loveliest spots in the county. Do you skate?"

"I played hockey in college."

"Excellent." She patted his hand, and her eyes gleamed with a knowing light as she added, "You're going to love it out there, Colt."

He wondered about that look as he made his way to the Trading Post to stock up on groceries before heading out to the lake. Bells chimed as he walked inside, and he waved at Sarah Reese, who stood behind the cash register speaking with an elementary-school-age boy holding a white ball of fluff in his arms. "I'm sorry, Josh, but my answer is final. I don't need a puppy. I have my hands full with Daisy and Duke."

"But Miss Sarah . . ."

"Good-bye, Josh."

Colt smiled as the downcast youngster departed the store, a dramatic pitch to his voice as he said, "It's okay, puppy. I'll find you a good forever home, no matter what."

Colt loaded his cart with staples. He enjoyed cooking, though he rarely had time to do so, and he planned to indulge in that activity during the next two weeks. He added a couple more steaks to his buggy, thinking that maybe he'd invite the Callahans out to dinner. He and Nic had been friends a long time, and he really liked her husband, Gabe. Plus he had to see the twins. Nic's Christmas card had said they were rolling over and trying to sit up. Then, picturing the teary-eyed redhead, he reached for the last rib eye in the meat case and murmured, "What the hell."

He chatted with Sarah while she rang up his groceries and asked how Lori was doing. "She's good. Anxious for college acceptance letters to begin arriving."

"Where does she want to go?"

"Texas A&M. She wants to be a vet."

"A vet, huh? What would she say about you turning down little Josh's puppy?"

Sarah laughed. "After working as Nic's vet assistant, she learned she can't bring home every animal in need. Still, she does go gooey at puppies."

"Most people do."

"Do you want a dog?" Sarah's lovely violet eyes gleamed with mischief. "I know where you can get one."

"Nope. I'm a short-timer here, as always, and my condo in DC doesn't allow pets, I'm afraid."

"Sounds like you need a new place to live."

Colt's smile sobered a little at that. "You may be right, Sarah. It's very possible that a new place to live might be exactly what I need."

He pondered the question on the way out to the lake. His job entailed so much travel that he'd never thought it fair to keep a pet. Still, he'd always wanted to have a dog. A big dog, like a retriever or a boxer. Maybe someday.

Celeste's directions to the house were spot-on, and when he made the final turn into the drive and saw the log cabin for the first time, he felt the last bit of tension inside him fade away. Thank God he wasn't in Washington right now. Celeste was right. He was going to love it here.

The cabin was decorated in what he thought of as mountain traditional—wagon-wheel furniture, elk and moose heads on the walls, and a bearskin rug in front of a huge stone fireplace. The master bedroom had a fireplace also, along with a king-sized bed and a sliding door that opened onto a deck with a hot tub.

"Awesome." A soak in the hot tub at the end of a day on the slopes had always been one of his favorite parts of skiing. And the stars in this part of the world were a sight to see. "Thank you, Celeste," he murmured aloud. "Excellent job."

He unloaded his car and put away the groceries, then lit a fire in the big stone hearth. He was careful and deliberate about the task, having witnessed some horrific results of carelessness over the years. As he watched the flames flicker and build, he told himself not to go there, not to think about his job at all.

He was burned out. Toast. He needed these two weeks to decompress, and he couldn't do that if he thought about work all the time.

He watched the yellow flames dance in the hearth until a flash of light against the window snagged his attention. Headlights, he surmised. Guess his neighbor had arrived home.

Curious as always, he moved to the window, where he spied a Jeep idling in the drive next door while an automatic garage door opener did its thing. He cupped his hand against the window glass to better see inside the Jeep.

When he identified the driver, Colt pursed his lips and let out a slow whistle. *Well now.* He dragged his palm along his jawline and considered his choices.

He could leave her alone. Maybe he *should* leave her

alone. But what was the fun in that? Glancing at the clock, he decided he'd give it half an hour. He'd let her settle in, and then he'd grab a measuring cup and go ask to borrow a clichéd cup of sugar—from his favorite redhead.

SEVEN

❧

Sage was in a mood. When she returned to the studio she maintained above Vistas after leaving Angel's Rest, her attempt to finish her work in progress failed miserably. Before the appointment with Celeste she'd been immersed in a fanciful piece of pixies and rainbows and having a wonderful time. Afterward, when she picked up her brush to complete the painting, she'd lost all enthusiasm for the subject.

It was all Colt Rafferty's fault.

She'd wanted to melt through the floor when she'd looked up to see the man. Twice now he'd witnessed her attacks. He'd almost been arrested because of her! It was mortifying, humiliating, and discouraging. And what was his response?

"My work is nice," she grumbled for probably the hundredth time since leaving the upstairs parlor at Angel's Rest. Oh, she hadn't missed that teasing glint in his eyes. Actually, it was better than the anger they'd reflected when he put her into the taxi in Fort Worth. But why did he have to latch on to her work as a way to annoy her? Why did she care? She didn't have a thin creative skin. She could take criticism. So why hadn't she stood up for herself? Why hadn't she said that what was "nice" were the checks she received from her "nice" paintings? Why was it that she always thought of what she wanted to say to him after the moment for saying it had passed?

That man had been a thorn in her side even before she'd met him. As a hobbyist wood-carver, he did do lovely things with wood, but she still didn't think it was right that he'd won first prize in the local-artists category at last year's art show. Not that she cared about the contest, because she didn't. Not too much, anyway. It was only a little, local thing, after all.

Okay, maybe she did care. Some. She possessed a competitive personality, but it wasn't that she expected to win the contest every year because she didn't. The nature photographer who'd moved to town last fall did some amazing work, and if he were to win this year's blue ribbon, well, so be it. But Marcus Burnes lived here. He paid taxes here. That should be the rule for anyone whose work was entered in the local-artists category.

"And why am I thinking about that, anyway?"

Was it because she didn't want to consider the real question—which was why, as she'd climbed into her car at the Angel's Rest parking lot, a few tears had slipped down her cheek? What was it about Rafferty? Why could he make her cry when she couldn't manage the feat herself?

At the end of an hour of wasted effort at the easel, she finally threw in the paintbrush and decided to call it a day. It was time to go home. She was tired and cranky and she wanted to curl up on her couch before the fireplace in her cozy little cottage and read. Maybe drift off to sleep. Sleep. Glorious sleep.

She couldn't wait to get home. She loved her lakeside place. When she'd first moved to Eternity Springs, she had lived and worked in the loft apartment above the gallery. Last year when the cottage's absentee owner listed it for sale, she'd jumped at the opportunity to buy it. Having a second studio was a luxury, but being able to set up her easel beside the lake to work on good weather days was worth every penny. Besides, she made enough income off her "nice" paintings to easily afford it. "So there, Mr. Wood-carver."

Although, come to think of it, she probably shouldn't indulge in a book tonight. At quilt group last week, she'd promised to complete her assigned task before this week's meeting. If she showed up without her finished squares, Sarah and Nic were bound to give her grief.

Of course, if—when—the nightmares woke her up tonight, maybe she could quilt instead of paint. On second thought, considering what she did with a paintbrush after her dreams, the idea of what she might do with a needle was terrifying.

Okay, then, she'd build a fire, put an audiobook on her iPod, and work on her squares. "Excellent compromise, Dr. Anderson," she murmured to herself.

Dr. Anderson? Whoa. Sage gave an internal shudder. Where had that come from?

"I so very much need one—just one—good night's sleep."

At the turnoff to her home, she noted tire tracks in the snow and recalled that Celeste had mentioned that her next-door neighbors, the Landrys, were having a visitor this week. The Texans regularly shared their vacation home with friends, so this wasn't an unusual occurrence, although it happened less frequently during winter than during the rest of the year. While Sage treasured the isolation of the point, she didn't mind having somebody within shouting distance in case of an emergency.

Once inside her cottage, she changed out of her slacks and a sweater and into jeans and a sweatshirt, but when she went to her closet for her slippers, her gaze lingered on her boots instead. Rather than curl up on the sofa, maybe she'd be better off taking advantage of the sunshine and the early end to her workday by strapping on her snowshoes and heading out for a hike. Strenuous exercise wouldn't hurt her goal of achieving dreamless sleep tonight.

Happy with her plan, Sage donned her boots, then headed for her coat closet and reached for her parka. She startled at the sound of a knock on her door, then remembered the tracks in the snow. *The new neighbor.*

She shrugged into her coat as she approached the door and opened it with a smile, which immediately died. Colt Rafferty stood on her front porch wearing a devilish smile and holding a measuring cup in his hand.

Sage's heart couldn't help but flutter. The man looked like he belonged out at the Double R Ranch atop a horse instead of riding a bureaucrat's desk in Washington, D.C. "Howdy, neighbor," he drawled. "Can I borrow a cup of sugar?"

Sage reacted instinctively and with an uncharacteristic rudeness. "I don't use refined sugar," she lied before slamming the door in his face.

She heard the scoundrel laugh, then he returned her rudeness with some of his own by opening the door and stepping inside. "I had expected something more neighborly from a citizen of Eternity Springs."

"Feel free to report me to the Chamber of Commerce." She returned to her coat closet in search of a hat, gloves, and scarf.

"Ah, c'mon, Cinnamon. Why the attitude?"

Sage wrinkled her nose.

"I don't think I deserve the cold shoulder," he continued. "Look, I'm sorry if I hurt your feelings earlier. I was teasing you."

She whirled on him. "You didn't hurt my feelings."

"All right. If you say so. In that case, let's talk about Fort Worth. I'd like to understand what happened. It's bothered me ever since. Did I completely misread you? I thought you wanted that kiss."

Sage sighed. "I owe you an apology, Rafferty. I'm sorry. What happened had nothing to do with you."

"See, actually, it did. I was the one kissing you at the time."

"I know. I'm sorry. Please, don't take it personally."

"Well, I have to take it personally. It was my mouth."

He wasn't going to let this go, was he? "You're a terrier, aren't you?"

"I'm safety engineer, an investigator. I spend my days searching for answers. If someone doesn't give me answers, I have to figure them out on my own."

"So you're trying to get into my mind? I didn't realize you have a psych degree in addition to all your numerous accolades, Dr. Rafferty." Sage pulled on a glove. "I've apologized. I figure that's all I really owe you."

His slow smile flashed his dimples. "In my estimation, you owe me another kiss. Sans the scream. Unless, of course, things get really crazy. Usually things get far more intimate before my attentions cause a woman to scream. But I am open to exploring that option if you're game."

"You're outrageous."

"And you like to throw around the attitude, don't you?"

"I'm an artist. Attitude is part of the package with artistic types. Look, today I had a bad day creatively, and when that happens, I'm better off not being around people—or safety engineers—until I've rid myself of the mood. So, if you'll excuse me, I need to take a walk."

"Exercise is a great stress reliever. Want some company?"

Outrageous and persistent. Sage wondered if he was really a used car salesman instead of a safety engineer. Fumbling with her other glove, she said, "No, thank you. I really need to be alone."

"Okay, then. Here's an idea." He paused and scooped

up the glove she'd dropped. Handing it to her, he continued, "You'll feel better after your walk. Why don't you have dinner with me? I put on a pot of chili a little while ago, and believe me, my chili is a treat you don't want to miss."

"Thank you, but no." She yanked her stocking cap over her head, opened the door, and smiled. "Good-bye."

His blue-lake eyes gleamed, and as his lips twitched with a grin, she had the sense that he'd been playing with her all along. When he strolled past her, he leaned down and brushed a kiss across her cheek before she could dodge it. "Enjoy your walk, Cinnamon. I'll see you later."

Then Colt Rafferty strolled casually away—a real feat, considering he had to tromp through snow up to his knees in some places.

As Sage watched him go, rather than the relief she expected, frustration swirled inside her. She felt the need to take one final shot. "Is that a threat, Rafferty?"

He halted and slowly turned around. The cold air fogged his breath as he called, "Nope, it's a promise. And while we're on the subject, there are a couple things about me that you should know, darlin', because they're written in stone."

"Oh, yeah?" she called back, even as she silently asked herself, *Why am I acting like a nine-year-old?*

"Yeah. And here they are. First, I always keep my promises, and second, Dr. Anderson, I always collect my debts."

With that, he gave a wave and continued his trek toward his cabin.

Sage blew out a long breath. This could be trouble. He could be trouble.

No, he *was* trouble. A mountain of trouble. How had he managed to snag the house next door as his rental? That was all she needed!

She watched him through the window as he plowed his way through the snow with relative ease. Those shoulders. That walk. That confidence.

Those blasted dimples.

All within a stone's throw. Or a mad dash. She blew out a breath that fogged the window glass. Despite the winter chill in the air, she felt flushed.

Lighten up on yourself, Anderson. She wasn't blind. Or dead. A woman would have to be dead not to be affected by Colt Rafferty.

And the audacity of the man! She owed him a kiss? Why, he could kiss her . . . *Oh, dear.*

Now Sage needed exercise more than ever, so she quickly donned her snowshoes and headed out. She walked hard, moving fast, pumping her arms and trying not to think about Colt Rafferty or kisses or how exhausted she was. She refused to think about nightmares. Or Africa. Or Peter. Eventually she worked off her snit and found the peace she was seeking. Some might call it the Zen effect at work. For Sage, it was the magic of Eternity Springs.

She turned and retraced her steps. Now she was able to enjoy and appreciate the beauty of a lakeside hike in a mountain valley on a sunny winter afternoon. She returned home shortly before dusk, weary but relaxed—until she spied the insulated cooler on her porch at the base of her front door.

Tensing, Sage glanced around suspiciously. She expected to see Colt dart out from behind a bush or a tree or pop up from beneath the snow. Energy hummed in her blood, and she was dismayed to realize the sensation wasn't anger or frustration but rather anticipation.

Only Colt didn't show. A full minute passed, and she was still alone.

Studying the ground, she counted the tracks between

her house and his rental. Two sets, coming and going. "Okay," she murmured. "Unless he flew over here, he has come and gone. Good. That's good."

She insisted to herself that she actually meant it.

She climbed her porch steps, then bent over the cooler and unzipped the lid. Inside, she found a covered stoneware pot wrapped in kitchen towels. The spicy aroma teased her senses and, in spite of her misgivings, brought a smile to her face.

Colt Rafferty had brought her a bowl of chili.

Midmorning the following day, Colt opened the door of the Eternity Springs Veterinary Clinic and stepped inside. "Hello, Mountain Girl."

Nic Callahan looked up from her paperwork. "Summer Boy!" She rose to welcome him with a hug. "This is a lovely surprise. I didn't think you visited Eternity Springs in the off-season."

"Ordinarily I don't," he replied, returning her embrace. "I got sent to detention at work, and this seemed like a good place to serve my sentence."

He took a step back and studied her. She looked a little tired, but more lovely than ever, dressed in jeans and a flannel shirt over a knit tee. "You look great, Nicole."

"Thank you. I feel great. The girls have both slept through the night every night for two weeks. That's a record."

"Congratulations." He glanced around the clinic and asked, "So, where are the little princesses? I'm anxious to see them. Do you have them in a kennel or something?"

She laughed. "Oh, I won't kennel my girls until they start crawling. They're with their daddy this morning—he bought a building on Fourth Street that he's remodeling—but they should be home in twenty minutes or so. You'll wait, won't you? We need to catch up. It's been too long since we had a chance to talk."

"That's why I'm here."

"Tell you what. My paperwork can wait, and I don't have an appointment for another hour. Let's go up to the house and have a cup of coffee. I have some of Sarah's oatmeal cookies in my cookie jar."

"Best offer I've had all week."

She slipped on her jacket and stepped outside, pausing to flip a sign beside a buzzer to read *Ring the house,* then she led him along a path recently cleared of snow to her back door. They hung their coats in the mudroom, and Nic introduced him to a brindle boxer with a crooked tail who came to greet them. "That's Clarence. He's Gabe's dog."

"Hey, boy. Aren't you a goofy-looking dog?"

Nic grinned. "He's so ugly he's adorable. Now, have a seat at my kitchen table and talk to me, Mountain Boy. Tell me about the trouble you're in at work."

While Nic made coffee, he opened up about the frustrations of his job. Talking about it to Nic helped solidify his thoughts, and he ended with, "I don't know, Nic. Sometimes I wonder if I'm just spinning my wheels at the CSB. I thought when I took that job that my work would help prevent accidents. So far, not a lot is changing."

"Then you'll figure out a way to make it happen." She set a mug of hot coffee in front of him. "That's what you do."

Colt wrapped his cold hands around the warm mug. He'd like to think Nic was right, but he definitely had his doubts.

"I do have an observation, though," she continued. "Would your frustration level be lower if you spent part of your summers in Eternity Springs? Maybe when you go back, you should negotiate for mental health trips to Colorado."

"You have a point." He sipped the coffee and mulled over his answer. "That's partially my own fault. I let the job take precedence over everything."

Nic placed a plate of cookies on the table, then took a seat across from him. "All work and no play makes Colt a grumpy boy."

He snorted and reached for a cookie. Nic said, "Seriously, though, we miss you, Colt."

"I miss you, too," he replied, meaning it. He took a bite of the sweet and added, "I miss Sarah's baking. I should have married her when Mrs. Roosevelt demanded it."

Colt referred to events that occurred after Sarah had publicly claimed that a summer guy had gotten her pregnant, but she'd refused to give his name and the guy had never stepped up. Pauline Roosevelt concluded that Colt was the evildoer, and nothing could convince her otherwise. She'd called Colt on the carpet one night in front of his whole family at Mountain Miniature Golf.

Nic smirked. "Sarah is still mortified by that. I don't think she's played miniature golf since."

Colt grinned and shook his head at the memory. "There is nothing quite like the righteousness of the innocent. Now, that's enough about me. Tell me all the news that is the news in Eternity Springs."

Nic snared a cookie for herself, then gave him the rundown on recent town events, ending with, "Things are so much better here economically than they were two years ago. The latest saying in town is 'Celeste certainly is.'"

"A Blessing," he said, making the connection. "I'm glad to hear such positive news. I will say I was surprised by the number of people on the streets."

"It's a beautiful, warm winter day."

"Warm? Nicole, it's twenty-nine degrees."

"And your point is?"

Colt laughed, and his gaze returned to a small painting Nic had hanging beside her phone. "That's an interesting picture you have on your wall."

"It's a rainbow. Sage painted it for us as a wedding gift."

He had wondered if it might be Sage's work, except that it seemed more genuine than the commercial stuff he'd seen from her. For one thing, the painting wasn't identifiable as a rainbow. It had the colors but not the shape. What she'd done with color and shadow and light made her rainbow moody, romantic, and, well, triumphant. "That doesn't look like her stuff. I don't see a single fairy or butterfly."

"Hey, Rafferty, don't be snotty. Those butterflies and fairies have made her quite the success."

"Whatever. They're just not my thing, I guess. This painting shows emotion. An emotion besides cheerful, anyway."

"I think what we have here is a case of one artist being jealous of another artist's talent," Nic offered with a knowing smile.

Colt snorted derisively. "Don't be ridiculous. So, what's the story with her?"

"What do you mean?"

"She's a doctor who gave up medicine. Why?"

Nic sighed. "I would tell you that I can't betray a confidence, but the truth is she's never told me the whole story." Interest gleamed in Nic's eyes. "Why do you ask? Are you interested? She is single."

"Considering her lack of enthusiasm toward me, I don't imagine it matters if I'm interested or not. Besides, I'm only in town for two weeks."

"A lot can happen in two weeks."

"Or very little. Little is probably best for me right now." Although if Sage Anderson came to his place looking for some sugar, he wouldn't turn her away.

Colt changed the subject by commenting on the baby photographs that covered almost every inch of the refrigerator. The twins were getting to the age where they were starting to seem like real people. Sitting up and smiling. Cute kids.

Nic's entire being lit up when she talked about her babies, Meg and Cari. He listened to her wax on about parenthood and marriage, and he felt a little wrench of envy that surprised him. He'd always enjoyed his role of favorite uncle in the Rafferty family; he'd never yearned to play father. Funny that he'd find the idea interesting now.

"I'm glad you're happy, Nic. Motherhood suits you."

"Thank you. It does."

He took another cookie from the plate as a knock sounded at the back door. Nic opened it to admit her husband, burdened with babies.

"I think this might have been the last time I try to take them both by myself, honey," he said, handing over one infant carrier. "At least until the weather warms up. The logistics of getting them in and out of places in a timely manner all but defeats me."

He noticed Colt and smiled. "Well, look what the blizzard blew in. Hello, Rafferty. This is a surprise. Welcome."

"Callahan," Colt said with a nod. "Thanks. Your wife has been plying me with cookies and gossip while we waited for you to come home. Now, let's see those little charmers of yours."

Colt admired the babies for a few minutes and earned a sweet smile from Nic by asking to hold one of them. After little Meg started rooting at his breast and fussing, he handed her back and Nic took both girls upstairs to nurse and nap. Gabe then settled a considering look on Colt and asked, "You're an engineer, right?"

"I am."

"I'm remodeling a building, turning an 1880s store into professional offices. I've run into something unusual. Could I talk you into tagging along with me to take a look at it?"

"I'll be glad to, although I'm a chemical engineer, not structural."

"You're a guy. That's what matters."

Nic called down from upstairs. "Sexist."

Gabe grinned and said, "I'm pretty sure I know what needs to happen. I just want a second opinion."

Ten minutes later, he was showing Colt an unusual support structure on an inside wall that left them both shaking their heads. "I know the building has been standing for over a century and a quarter, but I look at that and think, 'But for the grace of God.'"

"Yeah, that's what I thought. And I'm not a pro."

Gabe explained how he intended to rectify the situation, and Colt agreed with the idea, making one minor suggestion in the process.

"Thanks. Like most construction projects, this has turned out to be more than I'd anticipated. I was looking for a wintertime project. Should have stuck with my other idea."

"What was that?"

Gabe rubbed the back of his neck and gave an embarrassed grin. "Writing a spy novel."

"Oh, yeah?" As a resident of the nation's capital, Colt found his interest piqued. "You have contacts at the Agency?"

"Yeah." Gabe offered a faint, wry smile, then he changed the subject. "Since you're here, you need to take a look upstairs and see the real reason I bought this place. The view is spectacular."

Colt followed Gabe up to a second-floor office where a window was positioned perfectly to frame a breathtaking scene of Murphy Mountain and the craggy, snowcapped mountains beyond. "Bet the sunsets are gorgeous."

"They are."

"Whoever rents this office will have a hard time getting any work done. It's definitely a million-dollar view."

But when he turned around and caught a glimpse of the scenery from the office across the hall, he decided the view of Murphy Mountain, pretty as it was, couldn't compare. Across the hall, a window was positioned directly opposite a window in the building next door. The space between the two was small enough that a man of average height could climb out one window and in through the other without risking life or limb, and neither window had a curtain or shade to obstruct the view.

That's why Colt Rafferty could stand in Gabe Callahan's office and watch Sage Anderson apply paint to a canvas in her studio. She wore a tight green turtleneck sweater and formfitting jeans. Her long, auburn hair had been gathered and piled atop her head in glorious disarray. She had headphones over her ears and she gyrated her hips and shook her shoulders.

Listening to rock, Colt guessed. Hard, pulsing rock and roll.

He sucked air over his teeth and revised his earlier estimate. "Callahan, I take it back. What you have here is a two-million-dollar view."

EIGHT

At seven o'clock on the last Wednesday night in February, Sage hooked the tote bag holding her newly completed quilt squares over her shoulder and headed over to Nic Callahan's house for the Patchwork Angels meeting. She didn't want to go. She was running on fumes.

Despite her best efforts, she'd managed no more than four hours of sleep last night. She'd awakened about two from a return trip to the Zaraguina stronghold, and then she'd tossed and turned for an hour before giving up. She'd spent the rest of the night working on her quilt squares, which served her well for tonight's meeting but didn't exorcise her demons enough to allow her to get back to sleep.

She enjoyed the sewing. Making crazy-quilt squares from the fabric and embellishments of old wedding gowns appealed to her creativity. She loved working with the beads and laces, although piecing delicate silks and slippery satins tested her talent. Still, she'd always been good with a needle. After all, she'd been a darn good surgeon, which in many ways was just another type of artistry.

Sage waved to Larry Wilson, who was locking the door of the building supply center as she passed by. He called out, "Hey there, Sage. Sorry again for the delay in that special order of light fixtures for you. Glad they finally arrived. Bet you're excited to have the remodel team finally get to work at your gallery."

She tried to smile and agree with enthusiasm. After all, she'd hounded the poor man to death when the shipment was backordered at Thanksgiving. The major remodel of her gallery and studio originally had been scheduled to begin in October. One delay after another had moved the start date back, but shortly after noon today, she'd received a call from her contractor informing her that work would begin bright and early the following morning.

This was good news, since it meant the work would be done before what she hoped would be a busy tourist season. It was bad news because it meant that instead of spending her days in town working in the studio above Vistas, she'd be painting at the lake cottage. Although she'd planned to work at the lake during the remodel all along, now she wished the construction delay could have lasted another ten days or so—until after Colt Rafferty's distracting presence was gone.

"I'll simply need to be firm with him," she told herself. Just because the man was pushy didn't mean she couldn't push back. Rafferty was way too self-confident. Way too good-looking. In her experience, the good-looking ones invariably turned out to be jerks, and she had no use for jerks in her life. She had boundaries, and he'd need to respect them.

Gabe Callahan's dog, Clarence, met her at the front gate, wagging his crooked tail. She greeted him, scratched him behind the ears, then climbed the front porch steps and knocked on the door. Gabe answered holding one of his infant daughters like a football, and Sage was forced to concede that exceptions to her conclusions about jerks did exist. Callahan wasn't a jerk and he was definitely hot.

"Welcome, stranger," he said, grinning. "Nic will be glad to see you. Come on in."

"Thanks, Gabe." She smiled at the baby and said, "Hello, sweetheart."

Unlike almost every other female who came within reaching distance of the babies, Sage didn't stretch out her arms or ask to hold the child. Instead, she said, "Your little girls aren't so little anymore, are they?"

He grinned. "The little porkers were both over fourteen pounds at their last checkup."

"Is Cari over her ear infection?"

"Yes, thank goodness. Her pitiful crying made me feel helpless." The baby batted at his mouth with her little fist and babbled. Gabe caught the hand, kissed it, then said, "Nic and the others are all set up in the kitchen."

"Thanks." Sage hung her coat on the hall tree, then followed the sound of laughter to Nic Callahan's kitchen, where she found her hostess, Sarah Reese, Ali Timberlake, quilt shop owner LaNelle Harrison, and Celeste Blessing huddled over a cutting mat discussing the proposed arrangement of blocks. As Sage stepped into the room, Ali glanced up and said, "Hello."

"Well, I don't believe it." Sarah reached into the back pocket of her jeans, withdrew a five-dollar bill, and handed it to Ali. "You win."

Sage followed the exchange and scowled. "You bet on me?"

"Technically, I bet against you," Sarah replied. "I didn't think you'd show."

"That's mean." Sage folded her arms. "I said last week that I'd come tonight, and I always keep my word."

"You said you'd come to the band concert at school last night and you didn't."

"No, I said I'd buy a ticket, and I did. I never said I'd attend."

Celeste interrupted the exchange by saying, "What matters is that you're here now. We need your artistic eye, Sage. Help us decide how best to arrange our squares."

Sage glanced at LaNelle. "You're not doing it this time?"

The master quilter smiled. "No, not this time."

"She's not reading the Patchwork Angels email news-letter, either," Sarah observed.

Ali explained, "We decided to enter this particular project in the art show this summer. LaNelle is usually a judge, so she's recused herself from all efforts with this quilt."

"I'm only here to drop off the supplies," LaNelle said.

"And because your curiosity about our project got the best of you," Celeste suggested.

Amusement gleamed in LaNelle's eyes. "Caught me. Now I'd better leave before I get into any more trouble. Since Sage is here to oversee things, I know you'll do just fine with your design."

"Gee, thanks," Sarah said. "Glad to know you have so much confidence in the rest of us. Bye, LaNelle."

As Nic escorted LaNelle from the house, Sage turned to Ali and said, "I'm surprised but happy to see you back in town so soon this time of year. Any reason in particular for the trip?"

Ali's face brightened. "After reading the journals you guys uncovered written by my great-great-grandmother, I've caught the genealogy bug. I'm spending a few days here poring through the local history section of the li-brary, and today I found something interesting. Shall I share?"

"Absolutely," Nic said, returning to the room.

"Well, this goes back to the second generation of set-tlers in Eternity Springs. We know that Winifred Smith, who was Daniel Murphy's fiancée—the woman who he called his angel—disappeared on their wedding day and ended up a skeleton dressed in a bridal gown in Celeste's root cellar."

"Did you learn who her killer was?" Sarah asked. "I'm going to be jealous if you did. I've been looking into that mystery some myself when I have extra time."

"You don't have any extra time," Nic said.

"That's why I haven't discovered the killer." Sarah repeated her question to Ali. "Did you?"

"Nope. I found out something about Daniel Murphy's son Brendan and my great-great uncle Harry Cavanaugh Jr. They fought a duel over a woman. With rapiers."

"A sword duel?" Nic asked. "In the late 1800s?"

"Actually, the early 1900s. The woman was Caroline Hart. Brendan won the duel and the woman, but made a lifelong enemy of Harry in the process."

"Not good for Brendan Murphy," Sarah said. "The Cavanaughs had money, but the Murphys didn't. One of the best-known pieces of Eternity Springs history is that Daniel lost everything but his bad reputation."

Celeste spoke up. "The poor man was heartsick. His first wife had died, leaving him with young Brendan to care for, then he lost his angel, and the people in town turned on him. He had such a big, tender Irish heart, and it broke."

The women all looked at Celeste in surprise. She hastened to say, "I've been researching, too. Sorry to interrupt, Ali. Please go on."

Ali said, "Well, piecing together the information I found in the library and what I learned in the journals you guys found, I'm almost certain that the trunk of family heirlooms my dad inherited is really Murphy family heirlooms. I thought maybe . . ." She looked at Sarah. "Maybe Lori should have them."

Sarah sat up straight. Sarah's deepest, darkest secret,

known only to a very few, was that Lori's father was not a summer tourist, as Sarah had claimed, but the infamous Cameron Murphy. "I don't think—"

Ali held up her hand, palm out. "Let me finish. Cam's mother was a Cavanaugh. Lori has as much claim to the box as my children. Sarah, there are a few coins in the trunk. My father believes they could be quite valuable."

"College tuition," Sage pointed out, knowing how her friend worried about paying for Lori's education.

"This is cool, Sarah." Nic folded her arms and looked pleased. "At last, child support from Cam."

"I don't know," Sarah replied, her teeth tugging at her bottom lip. A cry sounded from upstairs, and as Nic left to check on her girls, Sarah said to Ali, "The trunk came to you. Well, to your dad."

"Fine. Then it's ours to give away. We want to give it to Lori. End of discussion."

"But—"

"Argue later, Sarah dear," Celeste said. "Let's get on to quilt business, shall we?"

Nic returned carrying a sleepy-eyed, whimpering twin rooting at her breast. As she settled down to nurse her little Cari, Sage followed Celeste's lead and studied the arrangement of blocks on the worktable. "I like the balance here. You all have done a good job with the design. And I think my own little contribution will fit in quite nicely."

She reached into her tote bag and pulled out her stack of finished squares. She placed the twelve-by-twelve-inch squares where her artist's eye said they fit best with the overall design. Upon seeing them, Ali said, "Oh, Sage."

Sarah looked and said, "Wow. These are gorgeous. Absolutely gorgeous."

In her blocks, Sage had used bits of lace, beading, and

bows to create bouquets of flowers. Each of the five squares was different; all were intricately detailed. After studying them a moment, Sarah added, "You are so talented, Sage. Now I'm really stressed out."

"Why?"

"Because the pressure is on. I said I'd do the piecing on this one, since it's my turn. And now that I've seen your squares, I think we possibly could win. But I'm gonna have to sew a straight line. Arrgh!" Sarah grimaced and covered her face with her hands.

Her friends laughed, and Ali reached out to pat her hand. "It'll be okay, Sarah. The contest entry is just for fun."

"Don't speak so fast, Alison," Celeste said. "If we're entering the art show, we darn well want a blue ribbon!"

"Here, here," Sage added. "I second that."

Nic looked up from her nursing child. "I knew Sage was competitive, but you, Celeste?"

"I am a proponent of always doing one's best," Celeste replied, primly lacing her fingers.

The others all laughed, and then the conversation shifted to plans for the next project. Sage did enjoy the comradery, but she was simply too tired to participate in the conversations with much enthusiasm. Subtly she watched the clock. Staying an hour should be long enough to fulfill her obligation, shouldn't it?

She was demonstrating her beading technique to Nic and paying minimal attention when Ali steered the conversation toward some charity work she did in Denver. It wasn't until she heard her own name that she truly tuned in. "I'm sorry, what did you say?"

"I'm finalizing activities for the kids' cancer camp at Angel's Rest in June. I need to submit the detailed plan to the insurance company for underwriting, and I'd like to add a second art program. Can I count on you to teach two art classes, Sage?"

"Art classes?" Sage repeated.

"Yes." Ali's smile dimmed a bit. "Remember, we talked about it right before Christmas?"

Sage went cold. "I didn't say I'd teach a class."

Obviously confused, Ali frowned. "Um, we did discuss it. You didn't tell me no."

Art classes to children? Teaching children? Sick children? Pediatric cancer patients? Everything inside Sage rebelled at the thought, and she snapped. "I certainly didn't tell you yes!"

That shut the conversation off abruptly. Nic, Sarah, and Ali appeared shocked and disapproving. Celeste's brow wrinkled in worry. Their reactions only annoyed Sage further. Couldn't they simply be her friends and leave her be?

With her defenses weakened by exhaustion, old fears and frustrations roared forth, and Sage lost her temper. "Excuse me, but I never committed to anything where your cancer camp program is concerned, and it's wrong of you to assume I'll go blithely along with the idea. You are my friend—not my mother, my doctor, my employer, or my priest. You don't get to tell me how I spend my time."

Ali drew back as if Sage had hit her. Sarah said, "Now, wait a minute—"

"No! You wait a minute." Sage surged to her feet. Her friends had crossed the line. Anger sharpened her tone, and she could feel her face flush. "All of you wait a minute. I went along with your little intervention because I recognized that in your own buttinsky minds, you thought you were doing a good thing. Not that anyone cared about how I felt. But this goes too far. These are children! Sick children!"

"Yes, they are," Ali said, obviously confused. "They're sick children and you're a doctor."

"A children's doctor," Nic interjected.

"And an artist. I'm not asking you to treat them," Ali explained. "I'm asking you to teach them to paint."

Sarah folded her arms. "What's your problem, Sage?"

Sage closed her eyes. They didn't understand. They couldn't understand. That didn't stop them from judging her, though.

Sarah wasn't finished. "You know, Sage, we've been trying to help you, but you won't let us. It's obvious that you have secrets—Nic and I figured that out when you moved here—and it's plain as day that you don't want to share them. Okay, fine. I understand about keeping secrets. My big secret is going off to college in the fall. So keep your secrets. But you can't expect us not to care. We're your friends. Look at yourself! I'll bet you've lost ten pounds since Thanksgiving, and believe me, it doesn't look good on you. You're falling to pieces!"

Sage's chin came up and she prepared to defend herself, only Sarah wasn't through. "You even blew off the twins' christening celebration. And you're one of their godmothers! What's wrong with you?"

Familiar guilt rolled through Sage at that. Her only defense for that sin was that Cari and Meg had plenty of other godmothers—Ali, Celeste, Sarah, and Gabe's three brothers' wives. However, that was a pitiful, weak excuse, and Sage wasn't going to float it. Nor was she going to explain that she couldn't overcome her aversion, that her only option was to stay away. These women didn't know what it was like. They couldn't know. And for their sakes, thank God for that.

"Now, Sarah," Celeste began.

"No." Sarah lifted her chin. "I'm sorry, Celeste. I know you said to let it be, but I don't see that letting it be solves anything. Ali needs Sage's help, and Sage should give it. Those children need her."

A flash of memory hovered at the edge of Sage's mind: white diapers and bright red—

"No." She shook her head hard, flinging the picture away. "No. I don't do children. Ever. For God's sake, have you not noticed? Do I volunteer at the school? Do I help coach the girls' basketball team?"

"You helped at the Valentine's daddy-daughter dance last year," Sarah said.

Well, she'd been different then. Stronger. But she couldn't explain, and while she searched for an acceptable comeback, Nic argued her case by quietly stating, "You won't hold my girls. You won't even touch them. You ask how they are, you give me medical advice, but you keep it all clinical. You've even distanced yourself from me since they were born."

Sage's breathing quickened. Pressure built in her chest and she closed her eyes. Nic's accusation was true. She *had* pulled away from Nic since she'd had her babies.

A lump rose in Sage's throat. She hadn't realized it— okay, admitted it—until this very second. She'd been trying to tell herself that this current state of emotional turmoil had occurred because of the trouble in December. Now, faced with Nic's accusation, she recognized that she'd been lying to herself. Her PTSD recovery had hit a wall last September when Nic had her babies, when Sage had delivered those two sweet, precious girls, then fled the house and fallen apart.

"It's hurt me, Sage," Nic added, driving the nail even deeper.

Sage wanted to disappear. To melt away into a puddle of nothing. *Someone throw water on me. I'm the Wicked Witch of the West. The Wicked Witch of Eternity Springs.*

But she couldn't melt into a puddle, and she couldn't

show weakness, because if she did, these women would pounce. They'd make demands. They'd press her for information. Without knowing what they were doing, they'd send her back to Africa. Make her relive the horror.

Well, that wasn't going to happen. She couldn't deal with pouncing, so she wouldn't show them weakness. Instead, she hardened her voice and said, "Well, sorry about that, but you're just gonna have to deal."

Turning to Ali, she added, "And you're gonna have to find someone other than me to teach your art classes." Her hands were shaking as she grabbed up her tote bag and said, "Sarah, you need to find someone else to pound on, because my emotional punching bag has been beaten to death. I'm going home. Please, do us all a favor and don't come calling. I cooperated during your little intervention, but that is over. I need my privacy now."

With that, she rushed from the kitchen, but not before she heard Sarah say, "Wow. She really let loose her inner bitch, didn't she?"

Sage was breathing as if she'd run a mile as she paused at the front door to pull on her coat. Her chest hurt. Her throat was tight. Pressure built behind her dry eyes.

"Sage?" Celeste Blessing came into the hallway outside the kitchen.

"No, Celeste. Please. I can't. I just can't."

Celeste linked her fingers in front of her. "It's okay, dear. You'll be okay. I'm praying for you."

Oh, God. Sage rushed out into the cold, zipping her coat and yanking on her hat and gloves as she hurried up the street. She went straight to her Jeep, thankful that before leaving the gallery she'd packed it with the art supplies she'd need during the remodel. She shoved the key into the ignition, started the engine, and put the car into gear before allowing it to properly warm up.

She kept her eyes straight ahead as she drove faster than was truly safe. Her breaths continued to come in shallow pants. The pressure behind her eyes built and built and built.

Shame swirled inside her. Shame and hate. She hated herself. Hated her actions. Her cowardice. She wanted to lie down and die. She should have died. It all came back to that. She should be dead.

Like everyone else.

She reached the turn onto the point in under five minutes. As she pulled onto the road that led to her cottage, she realized she was whimpering aloud. She arrived at the gate. Her cottage was dark, empty, and cold, while next door lights blazed and smoke rose from the chimney. Without conscious thought, she turned into the neighbor's drive, parked behind Colt Rafferty's rental, and literally ran toward his front porch.

He opened the door as she approached. "Sage? Honey? What happened? What's wrong?"

She simply stood there. Silent and aching and desperate. Beseeching. Searching for sanctuary. Looking for a soft place to fall.

"Oh, baby." He scooped her up into his arms and carried her over toward the fireplace and an old wooden rocker. He sat with her on his lap, cuddled her close, and rocked her as he murmured against her ear. "It's okay, Cinnamon. I have you. You're safe. Let it go, honey. You can let it all go."

So she did.

NINE

Since his job often brought him into contact with people in the midst of horrific circumstances, Colt was familiar with tears that poured from the soul. They were different from those that flowed from the heart or those from the part of the brain that registered physical pain. Soul tears had a unique depth, a singular intensity, that signaled pain that almost couldn't be borne. Soul tears were those that a person saved for the big things and shed on rare occasions.

The first time he'd seen Sage Anderson cry, she'd offered up soul tears. Here again, the same.

His own heart ached a little for her as he held her. His interest in the mystery of her increased. What was the genesis of her pain?

Because he was a man who tried never to overlook any possibility when attempting to solve a puzzle, he entertained the notion that she might have him fooled. Had he read her wrong? Maybe she was no more than a bubbleheaded drama queen who screamed over a kiss and lost it over something no more serious than a parking ticket. After all, the woman painted fairies for a living.

Following a moment's consideration, he shook his head. It simply didn't ring true. His instincts were telling him that this woman in his arms carried wounds as deep and as painful as any borne by those he'd encountered through his work.

"Attagirl," he murmured. She remained oblivious while he eased her out of her coat. "You get rid of all that poison. Just wash it away."

Her fist held the flannel of his shirt clenched in a tight grip. Her entire body trembled and shuddered. Little kitten mewls of pain escaped her. She was pitiful to behold, a strong woman brought low. He cuddled her a bit more tightly against himself and started to speak.

"I grew up in a midsized town in Texas about an hour from Houston. When I was eight years old, my dad bought a little runabout boat and we spent every day we could steal at the lake. We always packed a cooler with sandwiches and drinks, and we'd tie up or anchor in a cove or creek off the main body of water to have our lunch. After lunch, we'd diaperize—which in the Rafferty family lexicon meant wearing your life jacket upside down, with your legs through the armholes and the jacket around your butt like a diaper. That way you floated with your shoulders above the water without doing much work—it made it easier for my dad to drink a beer. Anyway, we'd float for a while and talk about baseball or the upcoming college football season—important things."

Sage sniffled and shuddered, and Colt couldn't tell if she was hearing him or not. Nevertheless, he continued. "My younger brother was one of the most annoying kids on the planet, a total show-off. He also liked to fish. We always kept a fishing pole or two in the boat. So one day during our float time after lunch, he decided it would be a good idea to fish while he was in the water. He diaperized, jumped in with this pole, and started casting. Think he was using a spinner bait, if I remember correctly."

Colt tugged a tissue from the box atop the lamp table

beside the rocking chair. He set it within reach of her hand, then continued his tale. "My aunt and uncle were with us that day, and Uncle John had just climbed back into the boat and begun to towel off when Jason called out, 'I caught one.' He'd hooked a six-inch sand bass."

He saw her fingers snag the tissue, and she brought it up to her face and wiped her eyes. Colt smiled. "Jason held his rod up out of the water and he was turning the reel, winding in the line, when all of a sudden that fish turned on him. Started swimming right toward him. Jason let out a yelp and started paddling backward, backstroking with one arm and holding the fishing pole out of the water with the other."

Sage held out her hand and wiggled her fingers, and he handed her another tissue. As she blew her nose, he said, "The fish swam right up his swim trunks and got wedged inside because of the life vest. Jason squealed and my mom hollered. Uncle Johnny laughed so hard that he fell out of the boat." Colt grinned at the memory, then added, "That was a great day."

A half minute of silence ticked by. Without lifting her head from his chest, Sage spoke in a soft, slightly peeved tone. "Why in the world did you tell me that story?"

"I don't know." He combed his fingers through the auburn curls that spilled down her back. "Just seemed like the thing to do."

"You were trying to distract me."

Of course. "Maybe."

Following another half minute of quiet, she added, this time with a bit of petulance, "With a fish story."

He stroked his fingers up and down her arm. "A good fish story, you have to admit."

He continued to rock her, and she remained snuggled up against him, limp and relaxed and awash in a fragrance that smelled of springtime. In that moment, Colt wouldn't have wanted to be anywhere else in the world.

Eventually she said, "Last time I sat in your lap and cried you kissed me."

"Yeah." His smile widened at that particular memory. "Unfortunately, the last time I kissed you, you screamed."

"I apologized," she said, stiffening a bit.

"Yes, you did."

"I wouldn't do it again."

He trailed a finger along her arm. "Well now, that sounds like an invitation."

She didn't respond, but he sensed her anticipation. It would be so easy to sink into that mouth, but following a moment's thought, and with a full measure of regret, he said, "As enticing as I find the idea, I think I'll choose a different direction today. I don't want to be predictable."

She sniffed with disdain, and seeing a little of her starch return only made him want to kiss her all the more. While the devastated Sage touched his heart, the prickly woman stirred him farther south, so to speak.

Colt liked puzzles and he loved challenges. Sage Anderson was both, all wrapped up in a gorgeous package. His sojourn in the snowdrifts promised to be more interesting than he'd expected.

He also liked women. A lot. He'd been involved in two separate long-term relationships since his "starter marriage" ended. He'd cared deeply for both women, and each time he'd believed they were headed for marriage. He had a few scars from the subsequent breakups, but nothing that had turned him off the idea of marriage.

Following that twinge of envy he'd experienced in the Callahan kitchen, he'd just about decided that in addition to that home and dog he wouldn't mind having, he might like a wife and children, too. Once he returned to Washington, maybe he'd step up his participation in the dating scene.

In the meantime, since he wasn't dating anyone seriously back home, he could consider making a play for the intriguing bundle presently in his arms. Yet he held back. She obviously had some issues to deal with. He didn't want to do anything that would make her situation worse.

Although sometimes a carefree, no-strings-attached fling improved a person's outlook. Maybe that was the medicine she needed.

He picked up a strand of her fire-streaked hair and let the silken curl slide along his fingers. "So, are you dating anyone right now?"

"No." Again she sniffed. "If I was, it'd be pretty scuzzy of me to be sitting here like this. I may be the Wicked Witch of Eternity Springs, but I'm not scuzzy."

Wicked Witch of Eternity Springs? "Why aren't you dating?"

"It's not really any of your business."

He expected her to push out of his arms at that point, but she remained right where she was, which pleased him. "Now, see, I can't agree with that. Look at it from my perspective. Say the reason for your, um, distress was a fight with your boyfriend, and you broke up, so you aren't lying when you tell me you're single. Say said ex realizes what an idiot he's been and comes rushing out here to beg your forgiveness. He might see your car stopped in the drive and your footsteps in the snow and follow you to my cabin. If he looked in the window and saw you in my arms, he might burst in and brandish his rapier and challenge me to a duel."

"Have you been talking to Ali Timberlake?"

"What?"

"Nothing. You're ridiculous."

"Made you smile, though, didn't I? I felt it against my strong, muscular chest." Her only response was a snort, but since it was a sleepy sort of snort, he allowed the silence to continue. Soon her body relaxed even more and he knew she'd fallen asleep.

Colt would have been content to hold her for hours, but when his phone rang and he recognized his brother's ring tone, he knew if he didn't answer, Jason would continue to call until he did. His brother was annoying like that.

Rising, he carried Sage to the sofa and gently laid her down. She stirred but didn't awaken. He covered her with a woolen throw and moved to answer the phone.

He saw that Jason had left him a voice mail, but rather than answer it, he returned the call.

Jason answered on the first ring. "Hey, bro. Did you get my message?"

"Didn't listen to it. What's up?"

"I'm headed your way tomorrow for a meeting at the Pentagon. Gonna be there a couple of days. Are you gonna be around? I'd love to see you."

Regret washed through Colt. "I'm not in Washington."

"Well, shoot. I knew my chances of finding you in town were slim, but I had my hopes up. We missed you at Christmas, Colt."

He closed his eyes. He'd been on call at the office and unable to get back to Texas. "It was a damned lonely holiday."

"So where are you this time?"

Colt hesitated, uncertain whether he wanted to share his professional frustrations with his family. Every Rafferty in the clan would feel the need to weigh in on the matter. The Raffertys were like that.

On the other hand, his relatives were smart, savvy, and for the most part happy with their lives. He could use their guidance. "I'm in Colorado. Actually, Jason, I'm in Eternity Springs. Wait until you hear why."

Warm and relaxed and oh so comfortable, Sage drifted awake slowly, an unfamiliar scent teasing her nose. Citrus, sandalwood, and musk—a masculine scent. A man. Her eyes flew open. *Oh, dear.*

A man's bed.

Colt Rafferty's bed.

Yesterday's events roared down upon her thoughts like an avalanche and made her want to burrow under the covers and never come out. The snit she'd thrown at quilt group. Sobbing on Colt Rafferty's shoulder. She'd been embarrassed the last time she'd done it. This time she was mortified.

She didn't remember him carrying her to bed. He'd taken off her shoes, but nothing else, thank goodness. How long had she slept? An hour, maybe? Two?

At that point, it registered that the light in the room was coming not from a lamp, but from the sun. Sage rolled over and sat up. Sunlight? She'd slept the whole night?

"I slept the whole night," she said aloud.

No wonder she felt so deliciously comfortable, so wonderfully rested. She'd almost forgotten how great sleeping through the night felt. Glancing around the bedroom for a clock, she spied one on the dresser to her right, read the time, blinked, then looked again. Eight-thirty? She'd slept, what, twelve hours? Wow. Just wow. If she hadn't been so mortified about the circumstances, she'd have leapt up and shouted hurrah.

She did allow herself a silent fist pump before throwing back the covers and quietly rising from the bed. With any luck at all, Colt would already be out and about for the day, and she wouldn't have to face him. Or he'd still be asleep in one of the loft bedrooms upstairs.

After a quick stop in the master bathroom, she took a deep breath and opened the door. The aroma of frying bacon swirled in the air. She probably wouldn't be able to slip out unseen. Okay, then. No big deal. She could handle a little mortification after twelve hours of sleep. Sage squared her shoulders, braced herself, and walked toward the living area—where she encountered a sight that took her breath away.

Wearing nothing but gym shorts and sneakers, Colt Rafferty sat with his back to her on a weight bench doing biceps curls with dumbbells. For a long moment she stood and stared. Heavens, he was gorgeous, the scars on his back notwithstanding. Old scars. Burns, she realized. *Wonder how he got them?*

Colt's muscles bunched, then released, bunched, then released, and Sage stood mesmerized. She wished the owner of this cabin weren't such a fitness buff that he'd outfitted his vacation cabin with exercise equipment.

She thought she might have made a little strangled sound, because Colt turned and gave her a slow grin that displayed those faint dimples of his to perfection. "Good morning, sleepyhead."

She swallowed hard. "Good morning."

"Do you feel better?"

"Actually, I'm pretty sure what I feel is mortified."

"Don't be." He set down the weights, then stood facing her. Sage swallowed hard a second time. The man had a six-pack.

To her relief, he grabbed the T-shirt draped over the handle of a treadmill and slipped it on. "Last night was the nicest evening I've spent in a long time. Nothing to be mortified about."

The nicest evening? Warily she said, "All I remember is crying on your shoulder."

"You were soft and warm and you smelled delicious. I enjoyed holding you."

The wicked glint in his eye compelled her to ask, "And that's all you did? Hold me?"

His expression went innocent. "What? You think I'd do something rude like cop a feel once you'd fallen into an exhausted sleep?"

She narrowed her eyes but decided to drop it. It was a no-win situation for her. "Well, I need to get home. Thanks for your patience, and I promise not to bother you like that again."

"Stay and have breakfast with me, Sage. It's ready, and I waited for you."

Under the circumstances, she couldn't bring herself to be boorish enough to refuse, though she had little appetite. "I'm not hungry, but I wouldn't mind a cup of tea," she conceded.

"Bacon and biscuits are ready. How do you like your eggs?"

"I don't—"

"I'm having mine scrambled. That okay with you?"

Why did everyone in town persist in fixing breakfast for her? Did they think she didn't eat?

"I have a jar of homemade raspberry jam that Nic gave me for the biscuits," he added.

Sage surrendered. "Scrambled is fine."

The tea was strong and hot and hit the spot and, to be honest, the food did, too. She expected to sit down to bacon and the third degree. Instead, to her surprise, he took the conversation in a completely different direction. "I talked to my brother last night and told him I was here and why. I realized my stress level already has dropped significantly. From the time I hit the city limits sign, I've hardly worried about my work. I've spent my time visiting with old friends and catching up on local news. It's been great. Just what I needed. I've decided to go do some Taylor River fishing today. The weather looks good for it, and maybe this time of the year, it won't be combat fishing out there."

"Combat fishing?"

"Battling for a fishing spot. Too many fishermen on the river in the summer anymore to be any fun. Anyway, the guys at the outfitters shop fixed me up with some Gore-Tex waders and the other cold-weather gear I'll need. I'm excited. It's hard not to relax when you're fishing. So what are your plans for the day?"

She thought about her explosion at quilt group and knew she probably should make the rounds to apologize, but she needed to think through what she wanted to say first. "It's a workday for me today."

"I need to stop by and see your gallery while I'm here. I'd have stopped in yesterday when I visited Gabe's building, but you had a Closed sign hanging on the door."

"The gallery is open by appointment only this time of year," Sage replied. She almost mentioned the remodeling that would begin today, but stopped herself just in time. She didn't need him wandering over for sugar of any sort while he was renting the house next door. "There's nothing to see there now, anyway. I send most of what I exhibit to another gallery during the off-season, although now that Angel's Rest is open and so well occupied, I don't plan to do it again next year."

Which was why she'd decided to remodel this winter.

He kept the conversation to small talk as they finished breakfast. She helped him clean up, then eyed her coat, which was hanging by his front door. "I need to get to work, and you need to catch some trout."

"Absolutely." He wiped his hands on a white floursack dish towel, then slung it over his shoulder and shot her a friendly grin. "You know, the spot I'm fishing is strictly catch and release, or I'd invite you over to dinner tonight for a fish fry."

While she searched for something noncommittal to say, he continued, "Although I'll bet there's a restaurant in town where we could get trout. My mouth will likely be watering for it after a day on the river hauling them in. How about it?"

"Thanks, but I already have plans," she replied, smiling weakly.

It wasn't strictly a lie. Tonight she had reserved for a chick flick DVD marathon.

"All right." He flashed an easy grin. "Maybe another time."

Sage slipped into her coat, reached for the doorknob, and paused. "Colt, I . . . um . . . about last night. I . . . well . . . you were very kind. Thank you."

"You're very welcome." He waited until she'd stepped out into the cold morning air to add, "Sage, in my job, I do a lot of listening. I've heard some seriously difficult stories. If you decide you want to talk, I'm here. If you don't want to talk, I'm still here."

She paused, looked up at a brilliant blue winter sky, and felt a wave of memory roll over her. She smelled the blood. Tasted the metallic flavor of fear. Terror and horror and grief all but brought her to her knees.

Sage swallowed the lump in her throat and fought her way back to the moment. Then, glancing over her shoulder, she met Colt Rafferty's solemn gaze. "You've never heard a story like mine. Pray that you never will."

Writers dream of making *The New York Times* bestseller list. Football players imagine how a Super Bowl championship ring would look on their hands. Poker players wait for the hand that draws a royal flush. Trout fishermen—serious trout fishermen—dream of landing a Taylor River rainbow.

The fish grew to record size and glorious color as a result of a steady diet of mysis shrimp flushed through the

Taylor Reservoir dam's bottom-release tube and served up as easy prey to the trout below the dam. Seven summers ago, Colt had watched another angler pull a twenty-pound rainbow from the water, and he had vowed to land one himself. Despite numerous tries since then, he'd never managed to coax one of the monster rainbows into taking his hook, much less actually land one. His excuse had been the wall-to-wall fishermen at the catch-and-release section right below the dam.

Colt told himself that today, with the temperature gauge in his SUV reading right at eleven degrees, he'd be shocked to find another fisherman on the river. After all, only an idiot would voluntarily wade into water to fish under these conditions. When he arrived at the Taylor River tailwater and spied half a dozen cars, he sighed aloud and prepared to join the other idiots. Luckily, the temperature had risen to a balmy seventeen by the time he gathered his gear and exited his SUV. It was a beautiful day, without a breath of wind or cloud in the sky, and he paused a moment to get his bearings. Multiple sets of footprints in the snow led toward the water's edge, but he recalled a particular pool a little farther downstream he wanted to try, so he struck off through the three-foot snowdrifts in the hope of finding an unoccupied spot.

The exercise, along with his cold-weather gear, kept him relatively warm despite the winter chill. He arrived at the riverbank and smiled to see that this stretch of the Taylor remained empty of fishermen. Excellent. Provided it wasn't empty of fish, too.

Colt spread out a waterproof tarp, set down his gear, climbed into his waders, then mulled a moment over his tackle. On the advice of Randy at the outfitters shop, he'd laid in a supply of long leaders and small tippet. This time of year, the fish hung out in the long, deep runs, where they could conserve their energy, so he planned to get down and dredge the bottom with nymphs such as midge patterns, worms, eggs, and other small beadheads.

Finally, with a grin on his face and hope in his heart, he waded into the river with his sights set on a flat-topped rock that rose out of knee-deep water. Randy had also advised that he'd last a lot longer on the river if he could keep his feet out of the water. Gore-Tex could only do so much.

Within minutes, he made his first cast and finally got his hook wet. By the fourth cast, a lingering tension flowed from his muscles, and as Colt relaxed, he started to think.

To be precise, he started to remember. He recalled fishing here with his dad and brother. As boys, he and Jason hadn't had the patience for fly-fishing, so after half an hour or so of casting but not catching, he and his brother would set down their fishing poles and go exploring.

He'd never forget the time they stumbled across Bear while out in the woods. Upon seeing Eternity Springs' own authentic mountain man—a tall, hairy bear of a man—they truly believed they had encountered Bigfoot. Colt laughed aloud at the memory.

"Now, that's a lovely sound to hear on a winter morning," came a feminine voice off to his right.

He turned to look, and his jaw dropped. "Celeste?"

She was dressed in white cold-weather gear but for a pair of gold waders. Her cheeks were rosy from the cold, her eyes shone a happy, brilliant blue, and her smile was the warmest thing in the county.

"What are you doing here?" he asked.

Her look went droll. "I'm baking cookies, of course."

Colt winced. "Right. Dumb question. I'm surprised to see you here, that's all."

"I try not to be predictable. It's one of my charms."

He nodded in acceptance, then asked the usual fisherman's query. "Having any luck?"

"Well now, that depends on how one defines luck. I have yet to catch a fish, but I have seen an elk this morning, and I've been able to listen to the music of water rushing over rocks. That's something I treasure, and I miss it this time of year when Angel Creek is frozen over. I'm here in this majestic place with a bright sun shining above, doing something that brings me pleasure, while my wool socks and waders have kept my feet relatively warm. I believe I'm having exceptional luck."

"You make an excellent point," Colt conceded.

They fished in companionable silence for a time. The sunshine warmed him, and Colt had a couple of nibbles, but he never managed to land a thing. In addition to being supersized, the Taylor River rainbows were smart, which made landing one all the more challenging.

As time passed, Colt's thoughts drifted to the last summer he'd spent in Eternity Springs. If he'd known then that he wouldn't make it back for three years, he'd have spent more time that summer fishing. He missed that particular perk of being a college professor.

What about the rest of it? As he pulled in his line to change flies, he considered the question. Did he regret leaving Georgia Tech? No. The academic world had its own brand of politics that he didn't like any better than Washington's. It certainly had its own overflowing supply of red tape, too.

He did miss the kids—well, some of them, anyway. Unfortunately for both students and professors, too often true learning was sacrificed to the work of making grades. What he'd enjoyed most was finding the occasional student whose mind was turned on to learning.

He'd recruited a few of those types of minds to the CSB over the past couple of years, and he had great teams working with him—smart, dedicated, compas-

sionate people. Not a slacker among them. With special-
ized work such as theirs, people made all the difference.
They were a joy to work with, and he needed to remember them when the bureaucrats—or bureau-rats—dragged
him down.

"I have a fishing tip for you," Celeste said. "You can't
frown a fish onto your line."

He glanced up to see that she'd moved to stand on a
rock a few feet away. She fished in the opposite direction
from him.

Colt grinned ruefully. "Maybe not, but nothing else
seems to be working, either." He hesitated a moment,
then confessed, "I was thinking about my job."

"Yes, I suspected as much."

"Working in Washington is as frustrating as trying to
land a Taylor River rainbow."

"And yet you stand here in freezing water on a cold
winter's day."

He sighed heavily. "I think I have a chance to catch a
fish. I'm not so sure about getting the necessary safety
regulations passed."

"You thrive on challenge, Colt Rafferty. Therein lies
your answer."

Colt was about to ask her to elaborate when her line
went taut. Over the next few minutes, he watched her
pull in a huge, colorful Taylor River rainbow. It was so
big, in fact, that she needed help holding it while she
freed the hook.

"I swear these fish are on steroids," Colt said. "I'll bet
this one weighs twenty-five pounds."

"It's certainly one of the heavier ones I've caught
here."

He gave her a sidelong look. "How many is that?"

"Hmm . . . I haven't been able to get away as much as
I like since Angel's Rest opened. This is only my third

time up here in the past six months. I think I've caught seven fish, counting this one."

"You average two a trip?" He didn't know whether to congratulate her or whine. "Whoa. What do you fish with, Celeste?"

"I tie my own flies, and it's my own special design. I call it an angel kiss." She gestured to the tackle box at her feet. "Would you like to try one?"

"I absolutely would. Thanks."

While Colt set about changing his tackle, he brought the conversation back to the question he'd been poised to ask before she hooked the monster. "What did you mean a few minutes ago about an answer?"

Satisfaction flickered in Celeste's blue eyes. "You fish for answers. Perhaps you've landed red herrings and you should try your luck elsewhere."

"Red herrings?" he repeated. "I don't understand what you mean."

"Think about it, dear."

At that, her line again went tight, and after she landed an even bigger trout, she declared she'd had enough fishing for the day and took her leave. Determined not to be outdone by a woman twice his age, Colt redoubled his efforts to catch one of the wily rainbows and tried every type of tackle in his box. Still, the fish eluded him.

When he reached the point of fearing frostbite on his toes, he admitted defeat and pulled in his line. He gathered up his gear and trudged back through the snow toward his car, cold, disappointed, but already thinking about the next time out. Arriving at the SUV, he spied something sitting on the center of the hood and he pulled up short. "What in the world?"

A hunk of wood—aspen—weighted down a piece of paper. He lifted it and removed the note, recognizing Celeste's handwriting.

"Of course. Who else would it be?" he murmured. He

opened the driver's-side door, slipped inside, and started the engine. As he waited for the vehicle to warm up, he studied the wood for a long moment, then read the note.

Dear Colt,

Do you recall the conversation we had when I first spoke with you about creating the sign for Angel's Rest? I asked you how you decided what to carve from any particular block of wood. You offered me a lovely explanation about how you'd hold a block of wood in your hands and open your mind to possibilities, and soon the image you were meant to carve would take shape.

I spied this piece of aspen as I left the river, and it occurred to me that you might find the exercise beneficial in regard to your current dilemma. Consider that this piece of aspen represents your path, your dreams and desires, known and unknown. Open your mind and your heart to all the possibilities.

Something wonderful is waiting for you, Colt. Open your eyes and see it.

Your friend,
Celeste

"Hmm," he murmured, folding the note and tossing it on the dashboard.

He glanced at the aspen log and shook his head. Celeste Blessing was a sweetheart, but she was also one strange bird. See his path in a hunk of wood? Path to what?

"I could carve a club to beat up the nine-to-fivers with, I guess," he muttered.

The auto heater began blowing warm air. Colt tugged off his gloves and held his half-frozen fingers up to the vent. Once he'd thawed out enough to feel again, he put the SUV into gear, pulled out onto the road, and headed for Eternity Springs. While he drove, he reflected on the day. Life should be full of days like today. Beginning with sharing breakfast with a beauty, then communing with nature for the majority of the day—even if the trout whipped his ass. Topping it off with a fish dinner with Dr. Sage Anderson would have been nice, but hey, no sense being greedy.

Thoughts of his neighbor at Hummingbird Lake lingered in his mind as he drove toward Eternity. Sexy Sage. Brokenhearted beauty. He'd been shocked to find her at his door last night. Despite the fact that she'd cried in his arms on two separate occasions, something about her made him doubt that she indulged in tears all that often. She was a mystery, an enigma.

She'd screamed when he kissed her, but she'd cuddled against him and slept like a kitten.

He blew out a heavy sigh. Shoot, it might be easier to get all the safety measures he wanted adopted by the appropriate agencies than to piece together the puzzle that was Sage Anderson, physician and artist. The woman had DEFCON 1 defenses.

Colt's route took him through Gunnison, and in the middle of town he stopped at a red light. As he waited for it to change, a display in the window of a flower shop caught his attention. He grinned. When the light changed, he claimed the parking spot in front of Columbine Flowers.

When he walked in, the woman behind the counter set down the paperback book she'd been reading and smiled. "Good afternoon. Can I help you?"

"I hope so. Could I get a flower arrangement made right away?"

"Absolutely. What would you like?"

"Something for a woman. Bright and cheerful. Friendly rather than romantic. And I'd like it in that vase." He pointed toward the ceramic vase in the window that had lured him into the shop.

The woman behind the counter blinked. "We usually send that to men."

"I can see why you would, but it's perfect for my purposes."

"All right, then. I'll have it ready for you in . . ." She glanced at the wall clock. "Twenty minutes?"

"Excellent." Colt flashed a satisfied smile, then asked, "I missed lunch, and I noticed the café across the street. Food any good there?"

"It's wonderful. I had today's special for lunch and it was beyond excellent."

"Oh, yeah? What's the special?"

"Fried trout."

Colt laughed. "Perfect. Absolutely perfect. I'll be back for my flowers after lunch."

"They'll be ready."

Colt gave the flower lady a quick salute, then exited the flower shop and crossed the street to the restaurant. Sometimes things simply fell into place.

Following a full and rewarding day at the easel, Sage fixed tomato soup and a grilled cheese sandwich for supper, then sprawled on the sofa, remote in hand, and was preparing to indulge in some University of Colorado basketball and their too-hot coach, Anthony Romano, when her phone rang.

For a long moment, she didn't move but simply allowed it to ring. It was probably Sarah calling, maybe Nic. She should answer and apologize for her outburst last night, but she simply didn't have the heart for it. So she let the phone ring until it stopped.

It rang again five minutes later. Again she allowed it to go on until it went silent after ten rings. When it sounded again two minutes later, she gave up and switched on her answering machine.

To her surprise, once her leave-a-message recording played, the voice she heard wasn't one of her ticked-off girlfriends.

"I know you're there," Colt Rafferty's voice rumbled from the answering machine. "I see the lights."

Listening to him, Sage felt her pulse rate speed up.

"I'm not gonna bother you tonight," he explained. "However, you need to go check your front door. I left something for you."

"More chili?" she said aloud.

"It's not supper," he continued, as if he'd heard her. "I had a trout dinner in Gunnison, and I all but licked my plate clean. Still, you need to bring it in before it freezes. I hope you had a great workday today and that whatever plans you have for tonight are pleasant ones. Speaking of pleasant plans, I'm gonna go soak in the hot tub and think of you. You're welcome to join me if you'd like, but I probably should warn you—I won't be wearing swim trunks."

Standing in the middle of her living room, staring at the answering machine, Sage swallowed hard. No trunks? Now that was just cruel.

"G'night, Cinnamon," he continued in a low, intimate tone. "Don't forget to check your front porch."

The machine clicked and fell silent. Sage sucked in a deep breath, then hurried to the front of her cottage. She flipped on the porch light and opened the front door.

Spying his offering, she began to laugh. Daisies, sunflowers, spider mums, and greenery emerged from a truly hideous ceramic flower vase that depicted a Taylor River rainbow trout.

Seeing it, Sage fell a little bit in love.

TEN

❦

Sage didn't see or speak to another soul for days. Her friends gave her the space she'd requested. Wanting to avoid any further confrontation phone calls might bring, she sent emails to Nic and the others apologizing for her outburst and asking them to respect the boundaries she'd drawn out of necessity. The notes they'd sent back remained a bit on the frosty side but did indicate a reluctance to allow the situation to permanently damage their friendship. Grateful, Sage told herself that the situation would improve with a little time, and she tried not to let herself fret about her relationships with her friends.

She also tried not to be too curious about the man next door.

She hadn't seen or spoken to Colt Rafferty, but that didn't mean he hadn't made his presence known. The man kept leaving gifts at her front door. A CD of Irish folk tunes. A butterfly carved from wood. A ridiculous four-foot-tall hot pink teddy bear that she knew had been for sale in one of the tourist shops downtown since she moved to Eternity Springs.

She loved it. She loved all the gifts. Each day she looked forward to opening her door. She found herself peeking through the curtains in an attempt to catch him coming or going. Frankly, she enjoyed the attention.

Sage had gone on a handful of dates since Peter's

death. They'd all been casual, and each time she'd felt awkward and unready to resume that part of life. Not only had she needed time to mourn Peter, she also recognized that dating was an exercise in futility. Relationships required openness and honesty, and that she simply couldn't give. She couldn't let anyone in.

Look at the damage her secrets had done to her relationships with friends. Imagine throwing a man— a lover—into the mix. Nope. Wouldn't work. Couldn't work. Not unless she was ready to pour out the whole ugly story, and even if she summoned the courage to tell it, there was no guarantee that the person who heard it would understand the enormity of what had occurred.

Words couldn't explain what had happened that day. Her nightmare paintings couldn't begin to depict the horror. How could anyone understand her, accept her for who she was, without knowing what had happened that hot African morning?

And if she did try to tell people, then what? Would they blame her? Pity her? Hate her?

Just like she hated herself?

No. She wasn't ready to go there. She simply couldn't do it. Not that she had abandoned all hope of working past the problem. She would never forget, but she trusted that eventually she'd learn to live with the memories. After all, she'd been doing pretty well before Nic's babies came. She had to believe she would claw her way back to mental health. She could do it. She simply needed more time.

In the meantime, due to the fact that Colt Rafferty's time in town was temporary—now less than a week, she believed—she could enjoy his attentions without worrying about the future because the future wasn't on the table. He was just a visitor. He lived thousands of miles away. He was safe.

Which was why, on the fifth day of her self-imposed

isolation, she picked up her phone and dialed the Landry cabin. Colt answered on the third ring. "Hello?"

"Is this the North Pole?"

He remained silent a beat, but when he spoke, she heard the smile in his low-timbred drawl. "That depends. Are you naughty or nice?"

"I'm nice. Definitely nice."

"Darn."

She chuckled at the regret in his voice, then said, "I'm so nice that I'm calling to invite Santa to a pot roast supper tonight if he doesn't already have plans."

"Ho ho ho." Now she heard delight in his tone. "What time should my bag of toys and I arrive?"

"Better leave your toys at home, big guy. This is a dinner invitation only. Seven o'clock would be good."

"See you at seven, beautiful."

Sage hung up her phone and glanced at the teddy bear she'd propped in a seated position on her cream-colored sofa. "We have a dinner date. We'd better get moving."

Not that she had too much to do to get ready. She'd managed six whole hours of sleep last night and she'd awakened in the mood to cook, which was why she already had a pot roast simmering on the stove, homemade bread rising on the counter, and an apple pie fresh from the oven. All she really needed to do to prepare was to primp. With a spring in her step, she headed for her bedroom with the thought of taking a nice warm bath. As she passed her studio, she paused, then stepped inside, grabbed the doorknob, and pulled the door shut. Her nightmare paintings were not for public display.

She added lavender-scented oil to her bath and managed to take a full hour getting dressed and ready. She chose brown slacks and a forest green V-necked cashmere sweater, dangling topaz earrings, and, just for fun, a barrette of fairy wings for her hair. At five minutes to seven, she took her bread from the oven and set it on the counter to cool. He knocked on her door at precisely seven o'clock.

Sage drew a deep, calming breath, checked her reflection in the hallway mirror, and answered the door. She burst into laughter. He was dressed in jeans and the top half of a Santa suit, and carried a dark pillowcase draped over his shoulder. Stepping back from the doorway, she waved him inside. "Where in the world did you find a Santa costume on such short notice?"

"Costume? What costume?"

She rolled her eyes and eyed the pillowcase. "I thought I told you no toys."

"No toys. Wine." He reached into the bag and pulled out a lovely Napa Valley cabernet that he handed to her, saying, "Okay, maybe I did bring a toy, too." Reaching inside the pillowcase once again, he drew out a small box.

"A Slinky!" Sage exclaimed with delight. "I love these things."

"I couldn't decide between that and Silly Putty, so . . ." He drew out the famous egg. "I got both."

"You're crazy." She removed the Slinky from the box, balanced it in her hands, and played with it. Her grin grew slowly but surely, and she felt a lightness of heart that she hadn't felt since . . . well . . . since the teddy bear showed up on her porch the day before. Glancing up from the toy, she asked, "Why the gifts?"

Unbuttoning the Santa top, he slipped it off, revealing a green cable-knit sweater beneath, and said, "You strike me as a woman who can use a few gifts."

"Why do you say that?"

"You have a beautiful smile and I haven't seen it enough. Besides, I've had fun picking out the presents. I like thinking about you during my day."

"You have quite a line, Rafferty."

"It's not a line when it's the truth."

She fumbled for a comeback to that and settled for inanity, "I'll go open the wine."

She escaped to the kitchen where she pulled the cork and checked her roast. She returned to the front room carrying the bottle and two glasses, and found him studying the brochure from Art on the Bricks in Fort Worth.

She folded her arms. "If you're going to criticize my work, you might want to hold off until after dinner or you're liable to go to bed hungry."

He set the brochure down and winked at her. "After spending the evening with you, I rather suspect I'll go to bed hungry whether I eat your pot roast or not."

She rolled her eyes. "Oh, for crying out loud."

He laughed. "Okay, here's an honest question. I've spent a good share of the past week working with wood, and it's made me curious about your creative process. How did you get started with fairies?"

Sage sipped her wine and savored the taste of cherry and oak as she recalled the day she had produced the work that changed the direction of her life. "It was the first year after I'd moved here. I woke up to a miserable, muddy day in late spring. It was dark outside, I felt dark inside, and I wanted some light in my world. I turned the TV on to the movie channel, and Julie Andrews was singing 'My Favorite Things' in *The Sound of Music*. I picked up my sketch pad thinking I'd sketch my version of the song, and the first thing that came to mind was Tinker Bell. It took hold of me then, and my list of favorite things ended at one."

Colt studied her thoughtfully. "Define 'it' for me."

"My muse. Sarah calls it my creativity wind. I don't dial into it every time I work, but when I do . . ." She shrugged. "I suspect it's what a crack high must be like. It's addictive. I think of it as the Force."

When he frowned thoughtfully, she gave in and ac-

knowledged his own artistry by asking, "What is it like
for you?"

Now his frown deepened into a scowl. "I'm a chemical engineer, not an artist. I carve for something to do, to
keep my hands busy. Anything I've ever carved has been
the result of deliberate planning and design."

Although his sentence ended, Sage sensed that he had
yet to complete his thought, so she remained silent. A
few seconds later, he added, "Until this week."

"What happened this week?"

His answer was slow in coming, but he finally replied,
"The day I fished the Taylor River I ran into Celeste."
His brow furrowed and his lips tightened, causing those
dimples to wink. "She has an uncanny way of cluing
into people, have you noticed?"

"Oh, yeah."

He told her about finding wood and a note on his car.
"After I left the flowers on your porch that night, I went
back inside and turned on ESPN. I watched a basketball
game. I don't remember picking up my knife or the
aspen log Celeste left me, but by the time the game
ended, the butterfly I gave you was almost finished."

Sage nodded. "The Force."

He glanced at her easel, where a half-completed painting of a rose garden sat. "I'm not sure I like your Force."

"Oh, I do. There is nothing I like better than losing
myself in the work."

With a smile, Sage suggested they sit down to dinner
while the bread was still warm from the oven. They discussed college basketball while they ate, arguing poten-
tial selections for the upcoming NCAA tournament. He
was sufficiently complimentary about her cooking and
had second helpings of everything and thirds of her
bread. When she politely but firmly refused his help
dealing with the dishes, he asked if she minded if he

started a fire in the fireplace. She joined him a few minutes later carrying slices of apple pie.

Welcoming flames crackled in the fireplace and Norah Jones played on the stereo. He sat on the couch with his boots off and his feet propped up on the ottoman. He idly pulled and stretched the Silly Putty while he stared into the flames. He looked totally comfortable, totally at home. As if he belonged here.

Sage handed him his pie, kicked off her own shoes, and sat beside him—not too close—curling her legs beneath her. "So, when are you heading back to D.C.?"

"Sunday."

"Are you anxious to get back to work?"

"I should be. My team deployed to an incident in Alabama this morning. Ordinarily I'd be chomping at the bit to join them."

"And you're not now?"

"Nope." He took a bite of his dessert, hummed appreciatively, and added, "I'm blaming it on Celeste and her block of wood."

"My butterfly?"

"The myriad of possibilities."

"I don't understand."

He didn't respond right away, but instead finished off his pie in three quick bites. Sage was wondering if she'd given him too small a piece when he set aside his plate.

"I don't really want to talk about it." He reached for her with one hand and smoothly took possession of and set aside her dessert plate with the other. Tugging her toward him, he suggested, "Let's neck instead. You won't scream, will you?"

He had the prettiest eyes. "Probably not."

He captured her mouth with his.

As far as changing the subject went, his method proved first-rate. Since Sage had been anticipating his kiss from the minute she dialed the Landry cabin to invite him for dinner, she neither resisted nor protested. She relaxed into the moment and allowed him to lie back and pull her atop him, sweeping her away into a warm, rolling river of pleasure.

He buried his fingers into her hair as he moved his lips over hers. His tongue explored her, stroked her, stoked her passion. He tasted of cinnamon and smelled like sin and felt like heaven pressed against her.

Sage sighed into his mouth. He growled in response. His hand began to move, skimming up and down her back. He slipped his hand beneath her shirt and caressed the sensitive skin at the small of her back with the callused pad of his thumb until she shuddered.

It had been so long since she'd indulged in any intimacy with a man—even intimacy as relatively innocent as this. When his mouth released hers and his lips trailed across her face, she tilted her head, offering her neck.

He nipped her there, and again she shuddered, sensation washing over her in waves like a sun-warmed surf caressing the sand. Pleasure. Yearning. Arousal. Delight. His hand slid down and cupped her butt, his fingers kneading her softly. When she realized she no longer felt his lips on her skin, she opened her eyes to see him watching her, an enigmatic look on his face. "What?" she asked.

"I'm trying to decide."

"Decide what?" When he failed to either reply or look away, she added, "I'm not going to sleep with you."

His lips twitched. "I'm not going to ask you to."

Okay, that was insulting. But when she pursed her mouth, preparing to fire a comeback, he put a finger against her lips and said, "Tonight."

She bit his finger and he laughed, then managed to flip their positions so that he lay atop her. He rose on his elbows and stared down into her face. "This is our first date. I won't take your clothes off. I won't let my hands stray to second-date territory. I won't let my mouth go the places it wants to go so badly that I'm shocked I'm not drooling. While I would love nothing more than to strip off your clothes and have wild mountain-goat sex with you, I'm trying to have more respect for us both."

Sage blinked. "Wild mountain-goat sex?"

He ducked his head and buried his face against her neck. "You smell and taste like summertime. Think that's why I'm so hot?"

"It's lavender and apples," she replied, deliberately ignoring the question.

"I love lavender and apples." He waggled his eyebrows. "You want to neck some more?"

Sage couldn't help it—she laughed. "Are you seventeen, Rafferty?"

"Twice." He grinned slowly and winked wickedly. "I'm experienced."

The glint in his eyes appealed to the part of her that had never met a contest she didn't want to win. "Experienced enough to handle me, big guy?"

His eyes widened, then gleamed. "Try me."

Sage placed her hand against the back of his neck and pulled his head down to hers, then proceeded to give him a blistering kiss. From that moment on, it was a battle. She wiggled and rubbed and worked her way back on top of him, which allowed her better access to his body. He'd promised not to strip off her clothes, but she had made no such promise, so soon she had his shirt open and her hands splayed across his chest. He had great pecs, firm and covered with a light layer of dark hair. His nipples were small and hard, and when she flicked her thumb across one of them, he sucked in an audible breath past gritted teeth.

Sage wanted to taste him, to tease him, so she trailed her mouth down his neck, gently nipping her way to his collarbone, then finally to his breast. His hands were clamped at her hips, his fingers tightened around her like a vise.

The bulge in his jeans was prominent, and Sage couldn't deny that seeing it, feeling it against her, both stirred her and satisfied her. She liked the fact that this man was that hard for her.

"You smell good, too, Rafferty," she said, blowing softly on the flesh she'd sampled. "Taste good, too."

"It's not lavender," he responded, his voice rough and raspy. "Irish Spring."

Sage grinned impishly and adopted an Irish brogue as she quoted an old commercial. "For the manly man."

Then she leaned down and licked the nipple she'd previously neglected.

"Ah, Sage. Please." His eyes shut, he grimaced. "You're killing me here."

"Crying uncle, Rafferty?"

"Uncle and aunt," he groaned. "Cousin. Niece. Nephew."

Then he opened his eyes, stared up at her, and said, "I could probably be talked into being easy."

Sage wavered. Being easy sounded awfully good to her right about now, too. She was hot and humming with arousal. Her bed was only steps away. It had been so long since she'd rolled naked with a man, and she'd never rolled naked with a guy as hot as Colt Rafferty.

But his line about respect had made an impression, and this was indeed their first date. She never slept with guys on first dates, and she suspected that if she indulged tonight, she wouldn't like herself tomorrow.

Besides, as long as she walked away right now, she could claim victory. That settled the question. "Nope. I'm done with you for tonight, Rafferty."

She sat up and stood, then turned away so that he wouldn't see her ogling his chest as he buttoned his shirt. To give herself cover and time for her breathing to return to normal, she picked up the dessert plates and carried them to her kitchen. She rinsed the plates and added them to the dishwasher, then turned to grab a dish towel to dry her hands. Colt stood in the doorway, holding the Santa suit top and his empty pillowcase in one hand. He watched her with a smoldering gaze.

"Leaving?" she asked, lifting her chin, proud that she managed to keep a tremor out of her voice.

"Yep." He strode into the room, his gaze locked on hers. She couldn't have looked away if her life depended on it.

He stopped close, too close. In her space. "I enjoyed this evening, Sage."

She forced herself not to back away. "I did, too."

"Thanks for the invitation."

Her mouth had gone desert dry. "You're welcome."

"I'll see you tomorrow."

"You will?"

The dimple in his cheek deepened as his mouth stretched in a slow, sensual smile. "Oh, yeah. I definitely will. G'night, Cinnamon."

Then he leaned down and kissed her, hard and fast, crushing her mouth with his, invading it with a plundering tongue. Her head began to buzz, her heart thundered. Her knees turned to water, and just as she reached for him to hold on for dear life, he stepped away. "Tomorrow."

Then he was gone and Sage was alone.

For the first time in a long time, she was lonely.

The frigid night air helped Colt cool down as he walked back to the Landry cabin, though he briefly considered stripping naked and walking into a snowbank. That mental image made him laugh, and he entered the cabin feeling pretty darn pleased with himself. Sage Anderson might be the most complex woman he'd ever met. She did it for him in so many ways.

He'd begun the gift giving on a whim with that bowl of chili. He'd continued because he enjoyed it, and because searching out the day's gift provided a welcome distraction from the storm of confusion Celeste Blessing had stirred up with him.

Consider that this piece of aspen represents your path, your dreams and desires, known and unknown. Open your mind and your heart to all the possibilities.

Celeste and her hunk of wood had him exploring all sorts of paths. He wasn't simply standing at a crossroads choosing whether to go north or south. He had east and west and every line of latitude and longitude on earth to consider. While he wasn't ready to commit to anything, he'd come to realize that exploring possibilities had its own rewards.

Colt slept well that night and awoke with a sense of purpose. He made business calls in the morning, worked on his latest carving project for an hour, then grabbed up the day's gift for Sage and headed next door.

This time, instead of leaving his gift for her to find, he set it to one side, then knocked on the door. When she answered a few moments later, the pleasant greeting on his lips died. She had dark circles under eyes that were red with fatigue. "What's wrong? You look terrible."

"Gee, thanks, Rafferty." She slammed the door in his face. Of course, he didn't let it stop him. He opened the door and walked right inside, following her back to her kitchen. For a beautiful woman, she looked like hell. How could a medical doctor allow herself to get into this position? "You didn't sleep again last night, did you?"

"I slept some." She shrugged. "I had a nightmare."

He frowned. "About me?"

She rolled her eyes. "You don't suffer from a lack of self-esteem, do you?"

He ignored that and pressed, "You should have called. I'd have come over."

"Go away, Rafferty. I don't have the energy for you today."

He folded his arms and studied her, debating whether or not it was a good idea to go forward with his plan for the day in light of her obvious fatigue. "When was the last time you got any exercise?"

She shot him a disgusted look and he clarified. "I'm not talking about sex, Sage. I'm talking about strenuous outdoor activity. Hiking. Skiing. Skating. Have you done anything physical since that walk you took around the lake last week?"

She closed her eyes and sighed. "Look, I appreciate what you're trying to do, but—"

"Want to see today's gift?"

She hesitated at that, which made up Colt's mind. She wasn't going to let him in, so he'd draw her out. He retrieved the gift from the front porch and dangled it in front of her. "Wanna play a game?"

"A hockey stick?" She gave him a look that said, *Are you crazy?* "You got me a hockey stick?"

"Celeste confirmed that you already have skates. I've been watching, and the kids don't show up to play until around four o'clock."

She took a step back. "I've never played ice hockey. I don't know the rules."

"We'll make up our rules." He could see that she was tempted, so he took a step forward and urged, "C'mon, Cinnamon. Come out and play with me."

She nibbled her lower lip, hesitating, before she visibly relaxed. "All right. For a little while, I guess. I need a few minutes to finish up something here. How about I meet you at the end of the point in half an hour?"

"I'll be there."

They spent an enjoyable hour on the ice. Sage proved to be an excellent skater and she quickly got the hang of using a hockey stick. The first time she managed to shoot the puck past him, she shouted with glee, did a spin, and gave a smile as big as Texas. With her rosy cheeks and the sunlight glinting off the red in her long curling hair, she was so beautiful that she made Colt's teeth ache. It was all he could do not to grab her and yank her into his arms right then. She declined his dinner-and-dip-in-the-hot-tub invitation, and he didn't press her. The fragile look she'd had earlier was gone. That was enough for now.

The following day he gave her a pack of peppermint-flavored lip balm and took her snowmobiling. The day after that he gave her a set of waders and coaxed her into fishing with him at the Taylor tailwater, which turned out to be a huge mistake because the darned woman caught one! He, once again, came up empty. How humiliating was that?

And yet the circles beneath her eyes didn't appear quite as dark as they had before.

The next day he showed up at her door, gave her ear-muffs and mittens, and challenged her to a snowball fight. That ended when the sexual hum he'd been feeling all week got the better of him and he charged her, knocked her down, and kissed her senseless.

After a few minutes of rolling in the snow with her, he lifted his head, stared down into her lovely eyes, and said, "I've never been this cold and this hot at the same time in my life."

Her laughter sounded like music on the air.

He stood and reached for her hand to pull her to her feet, saying, "Want to go into town for supper with me? I haven't eaten at the Bristlecone since I've been here, and I'm in the mood for one of Mrs. Hawkins' pork chops."

She hesitated, and he added, "C'mon. We can stop at the video store afterward and rent a movie."

An impish look entered her eyes. "I think the latest Nicholas Sparks movie is out in video this week."

He grimaced and rubbed the back of his neck. "You like those sappy romances with the unhappy endings?"

"Occasionally."

"Will watching it help my chances at wooing you into the hot tub?"

She gave him a considering look, and damned if his pulse didn't speed up. "Do you really want to be a stand-in for a Gerard Butler fantasy?"

"Hey, a good fantasy life is a sign of sexual health." He checked his watch. "How about I pick you up in an hour?"

"That'll be good." She gave a wave and headed for her house. Colt turned toward the Landry place, and she caught him completely by surprise when she pegged him between the shoulder blades with one last snowball. Her laughter rang out like church bells on the brisk winter air.

At the cabin, Colt thawed out in a long, hot shower, then checked his stock of wine and—just in case—changed the sheets on his bed. He drove over to Sage's cottage and knocked on her door precisely an hour after they'd separated.

He waited. She didn't answer. He knocked again. Still she didn't answer. "You are not going to stand me up."

He knocked one more time, then began fishing in his pocket for his cellphone. Suddenly the door swung open. She was barefoot, wearing a green silk robe and a fluffy white towel wrapped around her head. "Come in. I'm sorry. I'm running late. One of the galleries that shows my work called with a problem and the call dragged out. Give me ten minutes. Make yourself at home."

As she rushed back toward her bedroom, he watched the robe cling to her butt and called, "I'd be glad to come help. . . ."

She shot him a disdainful look over her shoulder and he grinned and added, "No rush, Cinnamon. Take your time." When she disappeared into her bedroom, he picked up the remote and turned on the television to fill the quiet. Thumbing through the channels, he paused at a station out of Denver.

The local news was on. A reporter was covering a charity event taking place at the Brown Palace hotel, and she was interviewing someone familiar—Ali Timberlake. When she mentioned a new children's program being established in Eternity Springs, Colt sauntered down the hallway toward Sage's room, intending to knock on her door and tell her what was on the television.

But as he approached her room, he saw that the door to her studio stood halfway open. Every other time he'd been inside her home, she'd kept the door to this room shut. Curiosity got the better of him and he peeked inside.

The painting on the easel stopped him in his tracks.

It was the last thing he'd expect to see on Sage Anderson's easel.

The canvas was large, maybe three feet square. She used shades of only two colors, red and black, and the images she'd fashioned had nothing to do with fairies or pixies or butterflies.

The images weren't even images, but rather impressions, bold strokes and slashes and circles that were raw and harsh and violent. Haunted and haunting. He was reminded of Edvard Munch's work *The Scream*. It was difficult to look at, but Colt found it impossible to look away. The work was as powerful as anything he'd seen hanging in a museum.

He shifted to one side to gain a different perspective and spied a stack of paintings leaning against the wall. Curious, he flipped through them. More of the same. All red and black. All violent. All terrifying.

Colt exhaled a harsh breath and murmured, "Dear Lord."

Was this what she saw when she shut her eyes? No wonder the woman didn't sleep. She was haunted by something far deeper than he had imagined.

Colt knew without a doubt that she'd be angered by his snooping, and for the first time, he wondered if he truly wanted answers to his questions about Sage. Disturbed, he exited the studio and returned to the living room.

He sat in front of the television and stared at it without seeing. What sort of hell had she gone through?

He once again took stock of what he knew about her and realized that despite the time they'd spent together the last few days, he hadn't learned all that much. Not about who she used to be, anyway. He'd discovered a lot about Sage Anderson of Eternity Springs, but for the most part, Dr. Sage Anderson still remained a mystery.

Maybe that was for the best. She obviously had her reasons for the actions she'd taken and for the privacy about those actions that she'd maintained. Maybe he should respect that. Maybe he should wait and let her come to him when she was ready.

On the other hand, given what he was considering, maybe he should redouble his efforts to discover what she was hiding.

What was best? How should he play this? She was beginning to trust him. If he pushed her, he might blow it. Maybe if he asked around the question, eventually he could get to the core.

Colt was still wrestling with the question when Sage came out of her bedroom looking like a million dollars in black slacks and a purple sweater. "Sorry to keep you waiting. I hate being late."

"Not a problem," he said, rising. He tried to regain his earlier, casual attitude. "You look great, Sage."

"Thank you. I feel great." Her smile was carefree, the look in her eyes warm. "You've been good for me, Rafferty. All the exercise has worked wonders. I'll need to be sure to keep it up once you're not around to make me do it."

Colt considered taking the opening she'd inadvertently offered, then decided to keep it light for now. Instinct told him not to push. Besides, he really was hungry, and he didn't want the conversation taking an appetite-spoiling turn. "I'll call you and remind you to go throw snowballs at somebody."

"You're such a friend."

"I am," he responded, meaning it.

The Bristlecone was surprisingly busy for a winter evening, with only two available tables upon their arrival. Colt ordered the pork chops he'd been craving while she selected chicken, and the dinner conversation revolved around normal date topics such as favorite movies and books. They were halfway through their meal when the front door opened and Nic and Gabe Callahan walked in.

"Oh, dear," Sage murmured.

Colt watched as, upon spying Sage, Nic hesitated. Gabe touched her on the shoulder and said something, then Nic nodded and veered toward their table. Sage wiped her lips with her napkin, then squared her shoulders. "Hello, Nic."

"Hello." Nic nodded at Colt, who stood and gave her a friendly kiss on the cheek. As he and Gabe shook hands, Nic continued, "I'm glad to see you out and about, Sage."

Colt wondered if anyone else noticed that his dinner date subtly relaxed. "I'm feeling better."

"Good."

"Would you two like to join us?" Colt offered, gesturing toward their table, which could easily accommodate four.

Gabe placed his hand at Nic's back and said, "Thanks, but my bride and I are out on a date. Nic's mom and aunt are visiting for a few days and they're babysitting."

"That's nice." Sage drew a deep breath, then met Nic's gaze. "I'd like to babysit for you sometime, Nic."

Nic's eyes widened in surprise. "Really?"

"Yes." Sage's smile turned a little wobbly as she added, "Although probably the first time out I should try it one baby at a time. Or maybe ask Sarah or Celeste to team up with me to watch them both."

Colt was surprised to see tears pool in Nic's eyes as she responded, "We could try that. Thanks."

"Good." Sage cleared her throat. "I'll look forward to it."

Colt thought he spied a sheen in Sage's eyes, too. He waited until the Callahans took their seats at a table across the room to ask, "Want to tell me what just happened here?"

Sage picked up her fork and pushed a green bean around on her plate. "Nic gave me a chance to apologize for a hurt I caused her, I did so, and she accepted it."

Colt frowned, then topped off her wineglass and his. "Women are the most fascinating creatures. So are the two of you okay?"

"Well . . ." Sage glanced across the restaurant toward the table where the Callahans sat. "We're better. It's complicated."

"Men would throw a punch or two and the trouble would be over."

"Women are more civilized," she said, shrugging. Then after a moment's hesitation, she added, "But they carry grudges longer. Sarah might like to go the punch-throwing route."

"You had a dust-up with her, too?"

"Like I said, it's complicated. Are we going to order dessert?"

He might be a man, but he was smart enough to recognize that she'd changed the subject. "Absolutely. What do you suggest?"

As they rose to leave after dinner, they waved to the Callahans and walked out into the cold. "So, are we still on to watch a video?"

"I'm counting on it."

"Thinking about Gerard Butler, huh?"

"Maybe."

She smiled a cat-and-cream smile that sparked heat in his belly—a good thing, since it was cold enough outside to turn his balls blue beneath three layers of clothes. "All right, but since the temperature is hovering somewhere around ten degrees, why don't we drive to the video store rather than walk?"

"No need to do either," Sage said as he helped her into her coat. "I have a DVD at home for us to watch."

"Oh?" Great. He'd hoped to influence the choice. "Let me guess—it's *P.S. I Love You*?"

A wicked smile flirted at her lips. "You'll see."

The ride back to Hummingbird Lake was made primarily in a comfortable silence. Under other circumstances, Colt's thoughts would have been centered on seduction, but tonight his mind kept returning to the paintings he'd seen in Sage's studio. He couldn't decide if he should ask her about them or not.

He was an old-timer here in Eternity Springs. He didn't have much time to ferret out her secrets—if ferreting was what he wanted to do. He wasn't so sure anymore.

At some point during the past week—maybe when they played hockey or when she lit up like a schoolgirl over the Slinky—Sage had become more than a puzzle for him to solve. She was no longer a beautiful woman who intrigued him, or fun company on days when solitude held no allure. She was more than a woman he wanted—rather badly—to sleep with. Sage Anderson meant more to him than that. She'd become important to him. He cared for her.

Which made his hesitation all the more confusing. Since he cared for her, shouldn't he want to know everything about her? Shouldn't discovering her secrets be of even greater concern to him now than when curiosity alone guided him?

This indecision wasn't like him at all. Seeing those paintings had truly thrown him off his game.

So ask her. Be blunt. Be direct. You'd better get the details before you go back to Washington and burn bridges.

He sucked in a breath, then blew it out harshly. He would ask her. He'd pick his time and bring up the paintings and see what he could glean from her response.

"Something wrong?" she asked.

"No. Not at all." Having reached the turnoff to Reflection Point, he glanced to his right, where Sage sat in shadow, and added, "Today has been a nice day."

"Yes, it has. It truly has." She turned her head, and he could just make out her smile. "I'm glad you asked to borrow that cup of sugar, Rafferty."

"Yeah?" He arched a brow. "Correct me if I'm wrong, but I don't believe you came across with any sugar."

"Well, play your cards right, G-man, and you might be surprised what you can beg from the neighbors."

In the process of turning into his drive, he almost turned into a snowbank at that. He shot her a look and wished for more light to see her better. Had she meant that to sound suggestive? With this woman, he simply couldn't tell.

He pulled the SUV to a stop and hit the remote to open the garage door, then glanced at her as soon as the automatic light pierced the darkness. She wore an enigmatic smile that told him nothing.

Once the car was parked, he walked around to open her door. "Be careful where you step. I found a leak out here earlier. There's some ice on the ground."

"Thanks for the warning." She took hold of his hand and didn't let go. His pulse jumped and he stifled a self-mocking snort. Good Lord, she had him revving like a seventeen-year-old again.

Inside, he gestured toward the great room. "Do you want to start the movie now or—"

"Now is good. Here." Holding his gaze, she reached into her purse, pulled out the DVD, and handed it over.

Colt glanced down at the box and frowned in confusion as he read the title aloud. "*Raising Cane*. The story of sugarcane production in nineteenth-century Texas?"

"It's a documentary about raising sugarcane. I've watched it before. It's very boring."

"O—kay." He looked at the blank screen on the television, then back at her. "I don't like my dates to be bored."

"Oh?"

There came that damned smile again, and Colt was suddenly reminded of the look in her eyes when she'd thrown that last snowball at him. He'd had it all wrong. Forget the nickname Cinnamon—he should call her

Vixen. She'd been leading him down the pine forest path all along, and he'd been too dense to recognize it.

Well, the blinders were off now.

"No. Boredom won't do." He reached out with his index finger to trace the V of her neckline, where her skin was as soft as the cashmere that caressed it. "Gonna let me entertain you?"

"What do you have in mind?"

"I thought we'd start with that dip in the hot tub."

"I didn't bring my swimsuit."

"That's handy." He skimmed his hand down her torso, grabbed the hem of her sweater, and whipped it up over her head. "You're not gonna need it."

ELEVEN

☙

Sage had never had hot tub sex before, so it was possible that what took place over the course of the next forty minutes wasn't unique in the history of hot tubs. However, it was definitely unique in the history of her world.

The man was a fantasy come to life. He did magical things with his hands, marvelous things with his mouth, and his penis . . . well, if a Hall of Fame for penises existed, surely he'd qualify for membership.

And she'd reached those conclusions prior to abandoning the hot tub for his bed. By the time he was finished with her, Sage didn't worry about nightmares. She didn't have the energy to complete a thought, much less to dream.

She lay spent, panting, and oh so satisfied as the clock ticked past midnight and a new day began. Colt groaned, lifted his head from the pillow, and said, "You are sleeping here tonight, right?"

Sage managed, barely, to roll her head in his direction. "That's some invitation."

"Nah, it's a warning. I couldn't be a gentleman and walk you to your door because even if I managed to get you there, no way I could get back home without collapsing in a snowdrift and freezing to death."

"Be quiet, Rafferty. I'm done with you. Let me get

some sleep." She closed her eyes, then smiled when he pulled her to him and spooned against him.

"Thank you, Sage," he murmured, kissing the back of her neck.

Sage slept like a baby that night, all through the night, and actually late into the morning. She woke alone, sore, and feeling better than she'd felt in months. Maybe even years.

She rolled from bed, scooped up the robe he'd obviously left for her, and availed herself of the master bathroom. Then she went looking for Colt.

He stood on the deck talking on the telephone. Seeing her, he ended his call, smiled warmly, and stepped inside. "Good morning."

"Hi."

He studied her a moment, then gave a satisfied nod. "You slept okay."

"I did. You?"

"I slept great." He took her hand and brought it to his mouth and kissed it. "Would you like some tea?"

"No, thanks. I need to be getting home. I have a haircut appointment this morning."

"What's your afternoon like? Want to hike up to Heartache Falls with me?"

"Oh." She frowned. "I need to work."

"I have to go back to Washington early tomorrow morning." He brushed her hair away from her face. "Come with me this afternoon."

She hesitated a moment, then nodded. "Okay."

"I'll pick you up. Two o'clock?"

"Okay."

He walked her back to her cottage, kissed her sweetly, then winked and strode away. Sage all but floated into her house.

She made her haircut appointment with minutes to spare—a good thing, since June Hart gave her customers grief if they were late. An hour later, washed and dried and sans split ends, Sage exited the beauty shop, squared her shoulders, and crossed the street to the Trading Post. She found Sarah on the cereal aisle, re-stocking Shredded Wheat.

Glancing up at her, the welcoming smile of her friend's face dimmed and developed a thin layer of frost.

Sage wanted to jump right in, but there were two other shoppers in the aisle. She smiled hesitantly, then said, "Hi."

"Hello."

Sage mentally hurried the shoppers on to the canned goods section. Sarah placed the last box of cereal onto the shelf, then picked up the empty carton. "Can I help you find something?"

Ouch. Sage glanced down the aisle. One shopper was gone, but Dale Parker couldn't seem to decide between Honey-Nut Cheerios and Raisin Bran. Okay, she'd do this with an audience. "Yes, you can. I'm looking for forgiveness." She reached out and touched her friend's arm. "I'm sorry, Sarah. You're a wonderful woman and a dear friend, and I'm so, so sorry that I hurt you."

As easily as that, Sarah's pique melted. She dropped the cardboard box and hugged Sage hard. "I'm sorry, too. Oh, Sage, I've felt so terrible about this whole thing. Ever since you came to town, it's been obvious that you're running from something. I'm you're friend and I love you. I guess my feelings have been hurt that it's still a big secret, especially since I told you my deep, dark secret about Lori's father."

"I know. I'm sorry. I love you, too." Taller than her friend, Sage dipped her head and touched it against the top of Sarah's. Quietly she said, "Something bad happened, Sarah. I'm not over it yet. I can't talk about it, not to anyone. I'm trying, but some of my wounds are still bloody."

Sarah hugged her again hard, then stepped back and met Sage's gaze. "Maybe rather than bloody, they're infected. Maybe you should lance them and let the poison out."

"Ee-yew."

"Just sayin'." She shrugged, then smiled tenderly and added, "I'm here for you, Sage, if you want to talk. Although you do look better. New makeup?"

"Thank you. It's a miracle remedy for baggy eyes. It's called sleep."

Relief and affection rose inside Sage. She was so lucky to have friends like Sarah and Nic. Now she had to figure a way to square things with Ali so she could stop feeling guilty about it. Then all she'd have to do was worry about following through on her offer to babysit for Nic.

Oh, dear. What have I done?

She repeated that question again later on her way back to the lake. She'd been in such a rush to get to the beauty shop that she'd hardly had time to think about Colt Rafferty and last night. Not that she'd put the events of the previous night from her mind—she was reminded every time she moved. She was deliciously sore.

Last night had been beyond anything she'd ever experienced. Maybe because it was the first time in her life she'd allowed herself to indulge in sex with no possibility of a future, but she suspected it had more to do with the fact that Colt Rafferty was incredible in bed.

The man was simply talented, period.

She was going to miss him when he was gone. He'd been good medicine for her this past week, so good, in fact, that she was glad he was leaving. So far he'd been a distraction. Were he not headed back to Washington, she feared he could be a disaster. He appealed to her in so many ways. She could see herself falling for him, and that could only lead to heartache.

She arrived home to find another gift on her porch, a bouquet of red origami roses with sticks for stems.

Grinning like a lovesick fool, she carried the bouquet inside and placed it in a position of honor—on an end table right next to the pink teddy bear. Then she went into her studio, frowned at the nightmare painting she'd left on her easel, and added it to the stack against the wall. She draped the stack with a sheet, not wanting the negative energy in her sights, then she took out a clean canvas and went to work. She chose to begin with a bright, happy shade of yellow. By the time Colt arrived at ten minutes to two, she was well on her way to creating what might be one of her best paintings yet.

"You're early," she said as she opened the door.

"I couldn't wait to kiss you again." So he didn't.

The buzz from his kiss on top of her creative high was almost enough to make her drag him off to her bedroom to have her way with him.

He broke the kiss, sucked in a breath, then stepped away. "Any more of that and I won't get to see Heartache Falls this afternoon, while it's still all frozen over. Celeste told me it's a sight to behold, and I promised myself I'd see it before I go back."

"Hey, you're the one who started it."

"Yeah, and I'd love to be the one to finish it, too. On second thought, if I want to see frozen water, I can look in the ice maker. Why don't we—"

"Cool your jets, Rafferty. Let me wash out my brushes and put on my cold-weather gear. I haven't seen Heartache Falls in winter, either."

He followed her back to her studio, where his gaze locked on the day's work. Sage folded her arms and arched a brow in warning. He grinned, a boyish but sexy flash of white teeth, and said, "I have a new appreciation for fairies. This painting is vibrant. It all but shimmers. It makes me smile."

She waited a beat, then nodded. "Okay. I guess you dodged that bullet."

"When it's done, I have first dibs on buying it, okay?"

For some reason that made her uncomfortable, so she simply replied, "We'll see."

She saw his gaze flick around the room and pause on the sheet-covered stack of paintings leaning against her wall. A shadow crossed his face. "I never intended to insult your talent, Sage. You are a fantastic artist."

"Thank you."

He looked down and away, then rubbed the back of his neck and sighed heavily. "I've heard it said that an artist's work allows a glimpse into his soul. Talk to me about those paintings, Sage."

He pointed toward the stack of nightmare paintings.

Immediately Sage stiffened and everything inside her went cold. *How could he . . . oh no.* Quietly she asked, "What do you know about them?"

He told her how he had spied one of the paintings through the open studio doorway when he came to tell her that Ali was on TV. Her stomach rolled. She felt sick. She wanted to be angry at him, but fairness wouldn't permit it. She had left the door open and the painting in plain sight, after all.

"I've never seen work so powerful. What do they represent?"

She closed her eyes. In her mind's eye, she saw children playing tag and women doing laundry and Peter throwing a baseball to a half-naked boy. When the images were swallowed by a storm cloud of red and black, she spoke past the lump in her throat. "It's private. The paintings are private. You shouldn't have seen them."

"I know." His blue eyes tender and sad, he added, "I almost wish I hadn't."

While she set about cleaning her brushes, he leaned against the wall, his arms crossed, signaling that he had all the time in the world to wait for his answers. When a full minute ticked by without a response from her, he said, "I have my own suspicions. Shall I tell you what they are?"

"Colt . . ." She set down the brushes, then turned and exited the studio, turning toward the kitchen.

He followed her saying, "It's possible that the paintings are a new artistic direction you are exploring, and nothing more. That doesn't feel right to me, though. I think the odds are better that this stack of paintings and your change in profession are somehow tied together."

"Look, it doesn't matter." She walked into the mudroom and reached for her coat. "Let's head up to Heartache."

"I think we have heartache right here. Sage, I didn't get the vibe last night that you were afraid of me, but if it's because of a man, something a man did to you . . ."

The coat slipped through her fingers. She licked her lips, then bent to pick it up. This wasn't the nosy investigator asking, but the lover. He wanted reassurance. She turned and looked him straight in the eyes. "I wasn't raped."

He studied her for a long moment, obviously trying to judge her truthfulness. "Why those two colors and only those two colors?"

She pulled on her coat and ignored the question.

Colt didn't let that stop him. "Gotta figure some sort of symbolism. Let see . . . black could be something positive, like power or formality or elegance. But the paintings don't feel like that to me. I think secrecy or mystery might fit. Or, of course, death."

He looked at her, wordlessly asking, giving her the opportunity to acknowledge the demons, but she couldn't. She simply wasn't ready.

A sad smile played about his lips. "Now, the red has a little more variety, to my mind. Red is energy and power and passion. Love. All good. But it's also the color universally used to represent danger. Then, of course, red is the color of blood."

"Stop," she pleaded. "Please, just drop it. It's personal and private and none of your business."

He folded his arms. "Sure it's my business. I care about you. I'm your friend. I'm your lover. What happened, Sage? What the hell do those paintings represent?"

"There. You said it. That's it." Her heart pounded. Nausea rose in her stomach. "Hell. It *was* hell. I don't want to think about it or talk about it, to you or to anyone else. Can you respect that boundary? Please?"

She grabbed her hat and gloves. She needed fresh air, fast. "I'm driving up to Heartache Falls. You're welcome to come with me—as long as you don't say another word about my paintings. Any of them."

She yanked her keys off the hook beside the door. "So. What's your choice?"

For a moment he appeared ready to argue. Then he surrendered with a shrug. "What paintings? Let me get my camera out of the SUV and we can go."

They made the drive up to Heartache Falls primarily in silence. Sage's emotions rolled and swirled and bubbled inside her like a mountain stream at spring melt.

The falls were a half-hour drive from town, followed by a twenty-minute climb along a mountain trail maintained by the Park Service. Sage was so agitated that she made the climb in fifteen, well ahead of Colt, who had lagged behind taking photographs and stopping frequently to enjoy the views.

Arriving at the overlook, she grabbed hold of the safety bar and gazed at the sight before her. Before when she'd visited these falls, water had poured over the precipice, tumbling and spraying and roaring downward. This was an eerily silent waterfall of icicles. It looked like God had snapped his fingers and frozen time, literally. Abruptly. In an instant.

Like Africa. Like my life.

One minute she had had a full, satisfying, rewarding life. An instant later it was gone. Over. Silent, frozen icicles. Black ice. Ice. Cold. Death.

She stood motionless for a minute—or an hour, she didn't know—her gaze locked on the icicles, her thoughts on a hot, dusty day years ago. She didn't hear Colt approach or notice that he'd taken a position beside her until he said, "Isn't that beautiful? Look at how the sun glistens off the icicles. It's so bright and sparkling—like a river of diamonds, don't you think?"

She hadn't noticed.

"How cold do you think it is right now? I'm guessing around twenty degrees. The sunshine works its magic, though. See?" He pointed toward the upper section of Heartache Falls. "The icicles in the sunshine are melting. Just a little, but they're definitely melting."

Sage stared. Sparkling sunshine and . . . yes. Water. Not ice, but a drop of water, sliding down the length of the icicle and falling free.

Liquid. Not frozen. Warmed by the sunshine and released.

Sage let out a shuddering breath and the words tumbled out. "I volunteered with Doctors Without Borders. In the Central African Republic."

He turned his head. His brows were arched in surprise, but he didn't speak. His silence encouraged her to continue.

"It was a lawless place. Dangerous. But Doctors Without Borders treats everyone. That's their mission. Doesn't matter what side of a conflict you are on. That's why they're allowed access. In CAR, our organization broadcast the mission far and wide, so the bad guys left us alone."

Colt listened, his expression interested but not judgmental, not the way her father's expression had been when she'd first told him she'd signed up to volunteer.

"I loved the work. These people had nothing, Colt, and what we gave made such a huge difference. It was so rewarding."

She couldn't bring herself to tell him about that day, the worst day, but she was able to tell him of the beginning of the end. "We were manning a medical clinic in a remote village. It was a beautiful morning. The heat in the afternoons was a killer, but that particular morning, the weather was lovely and people were happy. I'll never forget this set of twin boys. They were probably two and a half years old and their mother brought them for immunizations. They started playing a game of peek-a-boo with each other and they got to giggling. Soon they had everyone else in the room laughing."

She told him how in midafternoon, the Zaraguinas rode in looking for her. She told him about Peter and how he'd attempted to protect her and how they'd shot him.

"Your fiancé," he repeated, the rounding of his eyes betraying his surprise at that bit of news. "They killed him?"

"No." She shook her head. *Not that day.* "He recovered, but he couldn't stop them from taking me that day." *And I couldn't save him later.*

She remembered Peter, tall and lean and blond. So smart, so dedicated. Such passion for the mission. And for her.

She closed her eyes and when Colt moved behind her, wrapped his arms around her in a comforting embrace, she found the strength to continue. "They took me to another village, their stronghold. My reputation had preceded me because their leader, Colonel Ban Ntaganda, wanted me."

His voice tight and pained, Colt said, "Aw, Sage."

She realized then that he hadn't believed her before. Typical male. Although that wasn't fair. Peter had thought the same thing because, after all, they'd been living in the rape capital of the world. "Not rape. That's not what he wanted. They were kidnappers and—"

"You were a hostage? Held for ransom?"

"Not me." She shook her head. "The children. See, the people in the area were nomads, cattle keepers, and the bandits targeted their children because parents could sell their livestock to raise ransom money."

"That's evil." Colt's eyes glittered with anger and disgust. "Those poor kids."

"What happened that time was that a father had already sold his cows when Ntaganda kidnapped his children. The poor man had no way to pay the ransom and Ntaganda killed the kids. Right in front of their father."

Colt blew out a heavy, heavy sigh. "You saw this?"

"No. But it affected me. You see, the father went crazy. He somehow managed to get hold of a gun and he shot Ntaganda."

"And you were a surgeon," Colt said, finally getting it right.

She turned in his arms. Staring up at him, she confessed her horror. "I saved his life, Colt. He was an evil, evil man. I saved him. I never thought twice about it. I didn't think about those children or their father. I operated on the man, removed the bullet, cleaned the wound, gave him antibiotics, and told him how to avoid infection. I saved him, Colt."

"Ah, baby." He brushed the hair away from her face. "Of course you saved him. You're a doctor. That's what you did. You treated the sick and the injured. You took an oath. You'd have saved anyone who was bleeding to death."

Her throat tight, she murmured, "He was evil."

"Yeah, and he'd have killed you, too, had you refused to treat him." He met her gaze, his smile sad. "I'm sorry, honey. I'm so, so sorry. I know that has to be a heavy burden for you to bear."

And I've only told you part of it.

"I couldn't do it anymore. So I came here. To paint. To try to pick up the pieces."

"I understand. I do." He closed his eyes and held her tight, resting his chin atop her head. "I've seen some terrible things in my work. I deal with the aftermath of horror. You lived it, didn't you?"

"Yes," she whispered. *Even more than you know.*

He did understand, Sage realized, at least a little bit. That's why he listened and didn't judge. Didn't tell her to forget. He simply let her talk. It was a connection she'd been able to make with him alone.

"You know, honey, even before I got to know you, I knew I'd like you. You're beautiful, talented, smart, witty, so sexy that you make my teeth ache. What I didn't realize was how much I'd come to respect and admire you."

She shrank from the praise. "Why? I quit medicine."

"You didn't quit anything. I suspect Nic Callahan and her babies would agree. Look, you channeled your talents in a new direction. You are still contributing to people's lives and the greater good."

She laughed bitterly. "With butterfly paintings?"

"By bringing beauty into the world. That's nothing to dismiss, Cinnamon."

She burrowed her head against him. "I began painting as therapy. Light and bright and happy—that's what I needed to combat all the darkness inside me. Those paintings started out as my anchors so that I wouldn't get lost in the ugliness. Then, well, people liked them and they became my job."

Sighing, she added, "They've lost their mojo. Painting

butterflies and fairies and rainbows no longer holds off the black-and-red storm."

He hugged her tight. "I'm so sorry. Sometimes, baby, a storm needs to run its course. You just hang on and weather it as best you can and know that someday it'll pass. You'll know it in your bones. In the meantime . . ."

He waited until she looked up at him. "Throw in a unicorn amongst the fairies and the butterflies. He can use that horn of his to slay your dragons."

Now her laugh was genuine. Somehow, telling him had made her feel better. "You're ridiculous."

"Actually, I'm cold. You ready to head home?"

"Yes."

"Can I drive going back?"

"No."

He held her hand as they hiked back toward the car. About halfway between the falls and the car, he stopped and pointed into the forest. "Look. There, on the ground beside that rock. There's a flower coming up from the snow. It's freezing and that's a flower."

Sage looked where he indicated. "That's a snowdrop. They do bloom in February, they're the first flower of the year, but I've never seen one outside of a garden. Wow. It's kind of amazing to find one out here like this." She paused, then shook her head. "Are you familiar with the snowdrop legend?"

He shook his head. "No."

"It's beautiful." She smiled wistfully as she recited the tale. "The legend says that after Adam and Eve were expelled from the Garden of Eden, Eve was about to give up hope that winter would ever end. An angel appeared and consoled her, saying that even though the land was snowy and barren, spring would indeed follow winter. Then, as a token of his promise, he blew on the falling snowflakes. When the snowflakes touched the ground, they transformed into flowers. Snowdrops. Ever since then, snowdrops have appeared during the bleakest weeks of winter as a sign of the better times to come. They're a symbol of hope."

When she finished, Colt drew back. He gave her a doubting look. "You're kidding me."

"No, why would I do that?"

"That's just . . . wow." He shook his head. "Talk about symbolism."

"What do you mean?"

"Think about it, Sage. It's almost like that angel has been watching over you, and she's planted that flower to make a point."

Sage opened her mouth to protest, then shut it without speaking. Turned out she didn't have a response to that.

They said no more as they completed the trek to the car, and once there, despite her earlier denial, she tossed him the keys. She was suddenly tired, borderline exhausted. She dozed the entire way back to Hummingbird Lake and woke only when he pulled into her drive. "Wake up, sleepyhead."

"Wow. I can't believe I conked out like that."

"You needed the sleep." He stopped the Jeep and shifted into park. "Listen, I need to run an errand in town and do a few chores at the Landrys' place, but it shouldn't take me more than an hour. I have to leave Eternity Springs by six tomorrow morning to catch my plane. I want to spend the time I have left here with you. All right?"

He's leaving. That little fact had slipped her mind for a bit. Sage tried to ignore the little pang in her heart as she nodded and said, "I'd like that, too."

During the hour he was gone, she tackled some chores of her own, and while she worked, she once again realized that the solitude she'd prized out here on Reflection

Point now had a lonely feel to it. These past two weeks had changed her world, mostly for the better, but not entirely. She would miss Colt Rafferty when he was gone. However, after thinking it through while she mopped her kitchen floor, she decided that she still was glad he was leaving.

The man was like a dog with a bone, always pushing, always prodding, always wanting to discover a fact, solve a mystery, and piece together a puzzle. He did it in a nice way. Most of the time you didn't even notice he was doing it. Still, she'd had enough of it.

Sage would only be pushed and prodded so far.

With today's revelation, she'd pretty much reached her limit. Were he not already on his way out of town, she suspected she might have been forced to give him his walking papers. Because Colt Rafferty might push, but Sage Anderson planted. When she absolutely, positively, established a boundary or claimed a position, she sank her roots as deep as Murphy Mountain was tall.

She'd learned that she had to do it that way. It was how she managed to survive.

Her phone rang. It was Colt. "I'm at the Trading Post. Thought I'd pick up something to cook for dinner. Is pasta okay with you? In addition to killer chili, I make an amazing red sauce."

"Sounds great. While you're there, would you pick me up a gallon of skim milk, too, please?"

"Skim?"

She rolled her eyes at the pain in his tone. "Skim."

"Okay, see you in ten."

His red sauce lived up to his claims, but the meatballs she provided took the meal from excellent to sublime. She told him as much as she sipped a lovely Chianti. He fired back that he saved sublime for the bedroom.

She couldn't argue with that.

Especially after he insisted on proving his point,

which he did with delicious inventiveness, spectacular enthusiasm, and amazing stamina throughout the long winter night. She finally fell into an exhausted sleep an hour before dawn and she stirred only to half wakefulness when, sometime later, he kissed her and told her good-bye.

She awoke midmorning, and before she even opened her eyes, she knew something was wrong.

I'm not alone.

Her muscles tensed. Her pulse began to race. Colt was gone. She knew that. The bed beside her was empty, and yet. . . it wasn't.

Slowly, silently, Sage cracked open her eyes and peered through her lashes.

A wicker basket lay in the space Colt had previously occupied. Something was inside the basket.

He didn't. Her eyes flew open wide. "He did."

The gift he'd left was no stuffed animal or hockey stick or flavored lip balm. This wasn't a basket in her bed. It was a bed in her bed. A dog bed.

This time, his gift had a heartbeat.

Colt Rafferty had left her a puppy. A puppy! A little white puffball wearing a red collar tied with a big red bow, curled up and asleep on a purple pillow.

A folded gift card hung from a ribbon threaded through the wicker. In a state of shock, Sage reached for it and read his bold handwriting.

She's a bichon frise and she's lonely. She's had all her shots and Nic says she's healthy and ready to be loved. I left dog food, bowls, a leash, some toys, and a silly dog sweater Celeste pushed on me in a sack in your kitchen. (Please, though, don't humiliate the poor dog by dressing her up.)

She's ready for you, Sage, and you're ready for her. You bring smiles to the lives of others through your work. Let this little furball bring smiles to your life through play.

—Colt

"I can't believe he did this," she murmured as the puppy opened her round black eyes and blinked. "Of all the nerve."

She spoke to the empty room as if he were still there, as if he could hear her. "Rafferty, didn't anyone ever tell you that it's wrong to give pets as gifts? Adopting a pet is a big commitment. It's not something to do on a whim. Certainly not something to force on someone else."

She could almost hear him answering back. *This wasn't a whim, Cinnamon, but a well-considered, deliberate decision. She needs you. You need her.*

"No one is going to force me into keeping this puppy. I know where you got her. This is one of the Prentice family's pups. Little Josh Prentice has been trying to find them homes for a month. I'll load her up and take her back to them."

No, you won't. Look at her. Pick her up and hold her. She's meant to be yours. You know it's true.

The puppy rose to her little puppy paws, and her little puppy nub of a tail began to wag. Warmth flooded Sage's heart. "It's a good thing you're already gone, Rafferty, because I'd kill you otherwise."

She picked up the puppy and cuddled her close. When the dog lifted her little puppy face and licked Sage's chin with her little puppy tongue, Sage laughed and said, "I think I'll call you Snowdrop."

TWELVE

April
Tyson's Corner, Virginia

Colt leaned against his car on the suburban cul-de-sac as he waited for the realtor to arrive to show the house he'd made an appointment to see. While he waited, he pulled out his phone to check his email. Seeing another message from Sage, he grinned and clicked on the picture. He sighed and shook his head. "Of course. I should have expected this."

With tomorrow being Easter Sunday, she'd sent him a picture of the dog wearing bunny ears. This followed pictures of a little green leprechaun hat on St. Patrick's Day, a green sash in honor of the anniversary of the Girl Scouts' founding, a quilted sweater for National Quilting Day, and unfortunately, for the first day of spring, a green cape with a pink petal collar and a headpiece of pink and green antennae.

Colt had stuck a sympathy card in the mail to Snowdrop after receiving that one.

He glanced down at the lowered window of the passenger side door where his dog stood on the seat, his paws braced on the door, and his head poking out into the spring breeze. "I'm surprised that dog's coat hasn't turned pink from embarrassment."

Shadow let out a woof.

"You have a puppy!" a voice called out. "He is a puppy, right? What kind of dog is he, mister?"

Colt looked around to see a little boy—seven or eight years old, he'd guess—come speeding down the front walk of the house next door.

"Is he yours? Are you going to buy Mr. Barrington's house? Do you have any kids? Any boys?"

"Timothy Purcell, you leave the poor man alone." A harried-looking woman with a toddler on her hip stood at the front door.

She called out to Colt, "Sorry!"

"Not a problem," he replied as his realtor swung her BMW into the drive. To Timothy, he said, "I don't have any children, and Shadow is a Labrador retriever."

"That's too bad you don't have kids. Shadow has big paws. That means he's going to be a big dog." The boy called to the realtor. "Hey, Miss Cindy. This dog is a Labrador retriever!"

"Hello, Timmy. He's cute, isn't he? Hi, Colt. Sorry I'm late. Traffic was a bear."

"No problem." Colt pushed away from the car and lifted Shadow through the window, keeping him in his arms.

"If you want, mister, I'll hold his leash for you," Timmy offered. "Do you want me to show him the house, Miss Cindy? I give the best tours."

Cindy glanced at Colt, saw the smile and the shrug, and said, "Sure, Timmy. Thank you."

As the boy called out his plan to his mother, Colt set the puppy down and handed the leash to the boy. He then spent the most entertaining half hour he'd passed since leaving Eternity Springs over a month ago. Timmy knew the house inside and out, but it was his commentary that continued to amaze Colt. He pointed out the energy-saving features of the three-bedroom house and explained how they would not only lower the next owner's fuel bills but also help save the environment. He identified the trim paint as being oil based, not latex, and explained the differences between the two. He took great pleasure in explaining the mechanics of how the garage door opener operated.

After showing Colt the house, he led them outside. "I think you should probably let Shadow off his leash, don't you, Mr. Colt? That way he can explore the backyard and see if he likes it and if he finds any safety issues that need to be repaired before you would move in."

"Sounds like a good idea."

Colt watched the boy and dog take off and shook his head. "I wonder who will wear out whom first?"

"My money is on Timmy. He is a ball of fire." She hesitated a moment, then said, "When Frank Barrington offered me this listing, he asked me to introduce prospective buyers to the next-door neighbors. Frank loves the boy and he wants whoever buys this house to be aware of Timmy's, well, enthusiasm. The boy has an inquisitive mind, and, being a teacher, Frank has encouraged him to question and learn. He doesn't want the boy's spirit or imagination crushed."

"Sounds like Mr. Barrington is a good teacher."

"He's a law professor at Georgetown. Well, he was. He's taking a new position at Stanford. Do you have any questions about the house?"

"You mean that Tim hasn't answered?"

She laughed. He asked his questions, and she suggested other places he might want to consider. Colt shook his head. "I like this place. I don't want to keep the dog in the apartment any longer than necessary. Let me think it over tonight and I'll give you a call tomorrow."

"Great! I'll go in and lock up if you and Shadow want to leave by the gate."

"Sure." Colt stood, intending to cross the yard to retrieve his retriever, but he took a second to check his email first. Sure enough, Sage had sent another photo. This time the poor dog wore the Easter Bunny costume again, and this time she carried a carrot in her mouth. "I should sic the SPCA on her."

A smile played on his lips as he approached Timothy Purcell. The boy sat cross-legged on the grass with the puppy in his lap, absently scratching Shadow behind the ears as he frowned up at the tall tulip poplar growing at the back of the yard.

Colt followed the path of his gaze. "What's the matter? Did you see a critter of some sort?"

"No. I'm confused."

"What are you confused about?"

"Something we learned in school yesterday."

"What was that?"

"Photosynthesis."

"Photosynthesis," Colt repeated. He looked at Timmy, then at the tree. "Photosynthesis."

He sat beside the boy, stretched his legs out, and crossed them at the ankles. Leaning back, his weight propped on his elbows, he said, "Let me tell you about photosynthesis."

Denver

The Patchwork Angels' inaugural road trip took them to the Denver National Quilt Festival in the later part of April. There LaNelle was truly in her element as she visited with friends from other quilt guilds and used the opportunity for some expert example instruction for the Patchwork Angels. For the better part of the afternoon,

Sage steeped herself in the artistry of the textiles, the colors, the textures, the designs. She asked herself why in the world she didn't exhibit quilts at Vistas and made note of the names of two textile artists she intended to contact in order to correct that oversight.

After the show, they'd enjoyed a lovely dinner at Ali's house, though they'd been disappointed that her husband, Mac, hadn't made it home before the dinner party broke up. Despite Sage and her friends' growing friendship with Ali, they'd never met her husband. Mac's position as a federal court judge meant his days were filled to overflowing with legal work, charitable work, and after-hours social networking. When he'd called to report another late night on the docket, Ali had tossed her nightshirt and toothbrush in a tote bag and joined the Patchwork Angels at the quilt-themed B&B owned by a friend of LaNelle's for what turned out to be a grown-up version of a slumber party.

All in all, it had been a fun getaway. Now, though, the time had come to return to reality. The summer season kicked off in a few weeks, and playtime would be over.

"Road trips rock," Sarah said as she set her overnight case into the back of Sage's car for the return trip to Eternity Springs. "I had such a nice time."

"Me too." Sage closed the door, then took her seat behind the wheel.

Sarah sat in the front passenger seat, then twisted, reaching behind her to rub Snowdrop's head and greet her before fastening her seat belt. "After the way I whipped your butt at Trivial Pursuit last night, I halfway expected you to move Snowdrop's car safety seat to the front and make me ride in the back on the way home."

"Nah." Sage started the car. "The backseat is safer."

Sarah turned around to speak to the dog. "Now I know how I rate. Snowdrop, your mommy loves . . ."

She broke off, then frowned at Sage. "Sage, you painted that dog's toenails."

"We were awake in the middle of the night and it seemed like the thing to do. It's a great color, isn't it? Paint My Moji-Toes Red."

"That's just wrong." Sarah pulled two bottles of water from the tote bag at her feet, set them in the cup holders on the console, then settled in for the trip. "I know the whole costume thing is a dig at Colt Rafferty, but you are beginning to worry me. Your dog has more hair bows than my daughter ever did."

"You always said Lori was a tomboy. Snowdrop is a diva."

"And she has the rhinestone tiara to prove it." Sarah shook her head in disgust.

Grinning, Sage shifted the car into reverse as Gabe Callahan exited the bed and breakfast with his arms loaded with baby paraphernalia. Rather than driving west like the rest of their party, Gabe and his family were heading south to Texas for a Callahan family get-together. As she exited the B&B's parking lot, Sage gave her horn a little honk for one more good-bye.

"I still can't believe they're taking Clarence with them," Sarah said, referring to Gabe's dog. "They sure will have their hands full."

"Nic told me Gabe worried himself sick about the dog over Christmas."

"He did. He called every day to check on him, but he didn't need to fret. Clarence gets along fine with Daisy and Duke," Sarah said, speaking of her own golden retrievers. "I'd have kept Clarence this time, too, but Nic said Gabe's father wanted the whole family down in Brazos Bend."

As she waited to pull out onto the street, Sage glanced in her rearview mirror and saw Celeste exit the B&B along with LaNelle Harrison, Emily Hall, the owner of the town newspaper, and the town's librarian, Margaret Rhodes. LaNelle and Margaret were riding back with Emily.

"We have such a good group," Sarah observed as she waved good-bye to the others. "I can't say I'm sorry Marlene cancelled her plans to tag along. She can really be a downer."

"She's better than she used to be. Actually, ever since Marcus Burnes invited her to tag along on his photography shoot up in Rocky Mountain National Park, she's been downright cheerful. That romance is really heating up." Sage's thoughts drifted over the members of their group, and she added, "It's too bad Lori couldn't join us."

A shadow passed over Sarah's face. "It's not that she couldn't. She didn't want to join us. Well, join me, anyway. She might have come if it meant riding with you or Nic and not me. These days, it's like we're strangers— seems like all we do is fight."

"I think that's normal, especially for a mother and daughter as close as the two of you. She has to separate some in order to make that frightening leap that is going off to college."

"I know. Knowing it's normal doesn't make living it easier." She blew out a heavy sigh, then said, "Let's not talk about it anymore."

In the way of good friends, Sage and Sarah spent the drive in alternating bouts of conversation and silence. They talked music and baseball and the upcoming planning meeting for the summer arts festival. They had decided to dawdle their way home, so they took the scenic route and made frequent stops including a leisurely lunch. Sage enjoyed the trip tremendously and she was happy and relaxed and ever so glad she'd joined the Patchwork Angels for the road trip.

As they started up Sinner's Prayer Pass, Sarah said,

"Ali showed me that box of Cavanaugh stuff. I think I'm going to take her up on her offer to give those coins to Lori."

Sage glanced over in surprise. Sarah had been adamantly against this since Ali first told her about the find. "I'm glad to hear it. What changed your mind?"

"The reality of paying out-of-state tuition. Ali hasn't budged off her position of giving the box to Lori, and she says I'm just being stubborn."

"Ya think?"

"It makes me feel like a charity case, Sage."

"That is so stupid. Look, Cam Murphy is that girl's father and he has contributed nothing to her but his DNA. Whatever funds these coins bring to you won't be charity, they'll be a down payment on what that asshole owes you."

"Sage, please, let's not go there."

"I'm sorry. It just really chaps my hide whenever I think about it."

"Then let's think of something else. I saw the Marcus Burnes eagle photograph you put in the front window at Vistas a couple of days ago. It's gorgeous."

"He does wonderful work. It's visionary and unique. I'm surprised he's not a bigger name already."

"He's going to provide stiff competition for you in this year's arts festival. If you win a third-place ribbon, I think I'll move over to Gunnison for a month."

"Third place? Excuse me?"

Sarah shrugged. "Colt could send another piece."

Sage recognized that her friend was attempting to get a rise out of her, so she tried not to accommodate. Nevertheless, her voice sounded a bit thin as she observed, "Aren't you the funny one?"

"Hey, just sayin'. . ." Sarah laughed, dug a roll of breath mints out of her purse, and offered them to Sage before popping one in her mouth. "So, what were you and Ali huddled up about in the kitchen last night? You looked serious."

Sage hesitated, not wanting to dwell on a touchy subject when she was feeling so mellow. Although Ali had been thrilled with the news. Maybe Sage could finally forgive herself for being such a dweeb where the children's camp was concerned.

"I've exchanged emails and cards with Ali since the contretemps in February, but yesterday was the first time I'd seen her in person. I needed to talk to her about the art lessons for her charity program."

Sarah's eyes widened with surprise. "Is Ali still upset with you about that?"

"No. Not at all. In fact, when I tried to bring up the subject, I could hardly get her to listen. Once I got her attention, she was thrilled."

"You've decided to teach?"

Sage's stomach pitched at the thought. "No. I found someone better qualified to fill in for me. Last week, I spoke with Connor Keene. He said he'd be happy to lead the art lessons for her pilot program. I think the kids will love him. He's a storyboard artist for *Runamuka Ding*."

"The Saturday morning cartoon?"

"And soon to be a feature film. Yes."

"Oh, wow. You're right, the kids will love that. How did you pull it off?"

"He's a friend of a friend. Connor has the time and a special interest in childhood cancers. He lost a young nephew to bone cancer. He also couldn't resist the lure of Rocky Mountain trout fishing in June. I've arranged his travel and accommodations—he'll be staying at the Landrys' place—so you don't need to worry about any of that. He wants Ali to contact him at her convenience to discuss the nuts and bolts of what she'd like him to teach."

"That's really cool, Sage." Sarah thought about it a moment, then added, "I'm impressed. You figured out a way to make it work for everyone. So, are you ever going to tell us what the deal is with all that?"

Sage filled her lungs, then blew out a heavy sigh and braced for an argument. "No, not anytime soon."

"Okay."

When she realized Sarah really was going to drop the subject, Sage relaxed and enjoyed the rest of the drive. As they passed the Eternity Springs city limits sign, Sarah said, "It's back to the real world now, I guess. The summer season, sullen daughter, and . . ." Her voice broke a little. "Graduation."

"It'll be okay, Sarah. Your friends will be there to help you through it, both you and Lori."

"I know, and I'm grateful for it. There is part of me that wants to get it over with. Another part wants to stop time from moving at all. But, enough of that. I wonder if anything interesting happened in Eternity while we were gone? Maybe an elk wandered into the barbershop again or Bob Carson accidentally locked himself in the bank vault."

Sage turned onto Cottonwood Street and said, "We're home, so that means we'll find out in, what, five minutes?"

"Ten at the most."

At the corner of Second Street and Cottonwood, Sage responded to Mayor Hank Townsend's gesture to stop and roll down her window. "Glad I caught you," he said as she turned onto Second Street on her way to Sarah's house, which was across the street from her grocery store, the Trading Post. "Somebody was trying to track you down yesterday. A tourist. Wants to buy that eagle photo you have in the window at Vistas. He put his card through your mail slot, and asked half the people in town to be sure and let you know so that nobody bought it before he did. Seemed real important to him. I'd have sent him straight to Marcus, but he's up at Rocky Mountain National Park." In case she hadn't heard the latest gossip, he added, "With Marlene."

"Thanks, Hank. I'll look for it."

"So, did you ladies have fun on your trip? My wife sure hated to have to miss it."

"We had a lovely time," Sarah replied. "Tell Linda not to fret. We've decided the Patchwork Angels will do a road trip each spring and fall, so she can join us in October."

"Will do."

Hank stepped away from the car, and Sage completed her turn and drove the two short blocks to Sarah's house. As she slowed to make the turn into Sarah's driveway, across the street the Trading Post's door opened. Two people carrying grocery sacks and laughing with each other stepped outside.

Sage slammed on the brakes. Sarah jerked forward against her seat belt and glared at her. "What in the world?"

Sage couldn't speak. She couldn't breathe. She couldn't move a muscle. She sat in her car in the middle of the street frozen in shock.

The woman carrying a sack and a gallon of milk was her sister, Rose. The man with the six-pack . . . "Colt is here."

"Oh, yeah?" Now, Sarah perked up and she twisted her head to look. "Who is that woman he is with? She looks familiar."

Sage's mouth had gone dry as day-old toast. "She's my sister. I haven't seen her in years."

"Oh." After a moment of surprised silence, Sarah grinned impishly. "This is even better than an elk in the barbershop."

Colt saw Sage's car and cursed his timing. He'd had a nice romantic surprise planned as a way of sharing his news. *Okay, then. Change in plans. Not a problem.*

"Enjoy your stay at Angel's Rest," he told the woman with whom he'd shared an entertaining conversation about the space aliens on the cover of the tabloid while waiting to check out.

"Thanks. I am hoping I will," she responded, and in the process gave a little shrug that had him doing a double take because it reminded him so much of Sage.

The same Sage who hadn't moved since she'd slammed on the brakes.

He stepped out into the street, waving to Sarah as he walked in front of Sage's car and approached the already lowered driver's-side window. Her gaze was shifting between him and the tourist. Did she think he was with the other woman? He'd better make sure she knew otherwise.

"Hello, beautiful," he said to Sage, meaning it. "Hey, Sarah. I hear you two have been off gallivanting in Denver. Did you have fun?"

Sage simply stared at him. Sarah's grin grew bigger. "Had a blast. Didn't we, Sage?"

From her safety seat in back, Snowdrop yipped excitedly.

Sage finally found her voice. "What are you doing here?"

"How about we talk about it over dinner? Your place? Sevenish? Steaks? I'll bring everything."

"No." Her gaze returned to the Trading Post, and

Colt realized he had totally lost her concentration. He gave the woman another look and deduced that she had to be a relative. The short crop of hair was the same shade of auburn as Sage's. The eyes. Sage's reaction. Sister, maybe? One she wasn't overjoyed to see?

Well now, this was interesting. Another piece to fit into her puzzle. He couldn't wait to find out what this story was.

When Rose Anderson identified her sister as the driver of the car stopped in front of her, a truckload of emotion hit her head-on. Excitement. Grief. Fear. Anger. Nervousness. Sage looked as beautiful as always.

She wished she had something stronger than Snapple in her grocery bag.

The hot guy stepped away from the car as Sage opened the driver's-side door and climbed out. "Rose?"

"Hi, Sage."

"Rose, what in the world are you doing here?"

The accusation in her sister's tone prodded old wounds, and she reacted instinctively with an old childish taunt the sisters often had exchanged. "Hey, it's a free country."

The moment the childish words left her mouth she regretted them, so she quickly followed them with, "I'm sorry. I shouldn't have said that."

Sage's silence agreed with her.

Rose took a step toward the car. "Sage, can we go somewhere and talk?"

She held her breath as her little sister looked down and then away. A long moment later, Sage finally looked up and met her gaze. "Gee, Captain Anderson, why don't you call the office tomorrow and make an appointment?"

Rose sucked in a breath as the arrow struck home. She

heard the passenger in her sister's car say, "Whoa, Sage. That's cold."

"It's complicated," her sister said before Sage got back into the car and slammed the door. The man she'd been talking to in the grocery store hopped back as the tires spun and the car lurched off.

Rose stood staring after it until the car rounded a corner and disappeared. Weariness washed over her and made her feel old. Old, washed out, dried up, and useless. It would be so easy to plop herself down right here and cry, but she was trying to wean herself away from that habit.

She never noticed the guy approach until he stuck his hand out and said, "I'm Colt Rafferty. You're Sage's sister?"

"Yes. Rose Anderson." She shook his hand.

"What just happened here, Rose?"

She let out a shaky breath and said, "Look, I'm sorry. I just can't." She turned away from him and walked around to the side of the building where she'd left her bicycle. She deposited her grocery sack in the woven basket attached to the handlebars, then tugged the bike out of the rack and climbed on.

As she rode back to the place where she'd rented a room, she told herself that the tears trickling from her eyes resulted from the sting of the wind, even though the breeze was almost nonexistent. She also reminded herself that she'd known that healing the wounds in her relationship with Sage wouldn't be easy. But then, she should be accustomed to that. For the past eight months, nothing in life had been easy.

"So stop the pity party," she told herself. "That doesn't help a thing."

It was a lovely afternoon, in fact, and Eternity Springs was a picture-perfect town with flowers blooming everywhere she looked. Window boxes, flowerpots, hanging baskets, and flower beds adorned houses and businesses and churchyards. The air smelled of sunshine and forest and the aroma of baking cookies as she pedaled by a coffee shop called the Mocha Moose.

Tempted by the scent, she stopped and treated herself to a raspberry pinwheel cookie fresh from the oven along with a glass of cold milk. Comfort food. Sometimes a girl simply needed a cookie.

Her snack finished, she resumed her ride and a few minutes later walked the bike across the footbridge over Angel Creek and up to Angel's Rest. She parked the bike, then entered the converted Victorian mansion.

The older woman standing behind the reception desk looked up when Rose walked in, and she beamed. "Hello, dear. You must be our newest guest, Dr. Rose Anderson. Your resemblance to your sister is striking. I'm Celeste Blessing, the proprietor here. Welcome to Angel's Rest."

"Thank you, Ms. Blessing." Rose's smile went shaky at the warmth of the woman's welcome.

"Call me Celeste, please. I've spent hours on the road and I'm stiff as a lodgepole pine. I think I'll indulge in the soothing waters of our natural springs. I would love it if you would join me."

"Thank you, but I don't think—"

Celeste interrupted her, saying, "You know, your sister is one of my closest friends in Eternity Springs."

"She is?"

"Yes. Sage and I aren't Eternity Springs natives, so we had that in common, and it helped us bond. Now, I must run up and change into my swimsuit. Shall we meet back here in fifteen minutes?"

"Okay," Rose replied. "That will be nice."

To her surprise, the woman reached out and patted

her hand. "We'll have us a nice long talk. You know, I think Sage could use a big sister these days."

Rose smiled tremulously and spoke past the lump in her throat. "Actually, Celeste, I could sure use a sister myself."

THIRTEEN

With the sound of Sarah's scolding still ringing in her ears, Sage took the long way out to her cottage at Hummingbird Lake. She needed time to process the implications of what she had just witnessed.

Colt was here. Rose was here. Which problem did she want to think about first?

Thinking about Colt felt less threatening, so she concentrated on him. The man had come to Eternity Springs. He hadn't called or texted or emailed or sent a telegram or a smoke signal that he was on his way. So, what did that tell her? He was done with her? While it's true they'd spoken on the phone only a handful of times since he left Eternity, between the text messages and emails, they'd actually been in contact quite a bit. Sage had enjoyed the interaction. Based on his response, she believed he had enjoyed it, too. So why wouldn't he let her know he was visiting?

Was this just a quick visit? Had he thought to get in and out of town without her knowing about it? Surely not. Nothing happened in Eternity Springs that everyone didn't find out about eventually.

Maybe he'd wanted to surprise her. Maybe he'd planned on showing up with another gift. "Not another dog, I hope," she murmured. Glancing in the rearview mirror, she added, "While I do think you'd enjoy having a playmate at times, I'm afraid you're too spoiled to tolerate competing for attention on a regular basis."

Snowdrop let out a little whimper, and it reminded Sage that it had been a while since their last potty stop. Not a good idea with Snowdrop and her itty-bitty bladder.

She pulled into the parking area for the park at the northern end of the lake and let the dog out to take care of business, knowing it would take some time since Snow had to sniff extensively to find the perfect spot. While Snowdrop sniffed, Sage's thoughts threatened to drift toward her sister, so she forced them back onto Colt.

He had been the perfect man for her. Sinfully sexy, he had made her laugh. He helped her cry. He had given her such pleasure that sometimes in the teeth of the night she could lie in her bed and remember Colt and hold the nightmares at bay.

Yes, he had been perfect for her. Tall, dark, and temporary.

Safe.

"So what is he doing back in Eternity Springs?"

She could grab her phone and call him and ask. She could send a text or email. Doing that only invited trouble, however. He'd probably repeat his invitation, and she didn't think she could deal with him—with anyone—tonight.

"Hurry up, Snowdrop," she said, speaking more sharply than she'd intended and immediately feeling bad because of it.

Snowdrop, who had finally picked her spot and begun to tinkle, looked at her as if saying, *Are you kidding me?*

Sage smiled at her puppy and said, "Good girl."

Why was Colt in Eternity Springs? Could business have brought him here? Had an accident of some sort occurred in the area and she'd missed news of it? No.

She'd had the radio on part of the way home today. She had listened to news.

So if not his job, then what?

Why do you care? He doesn't owe you an accounting of his travels. We had a fling. It's over.

Snowdrop let out a bark. She'd finished and returned to the car, and she was waiting impatiently to be lifted back into her seat.

"You're right. Let's go home. Maybe take a nap. It's been a long day."

Fifteen minutes later, she pulled into her drive and discovered that her day was about to get longer.

Colt Rafferty waited on her porch, a grocery sack at his side.

Her grimace upon seeing him wasn't exactly how he'd hoped to begin.

She climbed out of her car moving slowly, tiredly, looking weary and sick at heart. *Aw, babe. What's the matter here?*

It didn't escape his attention that this time she didn't run to him and bury her head against him and burst into tears. Instead, she said, "What about the word *no* do you not understand, Rafferty?"

"Oh, come on." He tried his best smile. "You didn't mean it."

She shrugged, retrieved the dog from the car and set her on the ground. Colt squatted down, clapped his hands, and the bichon came running. "Hey there, darling. I can't tell you how glad I am to see you in your naked skin and not wearing some stupid little costume."

"Give it a rest, Rafferty. Please? I'm truly not in the mood for it."

She truly was in a sorry frame of mind. He knew without a doubt that the Snowdrop-in-costume bit had been something she truly enjoyed.

She climbed up the steps and walked right past him, slipping her key into the lock and opening her door. She didn't attempt to stop him from following—apparently she knew him better than that—but she didn't make him welcome, either. Colt gathered up the grocery sacks and followed her and the dog inside.

That's when he noticed the dog's toenails. "All joking aside, Sage, you painted her toenails?"

"It's called Paint My Moji-Toes Red."

"I'm sorry, girl," he said to the dog.

Sage walked into the kitchen, poured a glass of iced tea, then tossed it back as if it were bourbon. Refilling her glass and one for him, she asked, "What's for supper?"

"Steak. Baked potatoes. Salad. Since Sarah wasn't around to bake today, raspberry pinwheels from the Mocha Moose for dessert."

"I'm going to go take a shower." She headed for her bedroom, then stopped abruptly. Looking over her shoulder, she announced, "That is *not* an invitation."

"I'll scrub the spuds."

She stayed in the bathroom a long time. He did the prep work for dinner, then took the ball he'd brought for Snowdrop and let the dog out the back door. They played catch until Sage came outside wearing shorts and a green and gold Colorado University football jersey. Her hair was damp. Her feet were bare.

Colt wanted to cross the lawn and take her in his arms and give her the kiss he'd dreamed about since the day he left. Yet, everything about her, from the way she stood, to the way she moved, to the way she managed to look everywhere else rather than meet his gaze warned him to step carefully. She was fragile. Brittle. On the verge of breaking.

Not because of him, he thought, but because of her sister.

Well, maybe a little bit because of him.

He started with something easy. "Snowdrop has grown."

"Nic says she's going to be on the big side for a bichon. Especially a female. I've been in the car all day. Would you like to go for a walk?"

"Sounds great."

She didn't say anything as she donned her shoes and socks, lifted a dog leash from a hook by the back door, and affixed it to the dog's collar. The three of them stepped out into the late afternoon sunshine. Colt paused to take a deep breath of mountain air and smiled. He was here in Eternity Springs with Sage. The rightness of his decision settled over him like a song.

They took the path that trailed alongside the lake. He decided to wait for her to start the conversation. If she ever did, that is. She walked with her head down, her manner closed off. Luckily, Colt had the patience to wait.

His patience finally paid off when she asked, "What brings you to town, Rafferty?"

You, he wanted to say, but instincts told him to take it slower. The woman was skittish as could be. "I love this town. I'm happy here. When I went back to work after my trip here in February, I missed it." Walking beside her, he gave her a sidelong look. "I missed you."

Was that a hint of a smile on her lips? "You should have let me know you were planning a visit. I might not have been here. I almost stayed in Denver for a few extra days."

"I didn't exactly plan a visit."

"Even with a spur-of-the-moment trip you can spare time for a phone call."

"I wanted to surprise you. You liked my surprises in the past."

In a droll tone, she said, "Hey, what girl doesn't like a new tube of lip balm?"

She let out a long sigh, then said, "Okay, Rafferty, here's the deal. Under other circumstances I would hold out and teach you a lesson, but frankly, I can use a distraction right now. You assumed a lot by showing up here. I could have had a date tonight."

He jerked his head around in surprise. "Are you seeing somebody else?"

"I could be. That's my point. Just because we had a fling a couple months ago doesn't mean that you can wing back into town and pick up where you left off. You have no hold on me and I have no hold on you."

"What if I want to change that?"

She took a dozen steps before replying. "Colt, look. I enjoyed the time I spent with you, but that wasn't real. It was fantasy-land cabin fever, and I'm really not that kind of person. I like being your friend. I enjoy our long-distance communications, but I don't want to be where you go for vacation sex."

"Wow, you don't think very highly of me, do you? You think I came all this way for a booty call?"

"I don't know why you've come here. You haven't shared that piece of information with the class."

"I quit my job."

She stopped abruptly. "Why?" Then almost immediately, she added, "Don't tell me you got into another fight."

"I didn't get into a fight the first time," he responded. "I quit my job at the CSB because working there didn't allow me to accomplish the job I went there to do in the first place. I think I can be more effective outside government than inside."

"How is that? You won't have the big stick of government regulation in your pocket."

"I don't have that now. Unfortunately, I can't wave a

wand and get regulations put on the books and wave it again and get everyone into compliance. However, since I do have that government stick, people tend to spend all their time covering their asses and looking over their shoulders for lawyers instead of listening to what I have to say."

"All right, that makes sense. But what can you do outside of the CSB?"

"Do you remember the woman who came with me to your show in Fort Worth?" He told her about the chemical spill that had killed Melody Slaughter's husband and how when they'd spoken, Melody had expressed her regret that Colt hadn't given his presentation at the plant where the accident occurred. "She said the owners are good people, and that they'd have made the changes if anyone had identified the problem. I've seen that myself dozens of times. Owners don't want to have industrial accidents, but they also don't want to borrow trouble in the way of citations and fines. I've gone into business as a consultant, Sage. I have the paperwork all done."

Interest lit her gorgeous green eyes. "So you'll, what, inspect factories like an OSHA guy?"

"I'll do inspections, but instead of giving them governmental grief, I'll give presentations like I did in Fort Worth. I have some pretty horrific stories I can tell. They tend to get people's attention."

"People are ghouls," she snapped. Then she closed her eyes and gave her head a little shake. "So you'll travel all around the country?"

Now he hesitated, choosing his words carefully. "I will do some traveling. Based on the research I did prior to making this decision, I could go every week if that was what I wanted. But that much traveling would get old fast, so I decided to do something else, too. I'm going to return to teaching."

"Really? Are you returning to Georgia Tech?"

"No. I'm going to teach science classes. I'm pretty excited about it. I'll be sort of a roving teacher for everyone from kindergarten through high school. It'll give me a nice balance between travel and staying put."

"You have a Ph.D. You're going to teach first graders?"

"They have inquisitive minds. That appeals to me."

"I'll give you that." She nodded. "But what about middle school? Do you really want to attempt to teach thirteen-year-old boys?"

He grimaced. "Well, no job is perfect."

She laughed, then asked, "So, what school district is lucky enough to get your services, Dr. Rafferty?"

Well, here goes. Judging by her reaction so far, he suspected she might not throw herself into his arms out of joy when he told her. *Hope her response is warmer than the water in Hummingbird Lake.* "This one. Starting in September, I'll be teaching at Eternity Springs Community School."

Sage halted abruptly. "Excuse me? What did you say?"

"I'm moving to Eternity Springs. Actually, I have moved here already."

The expression on her face was a discouraging mixture of alarm and shocked dismay as she repeated, "You moved here?"

"Yes."

"Permanently?" Her voice squeaked.

"Barring the unforseen, yes."

She closed her eyes. "Can this day get any more worse?"

She's making Hummingbird Lake look tepid. "You know, that's downright insulting. I thought we were friends."

"We are friends. We're long-distance friends. You can't come here. This is my town."

Now she was getting under his skin. He folded his arms and said, "To quote your sister, it's a free country."

"Oh no." Her eyes rounded with concern and she took a step away from him. "Don't tell me Rose has moved here, too."

"I don't know anything about your sister." Colt reached out and took hold of her arm. "I'm not concerned about her. I'm concerned about us. What's going on here? Why are you so threatened by this?"

Her chin came up. "I'm not threatened."

"Yes, you are." Their walk had taken them to the small camping area south of Reflection Point, and Colt tugged her along toward a picnic bench beside the water. There he sat her down and said, "Talk to me. Tell me what's going on in that gorgeous head of yours. We were good together, Sage. I missed you when I left, and every time I received an email or a text or a call from you, I got a little charge. You must have enjoyed it, too, or you wouldn't have played the game. Am I wrong about that?"

Begrudgingly she said, "No."

"So then, why the panic? Why the cold shoulder?"

Rather than respond to his questions, she asked one of her own. "What do you want from me, Rafferty? Did you come here expecting to pick up where we left off? Did you think I've been pining away for you and all you'd have to do is say 'Honey, I'm home' and I'd throw myself into your arms and then drag you back into my bed?"

Well, a guy can always hope. "No, not at all. We had a fling. It was great, but that's not what I want with you now."

"Oh?"

Was that hope he heard in her voice? Wow. This woman was doing a number on his ego. Colt took a moment to debate his options. He could sound the retreat and regroup. That might be the most intelligent way to go about this. But in the past few weeks, he had adopted a more go-for-broke, lay-your-cards-on-the-table attitude, and so far it was working for him. He saw no reason to change that now. "No, I'm not looking for any more flings. I want a relationship. Long term. I'm tired of flings."

"Define relationship," she said, a bit of a wild look in her eyes.

"I'm thirty-four years old, Sage. I'm ready for a home of my own complete with all that entails—a wife, children, a yard for the dogs."

With a horrified gasp, she said, "You are not asking me to marry you!"

Inwardly Colt sighed. "No. We don't know each other well enough for that yet."

"Exactly!"

"But I want to know you that well, Sage. You are a fascinating woman and you've intrigued me from the very first. I want to know everything about you. I think I might be falling in love with you."

"Oh, God." She dropped Snowdrop's leash, put her elbows on her knees, and buried her face in her hands. "This is a catastrophe."

Colt's mouth twisted in a grim smile. This was the closest he'd come in years to saying the *L*-word to a woman and she called it a catastrophe. Pretty humbling moment, he had to admit.

He took a seat beside her on the bench. Snowdrop sat looking at them both, tilting her head from left to right then back to left again, wordlessly asking, *What is wrong with you people?*

"Careful there, Sage. You'll give me a big head from all the praise."

"Stop it. I am not responsible for your feelings. If I was the least little part of your decision to make this move, then you should have been smart enough to talk to me about it before you jumped off and did it. You would think a man with a Ph.D. would be smarter than that."

"Okay, then. Just for the grins, what would you have said if I told you that I thought you might be the one for me and I wanted time with you to explore the possibility?"

"I'd have told you don't waste your time. I'm not available, Colt."

"Why? Are you married to someone else? Involved with someone else? In love with someone else?"

"No, but—"

"So there is nothing tangible standing in my way," he interrupted.

"There's me," she said, her tone just a shade softer. "I *can't* have a relationship with you. I won't have a relationship with you."

"I'll change your mind."

"You are so infuriating."

"I'm determined. It may turn out that I'm wrong, that you are not the woman I'm meant to love, to live with, to make a home and family with. But I do know that if I don't give this, give us, the old college try, I'll regret it the rest of my life. Sorry, Sage, but I'm not taking no for an answer on this one."

"You have to. You can't force me to fall in love with you. You can't even force me to date you. This isn't Russia, Danny."

Colt looked down at Snowdrop. "What man can resist a woman who quotes *Caddyshack* during an argument?"

"Neither is it medieval England," Sage added.

That distracted Colt for a moment as he once again pictured her as the subject of one of Edmund Blair Leighton's paintings, only this time he pictured her naked. "Okay, you lost me on that one. How did medieval England get into this conversation?"

She waved a hand. "I was reading a historical romance last night."

"My mom loves those books." Colt scooped Snowdrop up into his arms and scratched her behind her ears, then stood. "So, are you about ready to head back? I'm getting hungry. The Trading Post had some excellent-looking steaks and Alton Davis swore by the bottle of cabernet I bought from him. It's a new-to-me label, but I told him I'd be back to hound him if he led me wrong. Besides, I can't be too late because I promised Beth Myers I'd pick up Shadow by eight o'clock."

"Your Lab. I forgot about your dog. You left him with the Myerses?"

"Yes. Beth and her dog were out in their yard when Shadow and I walked by on our way to the store earlier. Shadow and her mutt had a great time playing together, so Beth begged her mom to let her puppysit."

"You know what, Rafferty? I think it's time you learn what the word *no* really means. I'm not having dinner with you. I'm not letting you into my house. In fact, I don't think I'm going to let you hold my dog anymore." She stood and plucked Snowdrop out of his arms. "Go home, Colt. Wherever that is, just go."

"You have to eat."

"Yes, but I don't have to eat with you."

"Tell me why you won't."

"Won't what? Eat dinner with you? Date you? Sleep with you?"

"All of the above."

"No. N-O. No."

He grinned and those damned dimples winked. "I'll change your mind."

Aargh! "Why would you even want to? I'm a mess. You know that."

In that knee-bending, toe-curling, sexy low rumble of his he said, "I want you. I'm here and I'm staying and I'm not giving up. Hide behind your walls if you want, Princess, but I'm giving you official notice. You are under siege."

She couldn't help but be a little secretly thrilled. "Go away, Rafferty."

"You need to relax. Drink a glass of wine."

"Maybe so, but I'll do it by myself." Then she drew a deep breath and exhaled with a sigh. "Please, Colt? I still need to deal with my sister, and frankly, I don't have the energy to argue with you anymore right now."

She got to him with the sister argument. There was a story there, but she wasn't in any mood to tell it. And the sister had run off like she was being chased by a hell-hound, so yeah, there was definitely drama there. Fine. At some point Sage would spill and he'd be there ready to listen. For now, he figured he'd given her enough to think about. "C'mon, I'll walk you back."

"You go on. I think I'm going to sit out on the public pier and think for a little bit."

"All right. I'll talk to you tomorrow, then." He bent down and kissed her cheek, then started back the way they'd come.

He distinctly heard her murmur, "Not if I can help it."

He winced and kept on walking. All in all, that hadn't gone so terribly. It hadn't gone so great, but he had time. He'd given her his terms. He wanted her and he'd get her. Eventually.

He was now a permanent resident of Eternity Springs.

FOURTEEN

❦

Sage gave him a ten-minute head start. The talk about wanting to sit on the public fishing pier and think about her sister was bunk. First, if she wanted to sit on a pier, she'd do it on the one she shared with the Landrys. It was one of her favorite places to think. Second, she couldn't think about Dr. Rose Anderson even if she wanted to because her mind was filled with Dr. Colt Rafferty of Eternity Springs.

I think I might be falling in love with you.

Her knees felt a little shaky as she began the walk home. She'd made this same trek often, so she didn't need to pay attention as she went along, which was a good thing since she was so busy looking inward.

What was wrong with her? Colt Rafferty was a great guy. Intelligent, dedicated, swoon-worthy handsome, and a master in bed. He was kind, creative, and generous. Because of Colt, she had Snowdrop.

I think I might be falling in love with you.

Why did he frighten her so much? Because he was intelligent and dedicated. Perceptive. Persistent. He'd push and poke and prod without ceasing until he rooted out all of her secrets.

Would she even realize it? How was it that he managed to get her to tell him more than she'd even admitted to herself?

And then what? It was bad enough that she'd shared

as much as she had. What would happen if he learned the rest of it? Would that admiration in his eyes transform into disgust? Would he say the same things to her that her father had said when she went to him for absolution? Maybe. Probably. Her father had been a great guy, a generous man. He had loved her, too.

"And look what that got me," she muttered aloud, stooping to pick up Snowdrop, not because the dog signaled she'd grown tired, but because Sage needed the comfort of holding her.

At home, she brought her overnight bag in from the car and unpacked. She put a load of laundry into the washer, then read her mail and paid a few bills. She realized she'd inadvertently left her cellphone in her car, and after debating the matter for a few minutes, she went out to get it. She'd missed two calls, neither of which was from Colt or Rose.

Rose. Sage couldn't believe she'd come to Eternity Springs. What in the world was she going to do about her sister?

Maybe it was time she faced that dragon.

Sage eyed Colt's bottle of wine and thought, *What the heck.* She opened it and poured herself a glass while noting that Snowdrop lay curled up asleep in her bed in the living room. Grabbing a sweater, she opened her back door and stepped outside. She might as well walk down to the tip of the point and the fishing pier. After all, what better place to reflect on the misery of her family life than Reflection Point?

A few puffy clouds dotted the sky and the breeze had strengthened as the afternoon grew long. The air blowing in off the lake had a chill to it, so she slipped into her sweater before taking her usual seat at the end of the pier, her feet dangling above the water, her glass of wine sitting on the wooden pier beside her. Sunlight sparkled off the surface of the lake like diamonds, and she al-

lowed her gaze to drift along the shoreline before set-
tling on a leaf that floated on the water beneath her feet.

Rose.

Sage blew out a breath, watched the current spin the
leaf in a very slow circle, and remembered.

*Her apartment above the garage was dark, the blinds
and curtains blocking out all but the ambient light. She
lay curled in a ball amidst tangled sheets. The TV was
on, though the sound was turned off. The hum of the
window unit drowned out any sounds from outdoors,
and inside, the only noise to be heard was the buzz of
the fly that persisted in circling around her head.*

Maybe he thinks I'm dead.

*The image of flies landing on the bloody body of little
Aba Ballo flashed through her mind.*

Too bad I'm not.

*Beside her bed, the phone began to ring. Once again
she ignored it. She realized that she was thirsty, and she
considered getting up to get a drink. No. That took too
much effort. She drifted back to sleep.*

*How long she slept, she didn't know, but she awoke
to a new sound. Something different. Thump. Thump.
Thump. Someone was pounding on her door.*

*Sage grabbed her pillow and pulled it over her head,
muffling the sound, though not blocking it out entirely.
The pounding finally quit, and she relaxed back into
sleep.*

Until a loud bang bang crash *brought her sitting up in
bed.*

*Her front door flew open. Her sister swept inside like
an avenging angel. Sage sat on her bed and stared. She'd
kicked in the door. Rose had kicked in her door!*

"So you are *here," her sister said, her tone scathing
and accusatory. "Brandon said he saw a car in the driveway, but I didn't believe him. I told him you wouldn't be*

so selfish and disrespectful. I told him you wouldn't let me down this way. Let Dad down this way."

She stormed across the room and wrenched back the curtains. Light flooded into the room. Sage grimaced and shielded her eyes.

"Are you drunk?" Rose demanded, her gaze zeroing in on the empty vodka bottle on Sage's nightstand.

The bottle had been there for at least two weeks, maybe three. She'd brought it with her when she came home, drank it in the first week, then never roused herself to go out for more.

"What are you doing here?"

"What am I doing here?" she repeated before saying it once more in a rising screech. "What am I doing here?"

She advanced on Sage, her face red with fury, her eyes a little wild. "When I got hold of you in New York, you said you'd come. I called and called and called, but you didn't answer your phone. I waited for you for two weeks, Sage. Two weeks."

She glanced around the room, took in the suitcase, the handbag. The plane ticket. She picked it up and read the date.

Her jaw dropped. Her voice went faint and disbelieving. "You've been here all this time." She looked up, stared at Sage. "You were here. Ten minutes away from us. I don't believe this. How could you, Sage? How could you do this to Dad? How could you do it to me? You left me to do this on my own!"

Sage closed her eyes, the pressure in her chest so heavy she wasn't certain she could fill her lungs with air. What could she say? How could she possibly explain? What was she going to do? Tell Rose what their father had said to her?

She'd rather slit her wrists.

So she did nothing. Said nothing. Tried desperately to feel nothing.

Rose let out a little mewl of pain, and Sage looked at her. Her big sister was crying. Big, fat tears spilled down her cheeks.

In that moment, Sage was jealous, furiously jealous that Rose could cry. Her chin came up and she said, "Go away. Just go away."

Rose gasped audibly. For a long moment she stood frozen, not moving so much as an eyelash. Then she snapped her mouth shut, marched over to the bed, drew back her hand, and slapped Sage's face. "I came to tell you that your father is dead. I pulled the plug on him this morning."

Then she was gone.

Three days later, Sage attempted to attend her father's funeral. Rose's boyfriend met her at the door to the church and told her in no uncertain terms that she wasn't welcome there. She didn't see Rose to confirm the fact, but she didn't have the heart to force the issue. It had taken everything she had to get dressed and make the trip to the church. She had nothing left.

Two weeks after the funeral, Sage managed to drag her brooding self to the grocery store. Paying little attention to her surroundings, she stepped out in front of a moving car—an accident, she insisted, not sure if deep down inside she believed it. She bounced off the hood and onto the pavement, conking her head. The world had faded to black.

She awakened in the emergency room of a civilian hospital near the army base where Rose practiced medicine. She gave her sister's name as next of kin and asked the ER nurse to notify her sister.

When she returned a half hour later, the nurse was frowning. "I'm not sure your sister understood our message, Ms. Anderson. Her response doesn't make sense."

"What did she say?"

"She said that if you wanted medical care, you should call and make an appointment."

Her head pounding, her heart broken, Sage closed her eyes and drifted away.

Now, almost five years later, she watched as the leaf floating on the surface of Hummingbird Lake grew waterlogged and sank.

Heaving a sigh, Sage leaned back on her elbows and lifted her face to the sky. What was she going to do? What did she want to do?

She missed her sister.

She missed her family. And yet she'd made a new family here in Eternity Springs. Nic and Sarah and Celeste. Ali, too. Over the past few months, she'd grown especially close to Ali, despite—or perhaps due to—the fact that she lived in Denver. Email offered a certain intimacy that had allowed them both to share things they might not have said in person, she believed. Part of it, too, might be that Ali and Rose were close in age. Ali had slipped into that big-sister role so easily.

Sage didn't *need* Rose in her life. Shoot, Ali and the rest scolded as enthusiastically as Rose ever had. Sage had lost one sister and found four others. Well, three others. Celeste wasn't exactly a sister figure. Not exactly a mother figure, either. She was a combination mother, sister, confessor, conscience, girlfriend, best friend, cheerleader, and more. Sage had filled in all the roles Rose had occupied with other people. She was doing fine in her life without Rose, thank you very much.

And still, she missed her. Maybe because one other aspect of sisterhood did exist and no one else could fill it. Rose was the only one on earth who shared her history. No one else knew what it was like to live in the Anderson family. No one else knew what it was like to have the Colonel as a father. No one else on the planet had known Sage since the day she'd been born.

All that meant that no one else had the power to hurt Sage as much as Rose. She'd certainly exercised that power, hadn't she?

And now she was here.

And Sage still didn't have a clue what she wanted to do about it.

Colt stewed the whole eight-minute drive back to town.

Whether she liked it or not, Sage Anderson was a big part of his decision to return to Eternity Springs, and he'd never been one to let a little bump in the path make him take a different road. So what if she wasn't thrilled with his news? His timing had been bad. She'd been pre-occupied with her sister's sudden appearance.

A sister. Another mystery.

Colt made a quick stop at the Trading Post for more steaks. He rapped on the door at Sarah Reese's house and offered up a sheepish grin when she opened the door. "Have you already had your dinner?"

"No, why?"

"I struck out with Sage. I have beef and need advice, and Shadow would love to play with Daisy and Duke."

"Hmm . . ." She folded her arms. "I'm your second choice, huh? What a blow to my ego."

"Hey, you blew your chance to be my number one when you refused to go parking with me when I was a sophomore in high school."

"One of my life's great regrets . . . not. You were in your dad's minivan." She stepped back and waved him inside. "C'mon in and feed me, then you can tell me all about it."

Colt carried his grocery sack into Sarah's kitchen, where he found Lori painting her grandmother's nails. Ellen Reese was a lovely woman, an older version of Sarah, with middle-stage Alzheimer's disease. She remembered his family from their summers in Eternity and asked Lori three times in five minutes the name of the color the teenager had put on her nails. While Sarah put away the hamburger she'd been preparing to cook, he shared his news about his move.

"Wow. Big changes," Sarah said. Curiosity gleamed in her eyes, but he took the hint when she added, "I can't wait to hear more about it after dinner."

She put him in charge of her charcoal grill, and Lori accompanied him outdoors, asking him questions about living in Texas. "I can't believe you're old enough to be going off to college. When do you leave?"

"Mid-August. Right after the summer arts festival."

"Are you excited?"

"Yes. And scared. I'm told it's harder to get into vet school than medical school, and I want to be a vet so badly. What if I can't do the work? What if I screw it up? You were a college professor, right? Do you have any tips for me?"

"I do." With the fire ready, he spread the steaks upon the grill. As the juices hit the coals and sizzled, he said, "You do this one thing and I guarantee you'll be fine."

He paused, waited until she met his gaze, then told her, "Be true to yourself, Lori. If you're true to yourself in everything you do, every decision you make, you'll be fine and you'll achieve your goals."

"Wow. That's profound." Lori beamed a smile at him. "Thanks, Dr. Rafferty. I'll bet you were a great professor."

"I tried."

Her eyes glinted impishly as she added, "I'll bet the girls in your classes called you Dr. Hottie."

He frowned professorially. "Brat. You are your mother's daughter, aren't you?"

She laughed, then picked up a tennis ball from a basket of dog toys and stepped down into the backyard to play with the dogs.

Colt enjoyed the meal and the company, but he was glad when dinner was over and the dishes done and Sarah said, "I need to do a couple things at the store. Want to walk over there with me? Shadow will be fine with my dogs."

"Sure."

At the Trading Post, Sarah removed a set of keys from her pocket and opened the door. In another couple of weeks the store would switch to summer hours, but for now the place was empty and quiet and offered the perfect spot for its owner to turn on him and say, "Spill it. What happened?"

"I'm hoping you can tell me."

"You go first. You went out to see Sage?"

"Yeah." He summarized the exchange with Sage, short of sharing the fact that he'd floated the *L*-word, and ended it by saying, "I thought I knew what was going on with her. Now I'm wondering if I didn't have it all wrong."

"Our girl Sage is in many ways a mystery."

"Yes, one I need to solve. I'm not asking you to betray any confidences, but what's the deal with her sister?"

Sarah lifted her shoulders. "I don't know. I didn't even know she had a sister until today."

Okay, then. A secret sister was one big fat clue. Colt had thought that the trouble in Africa was the source of Sage's grief. Had he been wrong? Had he missed the mark entirely?

Family, he thought with an inward sigh. A good family was such a gift, but a bad family could do infinite harm.

"Did Sage tell you anything about her?"

Sarah went around behind the checkout counter and pulled out a manila file folder stuffed with papers. "Not really. She said they'd had a falling out, and then the two of them had that little snarky exchange that you saw. Then Sage drove around the block until she made sure that Rose—that's her name—had gone. I tried to get her to spill the beans about the estrangement, but no go. She's always been tight-lipped, Colt, and that didn't change today."

"That's frustrating."

"Ya think?" Sarah wrinkled her nose. "I love Sage. I truly do. But the woman has issues with a capital *I*. That's something I've learned to accept."

If all he wanted from Sage was friendship, he'd probably take the same route. But he wanted more than friendship. He wanted more from Sage.

"She's going to try to shut me out and keep me out."

"Maybe. If she feels like you are a threat in some way. Are you?"

"No. Maybe. I guess that depends upon the context." When Sarah gave him a sharp look, he explained. "I'm not out to hurt her. She means something to me, Sarah. She's important. But I won't let her push me away."

"Good luck with that. She's a stubborn woman."

"Yeah, but I'm persistent. I'll wear her down."

"With more gifts?"

"No," he replied, thinking it through.

Colt was a minor student of military history, and as such, he knew something about campaigns and sieges. It had taken the allied Greek forces ten years to conquer Troy. The British held Gibraltar against Spanish and French forces for more than three and a half years. It had taken General Grant seven months to conquer Vicksburg.

Colt hoped that winning Sage wouldn't take nearly that long.

"She's going to have to deal with me in some way every day. I'm not going away."

"Won't you be traveling with your new job?"

"I don't have to be in Eternity Springs for her to deal with me."

"Wow. You are determined, aren't you? You know, that is pretty romantic." She chewed on her lower lip a second before adding, "I want to ask one thing of you, though, Colt. Make sure you are doing this because it's real, not because you want to win the contest. You could hurt her."

"She could hurt me, too. That's a risk of being in a relationship. It's not a contest, Sarah, but there is a prize. I do want the happily ever after. I think I could find it with Sage. Time will tell."

"Dang it." Sarah picked up the folder and tucked it under her arm. "I'm beginning to think that *I'm* the one who missed the chance. Maybe I should have gone parking with you in your minivan after all."

She walked out from behind the counter, went up on her tiptoes, and kissed his cheek. "Good luck, Dr. Rafferty. I'll be rooting for you."

"Thanks."

"But fair warning—if you hurt her, I'll make you pay."

"I've known you for half my life, Sarah Reese. That goes without saying."

FIFTEEN

Sage arrived at Vistas the following day ready to paint. Despite a restless night, she awoke with the itchy energy that signaled an idea perking in her mind. She grasped hold of it like a lifeline and hurried through her morning routine before rushing off to work. She had two solid hours to work before opening Vistas, and the butterflies were flying, so to speak.

She adored working in her remodeled studio, though sometimes she didn't believe it herself. No one who had known her in her medical days would believe she worked in these conditions. Even in the African bush, Dr. Anderson's work area had been organized and uncluttered, her supplies pristine.

Here in the Vistas studio, she worked amidst a disorganized jumble. She had props of all kinds for inspiration—stacks of magazines, silk flowers and vines, funky furniture and fabrics, boas and beads. This was a mess, the perfect home for Sage Anderson, the artist.

She especially loved the lighting. She'd added two new skylights in the remodel. Along with the two front windows and the single one on the side, the new skylights created the perfect light, and when she walked into the room, the real world went soft and mellow and fantastical. As usual, she switched on her stereo and the sound of classic rock helped transport her into her creative world.

Here in her world of fairies and fantasy, Sage wasn't herself, but somebody new and unique and . . . clean. Here, she liked who she was, and each time she visited, she took some of that world away from her when she left. She felt a little bit cleaner each time she returned to the real world.

She hoped that eventually, she'd bring along enough of the clean back with her that she'd be the new Sage in both places.

Fleetwood Mac played in the background as she created. Using mostly blues and greens and yellows, she brought a world to life that made her smile as she stood at the easel, confident that the finished work would please her patrons. When the cuckoo clock on the wall that served as her alarm sounded ten o'clock, even though it was only nine thirty-five, she stepped away from the easel, turned to wash out her brush, and stopped abruptly.

Colt Rafferty sat on the sill of the open window of the building next door, directly across from her open window. "Hello, beautiful."

"What are you doing?"

"Not working, unfortunately. Too distracted by the scenery. It's obvious I'm going to have to move my desk. Say, do you want to go to lunch later?"

"Hold it. Stop. That's Gabe's building. What are you doing in Gabe's building?"

"This is my new office. I talked to Gabe last week. Got a great deal on the rent—he thinks the other office has a better view. He's a better architect than he is a businessman, I think."

While she gaped, he stepped across the narrow divide between the two buildings and into her studio. "You can't do that."

"It's barely four feet across. It's an easy step."

"I didn't mean that you can't do that. I meant that you *can't* do it."

He ignored her, looking around the room. "Wow. Your home studio wasn't like this. This place is a mess. What's up with that?"

But even as she drew a breath to defend herself, he approached her easel and said, "Sage, this is really interesting. Your work shows more depth all the time. You've grown."

"Good heavens, you are such a jerk."

"So, you gonna go to lunch with me?"

If she looked into the mirror on her right, she thought, she just might see steam coming out her ears. Instead she looked left at the cuckoo clock. "I have to open the gallery. See yourself out, Rafferty."

She left the room and headed downstairs, grimacing at the knowledge that she'd left her brushes filled with paint. She never neglected her brushes. Never!

Don't run away from him. Don't let him do that to you. Don't let him take your power.

"What power?" she muttered even as she hesitated. Turning around, she retraced her steps and was relieved—at least that's what she told herself—to find her studio empty once more.

She glanced through the window as she stood at the sink. He sat at a desk, talking on the telephone, flipping pages of a document in front of him. *Why, Gabe? Why did you have to go and rent that office to that man?*

She'd never get any work done now. She'd feel like she had someone looking over her shoulder all the time. She could move her easel, but she didn't want to do that. The entire remodel had been designed around her easel standing in that one spot. She'd have to get window blinds. No, that would ruin the light.

She'd get *him* window blinds. And curtains.

I think I might be falling in love with you.

"Oh, Colt." This was hard. If only . . . She closed her eyes. "No, don't go there. Go downstairs and open the gallery and make those phone calls you need to make."

She wanted to call Connor Keene's agent. Vistas was going to hang his work in June and they still had a few details to negotiate. Besides, the woman had promised her a cookie recipe Sage wanted to share with Sarah, and she'd forgotten to send it.

For the next twenty minutes, Sage managed to keep her mind off Colt and on business. She had just wrapped up a phone call with her own agent when the door chime sounded. She looked up and her welcoming smile died.

Rose stood just inside the gallery looking stiff and uncomfortable. Before Sage could get out a word about this being business hours and, as such, an inappropriate time for dealing with personal issues, Rose said, "You told me to make an appointment. That's what I am here to do."

Inwardly Sage sighed. As much as she'd like to avoid this, she knew it was stupid to put it off any longer. "Okay. I have something going on this evening, but I could meet you afterward. Say, eight-thirty. Here. Is that okay?"

"I'll be here."

Sage brooded about the appointment all morning. So unsettled was she about it that when Colt showed up at lunchtime and offered to buy her a salad at the Bristlecone Café, she let him. "Don't get any ideas, though," she warned as they walked up Fourth Street toward Cottonwood. "I need a distraction, and you are all I've got."

"Careful, Cinnamon. I'll get a big head from all your praise."

She rolled her eyes, then slipped her arm through his. "Tell you what. Let's call a truce during lunch, shall we?

Now that I'm over the surprise of your being here, I'd like to hear more about your plans. Where are you living?"

"For now, I'm at the Creekside Cabins. They have a fenced yard behind the office where they're letting Shadow chill when he's not with me, although I just learned about the doggie day care place that Celeste has added to Angel's Rest. Speaking of dogs, where's Snowdrop?"

"Today is her mani-pedi day."

He stopped abruptly. "You're kidding."

She grinned. "Yes, I'm kidding. The Landry kids asked if she could hang out with them today."

They arrived at the Bristlecone just as chaos erupted. Glenda Hawkins let out a scream and fell to the floor in a dead faint. Half a dozen people rushed forward; Sage hung back. Colt gave her an enigmatic look before addressing the couple at a nearby table. "What happened?"

"Her husband called," Marlene Lange responded. "She was taking our order and she asked Jimmy Turnage to answer the phone when it rang. He said it was Ralph."

Marcus Burnes added, "She didn't say much more than hello before she squealed."

By now, Glenda had come to and sat up. The knot in Sage's belly relaxed when she heard her say she was fine. Jimmy Turnage helped Glenda to her feet. Then Glenda shocked the entire restaurant by laughing out loud and calling, "Free lunches for all! Ralph won over eight hundred thousand dollars in Vegas, baby!"

The place erupted in cheers, and the celebration began. As word spread, the crowd grew. Laughter was the rule of the day as the people of Eternity Springs tossed out suggestions for how Glenda and Ralph could spend their newfound wealth. Sage ended up pitching in to help in the kitchen and her lunch hour turned into two and a half, but she didn't care. Not only did she enjoy herself, but the impromptu party gave her an extra hour and a half of distraction for the upcoming evening with Rose.

Colt had hung around, too, and as he walked back toward the gallery with her, he said, "You know, this is the sort of thing that made me want to move here."

"Lax lunch hours?"

"The sense of community. The town where I grew up had it, but I haven't found it anywhere else I've lived. Having that in your life enriches you."

Sage couldn't argue with him. Eternity Springs had offered her family when she'd had none of her own. Family. She sighed. "I'm going to talk to Rose tonight."

"That's good."

"I don't know if it is or not."

"Are you ready to tell me about what happened with you two yet?"

No, she wasn't. In fact, why had she mentioned Rose to him at all today? Doing so introduced an intimacy into their relationship that made the whole arm's length thing more difficult to maintain. "I think you and I both should get back to work. Oh, dear. Look, someone is waiting out in front of Vistas. I don't have so many customers this time of year that I can ignore them. I hope he hasn't been waiting too long."

As it turned out, the customer wasn't a customer of hers but an Eternity Springs resident waiting for Margaret Rhodes to get back from the Bristlecone and reopen the library, which was across the street and two doors down from Vistas. Once Sage shared the news of Ralph Hawkins' big win, the library patron decided to head over to the celebration himself.

As she unlocked the door to Vistas, Sage turned to

Colt and attempted to dismiss him. "Enjoy the rest of your afternoon, Rafferty."

"You too." He stepped forward and gave her a quick kiss on the lips. "Good luck with Rose. If you need me, I'm just a phone call away."

He walked away whistling, his hands stuck in his pockets. Sage couldn't help but sneak a look at his butt. The man did fill out a pair of jeans in a spectacular way.

Thoughts of Colt drifted through her mind off and on the rest of the afternoon. She had enjoyed having his company at lunch. Their interlude out at the lake last winter had been lovely, but more like make-believe than reality. Being with him at the Bristlecone today had been . . . ordinary.

Ordinary was so darned nice.

Against her better judgment, she allowed herself to imagine what it would be like to have a real relationship with Colt, to have an ordinary life with this man. It would be extraordinary.

It would be impossible.

He didn't want to stop with a dog. He wanted a family. That meant children.

Impossible.

Late in the afternoon, a still jubilant Glenda Hawkins floated in and purchased Marcus Burnes' photograph of a doe and her fawn drinking from Angel Creek. "I've had my eye on this one ever since I saw it hanging in your window, but I haven't been able to justify spending the money on it. It's the one treat I'm going to allow myself from this windfall."

"I think that's great. Where will you hang it?"

Glenda glanced around the gallery, making sure they were alone, then leaned forward. "Please don't tell anyone, but I'm about to burst with the news. Once things settled down at the restaurant, I had a long talk with Ralph. Guess what—we're going to move to Florida! It's been a dream of ours ever since we visited Nic Callahan's mom and aunt on our winter trip a few years ago. Billy is over the moon. He wants to be a pro golfer someday, you know. Florida weather is better for golf than what we have here."

"That's wonderful, Glenda. For you and Ralph and Billy, anyway. I can't say the same for Eternity. What will we do without the Bristlecone?"

"Hopefully you won't be without the restaurant. I plan to sell it."

"Well, your magic in the kitchen is what makes the Bristlecone so wonderful. I can't imagine anyone else being able to fill your shoes."

"That's sweet. Silly, but sweet. Thank you, dear. Now, you will keep the news to yourself, won't you?"

"Absolutely." Sage didn't expect to have to keep the secret long. Glenda Hawkins was the biggest gossip in town. Sage didn't see her keeping quiet about her own big scoop. In fact, she'd probably already told every person she'd spoken with since hanging up the telephone. Her suspicions proved true when, after closing Vistas for the day, she walked toward Angel's Rest for a Patchwork Angels meeting and three separate people stopped her and asked if she'd heard the news. "Ah, small-town life," she murmured. "Wonder how Colt will like this aspect of the community."

After that Sage's thoughts turned to the latest project of the Patchwork Angels, the small quilt they were making for the Alzheimer's Art Quilt Initiative. Lori Reese had suggested the project, and Sage had worked with her on the design. It was a labor of love for both Sarah and her daughter, and lately one of the few activities they shared without bickering these days. The graduating-from-high-school-and-going-off-to-college experience was proving difficult for them both.

She met up with said mother-daughter team at the

pedestrian bridge to Angel's Rest over Angel Creek, and Sarah quizzed her about Colt all the way to the Patchwork Angels workroom in the converted attic of the old Cavanaugh mansion. Sage was so busy fending off Sarah's nosiness that she had already set her tote bag on the table and pulled out her scissors when she spied the visitor. "Rose."

Celeste Blessing swept into the room. "Hello, dears."

Colt trailed in after her. Sage dropped her chin to her chest and sighed. If she was a conspiracy theorist, she'd believe that the world was conspiring against her.

Sarah said, "I'm surprised to see you here, Colt. Are you joining the Patchwork Angels? Are you packing a thimble and needles?"

"Afraid not."

Thank you, God.

"Celeste just wants me for my body."

Celeste laughed and pointed toward the far wall. "The boxes I need moved to the basement are over there."

Another couple of quilt group members entered the workroom as Celeste addressed the dozen or so women already congregated inside. "I suspect you all know Colt Rafferty, who is Eternity Springs' newest full-time resident. I want to introduce you to one of our guests here at Angel's Rest, Dr. Rose Anderson. Rose told me a story about a volunteer quilt project, and I asked her to share it with us today. Rose, the floor is yours."

Rose was so nervous that she felt sick to her stomach. Celeste hadn't said a word about Sage being part of this group. She never would have come if she'd known. Her sister undoubtedly would view it as an attempt on Rose's part to horn in on her life when, in fact, she'd agreed to speak to the quilt group because she was looking for a distraction before the meeting at eight-thirty.

What's done is done. You might as well just say what you came to say and leave.

"Until recently I was a internist on staff at a VA hospital in Pennsylvania, and when Celeste told me that your quilt group does volunteer projects, I mentioned one that I personally know is worthy of support. The organization is called Quilts of Valor. Part of what they do is to make quilts to honor and comfort our war wounded as a tangible way of saying thank you for their service, sacrifice, and valor. The idea is that the quilts are a hug from America for our combat veterans, that they are meant to be wrapped around our wounded warriors to show them that America cares."

"Just thinking about that makes me tear up," one of the women said.

"I know," Rose agreed. "I cannot tell you how much those quilts mean to our young men and women. They personalize a warrior's service and his or her sacrifice in a way that means so much. I think part of the reason is because quilting is part of America's heritage. They just seem to say home and say Mom and apple pie."

Sarah said, "I'll bet the vets treasure the quilts."

"They do. The quilts immediately become a family heirloom. But what I found most telling was how the warriors view their quilts when they're alone. I can't tell you how many times I walked into a room and found a vet teary-eyed over his quilt or sometimes simply running his hands over the stitches. It really is a wonderful, wonderful program. If your group is looking for a project quilt, I can't recommend Quilts of Valor highly enough."

One of the women asked how the donation process worked, and after Rose explained what she knew about it, another person asked if donations could be directed to Rose's hospital. Rose sneaked a look at Sage before she answered, "Actually, I'm no longer at the VA. I've left the service."

Sage's head jerked around. "You've what?"

"I punched my ticket."

"But . . . you're career army."

"Not anymore."

"Why not? What happened?"

"It's part of what I have to say at eight-thirty tonight."

Celeste looked from Sage to Rose, then back to Sage again. "For those of you who haven't made the connection, Rose and Sage are sisters."

As Rose watched Sage deliberate her next response, she had a flash of her sister standing before the Colonel, preparing to broach her request to stay out all night at the school-sponsored after prom. She'd asked Rose to make a special trip home to be there during the request to add sisterly support, and Rose had been happy to do so. Together they had overcome their father's objections, and once they were alone, Sage had squealed and thrown herself into Rose's arms and lavished her with praise.

Times had certainly changed.

And Rose wanted away from the audience.

As Sage opened her mouth to speak, Rose quickly interjected, "So, that's what I had to share with you all. Now, while you enjoy your meeting I have a date with one of the hot springs pools. I'll see you later."

She rushed out of the room and down the stairs to her second-floor guest room. There she grabbed her tote bag, a towel, and her swimsuit and continued downstairs.

Outside, she headed toward the hot springs pools. She only vaguely noticed that Colt Rafferty was wandering down the exact same path. She ducked into the hot springs changing facility, then reemerged a few minutes later in her swimsuit. She followed the path to the most isolated pool. There she kicked off her shoes, pulled her coverup over her head, then eased into the hot—and, frankly, smelly—pool.

It was heaven.

He gave her a whole half minute to relax. "Hello there, Dr. Anderson. You remember me—my name is Colt Rafferty. We met yesterday at the Trading Post. I'm dating your sister."

"Mr. Rafferty . . ."

He sat on one of the benches beside the pool Rose had chosen and began untying the laces of his hiking boots. "Call me Colt, please. Actually, it's more than just dating. I'm pretty sure I want to marry her, although in the spirit of full disclosure, she isn't nearly as certain about me. Sage doesn't talk about her family much. I'm curious. I take it you two have had a falling-out?"

He wants to marry her. Mr. Tall, Dark, and Dimpled. Well, great. She choked back a little semi-hysterical laugh. *Isn't that just perfect? He'll probably get her pregnant, too.* "Listen, Mr., uh, Colt. I don't think it's appropriate for me to talk about our family issues with you."

After all, she and Sage didn't talk about them.

Undeterred, he pulled off his shoes and socks and rolled up the legs of his khaki slacks. He sat at the edge of the pool and dipped his feet into the water. "I still can't get over the changes in Eternity Springs' pools. I vacationed here as a kid, and these hot springs were little more than a muddy mess. So, if you won't talk about troubles, how about easy stuff? Tell me what Sage was like as a girl. Was she ornery? A little angel? Did she chase butterflies even then?"

The man was so subtly persistent that Rose found herself answering without actually meaning to do so, and in the process she told him quite a bit about Sage, about herself, and even some about the Colonel.

"So was she artistic even then?" Colt asked. "Or did she always want to be a doctor?"

"Actually, as a child she wanted to be a painter."

"Oh, yeah?"

Rose nodded. "She always had great hands with a dexterity I coveted. A surgeon's hands."

"An artist's hands," Colt said.

"My hands." Sage stepped out of the shadows. She wore a one-piece bathing suit with a beach towel wrapped around her. "My business."

Rose shifted, sitting up straighter. Sage met Colt's gaze. "I'd like to speak with my sister privately. Would you excuse us, Colt?"

"Sure." He pulled his feet out of the water and stood. After Sage tossed him a towel, he dried his feet, pulled on his socks and boots, and rolled his pants legs down. He crossed to her sister and said, "I'll wait for you at the bridge."

"Don't bother."

"I'll wait." He stopped beside her as he left, gave her hand a squeeze, and kissed her cheek before moving off down the path.

For a long moment neither woman spoke. Rose didn't feel comfortable with the dynamics here, her seated in the pool and Sage standing over her. She'd just about decided to leave the pool when Sage tossed away the towel and stepped down into the water.

To break the silence, Rose asked an obvious question. "So, you decided not to wait until eight-thirty?"

"These hot springs pools stink of sulfur. Seemed like an appropriate place to have this talk."

Rose smiled wryly. Her sister had a point.

"Okay, Rose. Let's hear it. Say what you came here to say."

Giving in to nerves, Rose tapped her toes at the bottom of the pool. She tried to recall and launch into the statement she'd prepared and practiced dozens of times, but the words that came out were something else entirely. "I miss you, Sage. I want you in my life again."

"Gee, in that case, I guess you shouldn't have tossed me out of your life, hmm?"

"It was a bad time for both of us."

"I know it was for me. You had me thrown out of my own father's funeral, Rose!"

"That was Brandon's doing. I didn't know about it until afterward, I swear. I felt terrible about it when he told me what happened."

"So terrible that you rushed right over the following day to apologize, right? Oh, wait. My bad. That didn't happen, did it?"

Rose clenched her teeth. She'd never dealt well with Sage's sarcasm. Why hadn't she kept to her script? She'd put so much thought into choosing the right words in order to avoid a situation like this and then when the time came to use them, she went blank. *Stay calm. Keep your eye on the goal.*

"As much as I'd like to go back and change the past, I can't do that. All I can do is attempt to move forward. I'd like to move forward with you. I know I've hurt you, and I'm sorry about that. In the past year or so I've spent some time evaluating and reevaluating what is important to me. I figured out that a lot of the things I thought were important actually aren't. I also learned that things I told myself weren't important are the most important things on earth. Family is important, Sage. You are important to me. I'd like us to find our way back to each other."

Sage sank down in the water up to her neck. Above the bubbling of the springs, Rose heard her sigh. After a long silence, she asked, "Why now? Have you and Brandon finally set a date? You want family at the wedding and I'm all there is?"

"Brandon and I aren't together anymore. He married someone else. In fact . . ." She sucked in a breath against the pain, then forced out the words. "They're expecting a baby."

"You're kidding me." Sage's mouth gaped. "Didn't he always say he didn't want kids?"

"Yes." Rose was proud it didn't come out like a sob. "He changed his mind."

Sage muttered something Rose couldn't hear, then asked, "How long were you two together?"

Rose cleared her throat. "Seven years."

"Seven years." She blew out a breath. "Whose idea was it to split?"

"That would be Brandon."

"I'm sorry, Rose." She hesitated a beat, then said, "I never liked him."

Rose managed to keep most of the bitterness out of her voice. "Well, Brandon doesn't matter. That's behind me; it's over. I'm looking forward now."

Sage climbed to her feet. "Okay. Well, then. You just look forward. Personally, I'm up to my eyebrows with right now. The summer season is upon us, and I have a graduation party for a dear friend next week. Then I have a prominent guest coming to town to do a huge favor for me. I really don't have time to fret about forward."

She stepped out of the pool and reached for her towel. Rose said, "Sage. Wait, please. You're my family. We are the only family each other has. We should—"

"Stop it." Sage whirled on her, her voice fierce, her eyes glimmering with pain. "I'm sorry your boyfriend dumped you. I really am. Men so often suck. But you know what? I'm not all warm and fuzzy about being your backup date to the prom. It's insulting. You didn't sweep into Eternity Springs with an olive branch until Brandon left and you were alone. Maybe I would have been more receptive to the idea if I wasn't so obviously your last resort. Good-bye, Rose."

Ah, Rose, you really screwed this up. Sage had already taken three steps down the path away from her when Rose screwed up her courage and said, "Sage, I have cancer."

SIXTEEN

❦

Cancer.

The word knocked the breath from Sage's lungs and stopped her in her tracks. Cancer.

"My prognosis is excellent," Rose continued. "It's endometrial cancer and we caught it early. Actually, I should say I *had* cancer, not have, because I've finished treatment and everything looks good.

"I didn't come to Eternity Springs because Brandon dumped me or because I'm dying. However, facing that possibility made me confront the whole notion of death and decide what is and is not important in life. You are important, Sage. That's why I'm here."

A band of emotion squeezed Sage's chest, and she truly couldn't breathe. *Death. Rose. Africa. Wedding veils. Bloodstained baby rattles. Rose. Death.* The urge to flee grew so strong that she simply couldn't resist it. Turning a blind eye to the painful emotions etched on her sister's face, she blurted out, "I can't. I've gotta go."

She rushed up the path, away from her sister, away from the pain. Away from her own self-respect. The lack of compassion she showed her sister shamed her, but survival instinct was in control at the moment. She actually broke into a run as she exited the hot springs pool park and headed for home. If only she'd driven to Angel's Rest tonight. She'd hop in her car and start driving and maybe not stop until she reached . . . where?

Where else could she go? Eternity Springs was her sanctuary. This was where she felt safe. Where else could she go?

Then she saw him. Colt Rafferty, waiting at the footbridge over Angel Creek. Waiting, she knew, for her.

Not *where* could she go. To whom. To him. To those broad, strong shoulders and gentle, cradling arms. Arms she knew she could count on to hold her and protect her and save her from her demons, if only for a little while.

"Colt." He turned to face her when she called his name, and just as she expected, his arms opened wide. When she reached him, they wrapped around her and hugged her tight, and Sage thought that maybe, just maybe, she'd be able to breathe again.

"What is it, sweetheart? What happened?"

"I don't . . . I can't . . . can we get out of here?"

"Sure."

He kept her tucked against him as he led her toward Cottonwood Street, but when he would have gone south, toward the gallery, she stopped. She didn't think Rose would follow her to continue their conversation, but just in case, she said, "No. You're at Creekside Cabins, right? Can we go there?"

"Whatever you want."

They turned north. The cabins were only half a block away, and in moments he was ushering her inside. When he tried to let her go, she refused to let him do it.

Sage reached up and pulled his head down to hers and captured his mouth in a hot, desperate kiss.

She dragged him over and onto the bed. She yanked at his clothes, tugged at her own, and took him. It was fast and furious and fierce, and when it was over, they rolled apart, lying next to each other, breathing hard.

Colt rose up on his elbow. "I feel so used."

Sage groaned aloud, then rolled over onto her stomach. She pulled the pillow over her head and wanted to disappear. *I can't believe I did that. I all but attacked him.* Her voice muffled, she said, "I'm sorry."

"I'm not," he said, his voice filled with cheer. "That's the nicest thing to happen to me in weeks. Feel free to use me anytime. Often."

He reached out and stroked his hand gently down the indentation of her spine. "Why don't you tell me about it, Sage?"

"I can't." After a moment's silence, she rolled over. Staring up at the ceiling, she said, "Rose has cancer."

"Ah, baby, no. How bad is it?"

Finally, the tears came, flooding her eyes, but she blinked them back. "She said the prognosis is good. I didn't stay to hear any more. Colt, I am such a lousy human being."

"Why do you say that, Cinnamon?"

"It's so complicated. We have so much hurt between us." In fits and starts, she explained, "See, before he died, my dad and I . . . well, we had a fight. Except, it wasn't exactly a fight. He got angry. Disappointed in me. It hurt." After a long pause, she added, "Really hurt."

"Ah, Sage."

"Then he had a stroke and I didn't handle it well and Rose, well, we sorta broke."

"This was after you returned from Africa?" he clarified. When she nodded, he continued, "I'm not the right kind of doctor to make a diagnosis, but it sounds as if you had a textbook case of depression when your father died. Rose didn't cut you any slack for that?"

"I didn't tell her. No one knows, except for you."

He remained quiet, his silence giving her statement extra import. "Don't you think that could be part of the problem?"

"I can't talk to Rose. When I say our situation is complicated, that's a mild term to use."

Colt blew out a breath, then linked his fingers with hers and brought her hand to his mouth for a kiss. "While I'm always—and I do mean always—glad to sacrifice my body for the cause, I really think you should consider talking to someone with some letters behind her name about what's going on in that beautiful head of yours."

"I tried therapy." She tried to pull her hand away. He wouldn't let her go. "It didn't work for me."

"Maybe you need a different therapist."

Anxiousness began to replace the inner calm left in the wake of their sexual storm. "Maybe I do. Maybe sometime I'll go that route, but not now. Not yet."

"Why not?"

"I'm not ready." She sat up and pulled the white sheet up over her breasts. "You know, if I have enough time, I might whip this thing on my own. That's my intention, and I've been doing fine lately. But this thing with Rose—having her show up out of the blue, her news tonight—I wasn't prepared."

"That's the way life is, sweetheart. You can't always be prepared."

"Life isn't the problem. *Death* is the problem. I can't deal with it. I can't deal with death."

"Ah." He said it as if she'd just solved a particularly troublesome question. "That's why you gave up medicine."

"It's part of the reason why, yes."

"What happened? I'm guessing you lost a patient? In a particularly troubling way?"

The memory flashed. *The missionary school. A child being born.*

"Don't, Colt. Please." She closed her eyes as the past threatened to rise up and swallow her. She left his bed, reaching for the tote bag containing her clothes and saying, "I should go. Snowdrop is surely wondering where I am."

"She can wait a little while longer." He rose behind her and smoothly repossessed her tote. "You don't want to get dressed without taking a shower first. Not to be rude, honey, but you smell like rotten eggs."

"Ee-yew. Really?" She pulled away from him, embarrassed. She hadn't rinsed off in the showers at the changing hut; she'd grabbed her bag and ran. "Of course. Why didn't you say something? How could you stand me?"

"It was a sacrifice on my part, but I took one for the team. Now, though, let's get that shower. Since I now have your smell all over me, I need a shower, too. I'm living in the mountains now, so I'm all about conservation. I figure we'll just shower together."

For the first time in hours, Sage smiled. "To conserve water?"

He pulled her toward the bathroom saying, "Wait until you see what I can do with a washcloth."

Rose couldn't stop crying. She felt heartsick, defeated, and alone. So completely and totally alone. Even more alone than she'd felt last year during her treatment and Brandon's betrayal. As she showered in the changing hut, she lifted her face toward the spray and tried to wash away the tears and the trials. She decided she'd give herself the length of this shower to indulge in her pity party. Then she would march up to the house, pack her bag, and leave this little town. Tonight.

She'd drive to the next decent-sized town—what was it? Gunnison?—and spend the night there. Then tomorrow, she'd get up and go . . . where?

"Anywhere," she murmured as she grabbed a towel to dry off, then pulled her coverup over her swimsuit. It didn't matter where she went. She didn't have a job, but she could get one anywhere. She had enough savings to live on for a little while. She could take her time. She didn't have to make any big decisions right away.

What she did have to do was stop crying. Tears got her nowhere. Hadn't she learned that lesson? Using the corner of her damp towel, she wiped the wetness from her cheeks and used an old trick to shore up her defenses by summoning up an image of her father. *Soldier on, Rosemary.*

"Okay, then. I will. I'm going to look forward, move beyond, and make a new life for myself and fill it with people I like. People who like me. Sage simply won't be part of it, and that is her loss. Soldier on, Rosemary."

Yeah, right. Who was she kidding? It'd be a minor miracle if, once she got to her room, she didn't throw herself across her bed and sob into her pillow.

The room she'd been assigned at check-in was in one of the new dormitory-style buildings constructed on the estate within the past year. The shortest path from the hot springs to her room took her past a garden gazebo with a wooden swing suspended from its ceiling. As she approached, Celeste Blessing's voice floated out from the evening shadows. "There you are, Rose. I've been waiting for you."

Rose stifled a sigh. She should have expected this. She'd blabbed the entire sad story to Celeste earlier. Something about the woman invited the sharing of confidences. However, Rose didn't want to spill her guts again tonight. She'd make an excuse and keep on walking.

Even as Rose opened her mouth to beg off, Celeste said, "Please, join me."

Despite other intentions, Rose found herself veering toward the gazebo. When Celeste patted the swing beside her, she took the direction and sat beside the older woman.

Celeste smiled kindly. "It didn't go well, did it?"

"It's fair to say that's an understatement." Rose gave a brief synopsis of the events.

"I'm sorry, dear."

Rose's mouth twisted in a sad smile. "Me too. She surprised me, Celeste. I knew how mad she was at me over the whole mess when our dad had his stroke, but I didn't think she'd ignore the fact that I've been a cancer patient."

"I am certain she didn't ignore it. I suspect she's running away from it. That's what you need to understand, Rose. Your sister is in retreat."

"Retreat from what?"

"Pain. Despair. A winter of the soul so immense and so desperate that even someone as bright as your sister couldn't stand against it. So she retreated. She's managed to slow down the pace of it here in Eternity Springs, but she hasn't been able to plant her feet and fight."

"I don't understand. What has she told you?"

Her sneaker-clad foot against the ground, Celeste gave the swing a push. "While I never, ever betray a confidence, I can tell you that Sage is unusually quiet about her life prior to her arrival in Eternity Springs. What I know is from my own observation of your sister and her activities."

Rose remained silent for a long moment before saying, "I don't know. I don't guess it really matters. I gave it the good old college try, but I got nowhere and I'm done. I've had enough. I'm checking out, Celeste. Tonight."

"Oh, Rose. Running away is no solution."

"Isn't it? It seems to have worked for Sage." Celeste chastised her with a look, and Rose shrugged. "It's not running away. Not really. I need a new beginning. I need to figure out what that beginning should be."

"Do you have any ideas?"

"I'm a physician and I'm good at it. Unlike someone else we know, I have no intention of leaving that behind."

"Of course not."

Rose stood up and began to pace the gazebo's confines. "I may not have had the manual dexterity to be a surgeon, but that doesn't mean I'm not a good doctor. My instincts are excellent, my diagnostic skills superb. I am caring and compassionate and my patients trust me and trust in me. Medicine is more than just surgeons. My father always said I was born to be a doctor, and he was right. Dad almost always was right."

"Almost?" Celeste asked quietly.

"He was a strong, disciplined man with exceedingly high expectations. He challenged us to be our best and drove us to achieve. The worst thing in the world was to let our father down. If I left medicine, too, why, he'd turn over in his grave or come back to haunt me."

She whipped her head around and met Celeste's gaze. "Maybe that's Sage's problem. Maybe Dad is haunting her."

"While I am certain that the true reality of existence is beyond the human mind's comprehension, I doubt that it is in God's plan for a father to literally haunt his daughter over something as trivial as career decisions."

"Trivial!"

"What you do isn't as important as who you are."

"But being a doctor is what I am. It's who Sage is, too."

"Is it really?" Celeste gave the swing a push with her foot. "So, medicine was always your dream? When you were young, you and Sage both dreamed of being a doctor?"

The questions made Rose pause. She sat back down beside Celeste. "No, Sage wanted to be a painter."

"What did you want to be?"

Following a long pause, Rose said, "A writer."

"A writer!" Celeste exclaimed with delight. "What did you dream of writing?"

"Fiction. When I was young, I made up stories in my mind as I went to sleep at night."

"How fun. You must have such a creative mind. What type of fiction did you want to write? Do you still plot stories as you drift off to sleep?"

"I wanted to write mysteries—I loved Lilian Jackson Braun's cat books, but I haven't made up stories for a long time."

"Why not?"

Rose shrugged. "Medicine took over my thoughts. First med school and the army and then the job itself. I usually fell asleep the moment my head hit the pillow."

"And now? You're not working now."

"No." Rose exhaled a heavy sigh. "Since the diagnosis, that drifting-off time tends to be my worry moments."

"I see." Celeste patted Rose's knee. "Would you do me a favor? Would you walk with me back to the house? I have something I'd like to show you."

Rose hesitated. She should get packed and on the road. She wouldn't like tackling Sinner's Prayer Pass in the dark as it was. The thought of driving it while tired left her even more uneasy.

As if reading her mind, Celeste stood, saying, "This won't take long. Trust me. This is something you absolutely must see before you leave Eternity Springs."

Rose found it impossible to deny Celeste. "In that case, lead on."

The fragrance of roses swirled on the cool mountain air as they walked through the garden toward the Victorian mansion that was the heart of the Angel's Rest center. As Rose followed Celeste along the pavé stone path, she guarded against allowing her thoughts to drift toward Sage and instead focused on her immediate future. She'd call and book a room in Gunnison before leaving Angel's Rest. Since it wasn't quite high season in the mountains yet, she shouldn't have a problem finding a place to stay, but she'd rather not have that worry as she made the drive.

Celeste greeted the front desk clerk as they walked inside and asked how the teenager's grandmother was feeling following her recent gallbladder surgery. When that brief discussion ended, Rose said, "I'm in Aspen room seven, and I'll be checking out in a few minutes. Would you please get my bill ready?"

"Sure will."

Rose began dragging her feet as they approached the stairs she'd climbed earlier on her way to the Patchwork Angels workroom. She didn't think her sister would have returned to her quilt group, but . . . "Is the quilt meeting over?"

"Yes, it is. However, what I want to show you isn't in the workroom. It's a special little place I've prepared on the other side of the attic. Come along, dear."

Rose was relieved to know she wouldn't be running into Angels in this attic, but she wondered what in the world Celeste had up here that she thought Rose needed to see. When Celeste paused in front of a door and fished a set of keys from her pocket, Rose sneaked a quick look at her watch. If she could finish up here at Cavanaugh House in the next twenty minutes, take ten to pack her suitcase and get out of her room, she shouldn't be too late getting to Gunnison.

"Now, dear, before we step inside, I want you to promise me that you will keep an open mind for the next few minutes. Will you do that for me, please?"

Rose smiled indulgently. "I'll try."

Celeste swung the door open, flipped on a light switch, and motioned Rose inside. "This is our garret suite. It's been designed with creative souls—writers in particular—in mind. Since it's dark outside, you can't enjoy the view, but it's one of the loveliest pictures of snowcapped peaks in town. The furnishings are all prizes original to the house. Well, except for the computer, of course. I have a desktop set up here and we're equipped with Wi-Fi."

She opened a cabinet that revealed an entire modern workstation. "However, it's my opinion that the best seat in the house is the window seat. You'll note the convenient electrical outlet. A writer will be able to sit in the window nook all day long and write to her heart's content on a laptop. If writing longhand is more her style— I understand some writers do that still—we designed lighting just for that, too."

She gestured toward the nifty little adjustable wall lamp, then added, "Can't you feel the creative energy buzzing in this room?"

To Rose's surprise, she could feel it, and she felt herself responding to it at the same time her defenses rose. She wasn't stupid. She knew why Celeste had brought her here. "It's a wonderful room, but honestly, you don't think I'm going to hole up here and take a shot at writing?"

"Why not?"

"Well, because."

Celeste grinned. "Now there's a strong argument. I want you to notice that tucked away out of sight of the work area, but handy, too, is the sleeping area and a kitchenette. This suite is the only one in Cavanaugh House itself to have this feature. I had a friend who wrote novels, and he would shut himself up and not leave his apartment for days on end. I thought it was important for our garret suite occupant to be able to nourish not only her creativity but also her body. Rosemary, you could stay here and work on a book and no one would have to know."

Interest fluttered to life inside her, and Rose couldn't help but take another look around the room. What if . . .

"No." She shook her head. "I can't."

"Why not?"

"It was a childhood dream. A childish idea. Even if I wanted to give this a try, what do I know about writing?"

"You are a medical school graduate. I am certain you know how to do research. I don't doubt you can construct a strong sentence. Can you tell a good story? I don't know. Based on what you've said, I imagine you don't know, either. What I do know is that you won't know the answer until you try."

Rose stepped farther into the room. She did have her laptop with her. Maybe, just maybe, she had the threads of a medical thriller in the back of her mind. But she also had the echo of her father's voice.

You are a physician, Rosemary. You have been given a fine mind and the opportunity to excel. It is your duty to honor those gifts in service to others. You are a healer.

"I need to find another job."

"Pardon my asking, but is that due to financial concerns?" Celeste said.

No. Rose had always been a saver and she had a nice little nest egg built up. "It's because working is what I do."

"I see." Celeste tilted her head and asked, "When was your last vacation?"

"I haven't taken a real vacation in years."

"Then now is your chance."

A vacation? Well, a vacation was different. What would it hurt to take a little time away from reality? Away from expectations?

"Listen to this." Celeste twisted the latch on the windows and threw them open wide. The bubbling rush of Angel Creek drifted up to her like a song. "Isn't it lovely? The topography amplifies the sound. I adore the sound of a bubbling creek. That's what I listen to as I'm drifting off to sleep during these warmer months."

She patted the cushioned window seat. "Come here, my dear. Sit for a spell and listen to the night. It's so peaceful and, in its own way, healing."

Rose knew if she sat down, she probably was toast. The window seat looked like the perfect place to sit, to dream, to escape. It tempted her like chocolate brownies fresh from the oven.

What if she gave it a try? What would it hurt? She had nowhere else she needed to be. Nowhere else she wanted to be, to be honest. Maybe she'd hate it. Perhaps she would be lousy at it. It might be nice to give it a shot, and nobody would ever need to know. Medicine would be there waiting for her, just like always.

Celeste fussed with the fold on the filmy white lace window curtain. "We have another resident in town who is dabbling with a book. Gabe Callahan. He's a happy man now with a new wife and twin baby girls, but he's had a difficult time of it in his past. He says that he finds writing therapeutic."

"I could write a novel and name the villainess Sage," she grumbled.

"Now, Rose," Celeste chided. Then, in a more encouraging tone, she added, "Don't give up on your sister. She has been wounded and needs time to heal."

"I've been wounded, too," she responded. She felt a

bit embarrassed by her petulant tone, but still—she'd had the Big C.

"Yes, you have," Celeste said. "I am not discounting that at all. It's part of you, and as such, part of your relationship with Sage. As a physician, you know that not all injuries are physical, that some injuries take longer to heal than others, and that injured people heal at different rates."

"True, and some injuries never heal. Despite our efforts, some injuries kill."

"Absolutely. But if you'll look deep inside yourself, you'll recognize that in this case, the patient isn't dead yet."

The patient being her relationship with her sister, Rose understood. "Maybe not, but it's on life support."

"You've already pulled the plug on one family member. Are you honestly prepared to do it again?"

"Ouch."

"Sage is your sister. You are her sister. Each of you needs to forgive the other. True forgiveness can be difficult to achieve, but the reward is immense. Stay with us for a little while, Rose. Indulge your muse. Give yourself and your sister the time to find forgiveness."

Rose sat on the window seat and leaned against the comfy cushioned backrest. By their own volition, her feet lifted and she stretched out her legs. The seat fit her body so perfectly that it might as well have been built for her.

In that moment, she wanted to remain in Eternity Springs, in this garret suite, attempting to write a book and reconcile with her sister. She wanted it so badly that it frightened her. Reacting, she started to move, to flee this suite as fast as Sage had fled the hot springs park earlier. Even as she flexed her muscles, Celeste reached down to the window seat and said, "Look. It's a built-in serving tray. It's a perfect place to set your cup of tea."

Her gaze on the oh-so-perfect tray, Rose surrendered. "What's the security code for the Wi-Fi?"

SEVENTEEN

☙

June

At the end of the third day of the five-day children's cancer camp program at Angel's Rest, Colt sat with Ali Timberlake at a table set for four at the Bristlecone Café. Nic Callahan and Sarah Reese had excused themselves moments ago to visit the ladies' room. As a high school kid bused their plates, Colt gazed glumly out the window toward Angel's Rest and the footbridge over the creek where Rose Anderson basked in the attention of Connor Keene, cartoonist and wolf on the prowl. "Sage is going to hear about this and it's going to drive her crazy."

"Why is that?" Ali asked.

"Because Pencil Boy is the perfect pawn in the War of the Herbs."

A laugh bubbled from Ali's lips. "War of the Herbs?"

"Sage and Rosemary. I halfway expect their twin brothers to show up anytime now looking for their true love."

Ali visibly thought it through. "Parsley and Thyme? Are you a Simon and Garfunkel fan, Rafferty?"

"I'm a sucker who has somehow, without any intentional effort, found himself stuck in the middle between two hardheaded women."

Ali summoned Glenda Hawkins' attention with a little wave and gestured toward her tea glass. "They are both determined."

"Demented," he grumbled, taking a swig from his own glass of iced tea.

It had been six weeks since the sisters' scene at the hot springs at Angel's Rest. Four weeks since Rose went public with the news of her "extended vacation" and flew a bee right into Sage's bonnet that had yet to stop buzzing. The two women hadn't spoken to each other, but from what he observed, they each spent half their day trying to ferret out news about the other. Yet a part of him couldn't complain, because for the most part, he had been the beneficiary of Sage's snit about her sister.

She turned to him when she was in turmoil. That had gotten him back into her bed when he first returned to town, and despite a halfhearted attempt or two, she had yet to kick him out. His mistake—and in retrospect it had been a doozy—was to let Sage talk him into approaching Rose for the purpose of subtle interrogation.

He liked Rose Anderson a lot. She was friendly and funny and straightforward. She'd flat out asked him if he was a spy for her sister. He'd confessed that Sage was curious, she'd admitted to a similar state, and he'd launched into his newest part-time job—acting as go-between for the Anderson sisters.

He sighed and said, "So, how did the kids like Cartoon Man?"

"What do you have against Connor Keene?" Ali asked. "He's a really nice guy."

"He's a wolf. He comes on to every woman he meets—doesn't matter if they're sixteen or sixty. Single or married or . . ."

"Sleeping with someone?" Ali arched a brow. "Jealous, Rafferty?"

"He has octopus arms and he needs to keep them off my woman."

Ali laughed. "Well, he's great with the children, and he's been a wonderful addition to the program. He's even promised that if we do this again next summer, he'll come back."

"Oh, joy."

At that point, Glenda finally managed to break away from the other table of diners and make her way over to refill Ali's iced tea. Ali smiled up at her and asked, "How are the moving plans going, Glenda?"

"Pretty good. Our builder has promised the house will be ready by mid-August. We intend to be in and settled in time for Billy to start school in September."

"Any luck finding a buyer for the Bristlecone?" Ali gazed around the restaurant a bit wistfully.

"Not yet. We're not in a hurry, though, because thankfully our plans don't hinge on our ability to sell the Bristlecone first." As she topped off Colt's glass, she glanced out the window and clicked her tongue. "There's that wonderful Mr. Keene. He is such a nice man. So handsome, too. Don't you think?"

"He's adorable," Colt drawled in a dry tone.

Ali laughed as Sarah and Nic rejoined their table. "If you'll bring me our check, Glenda, we need to get moving."

"Don't we get to have dessert?" Nic protested. She looked at Sarah. "Didn't you make a chocolate cake for Glenda this morning?"

"I did."

"Then we need to stay and—"

"Nope." Ali grinned without remorse. "I promised Gabe I'd have you home by eight."

Nic threw Colt a pleading look. "Don't you want dessert, Colt?"

"Not enough to risk the wrath of Sage if we're late." He stood. "C'mon, Mrs. Callahan. I'll walk you home."

"Okay." Nic sighed audibly as she stood. Then she

gave Ali a genuine smile and added, "I had fun this afternoon, Ali. Working with those children was a joy."

"It was a joy for them, too," Ali replied. "You can always count on kids loving animals."

"We got lucky to have two litters of kittens for the show-and-tell part of the program."

"Speaking of litters," Sarah said, "you have five minutes to walk home before you're officially late."

Colt kissed first Sarah's cheek, then Ali's, and said, "Thanks for the meal. Y'all have a good night."

As they exited the restaurant, Colt gave the Angel's Rest footbridge one last look, and he was disheartened to see that Rose and Mr. Hollywood were still chatting up a storm. *I hope she knows what she's doing.* To distract himself, he asked Nic, "So, you don't seem worried about how your girls and Sage are getting along?"

"I'm not. This is the third time Sage has babysat for me. She did fine the other times."

Colt wondered if Nic knew that Sage got so nervous ahead of time that she couldn't keep a thing in her stomach. He decided it was probably best he didn't share that little fact.

The walk to the Callahans' took less than five minutes. They entered the house through the front door to find Sage sitting on the family room floor stacking wooden blocks for the romper-clad beauties to knock over. At eight months old and crawling, the blue-eyed twins sported short blond curls and various bruises that had Colt glancing from the babies to Sage to Nic in concern. Neither of the women appeared to be concerned, so he deduced that he need not be, either.

"Hey, you two," Sage said, looking up from the stack of blocks. "How did it go?"

"Great," Nic said as Gabe wandered out from the kitchen, a dish towel slung over his shoulder. "I had a wonderful time. The kittens were a total hit with the children. How did things go here?"

"We did just fine," Gabe told his wife. Hearing their mother's voice, the twins made a U-turn and crawled toward their mama. "Sage even juggled feeding them by herself when they woke up early from their naps and I wasn't back yet from helping you."

"Oh no." Nic winced.

Sage stood, brushed cracker crumbs off her jeans, and smiled. "I enjoyed it. I'm glad I was able to help. I don't think Meg and Cari are too traumatized by my inexpert care." Meeting Colt's gaze, she asked, "How was the mad scientist's presentation?"

"Dry ice is always a hit with the kids." Then, because he saw the tightness around her eyes, he said, "You ready to go?"

"Sure." Sage kissed Nic's babies good-bye, hugged both Nic and Gabe, then strolled casually out the door. She maintained her slow, carefree step until she was out of the Callahans' line of sight. At that point she sagged against the neighbor's front gate, bent over double, and drew in deep, shuddering breaths. Colt patiently waited her out, giving her his silent support, and when she'd once again gathered her strength, he clasped her hand in his and continued their walk, saying, "It's a beautiful night, isn't it?"

"Yes," she replied, giving a shaky laugh. They traveled half a block before she replied. "Why do you do it, Rafferty?"

"Do what?"

"Put up with my . . . weirdness. Why haven't you run as hard and fast as you can the other way?"

They strolled down Pinyon Street past Community Presbyterian Church, and when he spied the park bench surrounded by roses in the church's garden area, he steered her toward it. "Why am I not running?" he repeated. "That's easy, Cinnamon. It's because I love you."

She sucked in a breath and sank down onto the bench. "No, you *think* you might be *falling* in love with me."

"No. I've landed, and I'm sure. I love you, Sage. I want to make a life with you."

"Tell me this isn't a marriage proposal!"

The horror in her tone made him wince. "I don't have to worry about becoming egotistical when I'm hanging around you, do I?"

Sage leaned back against the bench and closed her eyes. "I don't mean to be insulting."

"I know."

"I just . . . I'm a terrible bet, Rafferty. I am such a basket case and I'm so afraid I'm going to hurt you. I like you too much for that."

"See, I'm making progress."

She sighed. "You don't give up, do you? You're like Angel Creek, always pounding away at the creek bed. Even during winter when the creek is frozen over, the current is still there beneath the ice, slowly eroding the rocks."

Colt sat beside her and linked her fingers with his. He didn't say any more, simply offered her his constant support. Following a few moments of silence, she asked, "Would you take me home, Rafferty?"

He wanted to release a frustrated sigh, but he refrained and reminded himself that he thrived on challenge.

They made small talk as they walked to the car and during the short drive out to Hummingbird Lake. He pulled into her driveway and switched off the ignition, and when Sage climbed out of the car, it didn't surprise him that she headed away from the house rather than toward it. The fishing pier was one of her favorite places around.

"Do you want me to hang around?" he asked.

"Please. I have something I need to say, Colt."

This time he couldn't stop the sigh. He'd known he was taking a risk by telling her that he loved her, but he'd believed she was ready to hear it. Judging by the serious expression on her face, he'd been wrong. Now he suspected she was going to try to dump him. *Not gonna happen, Cinnamon. You can try, but I'm not letting you win this one. I might make a strategic retreat, but this relationship is far from over.*

At the end of the pier, Sage spent a moment staring out at the water and the glorious orange, pink, and purple sunset crowning Murphy Mountain to the west. Colt saw her draw a deep breath, and he braced himself.

Turning, Sage drew a deep breath, then shocked Colt down to his soles.

Sage's knees had gone watery. Her mouth was dry and her heart pounded and a whole flock of butterflies had taken up residence in her belly. She couldn't believe she was going to do this. Colt Rafferty was a good man and she might well be able to ruin his life.

She blew out a breath, then said, "The last thing I want to do is to hurt you, and I'm afraid that's exactly what I'm going to do. You see . . . oh, I can't believe I'm doing this. I know it's a mistake. Colt, I love you, too."

His mouth dropped open. Sage laughed nervously. "Careful, Rafferty. You're around the water. You'll end up with a mouth full of bugs if you're not careful."

"Say it again, Cinnamon."

She relaxed a little bit. It wasn't often that she managed to surprise this man, so she took a moment to enjoy it before replying, "You'll end up with a mouthful of—"

"Oh, forget about it," he interrupted as he dragged her into his arms for a thorough kiss.

He finally lifted his mouth from hers, but he kept her wrapped in his embrace. Sage felt so safe in his arms, so much at home, that it gave her courage to say, "I love you, Colt, and I want to tell you why I'm such a basket case."

Against her ear, his warm breath murmured, "I love you, too, Sage, and I want to hear it."

"I've never told another soul."

"Okay." He waited.

If I tell him everything and he still wants me, then maybe, just maybe, we might have a chance.

She had to try to make him understand, although she doubted that would be possible. How could anyone who wasn't there that day ever understand? And yet, she suspected that this man, more than anyone she knew, might come close. "You are the first person who hasn't given up on me, Rafferty."

"I'm not going to give up on you, Anderson."

"I'm afraid. I have so much baggage."

"Actually, I've figured that one out." Sage managed to smile a little at the dryness in his tone before he added gently, "Talk to me, sweetheart."

Now she pulled out of his arms and paced the narrow width of the fishing pier. "I don't know how to start."

"How about at the beginning?"

She closed her eyes and rubbed her temples. She didn't want to go back to the beginning. She didn't want to let anyone else into her world. It was dark and ugly and full of pain. Her pain, bone deep, pain that at this point was stamped into her DNA.

Frankly, now that the moment was here, she was having second thoughts. She wasn't sure she wanted to share it.

The sights. The sounds. The smells. Oh, dear God in heaven, I don't want to go back to that place.

And the one time she'd tried, to the one man who should have supported her, the attempt had ended in disaster.

She walked up and down the pier. Finally Colt reached for her arm and pulled her to a stop. "Sit with me. You've made me tired just watching you."

They sat and Colt pulled off his boots and socks, then allowed his feet to dangle in the water. "Brrr . . . I thought the water might have warmed up by now but it's still just short of freezing. Honey, did something else happen in Africa?"

"Yes," she responded before she realized he'd tricked her with a distraction.

"Tell me about it."

Sage closed her eyes, dropped her head back and lifted her face toward the dying light. *In her mind's eye, she saw the children. She heard the singing from the missionary school. "Jesus loves me, this I know, for the Bible tells me so."*

A laboring mother's moan as she expelled a brand-new life into Sage's waiting hands. "It's a girl."

The sound of a truck.

No. Sage jerked her head down and banished the memory, but not before the old, familiar guilt flooded her body. Tears welled in her eyes and grateful, she allowed them to fall.

She wept silently, shedding healing tears that she believed were a gift from God working through the man she loved. As always, Colt was there for her, supporting her, waiting for her to trust him with the truth.

Trust. That's what everything hinged on, wasn't it? In her heart of hearts, she knew that in order to put that awful time behind her, to finally embrace the healing that Colt, her friends, this town and this valley offered to her, she would have to open up and tell him about her biggest secret, her greatest shame. Trust.

"It was six months after I . . . after the other incident I told you about. Peter and I and some nurses had traveled to a village down toward the border."

Colt reached out and took her hand, lacing their fingers. "We'd been there two days. People came from all over."

Jesus loves me, this I know.

She exhaled a shuddering breath. "A woman had been in labor for days. Adaeze."

Jesus loves me, this I know.

"Dr. Sage. Dr. Sage. You must help my wife."

Seated on the fishing pier of Hummingbird Lake, tears streaming steadily down her face, she said, "I did an emergency cesarean."

The sound of a truck.

Jesus loves me, this I know.

Sage tugged her hand from his and wrapped her arms around herself. She shook her head, rocking slowly back and forth, the pain inside her as sharp as a machete's blade. "I can't. I'm sorry. I thought I could, but I can't."

"It's okay, baby," Colt said, shifting behind her so that his arms wrapped around hers. He held her as she rocked, holding in the horror. "You will when you're ready."

I'm not ready.

Spit it out, girl. I don't have time for this nonsense. Daddy!

"Don't leave me."

"I won't," Colt murmured. "I'm not going anywhere. I won't let you down, love."

"Maybe not, but I'll let you down. I'm broken, Colt."

"Then we'll put you back together again."

Humpty Dumpty sat on the wall. Humpty Dumpty had a great fall. Jesus loves me, this I know. "All the king's horses, all the king's men . . ."

"Shush, baby." He rocked with her. "We'll fix you. I'm a great fixer. You wait and see."

Jesus loves me, this I know.

"How can you not know?" Colt demanded of the woman he hoped would someday be his sister-in-law. Since Sage had left with Snowdrop early this morning to spend part of her day off in Gunnison at the groomer's, he'd used this opportunity to invite Rose to his office. He'd been grilling her about her sister for the past five minutes, and his discouragement was beginning to show. "If she's this distraught five years after the fact, she must have been looney tunes when she arrived back in the States."

"I told you, I didn't see her," Rose responded. She sat in an office chair opposite his desk and her gaze kept straying to his window. "She was in New York, said she was busy interviewing and that she'd get home as soon as she could manage. We talked on the phone and she seemed fine."

She hadn't been fine, Colt knew. She'd needed her family. They should have been there for her. "Why didn't you and your father go see her? She'd been out of the country for some time, hadn't she?"

"We didn't know she'd come home," Rose explained, obviously annoyed. "I still don't know how long she'd been back before she finally called. Then, when she did come home, she didn't tell us ahead of time. I was away with Brandon that weekend, so she only saw Dad."

"How was she then?"

"Okay, as far as I know. He didn't tell me otherwise. Three days later, he had the stroke." Rose sucked in a breath, then let it out shakily. "When I called to tell her, she promised to come, to meet me at the hospital, but she never did. After Dad passed, I found out she'd come home, but she never came up to the hospital."

"Why?"

"I don't know. I wasn't exactly in the healthiest frame of mind myself at the time." She glanced from the window to Colt. "Why are there Beanie Babies sitting on the windowsill?"

She's changing the subject. She and her sister are more alike than either of them would admit to. "I leave gifts for your sister," he explained, deciding he'd pried enough for a moment. "She laughed at my reaction to seeing the science classroom at school for the first time. It's the home of our local mountain man's taxidermy collection. Have you seen it?"

Rose nodded. "Celeste showed me. She thought I might be able to use it in my book."

"How's that coming?"

"I'm enjoying the process. It's good therapy."

Which brought him back to the question at hand. Colt released a frustrated sigh. Two weeks had passed since his conversation with Sage on the pier, and so far he'd been unable to coax her into revisiting the subject of Africa. Even worse, she'd begun to pull away from him, attempting to push him back beyond the outer ring of castle walls he'd labored for months to breach.

He wasn't about to allow that. She'd given him the ultimate weapon for this particular war. She'd told him she loved him, and he'd be damned if he'd let her try to snatch it away now.

"What do you know about post-traumatic stress disorder, Dr. Anderson?"

Rose blew out a sigh and rubbed the back of her neck. "I used to work for the Department of Veterans Affairs. I've seen my fair share."

"I've seen it in my work, too. From what I can tell, your sister is a classic case. If you don't know what happened, I guess you don't know if she ever sought treatment?"

"No. Like I said, the timing stank. Our relationship didn't survive our father's death."

He gave her a narrow-eyed stare. "But you came to Eternity Springs to fix the problem, didn't you?"

She shrugged. "It was a thought. It didn't get a lot of traction. You know all this, Rafferty. Why are you asking these questions again?"

"Because Sage is stubborn and scared and she needs professional help. I need help convincing her to get it."

"Well, don't ask me." Rose's words held a distinctly bitter tone. "Ask Nic Callahan and Sarah Reese and Celeste. Give Ali Timberlake a call in Denver. They all are much closer to my sister than I am."

"Maybe that's true, for the time being, anyway." He'd talked to all of them already, in fact. "But you are her sister, Rose. She needs you in her life, and you need her, too. You should settle your differences with her for your own sake."

"Have I walked into the middle of an Oprah show?"

Colt shoved out of his chair and paced the office until he ended up in front of the window. He gazed across the narrow space between the buildings and stared into the studio where one of those frivolous fairy paintings stood half finished on her easel. "I think she's trying to do this all on her own. What's that old saying? Physician, heal thyself? Maybe she saw someone before she came to Eternity Springs, but she's not seeing anyone now. Until recently I thought she might be able to pull this off herself if I was around to help. Not anymore. This is bigger than I'd realized. Definitely beyond my pay grade. What am I going to do?"

"You really love her, don't you?"

He turned and met her gaze. "I do. I want to marry her, raise a family with her. I want to make a life with her."

Rose winced, sighed heavily, then pulled her phone

from her jeans pocket and asked, "What's your email address?"

He told her and she continued, "I know a psychologist who works at the Atlanta VA Medical Center. I'm sending you her contact information, and I'll send her an email telling her to expect your call. She might be able to give you an idea about where to go from here."

"Great. Thanks, Rose."

She stood and walked toward the door, then hesitated. "Does she ever talk about me?"

"She asks about you all the time. It's killing her to know that you're here writing a book but not to know the details. Plus, she wants to know if you've heard any more from Connor the Cartoon."

"Cartoonist," Rose corrected, a smile playing at her lips. "Actually, I have. Good-bye, Colt. Have a nice afternoon."

She was out of the door and headed down the stairs before he could pry any more information out of her. As he walked back to his desk, he fished his phone from his pocket and checked his email. Finding the message Rose had promised, he sat and picked up the land line, then noted the number and made the call. As it connected, his gaze drifted toward the empty doorway. The Anderson girls were two special women. Frustrating, but extraordinary.

The call proved to be a quick one, as the doctor he asked for was away from the office. He left a message and hung up as he heard the sound of paws on the staircase. Lori Reese was delivering Shadow back to the office following their daily run.

When the girl and his dog walked into his office, he said, "You're back early."

"I cut our run short," Lori replied. "Chase is only working half a day today, and we're going to go up to Heartache Falls for a picnic with some friends."

Now that Chase Timberlake was back for a second season as a trail rider at the Double R, he and Lori had begun seeing each other again. "That sounds fun. Thanks for exercising my dog today."

"He exercises me. This puppy has more energy than any other dog I've known." She unsnapped the leash and Shadow came running to Colt to say hello.

"Tell me about it." Colt scratched the dog behind his ears and wrestled with him for a moment. "Nic says he'll calm down in a few months. I hope she's right."

"When it comes to animals, she's always right," Lori replied. "I hope I'll be as great a veterinarian as she is."

"There's not a doubt in my mind."

They spoke about college for a few minutes, then when his office phone rang, Lori said good-bye and left. Lifting the receiver, he said, "Colt Rafferty."

"Hello, Mr. Rafferty. My name is Cynthia Watkins. I'm returning your call."

He leaned back in his chair. "Dr. Watkins, I'm so glad you did. Let me explain my problem."

EIGHTEEN

❦

A little after four, Sage returned to Eternity Springs with her long list of errands for the most part accomplished. Snowdrop sported a new haircut and a darling red, white, and blue bow on her head. It would look so cute with the outfit Sage had planned for her to wear on the Fourth of July. Colt would be so disgusted. Sage couldn't wait.

Their bickering over the dogs was one of the few areas of their relationship she felt confident about. Being in love with the likes of Colt Rafferty was not easy. The man was always pushing. He did it subtly, she'd give him that, but he never stopped. He believed that he could chase away her shadows. Sage had her doubts, and that uncertainty was holding her back.

She stopped by Vistas to check with her summer intern, Dorian, who was an art student at UCLA. "What did I miss?"

"We had a lot of lookers, but only one buyer. A couple from Southern California were very interested in the Bret Austin watercolors, and I suspect they'll be back. The wife really wanted them."

"Excellent. What did we sell?"

"Another one of Mr. Burnes' photographs. The mountain lion."

Sage nodded. "He's done phenomenally well with that series. Good job, Dorian."

"Thanks." The pretty brunette beamed. "You know, I was thrilled to get this internship because I thought working with you would help my art. I never expected to enjoy the selling part of the job this much."

"I know. The most fun is the first time you sell a new artist. I get almost as excited as they do. So, anything else interesting happen while I was gone?"

"Dr. Rafferty came in. He left a note for you in your office. Sarah Reese called to let you know that the Patchwork Angels meeting for tonight has been cancelled."

"Oh? Did she say why?"

The girl checked her notes. "Too many member conflicts. Someone has suggested suspending meetings for the rest of the summer since everyone is so busy."

Sage wouldn't mind that herself. This time of year they all barely had time to breathe—not that anyone was complaining. On the contrary. The citizens of Eternity Springs were delighted. This summer was shaping up to be an economic home run. *Thank you, Celeste Blessing.*

She stepped into her office and found a note taped to the jar of dog treats on her desk. It read, *Better check the studio.* To Snowdrop, she said, "What in the world has he done now?"

Sage couldn't deny the little spark of excitement. She and Colt were presently involved in a tug-of-war. She was trying to slow things down, while he was applying a full-court press. Unfortunately, he was winning.

She took the stairs two at a time. A white box tied with a fat pink bow sat in the middle of her studio floor. "The man and his gifts," she murmured.

She tugged off the ribbon and bow, tore apart the paper, opened the box, and . . . frowned. Exercise clothes? New sneakers? "What's the deal? Does he think I'm getting fat?"

She picked up the box and carried it over to her window. He sat at his desk, his back to her. He was talking on the phone.

Sage had never availed herself of the window route he took between his office and her studio—knowing her luck, she'd slip and fall. Tucking the box beneath her arm, she made her way downstairs, asked Dorian to keep an eye on Snowdrop, and made her way to the office building next door. By the time she'd climbed the stairs and entered Colt's office, he'd ended his phone call and he was making notes on a yellow legal pad. Looking up, he saw her and smiled. "You're back. Good."

Rising, he came around from his desk and kissed her hello. "How was Gunnison?"

"Fine. Thanks for the gift. I think. Are the exercise clothes a hint?"

"Nah, they're a convenience. I didn't know how late you'd be getting back and didn't want you to have to dash out to the lake to get your things before our class."

"Our class? What class."

"Our yoga class."

"Yoga."

He smiled that particular grin that made his dimples wink at her. "I signed us both up for yoga class at Angel's Rest. It starts tonight."

While she stood there in muted shock, he added, "I have your yoga mat over here. It didn't fit in the box."

She frowned in confusion. "Why in the world would you do that?"

"You're working too hard. Yoga is a wonderful way to relax."

"I don't need to relax. I can't afford to relax. This is the summer season. Of course I'm working hard." She scowled at Colt and added, "You've taken yoga classes?"

"No, but I'm always up for something new."

Speed skiing or skydiving or parasailing, yeah. But

yoga? "What's up with you, Rafferty? What is this about?"

"I thought it would be nice if we did this together. I'm working hard, too. Exercise is a good way to unwind."

Sage didn't believe him for a minute. "Then take your dog for a run. Shadow is always ready for that."

"Shadow can't do yoga. I want to do yoga."

"Why?"

He hesitated a long moment then said, "You're not buying any of this, are you?"

"I believe you signed us up for yoga classes, but beyond that, no."

Colt drummed his fingers on the desk, then blew out a breath. "Okay," he murmured. "I'm going to do this."

Standing, he came around from behind his desk, took her hands in his, and stared solemnly into her eyes. "I love you and I'm worried about you. Sage, I've been doing some reading and I've talked to a few people. I think you are suffering from post-traumatic stress disorder."

She opened her mouth in an exaggerated O and slapped her face theatrically. "Really? Wow. I guess you're a better doctor than I am, Dr. Rafferty. I never thought of that."

"Do I really deserve the sarcasm?" he asked, an annoyed frown on his face. "You've never shared your diagnosis with me. You don't appear to be taking any steps to treat it."

"That's not true. I'm working on it."

"Are you in therapy? Are you on medication to help the symptoms?"

"I'm using different methods."

He folded his arms and nodded. "Painting. That's pretty obvious. Are you still painting your nightmares, Sage? On the nights we're not together? Or, for that matter, on the nights we are together? I admit I sleep like a log; you could be getting up to paint and I'd never know it. Is painting the only way you're attempting to treat your PTSD?"

Now she folded her arms. He'd hit a nerve and her defenses were rising. "You're awfully nosy, Rafferty."

"I love you. I want to help you."

Then stop pressing me, she wanted to say. Instead, she snapped, "By signing me up for yoga?"

"I did some reading about how to help loved ones with PTSD. It suggested practicing relaxation techniques. I thought yoga would be a place to start, although Angel's Rest offers a number of classes you could take that might help."

Oh, Colt. He really was so sweet. If only he would understand that the shadows were too dark, too ugly. She couldn't go there by herself yet, and she'd be hanged if she'd drag anyone along with her. "I appreciate the effort, and maybe during the winter I'll give the classes a try. I'm too busy now. Besides, a walk along the lakeshore with Snowdrop relaxes me just fine."

"All right, then." He lifted his chin and forged ahead. "What about therapy? I have the name of a doctor who—"

"No," she interrupted, as the suggestion left her cold. Yoga was one thing, having therapy was another. Look what it had done for her in the past. *Daddy, I need to tell you something.* "Just drop it, Colt."

"No, I won't." He raked his fingers through his hair in frustration. "It's obvious you need more help than you are currently receiving. Everything I've read and everyone I've spoken to has emphasized how important therapy is to someone suffering from PTSD."

Now he'd pricked her anger. "I'm not going to discuss this with you. It's my past and my problem."

"You told me enough to know it's ugly, Sage. Until you deal with it, with all of it, it will only get uglier. I'm not asking that you tell me—although I'd listen if that's what you wanted. I'm asking that you talk to someone."

"No."

"Why not? I don't understand?"

"You don't need to understand," she fired back, flinging out a hand in emphasis. Then she pointed toward herself as she added, "This is *my* health we're talking about. *My* problem."

"Your problems are my problems now." He stepped toward her. "That's what happens when you love someone."

"Don't you understand?" She slapped both hands against her head. "That's exactly what I've tried to avoid. I don't want my problems to be your problems. I don't want to drag you into my darkness."

"Then let me lead you into my light, Sage," he said, his beautiful blue eyes warm and pleading. "Let me help you. Let a doctor help you."

"No! Drop it, Colt. I'm not going into therapy. I tried it. It didn't work for me." That, she thought, might be the understatement of the century.

She wasn't lying. She had entered therapy soon after she returned to the States, putting herself through six weeks of hell that culminated in the visit to her father.

Colt, being Colt, refused to let the subject go. Over the next ten days, he pressed her, cajoled her, and used both valid arguments and ridiculous ones in his attempts to ferret out her reasons for standing firm against his wishes. She explained as best she could manage, but the more they talked, the more frustrated they both grew. Finally, one evening after they'd attended the summer theater production of Eternity Springs' own Cellar Bride mystery and were walking to the Taste of Texas creamery to feed Colt's rocky road habit, he brought the subject up one too many times, and Sage let him have it. "Stop it. I refuse to listen to it one more time. If you so much as whisper the word *therapy* one more time, I swear, I'm going to scream."

"Now, that's not necessary."

"You're bullying me, Rafferty and I don't like it."

"Bullying? I'm not bullying you."

They bickered back and forth for blocks until Sage had completely lost her appetite for ice cream. It was the closest thing they'd had to a fight since they'd known each other. He wouldn't budge on this. And neither would she.

When the ringing of his cellphone interrupted his latest harangue, Sage was glad to give her ears a rest. Scowling, he fished the phone from his pocket, thumbed the appropriate button, and snapped, "Rafferty."

Sage caught her breath when the color drained from his face, leaving him ashen. Something bad had happened. Another industrial accident? He'd told her the other day that his old team was enjoying an unusually long stretch without incidents. Sage hated to think about what might have occurred. Seeing his reaction brought home to her how difficult his job must have been.

He listened for a full minute without speaking, his hand holding the receiver against his ear with a white-knuckled grip. "When did this happen?" he finally asked. "How many were hurt? . . . Okay. I will. Of course I will. I'll leave right away."

Then he closed his eyes and his voice cracked as he added, "Hang on, brother. She'll make it. She's a strong little girl."

Brother?

When he hung up the phone, he stood frozen in place for a long minute. He looked dazed and shocked, as if he'd aged five years. Sage placed a hand on his arm. "What happened?"

"My niece." His voice sounded strangled. "She and a

bunch of kids were on the way to church camp in a bus. A semi lost control and hit them. Two dead, fourteen injured, six of those critical. Rachel is one of those. The critical."

"Oh, Colt." Sage's heart twisted. "That's terrible. I'm so sorry."

He dragged a hand down his face. "I need to get to Texas as fast as I can. They're in a little podunk hospital in East Texas, but they'll be moving her as soon as possible. Most likely to Dallas. I gotta get to the airport."

He did an about-face and began walking back toward Creekside Cabins, where he'd left his car.

Almost running to keep up with his long-legged stride, she said, "What can I do to help?"

"Maybe call—" He stopped abruptly and jerked his head around. He focused on her, the look in his eyes fierce and intent. "You're a doctor. A pediatric surgeon."

Oh no. "Not anymore."

"Come with me, Sage."

No. No. No. "I'm not licensed to practice in Texas."

He waved that off, his expression desperate. "It's an emergency, but beyond that, I'm not asking you to practice medicine."

He took hold of her hand and started walking again. He thought aloud, obviously relieved to think that he had her—a pediatric surgeon—on his side. "It's perfect. You'll know what questions to ask, help us make decisions. The other families, too."

He expects me to come. He's not even considering otherwise. "Colt . . ."

"Too bad Jack Davenport isn't in town," he said. "He could give us a ride in his helicopter. We couldn't drive to Crested Butte in time to catch a flight out tonight. We'll drive to Colorado Springs. I wonder if we can get a flight to Dallas tonight." He sighed heavily. "It's at times like this I really miss my assistant. Amy would know . . . shoot."

He pulled his phone back out of his pocket and dialed a number. A moment later, he said, "Yes, it's Colt. Amy, I'm in a bind and need a big favor. Could you do your magic and tell me the fastest way I can get from Eternity Springs, Colorado, to Palestine, Texas? I need two seats."

"Colt!" Sage attempted to interrupt him, but he either didn't hear her or chose to ignore her.

"Thanks a million. I . . . wait, I'm getting another call." He checked the number, then said, "Call me back when you know something, please, Amy?"

He thumbed the number, then said, "Hey, Dad. Yes, he called me. Amy is working on getting me there the fastest way possible right now."

He listened for a few minutes, then said, "Ah, no. I can't imagine what their families must be going through. I think—wait, I think Amy is beeping in. . . . Sure will, Dad. You too. See you tomorrow."

Then, "Amy, what do you have for me? . . . Okay . . . Okay . . . Really? All right, then, that's what we'll do. Thanks so much. I owe you one."

He disconnected the call as they arrived at the Creekside Cabins. "Amy said we'd probably get there faster if we drive. Or if we drive as far as Amarillo tonight, we can catch a plane from there to Dallas tomorrow morning. If they haven't transferred Rachel by then, we'll rent a car and drive the rest of the way."

He finally fell silent as he fished his keys from his pocket and ran up the steps to his cabin's front door. Sage decided to wait until they were inside with some privacy to make him listen to her.

In the cabin, Colt headed straight for the bedroom and the closet with his duffel bag. "I'd rather not waste too much time packing. We can buy what we need once we get to Texas. Ah, jeez, Sage, all those kids. Imagine how afraid they must have been. How afraid they are now."

No, I won't. I know how children look when they are afraid. When they're bleeding. When they are dead.

"My brother and his wife are driving to east Texas now. Our folks are on vacation with some friends in New York, and they're going to fly out first thing in the morning. I think . . . oh, wait." Colt's gaze snagged on Shadow's bed on the floor beside his bed. "What'll we do with the dogs? Can Nic board them for us?"

At the moment, both Snowdrop and Shadow were at the doggie day care facility at Angel's Rest. Although it did have a manager, as the local veterinarian, Nic oversaw the operation.

Sage drew in a deep breath and said, "No."

"Why not? Are they full?"

"No, I can't go to Texas with you. I'm sorry, Colt, but I just can't."

This time, finally, he heard her. He turned around and met her gaze, his own eyes shocked and confused. "Why not?"

She tried not to babble, but she feared she only halfway succeeded at that. "This is what I've been trying to tell you, hoping to make you see. I'm too screwed up, Colt. I can't go be around injured children. I can't do it."

His mouth gaped open in disbelief, then he snapped his jaw shut. "Sure you can. You're stronger than you think. You need to do this."

"I'm sorry. I can't."

"They're little kids, Sage."

"I know. I can't do it."

He briefly closed his eyes, then pinned her with a pleading gaze. His voice cracking, he said, "I need you, Sage. Please."

She wanted to scream and throw something. She

wanted to fling herself on the bed and sob. She hated herself. Despised herself. This was the best man in the world. The man she loved. She was letting him down when he needed her the most.

A hospital filled with injured children. Crying children. Dying children. *Jesus loves me, this I know.*

"I'm sorry."

Anger tightened his expression and bitterness filled his tone. "Fine. Whatever. I don't have time for this."

Turning away from her, he threw clothes into his duffel bag and gathered his toiletries from the bathroom. Sage stood watching him, tears rolling down her face, wishing she was different, wishing she could let her memories go. She offered him the only thing she had to give. "You could call me. You could fax records and I'll study them. I'll answer any questions you might—"

"No. I'll find someone else."

With that, he zipped up his bag and was gone.

Colt didn't want to think about Sage and he didn't want to think about Rachel, and with a fifteen-hour drive ahead of him, he didn't want to be alone, either. So he did the only thing he knew to do to address the problem—he stopped by the doggie day care to pick up Shadow.

He wasn't prepared to arrive and find his dog sitting calmly in a tub of water, his body covered with bubbly white suds. Celeste Blessing wore yellow gloves and held a soft bristled brush in her hand.

"Celeste?"

"Hello, Colt. Oh, dear. You are earlier than I expected. I'm afraid I took your Shadow for a walk and he managed to persuade me to allow him to play in a mud puddle. He was just so darned cute about it that I didn't have the heart to tell him no. I thought I'd have time to get him all spruced up before you arrived to pick him up. I thought for sure you'd stop for ice cream after the play."

"No. Something came up. Let me help you get him rinsed off. I'm in a hurry."

"Settle down, son. I'll have him finished in five minutes. You can wait that long. Now, tell me why you're in a hurry. Is something wrong?"

"Everything is wrong," he grimly replied. In a dozen curt sentences, he summed up the evening's events, finishing with, "I shouldn't blame her. She's told me all along that she was damaged beyond repair. Guess I should have listened to her."

"Now, Colt, that doesn't sound like you." Celeste gently scrubbed Shadow's coal-black fur. The dog sat amazingly quiet in the washtub. "You are not going to quit on her, are you?"

"She quit on me," he fired back. "She won't even try to get help. I've asked and asked and I've given and given and given. Tonight I needed her and she gave me nothing in return. What sort of a relationship is that?"

"One that is in crisis, I would say." Finished with sudsing, she transferred his puppy to a basin of clean water and began to rinse the suds from Shadow's coat. "I'd also point out that Sage is making an effort for you. Emotional healing is not a broken leg. It does not happen on a timetable. She has made great strides in recent months. In Sage's case, however, it takes many little baby steps to cover the distance, so it's not always as obvious."

He closed his eyes. "She told me once that she's in a deep, dark well and she's not at all certain she'll be able to climb out."

"And yet you fell in love with her anyway. Or did you? Because if you truly loved Sage, I don't think you'd turn your back on her at the first sign of trouble."

"She turned her back on me," he shot back, temper heating the words. Furious and frustrated and afraid, he added, "I've tried with her, tried so hard. But it doesn't matter one damned bit. She won't let me or anyone help her. She quit. She quit on me."

"Did she? Really? Or did you ask too much of her too soon? I understand that Sage has let you down. Knowing Sage, she feels terrible for having done so. But you are not without some responsibility here. Be honest with yourself, Colt. You pursued her. You set out to win her. You pushed her. Sage fell in love with you despite her best intentions. She resisted you because she knew she wasn't ready. She knew that she still had a ways to go in her recovery. Now that circumstances have proved as much, it could be argued that if you walk away from her now, you have let her down as much as she has you."

With that, Celeste lifted Shadow from the rinse tub, set him on the floor, then leaned away while he shook. She picked up a fluffy white towel and briskly dried him off.

Colt sighed heavily, closed his eyes, and grimaced. "I don't know, Celeste. I'm too shaken up over Rachel to be able to think clearly."

"That's understandable. All I ask is that when you are able to consider your relationship with Sage, you take into account what I have mentioned here tonight. Fair enough?"

"Fair enough."

Celeste lifted Shadow into her arms and gave him a hug. Then she lifted his snout and stared into the puppy's big brown eyes. "You be a good boy on the trip, Shadow. You take care of your daddy. If he starts to get sleepy, paw at him. If he drives too long without taking a break, bark at him. If he gets too sad, climb up and give him your sweet little puppy kisses."

"I can do without dog slobber."

"I disagree. A person can never have too many kisses from someone who loves them. Now, go. Drive safely, and keep us posted on little Rachel's condition, okay?"

"I will."

Celeste handed the dog over to him, and Colt had to admit that the slight delay had been worth it. Shadow smelled a hundred percent better. He'd be a much more pleasant traveling companion. They headed for the door, where Colt paused and looked back at Celeste. "Thanks for everything, Celeste."

"You're very welcome."

"Can I ask you for one more favor?"

"Absolutely."

"Will you pray for us? For Rachel and my brother and sister-in-law?"

"Consider it done. And Colt, I have faith that little Rachel will fully recover from her injuries. Be at ease. I have good instincts about things like this."

"From your mouth to God's ear, Celeste."

She smiled indulgently. "Consider it done. Godspeed, Colt Rafferty."

NINETEEN

᪥

Sage lay on Colt's bed at the Creekside Cabins for a full hour after he left, sobbing her heart out into his pillow. She hated herself. Despised herself. Any doubts she'd had that she was indeed a horrible person had been laid to rest this evening. She was mean and awful and terrible and cruel and selfish and self-centered. She was every bad adjective in the language. She was making this all about her when it was really about Rachel and the rest of the injured children. The children. Innocent, trusting, fragile. Helpless. "Children," she wept.

She cried so hard and so long that she never heard the knock on the door, didn't notice the whoosh of evening breeze sweep through the room as the door opened. Didn't register the whispered, "Oh, for heaven's sake."

What finally got through to her was the wet rasp of a tongue against her tearstained cheeks. She opened her eyes to see Snowdrop's precious little face. Sage let out a little groan and hugged her dog tight, launching into another round of heart-sore sobs that lasted a good five minutes. Finally, it filtered through her head that Snowdrop hadn't found her way here all by herself. She opened her eyes expecting to see Celeste or Nic or maybe even Sarah. "Rose?"

Her sister sat at the bottom corner of the bed. "What's the matter, Goober?"

Her use of the old childhood nickname registered. In

that moment, Sage was just weak enough—or perhaps strong enough—to reach out to her sister. "Something horrible happened in Africa, Rose. Something so horrific that it haunts me still. I can't be around children and blood. I just can't."

Then she told her about the bus accident, Colt's request, and her refusal. "I am pathetic, Rose. Just pathetic. No wonder you hate me."

"I don't hate you, Sage," Rose insisted. "I miss you."

Sage looked up at her, tears flowing, and Rose reached out and tucked a loose strand of hair behind Sage's ear. "I think we got crossways when Dad died and we were both too wounded to be able to straighten the situation out. After that, well, we've always been hardheaded. We dug in with our positions and neither one of us was willing to give."

"You tried. You came to Eternity Springs. You're here."

"Five years after the fact." Tears pooled in her sister's eyes as she added, "I'm ashamed it took me this long to be ready to listen."

Sage bowed her head. "I don't think I'm ready to talk. Even after five years. I'm broken, Rose. Tonight proves it. I let Colt down. He's so wonderful, such a good man. I love him and I let him down."

"Oh, honey. The only thing tonight proves is that the mental health canyon you fell into is deeper than any of us realized. It's going to take longer than we'd like for you to climb your way out of it, but I know you, Sage Anderson. You're not a quitter. If Colt loves you as much as he claims, then he'll find some patience."

Sage swallowed the lump of emotion in her throat. "I let him down tonight."

"He asked too much of you tonight."

"He doesn't know that. I've told him some of what happened, but not the worst of it."

"Could you tell me?"

She closed her eyes, swallowed the lump in her throat, and shook her head. "I can't. I've tried to talk about it. I did one time, I told one person, and it was horrible. It only made things worse."

"You told a therapist?"

"No." Sage met her sister's gaze with a pleading stare. "I told Dad."

Rose sat back, and Sage could see her mental wheels turning. Long seconds ticked by before she asked, "Can you tell me about that?"

"He lashed out at me, Rose. He said some things that haunt me to this day." With this, tears began to flow freely again. "He told me to quit crying about it and to put it behind me and soldier on. He told me not to be a coward. That was our final conversation. He was ashamed of me, Rose. He was my hero and I let him down and now I've let Colt down. I hate myself!"

Rose sat back. "So, that's why you didn't come to the hospital when I asked."

"He wouldn't have wanted me there."

Rose dropped her head into her hands and groaned. "Oh, Goobs. Now it makes sense. I could never understand, but now it's clear as the water in Angel Creek."

"I'm sorry I let you down, too, Rose."

Rose reached for her sister and gave her a fierce hug. "Right back at you. I wasn't there when you needed me, and that kills me. But listen. I'm here now, and I want to say a couple of things. And you need to hear them. First, about Dad. This thing you can't talk about. You were traumatized in some manner, weren't you?"

Sage nodded, and Rose continued. "Do you remember that time I cut my finger while peeling potatoes with a kitchen knife?"

"You had to get eight stitches."

"Yep. Do you remember what Dad did?"

Sage thought about it. "Yeah, I do. He took you to the ER."

"That's right. Because he couldn't stitch me himself."

"He was too busy yelling at you."

"Oh, yes. My ears hurt as much as my hand. I don't know if you'll remember this, but he did try to treat me at home. He couldn't hold his hands still. Do you know why?"

"Because you were careless?"

"No, because he was afraid. The big, bad Colonel was scared, and when he got scared, he attacked. That's what he did. Later he apologized to me and asked my forgiveness. He said he was frightened for me, and that's how he reacted when he was afraid."

"That's stupid."

"That's a man for you. Sage, I'll bet my favorite pair of flats that whatever you told Dad—if it was as awful for you as I think it must have been—scared him. Rather than giving you the comfort you needed, he reacted to his fear for his little girl."

"No, he wouldn't . . ." Sage's voice trailed off. Hope flickered to life inside her and she added, "Do you really think he . . . ?"

"Yeah, I really do."

The sisters sat without speaking for a bit. Sage mulled over all that Rose had said. She'd love to believe it was true, that her father hadn't died thinking her a coward. It would lift such a burden from her soul and be her own personal miracle.

She looked at Rose. Her sister would have made it happen. "Why did you come here tonight?"

She shrugged. "Celeste asked me to bring Snowdrop to you."

"I'm glad you did." Sage licked her lips. "Rose, can you tell me about your diagnosis? I've been so worried about you."

With that, Rose's tears overflowed. Then, physician to physician, sister to sister, and woman to woman, Rose explained first the clinical aspects of her cancer and treatment, then the personal ones.

"Oh, Sage," she said, her voice cracking. "They had to take my uterus. I'll never have the babies I wanted. I let Brandon convince me to put the marriage off, and at the first sign of sickness, he bailed on me. Now he's married to someone else and has a baby on the way."

"He's scum. A selfish, scurrilous cad."

Rose snorted a laugh. "You still read historical romances, I see."

"Not to say I told you so, but I told you so. I really couldn't stand him." Now Sage was the one who reached for her sister and held her tight. "I'm so sorry. Cancer is such an evil disease. It's not fair. You should have had your babies. I know how badly you wanted them."

Pulling back, she added, "Maybe someday you'll hear something from the registry."

Rose shut her eyes, visibly flinching at Sage's oblique reference to the child she'd given up for adoption. "I'm afraid I've lost my faith in miracles."

"That's okay." Sage drew a deep breath and reflected on the momentous, stupendous changes she'd experienced within the past hour. Then her thoughts turned to Colt and dreams that might not be dead after all. "I have enough faith in them for us both."

Colt entered Children's Medical Center in Dallas on a run. He'd been in constant contact with his brother during the drive, and Jason had told him exactly where to go. Rachel was in surgery, still.

When the bus rolled over, she'd gone flying and landed on her head. She'd told a first responder that she'd heard her neck go pop. When she went to get up, her arms wouldn't move. X-rays revealed broken bones in her neck pressed against the spinal cord. The ligaments, joints, and a disc were injured. One of four main arteries that feeds the brain was kinked.

"They took great care with her neck while transporting her, thank God," Jason had told Colt while he waited to board his flight at the airport in Amarillo. "Her pediatric neurosurgeon says that had she moved any more, she would have compressed the spinal cord to the point that she would have functional loss."

"And that means . . . ?"

"She would have been paralyzed from the neck down."

Those words had haunted Colt the rest of the trip. The last time he'd seen his niece she'd been playing tag with the neighborhood kids.

At the doorway to the waiting room, he hesitated. His sister-in-law, Ann, sat in a chair, her arms wrapped around herself, rocking, staring unseeing into space. Jason stood staring out a window, his hands shoved into his pockets. He'd aged ten years since Colt had seen him last.

Colt sucked in a bracing breath, then stepped into the waiting room. "Ann? Jason?"

Ann flew from her seat and into his arms. She mumbled mostly unintelligible words against his chest, though he did make out "Glad you're here."

He met his brother's tortured gaze, and asked, "What's the latest?"

"Nothing new since we hung up. Thanks for coming, Colt."

"I wouldn't be anywhere else."

The waiting was misery. The doctors had warned Rachel's parents to expect a lengthy surgery, but the wait seemed like days. Especially when her loved ones knew that the operation carried significant risks. Moving even a few millimeters during surgery could injure her spinal cord or cause the kinked artery to push a clot into her brain, resulting in a stroke. Yet surgery had been her only option.

Every so often, a nurse arrived with updates. Each time the Raffertys spotted her face through the window in the door to the surgical suite, they held their collective breath. After the third such event, Colt realized that seeing the nurse was a good sign. If something bad happened, it would be the doctor who came out to meet them.

When the surgery passed the six-hour mark, Ann let out a frustrated wail: "Why is it taking so long?" Then she burst into tears.

Her husband sat beside her, took her into his arms, and spoke quietly, reassuring her, drawing strength from her and offering her his. They leaned on each other, supported each other during this, the most challenging moment of their lives. Watching the couple, Colt was reminded that this was what he wanted in a relationship. Shared burdens were eased burdens. Why couldn't Sage see that?

Seven hours after the surgery began, Rachel's doctor walked into the waiting room, a big smile on his face. Seeing it, a knot of tension released inside Colt.

"She did great," the surgeon said. "We're not out of the woods yet, but I have to say I'm much more optimistic than I was the first time I saw her X-rays."

He summarized the procedure in detail, then ended by saying, "So she has a titanium plate, ten screws, and two rods in the back of her neck to hold it in place. We won't know how badly the spinal cord has been damaged for a while yet. The next seventy-two hours will be key."

"What about the stroke risk?" Jason Rafferty asked.

The doctor hesitated. "I'll feel better about everything after those seventy-two hours."

"Can we see her?" Ann asked.

The doctor nodded. "One at a time and only for a few minutes."

After Rachel's parents spent their allotted time with her, Colt paid a brief visit, then almost wished he hadn't. Seeing her lying in bed, pale and immobilized, all but broke his heart. He could only imagine how Jason and Ann felt.

He'd spent his fair share of time in hospitals as part of his job, and the visits had all been tough. This was different. Having the patient in the bed be one of your own took the horror to a whole other level. He wanted this child to recover, to walk again, to continue those piano lessons she'd begun at the beginning of summer. Most of all, he wanted her to live.

Blinking back the wetness that pooled in his eyes, he gently placed his hand atop hers. "You be a fighter, Rach. We are all counting on that. I love you, sweet pea."

The nurse shooed him out of the recovery room, and he found his brother and sister-in-law in each other's arms once again. This time, Jason was the one who'd broken down and Ann the one offering comfort. Again, thoughts of Sage whispered across his mind. He wished she were here.

Had he expected too much of her? Was Celeste right? Maybe so, but that didn't negate the fact that he needed her with him. He could use a shoulder to lean on right now. Hospitals were lousy places to visit alone. Shoot, he didn't even have his dog to support him—Shadow was now boarded at a vet clinic that Nic had arranged for him not far from the hospital.

What's with the pity party, Rafferty? Stop it. Just stop it. Rachel didn't stroke out, and she might have dodged the paralysis bullet. You should be on your knees thanking the good Lord.

He gave his head a shake. He was getting loopy. Standing, he dragged a hand down his face and spoke to his brother. "I'm going to hunt up some caffeine. Can I bring you guys anything?"

Jason looked at his wife, who shook her head. "Maybe a soda?" he asked.

"Sure."

As Colt roamed the hospital halls, his thoughts drifted back to his old job. How many hospitals had he visited over the years? Dozens, certainly. He'd done hundreds of interviews. But very few of children. Never in a children's hospital. He couldn't imagine working around seriously ill children all day, every day. It would wear down a man's soul.

Or a woman's. *Ah, Sage.*

The stained-glass windows of the hospital chapel caught his attention, and something compelled him to open the door and step inside. He was surprised to see Rachel's surgeon sitting on a pew in the middle of the chapel, his head bowed.

Colt sat in a pew across the aisle from the physician. A moment later, the man finished his prayer and looked at Colt who hesitantly asked, "Everything okay, Doc? Something you're not telling us?"

The doctor gave a tired, crooked grin. "I'm a religious man. I saw something today that reaffirms those beliefs."

"What's that?"

"This is no promise, Mr. Rafferty, and time may very well prove me wrong. Ninety-nine times out of a hundred, patients with the sort of injury Rachel suffered are paralyzed. In this case, I am convinced that God wrapped his hands around her spinal cord while those bones went flying everywhere. I think she'll walk again. I may be wrong. Like I said, this is no promise, but I feel very positive about her chances."

"Thanks, Doc. I'm beginning to feel that same way, too. She has lots of people praying for her." An image of Celeste surrounded by her collection of angel figurines in a room at Angel's Rest flashed through his mind, and he silently repeated the words he'd spoken before leaving Eternity Springs: *From your mouth to God's ear.* "I think our prayers are being heard."

Forty-eight hours later, with her mother, father, grandparents, and uncle Colt at her bedside, Rachel Rafferty wiggled her toes. Overcome by emotion, Colt turned away to collect himself and gazed out of the room's window which overlooked the hospital's front entrance.

Sage stood facing the front doors. He blinked, looked again, and decided that yes, she was there. He wasn't seeing things. She wore a yellow sundress, and she had that waterfall of auburn hair piled atop her head. She held her sunglasses by the earpiece and twirled them in a slow circle as she stared at the hospital entrance.

"I'll be right back," he said to his family, although no one noticed, their complete focus on the miracle child in the bed.

He had to wait an agonizingly long time for the elevator, and when he finally reached the ground floor, he dashed for the front door, burst outside, and gazed about frantically.

Sage wasn't there.

He hurried back into the hospital and stopped at the visitors' desk. "Did a woman just ask for a room number for my niece, Rachel Rafferty? A beautiful, redhaired woman? She's wearing a yellow dress. It would have been in the past few minutes."

"No, sir," a pleasant older lady responded with a smile. "No one has entered the hospital in the past few minutes. My shift is over and my husband is on his way to pick me up. I've been watching the doors."

"Thanks." Colt hurried back outside. He studied the

entrance area, walked the parking lot, even tried calling her cellphone, but the call went straight to voice mail. Sage was gone.

"But she tried," he murmured, a smile playing on his lips. "She tried."

TWENTY

At her cottage beside Hummingbird Lake, Sage's phone rang. She picked it up and heard Sarah Reese say, "He's back. I was coming out of the post office and I saw him drive by. He smiled and waved. Looked like he was headed for the Creekside Cabins."

"Okay, then." Sage exhaled a heavy breath. "He'll find my note. I have to call Rose. Thanks for the heads-up."

"Good luck, girlfriend."

Sage placed the call, and her sister answered on the first ring. Two minutes later the arrangements were completed, and Sage ducked into the bathroom, freshened her makeup and brushed her hair, then checked on Snowdrop, who lay snoozing on her bed in the laundry room beside the spinning dryer, one of her favorite places in the house. Then she exited the cottage and headed for her own favorite place, the private fishing pier on Hummingbird Lake at the tip of Reflection Point.

A quarter of an hour later she heard the car. Since she trusted Rose to have briefed Colt on her intentions, she kept focused on the effort at hand. When she heard footsteps on the pier behind her, she braced herself and darted a quick look.

Rose's eyes appeared anxious, her smile encouraging. For almost the first time since she'd known him, Colt's expression remained unreadable. *Well, at least he came.*

Sage turned, focused on the water, blew out a breath, and began. "First, I need to tell you, Colt, that I'm so happy to hear that your niece will recover from her injuries. Celeste passed along the good news.

"Now, I'm going to talk about Africa, and I'm asking you both not to interrupt me. Rose doesn't know the beginning of the story, so first I need to bring her up to speed."

Besides, she'd told this part of the story before. She knew she could do it. *It'll be a good lead-in to the rest of it.* In a quiet, steady tone, she recited the events of the day she had dug the bullet out of Ban Ntaganda, thus saving his life. When she finished, she said, "Would you two come sit beside me?"

"Sure, honey," Rose said, her voice heavy with emotion. She gave Sage's right shoulder a squeeze and took a seat beside her. Sage noticed then that she wore flip-flops decorated with silk sunflowers. That was a new look for her sister.

Colt didn't speak, but he took a seat on her left. He had removed his shoes at some point, and now he allowed his feet to dangle in the cold waters of Hummingbird Lake. Sage let out the breath she'd been holding. He'd come this far. Maybe he would listen to her later, too, when she explained that she had at least tried to join him in Texas.

The scent of wood smoke swirled in the air as Sage clasped her sister's hand, then hesitantly offered her other hand to Colt. When after a moment he took it, she closed her eyes, and something within her relaxed. He was here. Despite everything, he was here for her. *I just might be able to do this.*

Then, for the first time ever, Sage consciously returned her thoughts to that violent day that had changed her life forever.

"It was our second day in the village. We'd arrived

shortly before dark the previous day, Peter and me and three nurses, two men and a woman from England. We set up shop in the two-room missionary school and were working before the sun was fully up. We treated cuts and colds and infections. Midmorning, a man ran in and told us his wife was in labor and having trouble. They lived in another village, but once he heard we were there, the husband had borrowed a truck and brought her to us. She'd been in labor three days and was weakening."

Sage took a deep breath and allowed herself to remember.

Shimmering waves of heat rose from the dusty, parched earth and danced to the tune of "This Little Light of Mine" sung by children in the mission school as Sage slipped her arm around the laboring woman, supporting her through the pain of her labor. The summer sun beat down upon them, cruel and unrelenting. Sweat rolled down Sage's face, stinging her eyes as she said to the newcomers, "Let's get into the building and I'll take a look."

If the situation was as the father claimed, she'd be prepping this woman for a C-section within minutes. She'd prefer to avoid it if possible, but if this labor truly had lasted three days, it needed to end.

Blankets draped over a rope stretched between two beams shielded the laboring mother as Sage performed a quick examination. This baby was in the breech position and in distress, and the mother was fading. "I have to do a C-section here," she called out to the other medical professionals in the room. "Can one of you assist me?"

Peter joined her and they went about preparing the setting to be as clean as possible. This was, she thought, man versus nature at its most basic. If left to nature, both this baby and her mother would die. They might yet—infections in this part of the world were common and brutal—but at least with her help, they had a fighting chance.

This was why she'd become a doctor, why she volunteered with DWB. Her calling, her passion, her joy was to save lives.

In some part of her subconscious, amidst the sound of children now singing "Jesus Loves Me" next door, she noted the noise of arriving vehicles, though she remained focused on the task at hand. Peter administered anesthetic to her patient and she picked up her scalpel.

"Yes, Jesus loves me."

The procedure itself would take but a few minutes. She placed the scalpel against the skin and made the cut.

Shouting. Angry voices. Echoes of an argument, she surmised, paying them little mind.

"Yes, Jesus loves me."

As a surgeon at work, she dared not allow her attention to wander. If she stopped, they'd die.

"Yes, Jesus loves me."

"What's that?" Peter asked as his big, tanned hand dabbed the seeping blood away with white gauze. "Sounds like a fight."

"What?" Sage lifted the child—a girl—from her mother's womb.

"The Bible tells me so."

With sharp, shining scissors, Peter cut the umbilical cord.

The bullet struck him in the forehead and blew off the back of his head.

From that moment on, seconds passed like days. Before Sage could even process what had happened, before Peter's body toppled to the floor, before the new life in her arms let out its first cry, the room was overrun with men wielding guns and machetes and shouting loudly.

Pop pop pop. Rat-a-tat-a-tat. "No!" cried one of the

British nurses. "Please, don't. Please, I have children. I—" Rat-a-tat-a-tat.

The baby breathed and cried and Sage brought her up to her chest, cradling her against her own bosom. She saw the gun barrel turn her way. Funny how smoke curled up from the end of the gun that way. The black hole.

The children next door were crying and screaming. Rat-a-tat-a-tat. Sage started to sing, "Jesus loves me, this I—"

A gruff voice shouted, "No. Halt. She's Dr. Sage."

The gun lowered. The baby continued to cry.

Outside, the blended sounds of gunfire and screams abruptly cut off intensified.

The gruff-voiced man grabbed hold of her arm and dragged her away. Sage turned her head and looked back at Peter's body just as the machete came down on the neck of her patient, mercifully still asleep from the anesthetic. Her arms clasped the child more firmly in reflex. So tiny. So helpless. So innocent.

Outside, she saw two flatbed trucks stopped in the center of the road in the middle of the village and . . . carnage. Blood splattered the hard-baked earth. Bodies lay everywhere. Men. Women.

Children.

The volume of gunfire, of screams, decreased. For the most part, the screams had gone silent. All around her, villagers lay either dying or dead. The physician in Sage told her to run to the injured, to attempt to save the dying. The punishing grip around her upper arm wouldn't allow it.

One by one, the Zaraguinas returned to the trucks, lining up behind them, good little tin soldiers all. She saw one villager alive and standing, a boy of about eleven or twelve. He didn't appear to be afraid, but rather in shock, unable to comprehend the butchery *that he'd witnessed. Sage suspected her own expression looked the same.*

Now the gunshots came in singular pops, moving from the far end of the village toward her. The baby in her arms found her own fist, and sucking it quieted her cries.

The sun baked down. Sage sang softly,"Yes, Jesus loves me. Yes, Jesus loves me."

The passenger-side door of one of the trucks opened. A man stepped outside. Ban Ntaganda.

Sage's gaze dropped to his left leg as he sauntered toward her. No limp. She'd done a good job. She hummed the children's hymn softly as her body trembled.

The stench of death filled the air as he stopped ten feet from her. His gaze raked her up and down. "Dr. Sage. You saved my life. I return the favor."

Sage closed her eyes in Africa.

In Eternity Springs, Colorado, she opened her eyes and said, "They took the boy with them, the eyewitness, to announce the massacre, which was punishment for the village elders having refused to pay the demanded tribute to the rebels. Cattle. They'd asked for twelve head of cattle. The village leaders refused because those cattle were the source of income for the village. So Ntaganda murdered everyone in the village. Men. Women. The children in the mission school. Everyone except for their witness and me. We were the only ones left."

"The newborn?" Rose asked, horror in her tone.

Sage realized then that her sister had been squeezing her hand hard. She shook her head. That part she couldn't say. She couldn't bear to go there in her mind, and she never would.

She stole a glance at Colt. He stared straight out at the lake, his lips set in a straight, firm line, his expression as hard as granite. But his hand held hers with tender, gentle care.

She swallowed hard. "I don't know how long I stood there. I've never heard such quiet in my life. Utter stillness. No animal sounds. No birds. Nothing. Everything was silent." She drew a deep breath, then exhaled harshly. "Until the flies began to buzz."

"What did you do, Sage?" Colt asked, his voice raspy. "How did you get out of there?"

"The missionaries had a radio. I sent out a mayday. It took two days for someone to show up." Sage released Colt's and Rose's hands, then rubbed her eyes.

"You were there with all those bodies? All alone?" Rose cupped her hands over her mouth. "Oh my God, Sage. I can't imagine. The heat . . . the stench. What did you do?"

There simply weren't words to describe it. In fact, she was fairly certain that she'd blocked a lot of the time out. So she simply said, "I waited. They finally came and, well, that's my story, the source of my, well, weirdness."

"It isn't weirdness. You lived through something unspeakable. Something so horrible, I can't even begin to wrap my brain around it. I'm so, so sorry." Rose threw her arms around her sister and hugged her hard, then leaned back. "And you told this to Dad?"

Wearily, Sage nodded. "I did. He's the only one I told."

"And he reacted poorly. Shame on him. But after hearing this, I'm more certain than ever that he simply couldn't handle the hurt he felt for you. Then before he could make it up to you, he had the stroke."

"If you're right and he was upset about me, maybe the extra stress . . . ?"

"Absolutely not." Rose shook her head. "His blood pressure was off the charts and had been for some time.

He and I discussed it because his treatment regimen wasn't proving effective, so don't add that worry onto your shoulders. They already have enough to bear."

Sage gave a little sigh of relief, and Rose continued, "This is the most horrible story I've ever heard. I'm so, so sorry you went through this, Sage. It's no wonder you laid down your scalpel and picked up a paintbrush. I'm amazed you came out of that village able to speak a coherent sentence. Going through what you went through would have driven me insane."

"I'm not mentally healthy."

"Maybe not entirely, but you're getting there. I think you took a great big step here today." Rose gave her sister another hug, then looked from Sage to Colt and back to Sage once more. "Now, I think I'll mosey back to Angel's Rest. I have a chapter to finish, and you two need to talk. Colt, you can find your own ride back to town, right?"

Continuing to stare blindly out at the water, Colt nodded. His voice sounded scratchy and rough when he replied, "Thanks, Rose."

Sage stole a glance at Colt, then said, "I'll walk you to your car."

Once the sisters were out of earshot of Colt, Sage asked, "Well, what did you have to promise him to convince him to come?"

"Nothing at all. He acted like he wanted to talk to you."

Glum, Sage kicked at a stone. "Probably can't wait to call things off between us."

"Now your self-pity is showing. Stop it. It's unattractive."

"It's not self-pity. It's sadness. I can't be the woman he needs and deserves."

"Sure you can," Rose scolded. "You took a big step

forward just now. You are healing, little sister. Slowly but surely. I am so proud of you. I admire you so much."

"I love you, Rose."

"I love you, too. And so does that man down by the lake. Have faith in him, Goober, and in yourself."

Sage sighed and smiled. "Are you ever going to quit calling me that stupid name?"

She is an amazing woman. Colt was shaken down to his core. *Poor, poor Cinnamon.* He'd known that whatever had her spooked was bad, but he'd never guessed it would be this horrific. And here he'd been pushing her into therapy. Who would want to talk about that? Who would want to remember it? No wonder she painted nightmares. She'd lived them.

He needed to move, to run, to exorcise the anger and the images her words had placed into his brain. His gaze landed on the rowboat tied at the end of their pier. That'd do. A minute later, he'd loosened the line, manned the oars, and headed out.

He rowed hard and long, digging the oars into the water, wishing the ungainly rowboat was a slim skiff that he could send skimming across the lake. As it was, he got the boat going a decent enough speed. Most important, he drained himself of the sharp edge of his anger. He could probably talk to Sage now without erupting like an idiot.

He was still furious, and if he could transport himself to Africa and stab this Ntaganda guy through the heart, he'd do it in an instant.

The world could be an evil place with evil people doing evil things. To think that gentle, tender-hearted Sage witnessed something like that, lived through something like that, made him want to howl to the moon.

Thinking about that poor newborn baby brought tears to his eyes.

Now he understood why delivering Nic's babies had caused such a reaction in Sage and why babysitting the pair had taken so much out of her. The woman had grit. Pure grit. He'd never admired her more. He'd never loved her more.

He gazed toward Reflection Point. Sage wasn't waiting for him on the pier. Okay, then. She'd probably gone looking for Snowdrop to hug. He'd hunt her down. He had something to say to her. Something he'd considered long and hard during the trip from Dallas back to Eternity Springs.

He rowed back to the pier, secured the boat, then walked with steady determination up to her cottage. There, he made a perfunctory knock on her back door, then stepped inside. He found her in her studio, working on a portrait of Snowdrop.

"No butterflies? Fairies?"

"Just Snowdrop."

"Comfort painting."

She smiled a little sadly, but didn't respond. Colt stepped farther into the room. He knew what he wanted to say, but he didn't know the best way to say it. Ease his way in, or just say it flat out? He watched her add a spot of white, a bit of light, to the chocolate brown of Snowdrop's eyes, and decided to jump into the deep end of Hummingbird Lake. "I love you, Sage Anderson. I want to spend my life with you. Make a family with you. Look at me, please?"

Slowly she turned, and their gazes met and held. "Marry me, Cinnamon. Let me be your soft place to fall."

The paintbrush slipped from her fingers and clattered to the floor. The pain in her eyes caused his stomach to drop to his knees. "Oh, Colt. Don't do this, please. I am nowhere ready for this. I am the most screwed-up person in the world. I let you down when you needed me the most. That's what I do. It's who I am. I'm trying to change, but who knows if I'll ever pull it off."

"I saw you outside the hospital."

Her eyes rounded. "You did?"

"It was a few minutes after Rachel first moved her toes. I ran down to find you, but you were gone."

"I stood out there for over an hour, Colt, but I couldn't make myself go inside. It perfectly illustrates my point. I travel all the way to Texas, but I can't go the last few steps. Like I said, I am the world's most screwed-up person."

"You survived, Sage."

"Yes, I did. I survived and I'm existing and I'm trying to learn to live again. But marriage?" She shook her head. "You're pushing me, Rafferty. You're always pushing."

"Yeah, I tend to do that. It's a fault of mine."

"Well, you need to back off. I'm not ready. I may never be ready. First I have to be whole."

"Fine, then." He folded his arms, lifted his chin, and shrugged. "I'll wait."

She lifted her face heavenward and let out a noise of frustration, "Arrgh! There you go again. Listen to me, Rafferty. I won't be pushed."

"I'm waiting. Waiting isn't pushing."

"From you it is."

"Wrong. This would be pushing." He crossed the room, dragged her into his arms, kissed her passionately, then tilted her chin and stared down into her dazed eyes. "Marry me, Sage. I want to wake up with you each morning and lie down with you each night. You bring color into my world and happiness into my heart. You complete me."

Tears pooled in her eyes and overflowed. "I hate you."

"I know," he murmured, kissing the salty wetness away. "Of course, that only makes you love me more."

She laughed sadly and wrapped her arms around his waist. "I need to see a therapist."

"I'm not touching that with a ten-foot pole."

Sighing heavily, she stepped away from him. "Rose knows someone with the Department of Veterans Affairs. A psychologist in Georgia. I flew there after I left Dallas and met with her twice."

"That's great news, Sage."

"She has a two-week vacation coming up. She had planned to go to Oregon, but Angel's Rest intrigued her, and she and I cut a deal. She said if I worked up enough gumption to tell you and Rose about Africa, then she'll spend a working vacation at Angel's Rest. She thinks we could accomplish a lot with a handful of face-to-face sessions followed up by phone calls."

"Excellent. What would you think about a December wedding?"

Sage doubled up her fist and punched him in the stomach. "Quit pushing. I mean it. We are not engaged!"

"All right, already. I'm not pushing. No pushing. I'm waiting. We're not engaged." After a moment's pause, he added a note of worry to his voice as he asked, "Are we still sleeping together?"

She folded her arms, rolled her eyes, and sighed with disgust. "Really now, Rafferty. What do you think? Just because I have a mental problem, it doesn't mean I'm stupid."

"I knew that." He swooped in and swept her up off her feet. Carrying her toward the bedroom, he said, "Let's see about a proper welcome home, shall we? I missed you."

"I missed you, too. I love you. I'm trying my best to beat this thing."

He laid her on her bed, then knelt over her. "Don't worry about it another minute. We have all the time in the world. I'm going to prove it to you. Tonight."

TWENTY-ONE

August arrived and with it, the annual summer arts festival. Every rental in town was booked, all the campgrounds reserved. Eternity Springs bustled with the arrival of artists and tourists, and townspeople simmered with excitement over the frequent and gratifying *kaching* of cash registers. Celeste's economic improvement plan was proving to be an extraordinary success.

It was always Sage's favorite week of the year, and this year she looked forward to it more than ever before. Colt was due back today from a two-week consulting trip to factories on the West Coast. She'd missed him terribly.

"You need to settle down," Sarah scolded as Sage checked the street yet again for a sign of his truck. "This is supposed to be our chance to relax."

"She's right," Ali Timberlake agreed. "I'm getting tired just watching you."

Sage, Nic, Ali, Sarah, and Celeste had met at the Mocha Moose for lunch prior to delivering the Patchwork Angels' entry into the textile competition. Judging would take place tomorrow, with the winners announced the day after that. Sage was convinced they'd at least place in the contest. Of course, as always, she was shooting for the blue ribbon.

"You guys shouldn't be surprised." Nic dipped a carrot stick in ranch dressing and took a crunchy bite. "She's this way every year before the judging."

Celeste asked, "Which painting did you decide to enter, dear?"

Sage's mouth twisted. Colt had urged her to hang one of her black-and-red paintings, and while she'd made progress since beginning therapy, she still had a ways to go. She wasn't about to show the world the black-and-reds. "I settled on the one of Snowdrop."

"I love that picture," Nic said.

"Me too," Sarah added. "You know, a real friend would paint Daisy and Duke for me as a pick-me-up since I'm so distraught over Lori leaving for college."

Sarah said it as a joke, but no one laughed. With the red-letter day less than a month away, Sarah had become as big a basket case as Sage. Ali sighed and said, "Why would she paint your dogs? If Sage does a painting for you, it should be of Lori. I sent Caitlin to the photographer for a set of going-off-to-college photos."

"I'd rather have my dogs," Sarah said glumly. "I get along with them. They still love me."

"Now, Sarah," Celeste scolded.

"Don't be stupid." Nic polished off her turkey sandwich with finger-licking pleasure. "Lori loves you. You love Lori. What we have here is separation anxiety in full swing."

"No." Sarah hooked her thumb toward Sage, who had risen to check the street for Colt's car once again. "That's separation anxiety."

"Stop it." Sage gave her hair a toss. "There's nothing wrong with missing the man I love."

"No, there's not," Celeste agreed. She dabbed her mouth with her napkin, then added, "Nothing wrong with marrying the poor man, either."

"Celeste!" Sage protested while the other women laughed.

Sarah stood and said, "This has been fun, but I need to get back to work. Let's go deliver our baby to the contest, then Nic can get back to her babies—"

"They're almost a year old," Nic said. "They're toddlers now."

"—and I can go argue with mine," Sarah finished. "If we wait too much longer, Colt will be back in town and Sage will be too busy making her baby to tag along with us to enter our quilt."

"I hate you," Sage said.

Sarah blew her a kiss as Nic lifted the quilt, folded and protected inside a pillowcase, from an empty chair. Celeste swiped the check off the table and said, "My treat."

As they exited the Mocha Moose, Sarah and Ali discussed their pending empty nests while Nic placed a phone call to Gabe checking on the girls. Sage refrained from calling Colt again for an updated ETA, but just barely. Soon they arrived at the remodeled old firehouse that served as the home of the Eternity Arts Association. The festival entries were being hung in the theater for judging before being moved to the exhibit tent when the festival opened. At the registration table, with fanfare, Celeste filled out the entry form for the Patchwork Angels' quilt, named *Journeys*. Sarah handed over the fifty-dollar entry fee.

The quilt was hung, lighting applied, and the group admired their work. Sage was as proud of the group project as she'd ever been of one of her own paintings. "We're gonna win the ribbon," she said. "You can bank on it."

With the quilt business done, Nic and Sarah departed, but Celeste lingered while Sage entered her painting of Snowdrop into the local artists competition. After it was hung, Celeste studied it and smiled. "Your love for that little dog shines in your work. Have you sketched Colt yet?"

Thinking of the nude pencil sketches she'd done without his knowledge while he lay sleeping, Sage opened her mouth to say no, but she couldn't lie to Celeste. "Artistic things. Nothing for public consumption."

Celeste chuckled, "Drawing nudes of the man? I'll bet they're . . . powerful."

Sage felt her cheeks flush with heat, then was happy to see a distraction walk into the room. Waving, she said, "There's Rose."

Her sister carried a gift-wrapped box tied with pink-and-blue ribbon. Seeing Sage's wave, she crossed the room to them. "I stopped in to see the quilt the Patchwork Angels made. Is it hung yet?"

"It's around on the other side."

Rose studied the painting of Snowdrop and smiled. "You are truly talented, Goober. That makes me want to pick her up and hug her. Of course, I take full credit for the fact that you're a superstar painter, since I forced you to take those art classes when we were girls."

Sage looked at Celeste. "She wanted something to keep me busy so she could hang out with her boyfriend at the tennis center."

"Sometimes seemingly small decisions can have far-reaching consequences," the older woman observed, then gazed pointedly at the box in Rose's hand. "You have a baby gift for someone?"

"I do. I'm on my way to the post office." Rose stood proudly as she added, "It's a baby gift for Brandon."

Sage couldn't hide her surprise. "That's a big statement from you."

"It is, isn't it?"

"You've forgiven him." Celeste reached out and gave Rose a hug. "I'm so glad for you, Rose."

Sage saw her sister soften as she hugged Celeste in return. "You knew exactly what to say and when to say it to show me the error of my ways, Celeste. 'Grudges are germs to the doctor who nurses them.'"

"Cute," Sage said.

"That was the catchy part."

"No, fishing was the catchy part," Celeste corrected. "For me, anyway." To Sage, she added, "Your sister isn't much of a fisherwoman, but she did open her heart to possibilities while making the effort."

Rose nodded. "I can see why those guys at the outfitters shop say fishing can be a religious experience. Celeste took me up above Heartache Falls. It was so peaceful and beautiful and uplifting."

"God's country." Celeste all but glowed as she said it.

"I realized that I'd been thinking too small. Life is big. I need to look at it in a big way. The first step in doing that was letting go of small. Holding on to my anger at Brandon was small. So"—Rose lifted up her package— "I'm going big."

Celeste clapped her hands. "Excellent. I'm so glad. Rose, you have come a long way and, I'm proud to say, have earned this."

She reached into her tote bag and withdrew a small white jewelry box, which she handed to Rose. Rose lifted the lid and said, "Oh, it's pretty. It's an angel's wings on a chain."

"My design," Sage said, narrowing her eyes. "You gave her an Angel's Rest medal?"

"A blazon, dear." To Rose, she explained, "This is the official healing center blazon awarded to those who have embraced healing's grace. Wear it next to your heart, Rose Anderson. Carry the grace you found here with you along whatever life path you travel."

Rose's expression went bright with delight. "It's lovely. Simply lovely. What a positive sentiment and statement it makes. Thank you, Celeste. I'll wear it with pride and pleasure."

She slipped the chain over her head, preened a moment, then added, "Now, if you guys will excuse me, I want to take a peek at the quilt, then get to the post office before it closes for lunch. See you all later."

As Rose walked away, Sage crossed her arms. Her toes began to tap. "I can't believe you gave her an Angel's Rest medal."

"Blazon."

"She's not a permanent resident. Why does she get one?"

"She earned it."

"By sending a baby gift?"

"It's a huge step for her."

"I've made huge steps."

"True, and I have faith that someday, maybe even someday soon, you will fully embrace healing's grace and earn a blazon, too."

"But not yet?"

Celeste patted her hand. "I need to move along. I have an appointment to get my hair cut in a few minutes, although I'll probably stop back by here afterward—I love to see all the contest entries come in. It's so exciting. Good-bye for now. I enjoyed our lunch, dear. Have a great afternoon."

Sage pursed her lips. Her toes continued to tap. Her gaze on her departing sister, she barely noticed who walked in the door.

Colt sauntered up carrying a canvas bag. "Hey there, beautiful."

She hardly spared him a glance. "Rose got an Angel's Rest medal."

Colt looked toward the door, then back at Sage. "Okay. Hey, I missed you, too. Yes, the trip went well. Thanks. I knew you'd be on pins and needles waiting for me to get home and that you'd throw yourself into my arms and smother me with kisses, so I hurried and risked my life driving too fast over Sinner's Prayer Pass."

"I'm sorry. What did you say?"

"Ouch." He clapped a hand against his chest and said, "If I start to bleed out from the wound, would you tell my brother that he gets my baseball card collection?"

Sage had the grace to be embarrassed. "I'm sorry. I was distracted." She went up on her tiptoes and kissed him soundly on the mouth. "Welcome home, Rafferty. I missed you."

"That's better." He went back for another kiss, this one enthusiastic and long enough to cause some catcalls in the theater.

"Why don't we go home?" Sage suggested when they finally stepped apart.

"Sounds great." He slipped his arm around her waist. "Let me take care of something here real quick and then we'll go."

He steered her toward the registration table. "Hello, Marlene. I have an entry for the local artists competition."

"You do?" Sage was surprised. She hadn't noticed him working on anything before he left town.

"Since I couldn't put my hands on you, I put them to work thinking about you." He set the bag down, reached inside, and drew out a cloth-draped shape. He removed the cloth to reveal the graceful figure of a woman with wings on her back and a butterfly in her palm.

"That's fantastic, Colt," Marlene said. "It's Tinker Bell."

"No." He grinned down at Sage. "I call it *Paradise*."

"Well, I thought for sure Marcus would win with his photograph of the mountain lion at the edge of Hummingbird Lake, but with your *Paradise,* you'll give him a real run for the money."

"Excuse me?" The question burst from Sage's mouth.

"Nothing personal, Sage. Your little dog painting is nice, but this . . ." She gestured toward the carving. "This is powerful."

"Powerful."

"Delicate, but at the same time, strong and beautiful. Powerful."

"Thanks, Marlene." Colt filled out the registration form, took a folded check from his pocket, then handed both items to Marlene. He winked at Sage and asked, "You ready?"

She stared at the carving. "He's powerful," she muttered. Her foot started tapping. "She got an Angel's Rest medal."

"A blazon," Colt corrected. When Sage lowered her brow and glared at him, he said, "C'mon, Cinnamon. Lighten up."

"I hate it when people say that to me."

He actually had the gall to laugh. "You're not afraid of a little friendly competition, are you?"

If Sage were a cartoon figure, steam would have been coming out of her ears. "Afraid of competition? Me?"

Colt shrugged. "I didn't think so. Maybe you simply don't agree that my pixie is more powerful than your Snowdrop." To Marlene, he asked, "Who are the judges this year?"

"I'm one of them," she replied, her smile bright.

Sage focused on the carving. It was beautiful. She knew it represented her. Delicate but strong. That's how he saw her. He carved this because he wanted her to realize how he saw her. "You did this on purpose, didn't you?"

"Excuse me?"

His innocent look didn't fool her. "You're trying to

goad me into taking another step along Recovery Road, aren't you?"

"What in the world are you talking about?"

"You think that I'm too competitive to hand you the blue ribbon by keeping my most powerful work in reserve." She gestured toward his carving. "That is your way of issuing a challenge to me."

"Honey, if I wanted to challenge you, I'd say it. When have I ever held back from saying anything to you?"

"You're sneaky smart, Colt Rafferty."

"You're paranoid. C'mon, let's go. I have a to-go order placed at the Bristlecone, and I brought a sublime bottle of wine with me from California. I've been dreaming of watching the sunset from Reflection Point since my second day away from town."

Sage took one last look at the carving, then turned and left the building with Colt. They picked up his order at the Bristlecone and headed for the lake. But as they discussed his trip and she caught him up on the happenings in town, her thoughts drifted to his carving. While they ate their dinner and enjoyed the wine that proved to be as good as he had promised, she pictured the Angel's Rest necklace hanging around her sister's neck. When they walked hand in hand down to the end of the point to watch the sunset, Sage watched a yellow butterfly dance on the air, then alight on the trunk of a fallen tree, and her thoughts returned to her painting of Snowdrop. Of Colt's carving. Of her sister's necklace.

He did distract her completely while he made slow, sweet love to her, but when he drifted off to sleep, she lay awake thinking.

At two in the morning, she slipped out of bed and went into her studio.

Colt opened his eyes and smiled into the darkness.

* * *

The summer arts festival opened to fanfare, funnel cakes, and a fish tank for the under-ten set. Spruce Street was closed to traffic and square white tents lined the space from First to Eighth, displaying the wares of artists and artisans from across the nation. On the south side of First Street, in the grassy park area where Angel Creek made a bend around the town on its way to Hummingbird Lake, a large tent had been erected to display the contest entries.

Colt sat on a park bench along Angel Creek that offered a view of the front of the contest tent, eating the breakfast burrito he'd purchased from one of the food vendors after separating from Sage at the front door of Vistas. It was nine forty-five. Contest entry closed and judging began in fifteen minutes. He expected Sage to show up any minute now.

It hadn't missed his notice that she'd left the cottage with a portfolio this morning. He'd almost asked her what was inside, but instinct told him to keep his lip zipped. Encouragement or pressure or even goading wouldn't help her to take the next big step in defeating her monsters, he knew. It had to come from inside her, and he was betting she'd pull it off.

At twelve minutes to ten he spotted her. She carried the dark brown cardboard portfolio she'd brought from home with her this morning.

"Attagirl," he murmured to himself. When she hesitated at the opening of the tent, he quietly said, "You can do this. You're strong."

She moved forward, stopping at the registration table. He saw her set the portfolio on the ground, wipe her palms against her slacks, then speak to the woman at the table.

He groaned to himself when she suddenly shook her head and turned away, then started to leave. "Ah, Cinnamon. Buck up. You can do this."

As though she'd heard him, she halted. He saw her shoulders lift as she drew a deep breath, then fall as she exhaled in a rush. She pivoted, marched back to the tent, set down her portfolio, and whipped out a painting. Done in shades of black and red. A nightmare painting.

"You go, girl," he said, grinning. He polished off his burrito, licked his fingers, then stood. Good thing he'd shopped for an engagement ring while he was on his trip. Looked like he'd need it sooner rather than later.

Colt took a leisurely route back to his office. He browsed the booths, bought a birthday gift for his mother, and indulged in a second breakfast burrito since the first had been so tasty. He arrived back at his office shortly before his scheduled conference call at ten-thirty, and by eleven-thirty, he had another road trip scheduled and a fishing trip with Gabe Callahan arranged up on a private stretch of land above Heartache Falls where the trout were said to compete with Taylor River rainbows. "I'll believe it when I see it," he said to himself, though his pulse sped up at the possibility.

At lunchtime, he exited the office building and sauntered back over to Spruce. When he arrived at the tent where Sage had items from Vistas on display, he was surprised to find her huddled up with Sarah, Nic, and Ali. All four women had concerned looks on their faces. "What's up?"

"Some man is going around town looking for Marcus Burnes and making crazy accusations," Sage said. "He talked to me about fifteen minutes ago. I didn't know what to tell him."

Sarah said, "I sent Lori and Chase to the sheriff's office looking for Zach. Then a few minutes ago, Marlene ran by here in tears."

"What was this guy saying?"

Sarah gestured toward one of Burnes' photographs that Vistas had on display. "He claimed that Marcus

Burnes isn't his real name, that his real name is Donald Bebe and that he jumped bail in Oregon on . . ." She winced as she finished, "Child pornography charges."

Colt's brows winged up, and he looked at Sage, who said, "I didn't do a background check or anything on him. I bought his photographs. He never claimed any formal training, so it never occurred to me to check."

"Who is the guy making the claims?"

"He said he's the father of one of the abused boys," Ali said. "Someone he knows was here earlier this summer and he said he picked up a brochure about the arts festival. It has one of Marcus' photos on the cover. Donald Bebe had a legitimate business as a nature photographer, too. The father said he recognized the work and came to Eternity Springs to have him arrested."

Sage nibbled at her bottom lip. "I hope it's all just a mistake."

"Me too," Sarah said. "Child porn is . . ." She shuddered.

"Evil," Sage said, her tone flat.

"Well, this is all conjecture and gossip," Ali said. "We'd be wrong to condemn the man until all the facts are known."

The women looked at one another, then all looked at Colt. Sage said, "Go find out the facts for us, Rafferty."

"Hey, it's none of my business. Why don't we—" He broke off abruptly at the sound of the screams.

The gunshots had him tackling the women, forcing them to the ground in search of cover.

Gunfire.
Screams.
Jesus loves me, this I know.
Bang. Bang. Bang.
The darkness threatened, black fingery shadows reaching toward her like B-movie monsters. She started

to shake and shiver and shudder like aspen leaves in a gale, but Colt's voice reached through the fear.

"Hang in there, Sage. It's okay. We're okay. This is Colorado. We're in Eternity Springs. You're home."

Eternity Springs. Not Africa. Eternity Springs.

"What's going on?" Sarah asked, and the same time Ali said, "The kids! Where are Chase and Lori?"

"Stay here," Colt demanded. "I'll find out."

Even as he stood, Sage heard the calls. "Doctors. We need doctors." As Sage climbed to her feet, Chase Timberlake ran up, saying, "Ms. Reese. Come quick. Lori's been hurt."

All three women gasped and the Vistas tent emptied, the women on Colt's heels, running north on Spruce toward the crowd gathered at the Sixth Street intersection. As they arrived, Sage heard her sister's voice firing off orders like a battlefield medic.

Rose knelt on the ground beside Lori. Her leg was bleeding. Zach Turner barked orders into a phone, cradling a bloody arm. Shoulder wound, she deduced. Marcus Burnes was on his side with what appeared to be a chest wound. A stranger sat restrained by Mayor Townsend and two others. He was crying, his face drained of color. "I didn't mean to hurt the girl. Dear God, forgive me. I didn't mean to hurt the girl."

"Somebody get my sister!" Rose shouted.

Sage moved forward. "I'm here. What do we have?"

"Leg wound, in and out. She'll be okay. Same for the sheriff. Burnes is bad. He'll bleed out without your help."

Burnes. The child pornographer. "What about the doctor at Angel's Rest?"

"Oh his way," Zach Turner said, "but it'll take him a few minutes to get here. Helicopter is on the way for Burnes."

A child pornographer. An evil man.

Another evil man.

"You do it, Rose. I'll take care of Lori. Nic, you want to see to Zach?"

While the veterinarian hurried over to the sheriff, Sage's sister glared at her. "You're the surgeon. You have a surgeon's hands. He's bleeding out."

Jesus loves me, this I know.

Another evil man. *Dear Lord, why?*

Sage's heart pounded. Her mouth went dry and her hands trembled violently. She shut her eyes.

Time hung suspended as a kaleidoscope of memories whirled through her mind. Africa. Her father. Standing outside the hospital in Dallas. Paintings in red-and-black.

Another evil man.

And I am neither judge nor jury.

Sage blew out a breath and twisted her head around, locating Colt. "I have to help him."

"Of course you do, sweetheart."

Stepping forward, someone slapped some latex gloves into her hands. She pulled them on, knelt, and set about saving the dying man's life.

An hour later, having turned over her patient at the hospital in Gunnison, Sage ducked into their physicians' locker room for a shower and changed from bloody clothes into a pair of clean blue scrubs. She exited the hospital and discovered Colt sitting on a wooden bench, waiting for her.

"How did you get here?" she asked. "It's a two-hour drive."

"A friend of Gabe's has his own bird. The guy who owns Eagle's Way."

"Jack Davenport."

"Yeah, that's him. He was in town, so Gabe called him and he brought me down. I thought you might need me." He paused, gave her a thorough once-over, then added, "I was wrong, wasn't I?"

Sage smiled and took hold of his hand. "Oh, I need you, Rafferty. I definitely need you. But I don't *need* you."

"That makes total sense." He touched her cheek. "You look good in scrub blue, Dr. Anderson."

"Thanks, but I don't think it really suits me. Prints hide paint splashes better than solids."

"Ah."

"I called home. Sarah told me Lori's okay, and they were able to treat Zach's wound at the clinic, too."

"So I understand." He hesitated a moment, then said, "The father has been arrested."

"Yes, and Marcus Burnes will be, too, as soon as he's out of surgery. Sarah told me the sheriff's office verified the shooter's claim. Marlene is brokenhearted." Then, ready to have the unhappiness behind her, Sage asked, "So, Rafferty, how are we getting home?"

"Well . . ." He rubbed the back of his neck. "Celeste called and asked a favor. Seems she's had her motorcycle here in the shop, and she asked if we'd ride it back for her. Would you mind?"

"Her Gold Wing?"

"Yep. She also said there's something for you in the tour pack."

"I'd love to ride her Gold Wing."

He grinned, and those devilish dimples of his winked at her. "Good, because I already had it brought over. So, you ready to go?"

He held up the keys. She laughed, swiped them out of his hand, and started for the motorcycle. "I'm driving."

"Oh, jeez."

Her heart lighter than it had been in years, Sage almost skipped to the parking lot where Celeste's ride awaited them. Before climbing aboard, she opened the tour pack, looked inside, and spied a small white box. Sage picked the box up, lifted off the lid, and gasped.

"Whatcha got?"

She grinned up at him, then strutted her shoulders and held up the Angel's Rest blazon. "I earned my wings."

"Well, aren't you special."

"That I am." She slipped the necklace over her head and snapped the trunk closed. Flinging her leg over the bike, she accepted the helmet he handed her and said, "Climb on, cowboy."

"Anytime you ask, Cinnamon. Anytime you ask."

She started the engine and drove sedately out of town, but once she hit the open road, she throttled up and let out a joyous laugh.

She had slain a monster today. Conquered a mountain. Destroyed a fearsome foe. She didn't expect that the nightmares were over for good, and she'd probably still suffer flashbacks from time to time. She'd never stop mourning the events of that horrible day. But now, finally, she knew that she'd survived them. "I'm a survivor, Rafferty," she shouted.

"That you are, woman."

"So marry me, Rafferty!"

His hands tightened around her waist. "What did you say?"

"I said marry me."

He leaned forward. "You just asked me to marry you?"

"Uh-huh."

"As we're riding down the highway at seventy miles an hour?"

"Sixty-five. Within the speed limit. So what's your answer, Rafferty?"

"Pull over."

"Not until we get to Eternity Springs. What's your answer, Rafferty?"

"Yes, dammit. I love you. Don't wreck this motorcycle before I can give you a proper kiss."

"I won't. I love you, too. Now, hold on, Rafferty. I intend to give you the ride of your life."

Colt spent the rest of the ride to Eternity Springs teasing her. She had to keep her hands on the steering, but all he needed to do was keep his hands on her. Putting his mouth on her was a nice little extra. As they flew down the road toward Eternity Springs, he made it his goal to torture her to the point that she'd surrender, pull off the road, and let him lead her into the trees for a little . . . nature hike.

It became a contest. A war. Yet another siege.

He should have known the woman was so filled with power that she'd withstand his sensual assault. Still, he could tell that he'd gotten to her. All that shifting she did in her seat wasn't to help keep her balance.

When they finally crossed the Eternity Springs city limit, he heaved a sigh of relief. Forget her seat shifting. Sitting on this motorcycle with a log between his legs had grown downright uncomfortable. At least they'd be home in a few minutes.

With Spruce blocked off to traffic, he expected her to take Cottonwood on around the edge of town, and she did just that. But as they rounded the curve onto First and their route took them past the contest exhibit tents, she slowed.

She pulled off the road a short distance from the tents and said, "Let's check the winners, shall we?"

He groaned. "Can't it wait until tomorrow? The results aren't going to change."

"What's the matter, Rafferty?" She switched off the

motor and climbed off the bike. Removing her helmet, she shot him a saucy smile. "Are you afraid that this year I won the blue ribbon?"

Colt couldn't take another minute of it. He yanked her into his arms, bent her over backward, and planted a blistering, extended kiss on her lips. Vaguely aware of the murmurs of the crowd, he realized they had an audience, and released her with a flourish. "Me, afraid, Sage Anderson? Not hardly."

She stood with her shoulders back, her chin up, and that gorgeous hair glistening in the afternoon sun. "So, you really think your carving might have won?"

"Doesn't matter." Colt gave her a wink, and his grin flashed his dimples. "You might have won the blue ribbon, but darlin', I won the prize."

ACKNOWLEDGMENTS

New beginnings are exciting things. For this one I'd especially like to thank my awesome, talented, oh-so-keen-eyed editor, Kate Collins, and my agents, Meg Ruley and Christina Hogrebe, for their support and guidance and belief in this series. You ladies rock. Also, to my dear friends Scott and Christina Ham, who knew just the motivation to give me to find my way to Eternity Springs, and to Mary Dickerson for being my reader, my red-liner, and most important, my friend.

Read on for a preview of
Emily March's next novel
in her Eternity Springs series:

Heartache Falls

In the bedroom she shared with her husband, Ali Timberlake tucked her makeup case neatly into her suitcase, then zipped it shut just as her husband emerged from his closet, a duffel bag in one hand. "Are you sure about this, honey?" Mac asked, his brow knitted with concern. "We can still change the plan."

"Right," Ali replied, her tone dry. "And for the rest of my life I'll get to listen to Stephen and Chase talk about the one that got away."

"Hey, we can go fishing in Alaska another—"

Ali interrupted. "No, it's okay. I'm glad you're getting to go. It's a minor miracle that your schedule and those of the boys meshed this time. If Caitlin wanted you with her, that would be different, but she's flexing her wings and feeling independent and ready to take on Vanderbilt University."

Her lips twisted as she added, "Frankly, I'm not sure she really wants *me* to go with her to Nashville. We haven't exactly been getting along very well lately."

Her husband tossed his duffel onto their bed, then gave Ali a rueful look. "She did tell me you packed her toothbrush three days ago. She thinks you can't wait for her to go."

"After the way she's been acting lately, can you blame me?"

"Now, sweetheart."

"Oh, I know." Ali shrugged and waved her hand in a dismissive gesture. "She's emotional. I'm emotional. It's not every day that your youngest child and only daughter goes off to college for the first time."

"Exactly." Mac grimaced and rubbed the back of his neck. "That's why I think I should be there. The boys could go to Alaska without me. No reason why they couldn't."

He truly appeared torn, so Ali swallowed her own misgivings and pasted on a smile. "Actually, there is. This is a father-son trip. You can't very well have a father-son trip if the father is a no-show. You went with me and Cait to orientation, and that was the important trip. This will be fun for me and Caitlin. An August road trip. A mother-daughter adventure. We'll do just fine."

He gave her a long, searching look, then nodded. "Okay. If you're sure."

"I'm sure." She smiled with a brightness she didn't feel. "Now I'd better get downstairs and see to breakfast."

"Leave your suitcase. I'll carry it down when I come."

"Thanks."

Ali tried to shake off her melancholy as she made her way downstairs to prepare a meal for her family. She wanted today's breakfast to be extra special since this was Caitlin's big day, the day she flew out of the nest and off to college. It was also the first time in months that the entire family would sit down to a meal together and likely the last meal they'd all share until Thanksgiving.

Throughout the children's lives, Ali had made the family supper a big deal. It was the Timberlake family together time, and everyone was expected to make a real effort to be there. Since Mac had worked at her father's firm while the kids were growing up, she had invoked the boss's daughter privilege in that respect alone. Mac had rarely missed dinner with the family. That had changed since he took the seat on the bench, but by then the crucial years were behind them, the precedent had been set. Their family was stronger because of it.

After today, family meals would be few and far between.

Ali briefly closed her eyes. *Don't go there.*

She'd have the kids set the table in the dining room and make it a celebration. Maybe even use her mother's china. The kids would complain about having to hand-wash the dishes, but if you didn't go to the trouble to make an occasion an occasion, it became just one more meal in a lifetime of meals.

Mentally she reviewed the contents of her fridge and pantry. Yes, she could do a Hollandaise sauce. She had fresh spinach. If she did eggs Florentine, at least the boys would have one serving of a vegetable today. Fresh berries. She could do pigs in a blanket for Caitlin. They were her favorite.

As she approached her kitchen, the aroma drifting in the air gave her warning. Bacon? Someone was already cooking? Her eyes rounded with surprise. What alternate reality was this?

Ali stepped into the kitchen and halted abruptly. The kitchen table was set with a "Bon Voyage" paper tablecloth. A Sponge Bob Square Pants paper centerpiece adorned the center of the table. Paper plates proclaimed "Happy St. Patrick's Day," and helium-filled Mylar balloons that read "Over the Hill" had been tied to the back of each of the chairs.

Each of her three grown children turned to look at her, and Ali desperately wished she had a camera. Stephen, looking like a lawyer already with his neatly trimmed hair, freshly shaved face, and button-down shirt. Chase, the outdoorsman, with his three-day beard and longish hair drawn back and tied at the nape of his neck with a leather lace. And Caitlin, blond and beautiful and brimming with life, a typical college coed. Ten minutes ago these young adults had been grade-schoolers riding their bikes on the sidewalk. Where had the years gone?

Familiar impish grins spread across their faces, telling Ali that they were tickled pink that they'd surprised her. *Some things never change, thank goodness.* They'd recognized that this was an important family moment. Something she'd tried too hard to teach them had stuck. Happiness bloomed inside Ali like a springtime flower, and she didn't try to keep the smile off her face as she said, "Caitlin, did your brothers actually cook for you to mark your special day?"

"Sort of," Caitlin replied, glancing at the boys. "But not exactly."

"We are cooking breakfast," Stephen clarified as he removed the last piece of bacon from the frying pan and placed it on a paper towel to drain. He was a younger version of Mac, with his father's dark hair and brown eyes that now sparkled mischievously. "I know it's shocking, and I'm glad we didn't give you a heart attack. At your advanced age, I worried about that."

"Just because you are in law school, young man, doesn't mean I can't still send you to your room," Ali fired back. Her gaze fixed on the table, she asked, "Happy St. Patrick's Day?"

"We shopped the bargain bin at the party store," Chase explained. "G'morning, Mom."

"Good morning, son." She eyed the activity at the stovetop, counter, and kitchen table. Apparently the menu included bacon, scrambled eggs, toast, orange juice, and of course Chase's favorite, Froot Loops. "So, who is going to clue me in? What does Cait mean when she says 'sorta'?"

Chase opened his mouth, but Caitlin stopped him with an elbow to his side, then pushed the lever on the toaster and gave Stephen, their eldest, a look that said, *Go on.*

"We thought it was important to mark the occasion because today is a special day," Stephen said as Mac joined the family in the kitchen. Mac placed his hand on Ali's shoulder while their eldest continued, "The last of your chicks is officially flying from the nest today. It *is* a special day for Caitlin, and that's why we bought her a princess crown to wear during breakfast. But it's also a special day for you and Dad. We thought it was an appropriate time for the three of us to tell you both how much we love you and how much appreciate all you've done for us."

Oh. Ali brought a hand to her chest. *Wow.*

Stephen nodded toward Chase, then cracked another egg into a bowl. Ali's middle child flashed his father's grin, then said, "I'll keep my part short because I know you, Mom. You'll start bawling, and we don't want you dribbling snot into your eggs."

"Cha-a-ase!" Caitlin protested as the toast popped up.

"Well, it's true."

"Yeah, but you don't have to be gross about it. Are you ever gonna grow up?"

"Probably not."

Probably not, Ali silently agreed. Chase had been such a terror, such a daredevil, when he was little. Such a challenge to parent, yet so much fun.

"You are the greatest mom in the world, Mom," he continued. "You've always been there for us, and we always knew we could count on you. I was always proud that you were my mother."

Ali started blinking. She was moments away from bawling. *My kids know me so well.*

Chase made a sweeping gesture toward Caitlin. Ali's daughter, now a young, idealistic woman, stepped forward. Lacing her fingers, she spoke with solemn sincerity. "You guys gave us a firm, stable foundation on which to build our hopes and dreams. That's something few of my friends had. Actually, none of my friends had the great home and family life we have had. I know that makes me a stronger person, and it makes today easier for me.

"Today is my Independence Day, but it's also your Freedom Day. Especially for you, Mom." Then, with a loving smile, sweet, tender-hearted Caitlin shot the arrow through the very center of Ali's heart. "You're not a stay-at-home mom anymore."

Mac's hand gave her shoulder a reassuring squeeze while Ali stood there bleeding.

"So," Caitlin continued, "the boys and I thought it'd be nice to mark this special day with a special thank-you—a family meal we prepared."

"Besides," Chase piped up, "we knew if we didn't do something first, then you'd go all out and we'd be stuck washing Grandmother's dishes."

Ali couldn't speak past the lump of emotion in her throat. Mac stepped forward and covered for her. "This is a real nice surprise. How long before it's ready? I'm starved."

Breakfast was delicious, boisterous, and fun. The kids teased each other as usual, and for just a little while Ali could pretend the old days were back. All too soon, however, breakfast was finished, the paper plates relegated to the trash, and the pots and pans washed and stored away. Mac glanced at the clock. "You girls had better hit the road. Kansas City is a long drive."

"Don't remind me," Caitlin groaned. But excitement shone in her eyes as she hurried upstairs, saying, "I'll be ready in five, Mom."

A few minutes later, out beside the car, Mac studied the load and grimaced. "We should have shipped half of this stuff. If you have a flat tire . . ." He exhaled a heavy sigh and shook his head. Then he gave Ali a long look and said, "Last chance."

"We'll be fine."

"I'll worry about you being on the road for the next week."

"I'll worry that you'll be eaten by a grizzly bear, too."

Caitlin bounded out of the house carrying her purse and a tennis racket that she somehow found space for in the back of Mac's SUV. She exchanged hugs and more good-natured teasing with her brothers, then her father took her hands. Mac's voice was a little gruff as he spoke his traditional farewell, "Be careful, kitten. Wear sunscreen. Drink lots of water."

"*Dad*-dy!"

Mac grinned, then pulled her into his embrace and hugged her hard. "Seriously, though, do be careful. Listen to your instincts. Go to class. Make smart decisions."

"I will, Daddy."

He kissed her forehead, then said, "I'm so proud of you, Caitlin. I'm going to miss you so much."

"I'll miss you, too, Daddy, and I'll be home for Thanksgiving before you know it. Shoot, with the hours you've been working, you won't even notice I'm gone."

"Finally, something good to come out of all of those hours." He gave her one more kiss, one more hug, then opened the door for her. "Buckle your seat belt. If you're driving, don't talk on the cellphone, and especially don't text."

Caitlin rolled her eyes as she slid into her seat. "Good-bye, Daddy."

"Bye, baby." He shut the passenger door behind her, then walked around to the driver's side, where Ali was fitting the key into the ignition. "Alison, you drive carefully. Call me when you stop for the night."

"I will." Ali lifted her face for his quick kiss. "You guys be safe, too, and have a wonderful time. I hope you catch dozens of fish."

She started the car, and she and her daughter drove off for their grand adventure.

As road trips went, it proved to be one of the most pleasurable Ali had ever experienced. She and Caitlin shared a similar traveling style. They agreed on what music and audiobooks to listen to. They both wanted to stop every two hours, and they liked driving late into the night and sleeping in the next morning—just the opposite of Mac's preferences. What Ali enjoyed most were the hours on end spent in conversation with her only daughter. They talked about everything under the sun—family, friends, old memories, new dreams, wishes, and desires. Ali knew that she'd remember and treasure for the rest of her life this time spent with Caitlin.

Eventually the conversations ended. The trip ended. Four days after leaving Denver, in a slightly different version of the scene Caitlin had had with her father, Ali told her daughter good-bye in the parking lot outside her dorm. They hugged, they kissed, and they declared their love for each other, but Ali could tell her daughter was distracted. Her suitemates were waiting for her to go shopping for their coordinating bathroom accessories.

Ali made it three whole blocks before she burst into tears. She pulled into a convenience store parking lot and buried her face in her arms against the steering wheel. She cried long, hard tears, pouring out her sadness and her grief, sobbing out her sadness and her sorrow.

Finally, when she'd drained her tears and used all the tissues in the box, she went into the store and used the facilities, then picked up a new box of tissues and a packaged brownie. For a long moment she eyed the selection of tall-boy beers. Sighing, she chose a Coke instead, paid for her selections, then resumed the long drive home.

An hour into her trip, she tried to call Mac, but of course his phone went to voice mail. Her men were out in the wilds of Alaska, where cell phone coverage wasn't exactly grizzly-to-grizzly. She tried to call her father, but his phone, too, went to voice mail, and she recalled that he had a golf vacation this week. Charles Cavanaugh didn't carry a cell phone in his golf bag.

She drove another fifty miles, then dialed one of her friends in Eternity Springs. She had a nice long conversation with Sage Anderson, recently engaged and planning a Christmas wedding. Afterward, Ali tried Mac again.

Silly of her, really. Mac wasn't there. Mac was rarely there anymore.

"Don't be snotty," she scolded herself. Mac had an important job that kept him extremely busy. Hadn't she known from the very first that this was what she could expect if she shared her life with Mackenzie S. Timberlake?

When she'd met Mac her freshman year at Notre Dame, he'd had a well-defined plan for his future. He'd not deviated from his plan in all the years since—well, except for the surprise they had named Stephen. Following his undergrad years, Mac had gone to Stanford for law school, then on to private practice at her father's law firm. While the family connection had landed him the job, he'd earned his partnership all on his own with hard work, a brilliant mind, and excellent instincts. He'd achieved his goal of a federal court judgeship three full years ahead of the timeline he'd outlined to her on their second date. A man didn't accomplish so much at such a relatively young age without a full share and more of discipline.

Of course, she'd had a plan for her future, too, but the

surprise currently attending law school had altered her plan permanently. She'd graduated from college with a degree in business she didn't want, the dream of culinary school in mothballs because of the baby already on the way. While Mac built his resume, she'd wiped snotty noses, organized PTA fund-raisers, and spent a good portion of her day in a minivan toting kids from one event to another.

She'd loved it. She might never have fulfilled her own workday dreams, but she'd settled comfortably into her role as a stay-at-home mom, and the entire Timberlake family had thrived.

And, eventually, outgrown her.

That's okay, she told herself. It wasn't like she didn't have a life of her own separate from the kids. She'd still keep busy. She had her volunteer work. Her classes at the gym. She thoroughly enjoyed her occasional trips up into the mountains to Eternity Springs. She'd find plenty to do to fill the hours now empty of baseball games or debate matches or dance recitals.

Maybe she'd leap headlong into the whole quilting thing. She could join a guild in Denver. Meet a whole new group of friends. Except Ali already had lots of friends. She didn't want more friends. She wanted her family.

She was a stay-at-home mom who'd completed her job. Lost her job. A thundercloud of self-pity built in her emotional sky, but she fled from it, tried to outrun it, by lecturing herself aloud. "You haven't lost your family. They just don't live with you anymore. In lots of ways, that's a good thing."

She'd no longer have sweaty gym socks stinking up the boys' rooms or a clutter of makeup spread all across the upstairs bathroom vanity. Those were good things. She wouldn't have to lie awake in bed worrying until her kids made it home by curfew—or not. Another good thing. And one of her friends had told her that the best thing about having an empty nest was that now she and her husband could have sex on the staircase if they wanted. Personally, Ali couldn't imagine that being too comfortable, but hey, she was willing to try anything once.

"I'll just put that on the calendar," she decided, feeling marginally better.

So she'd finished the stay-at-home mom years of her life. Big deal. She hadn't lost her family. She still had Mac. Maybe they could use this time to reinvigorate their relationship. Enjoy an empty-nest honeymoon of sorts. Spend time and energy on each other instead of the kids. Why, this could be the best time of her life. Of their lives.

Thank goodness she still had Mac.

"The Desai case?" Mac repeated, one week after his return to work following his Alaskan vacation. Desai was a high-profile case of attempted domestic terrorism. "I thought that went to Judge Harrison."

The court clerk nodded. "It did, but Judge Harrison had a heart attack this morning on his way in. We heard fifteen minutes ago."

"Oh, no. How's he doing?"

"It's serious. His son took my call and said he's not out of the woods entirely, but they do expect him to survive."

"That's good news."

"Yes, but the son also said the doctors are talking about retirement."

Mac hated to hear it. Harrison was a brilliant jurist and an affable colleague. He'd be missed.

"The case has been reassigned to you, Judge Timberlake. You have a hearing that starts in twenty minutes."

"Twenty minutes! What sort of hearing?"

"The U.S. attorney wants a search warrant executed today. We have FBI, DEA, and the Denver police headed in." The clerk handed over a file. "It's a good thing you had your vacation. This thing is liable to have you tied up for months."

Mac stared down at the bulging file and sighed. He should call Ali and warn her that he might be late. He was pretty sure she'd dropped the word *special* when she'd referenced dinner tonight.

As he headed for his office to make the call, his secretary, Louise, stopped him with a problem. From that moment on, the Desai case consumed him, and he didn't leave the courthouse until well after 10:00 P.M. It wasn't until he walked into his dark house and smelled the faded aroma of his favorite, veal parmigiana, that he remembered that he'd never made that phone call, and his stomach dipped.

Next he recalled that she'd mentioned something about special plans for the evening, and his stomach dropped even more.

Sure enough, when he peeked into the dining room, he saw the table set for two with her mother's china. *Oh, hell.*

Mac rubbed the back of his neck and inwardly groaned. He'd screwed up. Big time. He knew this was a difficult time for his wife, and he'd been trying to be extra sensitive to her wishes and desires. Luckily, she'd appeared to be happier since he returned from Alaska and she returned from Tennessee. He had hoped that Ali would find the anticipation of Caitlin's departure for college more upsetting than dealing with the actual aftereffects of it, and so far, it appeared that would be the case.

But letting her down like this tonight sure didn't help the situation. "Timberlake," he murmured, "you're an ass."

He slipped off his jacket and loosened his tie as he climbed the stairs to their bedroom. The room was dark, the figure in the bed unmoving. Attempting to be as quiet as possible, Mac readied for bed, then slipped between the sheets.

He breathed in the familiar lavender scent of the lotion she habitually smoothed over her skin before bed and edged closer to her warmth, trying not to wake her as he put his arm around her, seeking, and finding, that sense of homecoming she offered him even after all these years.

"You're home," she said.

Mac closed his eyes. *Damn.* "Sorry I woke you. I'm sorry I'm so late. I know I should have called."

"Where were you?"

She said it like a question, not an accusation, so he breathed a little easier. "I had a hearing. A new case. We ended up ordering in dinner."

"Oh. Okay."

She sounded tired—very tired—so he decided to wait until the morning to offer any further details. He kissed her shoulder and spooned her tight against him. "Goodnight, babe. Sleep well."

"You too."

Mac waited for her to continue their usual nighttime ritual, but her regular breathing told him she'd fallen back asleep. Disquieted, he drifted off plagued with a sense of foreboding.

When was the last time they'd gone to sleep together without exchanging the words "I love you"?